FOG OF WAR

By LeAnn Robinson

COPYRIGHT

Fog of War Copyright © 2023 by LeAnn Robinson. All Rights Reserved.

All rights reserved. No part of this book may be reproduced in any form or by any electronic or mechanical means including information storage and retrieval systems, without permission in writing from the author. The only exception is by a reviewer, who may quote short excerpts in a review.

Cover designed by LeAnn Robinson, using an image created with Midjourney
ISBN: 978-1-948768-17-7

L. D. ROBINSON © 2022

To my mother, Gladys Pratt Dennis, who was the first woman in the military I ever knew.
(She was a WAVE in the U.S. Navy during WWII.)

L. D. ROBINSON © 2022

Prolog - Attack of the Nabbers

The force fields were still on, so Galth's sense of movement wasn't providing any information, but the waves below him seemed to be slowing. They were about to reach land, and what had from orbit looked like a long straight coastline was now filled with crenulations and bays and dotted with structures built by the aliens of this newly discovered planet, third from its yellow sun, aliens so perfectly matched to their own physiology that it would be hard to tell the difference between them, a rare find in the Galaxy. Galth turned to the pilot, Krelg, ready to complain.

But Krelg's frown was deeper than Galth's. "Demons of the Night Sea," he said as he stared at the ground ahead of them. They were high enough to see over the trees and the tall buildings, high enough to see the length of a long curving road right next to the ocean, splitting the water from the squared-off

L. D. ROBINSON © 2022

structures, a perfect landing place for a harvesting mission. Krelg stood only a few inches from the front wall, control pad in hand, leaning forward against the dark bulkheads and the viewscreen, like he could see the road better if he got closer.

"What's the problem?" Galth said. Each of the five landing spots on this nice little planet had been pre-selected, so any difficulty Krelg claimed for the target he had been given would reflect badly on Captain Zolbon and his staff, and Galth knew enough about Zolbon not to cast any blame in *his* direction. You could get sent out the airlock if you weren't careful.

Krelg huffed. "There's something in the middle of the road."

"Something?" Galth shook his head. Krelg was a senior pilot, with much more experience than Galth. He should realize that such a vague word would mean little when describing alien terrain or structures. "I don't see anything, except some bushes." Bushes would be easy to deal with, easy to knock over, or if necessary, Krelg could burn them to the pavement when he put on his brakes to slow their descent.

"Looks like it's made of concrete," Krelg said, pointing to the viewscreen, running his fingers up and down the center of the long street. "Like a narrow container, holding the dirt the bushes are growing in."

Galth looked closer. Yeah, okay, he could see it now, a strip of material several feet wide and equally tall, painted in stripes of black and white, filled with soil and the dark green shrubs, and running the entire length of the road, all the way up the coast, only missing where other roads intersected with the target street.

Krelg let out an exasperated huff. "If we try to land on that, we'll tip over."

Galth nodded. The shuttle was designed to land flat on the ground, no legs or struts holding it up. And it was too wide to fit between the barrier and the buildings, even if they plowed away all the surface vehicles parked along its length.

"Maybe we should land in the intersections?" the sensor operator said. He stood on the other side of Krelg, his attention on his control pad screen.

"Too far from the building entrances," Krelg said. "Call the ship, tell them we need an alternate landing spot."

Galth stared at him.

"Close your mouth," Krelg said.

Galth snapped his teeth together. He hadn't even realized his jaw had been gaping. But that order was the most idiotic thing he'd ever heard, and he was not about to tell the captain their landing spot was inadequate.

"Do it," Krelg barked.

"I don't see a problem," Galth said. "You want to convince him, you make the call."

Krelg gave him a quick eye roll. He had stopped the shuttle's descent, and now they were casting a dark shadow over the road, the trees, the sidewalks, and all the people down there, the potential victims, were running away, surface vehicles jamming the street in a rush to get away from the threat from above.

L. D. ROBINSON © 2022

Not that any of those quivs knew what the threat was. If they had known, they would have been running even faster.

"Take the helm," Krelg said, pressing a button on his pad to release his own control over the shuttle. Then, he called up a communications screen.

Galth quickly assumed command of the helm, then maneuvered the shuttle back around, making a circle out over the bay, back down to a point beyond where the target road ended, now hovering over the water, perfectly lined up with the street, the barrier, and the buildings where all the people they planned to harvest still waited, thinking they were safe inside.

Just to be certain, Galth double checked the course he'd laid in.

Krelg looked up from his call. He'd barely made contact with the bridge above them, and they were asking if he was ready for their ship to fire down on the planet from orbit.

"Tell them, 'almost'," Galth said, turning up the intensity of the forcefields designed to hold everyone in place and putting shields on full to protect the hull from damage. Then, without any pause, he slid the acceleration control forward.

"What are you doing?" Krelg bellowed, grabbing at Galth's control pad.

The shuttle dipped to ground level, skimming over the water, heading directly toward the lone tree that stood between them and the target street, following Galth's pre-programmed route. By the time Krelg wrestled back control, they would be stopped and in position to begin their work.

"Are you out of your mind?" Krelg screeched as the shuttle's nose smashed into the tree, shattering its fragile trunk, leaves and bark spraying into the air. An instant later, they rammed into the concrete bush holders. Dirt and bits of concrete rose up like ocean waves. Leaves and branches from the bushes plastered themselves against the front of the shuttle. Even a couple of the colorful surface vehicles got caught up in the crash, one boxy conveyance spinning end over end before it thudded to the ground.

And all the shuttle crew just stood there, like nothing had happened, like the ship had not been buffeted and slammed around, like the sudden deceleration from hitting the barriers had been a slow, even braking, all thanks to the force fields.

Galth smiled and pressed the button on his pad to return control to Krelg. "The helm is yours."

Krelg glanced back at the viewscreen, his expression angry or befuddled, with a hint of frustration, because there wasn't much Krelg could do about it now. A brittle stick from one of the bushes slid down the view, hitting a leaf and knocking it off the front of the shuttle. "Ready," Krelg said into his pad, still in contact with the ship in orbit. He turned off his communications, then glared at Galth. "If the shuttle is damaged, I'll dump you into the middle of this ocean." He pointed out the window, to a wide swath of water lapping at the shore.

L. D. ROBINSON © 2022

"There may be a small dent or two," Galth said with a confident smile. "Nothing that can't be fixed." Now, his role as co-pilot was over, and he had little to do while the ground crew began their preparations of the building, blocking off all exits but the one that led to their shuttle. Meanwhile, the ship in orbit had fired down on the building, creating a conflagration that would force all the people inside to evacuate. In no time, and with nowhere else to go, quivs would be pouring into the cargo hold. And they would get a lot of victims, because Galth's move had given them more time to harvest than they would have had if they had needed to move to another spot. He expected he would get a big reward for this, in spite of Krelg's evident annoyance.

"Approaching vehicle," the sensor operator said.

"Handle it," Krelg commanded. Galth glanced over at Krelg's control. The man was running diagnostics, like he thought the shuttle couldn't handle a rough landing. What a stupid worrier.

A large red vehicle approached, red lights flashing from the roof, siren blaring so loud Galth could hear it through the walls of the shuttle. It looked harmless enough. No weapons he could see. Not that the weapons carried by these backward creatures were any threat. They were projectile launchers, mostly, their damage based on the kinetic energy of the small bullets they spewed out, something the shields could handle without an issue.

The red vehicle stopped just beyond the last of the pieces of overturned barrier, and several short, brown-skinned men dismounted, scurrying around the vehicle, pulling out long cloth strips of some kind.

"Those are tubes," the sensor operator said. "They're going to spray water on the building."

"No, they're not," Galth said with a smile. He switched screens on his control pad to the weapons view, aimed the smaller of the energy cannons at the vehicle, then fired.

A flash overwhelmed the viewscreen, turning it dark, and when it came back on, there were no men around the red vehicle, and it was not red anymore. Didn't look much like a vehicle, either. Only a blackened frame remained, the rubbery wheels melted and smoking.

Galth chuckled. "Is that the best they can do?"

"There's someone else," Krelg said, pointing at a man with some sort of strange weapon resting on his shoulder. He stood behind a tree, leaning around it just enough to point the wide, glassy end of the weapon at them.

"That's one strange looking gun," Galth said, fingering his weapons control to get a shot at the man.

"Not a gun," the sensor operator said. "Some kind of recording device."

"Recording?" Galth lowered his control pad. "Should I shoot him?"

"He's not a threat," Krelg said. "Maybe you can coax him into the shuttle, though."

Galth frowned. Was Krelg kidding? If he went out there, he wouldn't have the protection of the shields anymore, and those damned projectile weapons could do serious damage to flesh and bones. And speaking of projectile weapons, behind the man with the recorder, a couple of other men approached, carrying small guns, pointing their narrow, dark ends at the shuttle.

Maybe Krelg wanted to get rid of Galth, take credit for the removal of the barriers for himself. Galth needed to be careful here.

"Go help the ground crew," Krelg said. "Looks like these two quivs are about to cut through the exit barrier."

Galth watched the men as they approached, one with a large knife, crossing the street while hunched over, as if their being smaller targets would make it difficult for Galth to hit them. He pulled his blaster from his belt and waved it in the air. "I think they're about to lose their heads."

Krelg nodded with a chuckle. "Good target practice. Enjoy."

Chapter 1 — Mounting Fear

Two weeks later...

If tension could be put in a bottle, Colonel Patrice Sullivan would have the perfect weapon, but even in the midst of all the fear, she wasn't expecting to hear a soul shattering scream.

She dropped her pen mid-signature and bolted for the door, catapulting her chair into the wainscotting. In the outer office, everyone else just stood there like idiots, like the building had just been called to attention, like there was no emergency to attend to. Just as well. She didn't need them in her way.

Spinning around the door frame to the hall, she found a crowd of soldiers choking the doorway into the S-2 suite, obviously the place where all the action was unfolding. "Clear these people out of here," she shouted, and a nearby MP leapt into action, commanding the others to disperse.

She shouldered her way through the cluster, and they jumped back as soon as they saw the silver eagles on her shoulders, or maybe it was the scar on her cheek. She burst into the intelligence offices. Across the room, a pointed object pressed against the dark skin of a female sergeant. Behind her, the assailant stood in front of the window, silhouetted by the afternoon sun, a halo of light around his short red hair throwing his face into shadows, made worse as he ducked behind his victim's black curls. Taller than the woman, he gripped her tightly around the shoulders, while she trembled, her eyes so wide they looked like they had their own light source.

Major Li, the officer in charge, crept up to Sullivan.

"Who is he?" she said softly.

"Name's Steed. Only been here a few weeks."

Her eyes narrowed. He held a pair of scissors, their silver blades glinting under the neon lights. No blood yet. Thank god.

Sergeant Finley, the victim, and one of the sharpest soldiers in the entire section, swallowed while she pushed her head back into Steed's shoulder in a vain attempt to distance herself from the weapon.

"Take it easy," someone else said. Sullivan glanced in the direction of the sound. Sergeant Clark, from operations, an MP rather than an intelligence soldier, gestured for calm.

That was good. He would know what to do. All she had to do was give him the opening.

"So, Steed," she said, "what's the problem here?"

It took Steed a second to realize he'd been spoken to, and then he surveyed the room, eyes landing on Clark, standing so still he could have been a mannequin.

"Steed?" Sullivan said again. "You know who I am? I asked you a question."

"Um," he said, closing his eyes.

Sergeant Clark inched closer.

"I won't go," Steed finally blurted, now breathing heavily, eyes dancing as he scanned the room.

"Go?"

"You can't make me!" His voice cracked, and now his weapon hand trembled, and Finley sucked in a frightened breath.

"Go where, Steed?" Sullivan said, voice as calm as she could manage, even though her stomach whirred like it was filled with a dozen dragonflies, wings buzzing madly.

Steed stared at her, then lowered the scissors a fraction of an inch. "An alien attack."

Sullivan glanced at Major Li, who shrugged apologetically. "I had him watching the videos from Mumbai."

Great. So, he'd spent several days watching police officers get their heads blown into red mist. No wonder the guy was so terrified. She turned back to Steed. "Okay. I understand." She waited for him to make eye contact, to show that he was in a mental state where he could comprehend. "And I can tell you, you're not going to be sent there."

Steed pressed his weapon against Finley's neck. "That's not true! I've seen the orders! We're all going!"

"Lord, help me," Finley whispered, a tear hovering between her eye and cheek bone, like it couldn't decide whether to fall.

God, he was over the bend, so nuts he wasn't going to believe anything. Patrice's mouth had gone dry, and she struggled to think of how to reassure him. "I saw the orders, too. But not all of us are actually--"

"Don't lie to me!"

"Easy. Easy," Sergeant Clark said. He sounded like a farm boy talking to a spooked horse, voice calm, hands out, palms facing downward.

Steed's eyes danced, jerking in frantic saccades, and a trail of spittle drew a line over Finley's collar. "I saw that policeman get his head blown--" His voice broke.

Clark cocked his head.

"Steed," she tried again, "it's the infantry soldiers who'll face down the enemy. Not... not an intel specialist in an MP brigade."

"And if they fail?"

She closed her eyes for a split second. Damn, he'd read those orders more carefully than she had expected. "Okay. Then how can I reassure you?"

He froze.

You don't know, do you? she wanted to say. Stupid ass, you need to think these things through before you go postal on us.

Sergeant Clark took a slow-motion step toward him.

Steed spun his head toward Clark. "Get back! Right now! I'll kill her!"

An invisible hand grabbed Sullivan around the throat. Now, her bladder was painfully full, ready to burst. "Do what he says," she instructed Sergeant Clark.

Clark's expression turned dark, but he nodded, then returned to his original position. Thank God he knew how to follow orders in a tough situation.

She had to recover Steed's attention. "How about a transfer to another unit? Some outfit that isn't going to be deployed?"

"Um..." Steed glanced at the sergeant standing nearby. Then he looked at Major Li. Finally, his eyes returned to Sullivan. "Yeah." His hand lowered the scissors slightly, so that the point no longer pressed into his victim's skin.

"Okay," Sullivan said, putting a deliberate brightness in her tone. "I'll go over to S-1 and get the transfer paperwork started."

Another micro lowering of the weapon.

She pulled a small green notebook from her cargo pocket, and a pen from the slot on her left sleeve. "I'll just need a little information."

"Uh, right."

"First, your social." She put her pen to the paper as though she planned to write.

"Five, one, eight," Steed began.

"Five," she repeated, like an idiot struggling to write the numbers, "eight…"

"No. Five, one."

"One." She glanced back at him, saw the scissors lower another half inch. Sergeant Clark remained in her peripheral vision, as still as a cat waiting for the right moment to pounce.

"Okay. Five, one, one…"

"No." Steed huffed, and the scissors lowered again.

SSG Clark leapt at Steed, grabbing the hand with the weapon, and slamming it onto the table. Finley spun as Steed lost his grip on her.

"Ow!" Steed shouted, fingers cracking open. The scissors clattered on the metal surface.

Sergeant Finley dashed around the table and into the arms of a female lieutenant, sobbing.

In less than two seconds, Clark had both of Steed's hands on the tabletop, feet spread wide. "You have the right to remain silent," he began.

Another MP joined him, proffering handcuffs. "Yeah, you're going to another unit alright. Like, Leavenworth."

Major Li grinned. "That was awesome, ma'am."

Sullivan let out a long breath. Felt like she had been holding it the whole time. "Get Finley checked out by the medics."

Li came to the position of attention, then nodded. "Of course."

"Then make sure she gets counseling."

"Right."

"And keep me informed." She headed to the latrine, and only when she'd closed the door to the stall did her knees turn liquid.

Back out at the sinks, a good splash of water on her face brought her back to the present, to the place where a person pushed her feelings away because there wasn't time for such luxuries. Water trickled over her cheeks, over the jagged scar below her right eye. She touched it.

Can't trust anybody.

A quick wipe with the towel, and she went back to her office, where she flopped into her chair. Her large, wooden desk usually felt like a shield between her and anyone who would threaten her, but not now. She pulled up the unit orders on her computer screen and scanned the first section again, the part that talked about the enemy they expected to face.

Too little information. The aliens had only attacked Earth once, two weeks earlier, hitting five cities in the Eastern hemisphere, where they grabbed tens of thousands of people, stuffed them into the alien spacecraft, then sped back into the blackness of space. No contact with governments, no demands, no hints they wanted to conquer.

And nobody knew when they would return.

L. D. ROBINSON © 2022

Chapter 2 — Alien Captain

Beglash of Kernish, Captain of the Imperial war ship *Blood Fury*, stepped through the door of the communications center, hands balled into fists shaking in triumph. He had won. The little guy, the one who had been picked on and belittled, finally, he had scored his victory, finally he had been given a mission worthy of his ship and his command.

The dark possibility of failure flitted into his awareness, and he batted it away. He would succeed. No need to ruminate over what might go wrong.

There was too much satisfaction to enjoy, especially as he remembered the dark look on Ramed's face when the Admiralty agreed to send Beglash's ship on the next harvest. They trusted he would succeed, even if Ramed continually whispered doubt. Even better, once his mission was accomplished, Beglash would have a chance to exercise the kinds of influence other captains, those with more prestige, had already wielded. Beglash's son, two years overdue for manhood, would finally go to the front of the line.

Unable to repress his smile, he started down the outer utility concourse of Dakhesh's principal space port, the left wall studded with doors and passages, the right almost deck to deck windows, displaying the glorious beauty of space, the view only occasionally blocked by long umbilicals snaking from the port to the ships docked there, maintenance shuttles flitting about, and even the occasional team of mechanics floating outside a damaged ship's charred skin, doing whatever repairs they had been assigned. He stopped and watched with amazement the delicate weightless dance as jetpacks puffed and men spun feet over head. Something blue flickered in the dim light, and Beglash's stomach jolted.

Those men in blue shirts were everywhere, even out here, even off the planet.

Time to get back to his mission.

And how hard could it be? For a successful harvest, he just had to remain hidden from the Enforcers, and he was good at that. He had trained his crew in every trick to keep those sinking meddlers from ever knowing his whereabouts. This time would be no different.

He hurried around the curved walkway, anxious to get to his ship, approaching the safety wall, which held massive doors that would slam shut should any of the compartments be breached. Without those walls, he would already be in view of the *Blood Fury*.

"Look at you!" someone said in the far room, voice booming. It sounded like Zolbon, a one-time friend, but that relationship had died years ago. Zolbon was the last person Beglash wanted to talk to right now.

Beglash stopped before he reached the door. He would wait until the loud person was gone.

"You look like a man!" Zolbon continued. "Last time I saw you, you were only this high!"

"I'm not a man," another voice answered, a rich baritone with a touch of reticence there. "My father says there are a hundred thousand boys ahead of me in the line."

Beglash's knees turned to water. Was that his son, Grelid? Admitting all these terrible truths to his father's greatest rival? Waves and foam, this couldn't be happening.

"Well," Zolbon continued, "that certainly is a problem. If only there was something I could do to help."

Son of a whore. That lying Zolbon could help if he really wanted to. Right now, he could get the ministry of ritual to do anything he wanted, but he was having too much fun laughing at Beglash's lower status.

But wait. Beglash had just brokered that exact deal with the Ministry. No reason at all to slink into the other room like a *wilp*. Beglash lifted his chin and walked through the blast doors.

Zolbon, his thick belly protruding markedly from his vest, faced Grelid. The boy's mother stood behind him, looking as timid as Grelid sounded. "But when you get to the front of the line… what a mighty warrior you'll be," Zolbon continued, reaching out in an expansive gesture. "You must have gotten that from your mother's side of the family."

Heat rose into Beglash's face. It took all his discipline not to attack Zolbon from behind. After all, it wouldn't be a good idea to kill the hero of the empire.

"Hello, father."

Zolbon spun around, a little guilt on his face. But he quickly recovered and put on a magnanimous grin. "Oh, Beglash, my friend!"

"Zolbon."

"Come over here." Zolbon motioned to the other side of the wide hallway, as though he were about to share state secrets and didn't want the uninitiated to hear.

Beglash should refuse, but it wouldn't be good for his son to see him having a spat with another captain. He nodded, not letting up on his frown. Zolbon joined him near the inner wall.

"So," Zolbon said, voice lowered, while slapping a beefy hand on Beglash's back. "I hear you got a new mission to my planet."

Beglash coughed. Just because they were calling it "Zolbon's planet" didn't mean it belonged to the man. In fact, Beglash looked forward to finding out what the inhabitants called that planet. And he wanted to see the look on Zolbon's face when the man lost the honor of having a whole world named after him.

"News travels fast," Beglash said.

L. D. ROBINSON © 2022

"You'll do fine," Zolbon said, a note of fake reassurance in his tone. He pointed out the window, where the *Blood Fury* stretched out from the spaceport, looking like a leech hanging from the belly of a sea *righul*. The black paint of its exterior was a little too shiny, and the spindly engine pylons looked like they could easily break off. "A fine little ship you have there."

Beglash forced a smile, like he was proud of running the smallest of all the imperial ships outfitted for battle. Like he took Zolbon's comment as a compliment. Like he hadn't noticed that Zolbon's ship was five times the size of his own. "You have a good eye for quality in the fleet."

Zolbon's smile flickered momentarily, then a soft chuckle worked its way down his ample belly. Beglash glanced at the other captain's belt. What would Zolbon say if Beglash commented that Zolbon needed a larger ship just to accommodate his girth?

Zolbon lifted his brows, making a gesture with finger and thumb close together and running horizontally. "It's very sleek."

"The Enforcers will never spot it," Beglash added. Not so much because it was small, but because Beglash was skilled at evading. And patient. He could wait until they were finished with their patrol of the system before he made his move.

"Ah, yes," Zolbon said. "How is your crew? Well disciplined? Courageous?"

Beglash narrowed his eyes at his rival. How much did Zolbon know about Beglash's personnel problems, about the shortage of sensor operators, the assignment of inappropriate crewmen to his bridge? Had he helped Ramed in planning how to sabotage the *Blood Fury*?

That was unlikely. Zolbon barely knew Ramed and had little regard for any officer unqualified to serve in space. Best pretend everything was fine. "They are all excellent," Beglash said, "except for one, a pilot named Galth, recently transferred from another ship." When Zolbon's eyes narrowed, Beglash knew the other captain remembered Galth. "Evidently, they didn't teach him any discipline where he came from."

Zolbon jerked his head back, like he'd been slapped. "Oh, really? What was his former ship?"

Beglash had to force himself not to smile, not to laugh in Zolbon's face. Instead, he shrugged. "I don't recall," he lied. "But it doesn't matter. He'll learn soon enough."

Nodding, Zolbon appeared to brush off the insult. "Are you certain your crew can handle the mission?"

"It'll be difficult," Beglash said, "but we're ready."

"Just the reason I wanted to talk to you," Zolbon said, again indicating the *Blood Fury* with his hand. "Even with such a… stealthy ship, you may have problems avoiding the Enforcers."

"And?"

"And so, I'm offering my assistance. If you can't make it into the system without them seeing you, I can bring my ship in and provide a distraction. Maybe I can even lead them back into interstellar space. Give you plenty of time to harvest..." He glanced at the *Blood Fury*, eyes roving it from one end to the other. "... as many quivs as your ship can hold."

So Zolbon could take credit for the harvest? Not as long as Beglash was breathing.

"Or," Beglash said, "perhaps they'll be in another system, like when you went there."

Now, Zolbon's smile looked strained. "I'll be available, if you need me."

"Yes. Don't do anything until I call you." With a forced grin, Beglash slapped Zolbon on the arm, then strutted toward his family waiting near the window.

"Grelid," Beglash said, "I'm pleased you came to see me off." He gestured for them to gather close, as though he didn't want anyone, make that Zolbon, to hear anything. "The Minister of Ritual has sworn that if I'm successful in my next mission, then you," he poked his finger in Grelid's direction, "will be moved to the front of the line."

Grelid clapped his hands and made a quick jump of excitement. "Great embrace!"

Of course, that was only half the agreement, but Beglash had no reason to tell them the rest of it. That would only worry them needlessly. Beglash planned to return with a ship full of Dakh Hhargashian equivalents or quivs as they were called, so many that everyone in the fleet would wonder how he got them all into his small cargo hold.

Yes. That small blue planet and its billions of inhabitants weren't going to know what hit them.

L. D. ROBINSON © 2022

Chapter 3 — Alert

Phone... ringing... ringing...
Three oh seven... way too early.
Dark outside.
Ringing.
Shit!
Patrice jolted up, fingers clawing at her cell phone, which danced as it vibrated on her nightstand, playing Stars and Stripes Forever, the ringtone she'd set for calls from the staff duty officer.

"Sullivan," she said, her voice croaking from disuse. She cleared her throat, grabbed another gulp of air, her lungs working like she'd just run five miles flat out, her heart sprinting as the possible emergencies dog-piled into her awareness.

The man on the phone identified himself, one of the many young officers in the brigade, someone she barely knew. "We've been alerted," he said. "Another ship's been spotted in outer space."

Hell. Everything Private Steed had fretted about exploded in her mind, the chaos of an attack, the hopeless struggle as first responders tried to stop the death-ray armed men while militaries scrambled to reach the scene before it was too late. She flipped on her bedside lamp, then rushed to the chair in the corner, where she'd laid out her uniform for the next day. "I'll be right in."

No time to think now. Her uniform went on in record time, boot laces tightening with a single pull. She grabbed her duffle from the closet, something she kept always packed, then headed for her front door.

Just as she reached for the doorknob, she remembered she no longer lived alone. Old habits had almost had her out the door without a word to anyone.

She left her bag by the door and went back down the hall, then slipped open the door to the other bedroom. Slivers of light illuminated the curves of her mother's body, curled under the off-white blanket, knees drawn to her chest, as if only in her sleep could she admit her vulnerability.

Patrice closed her eyes while her inner critic berated her. This was no place for her mother to live, where you never knew what was going to happen next, where Patrice could not always be there to assure her mother's needs were met.

She took a deep breath. Neither of her siblings had any better circumstances. This was what they'd decided upon, and that was that.

If only the instability of Patrice's life hadn't intruded so soon.

Mama stirred. "Charlie?"

"It's Patrice, Mama." She walked over to the bed, skirting around the piles of still unpacked boxes, then sat on the edge of the mattress. "Just wanted you to know I got called in early."

Mama's face looked confused, and Patrice held her breath. *Please don't call Dad's name again...*

"At three in the morning?"

Patrice exhaled as a smile crept onto her face. "Happens all the time. After you've lived here for a while, you'll get used to it."

"Oh." Mama's laugh sounded like Patrice's grandmother, old and craggy. She sat up, leaning against her elbows.

"But I might not be home soon, so I want you to call Steve, okay?"

"Where will you be?"

Patrice glanced at the nightstand, where Mama had stuck a framed photo of her and her husband, Patrice's dad, a casual shot with him running his fingers through his ample head of hair. Son of a bitch hadn't even given her a real wedding with a professional photo she could put up. They'd defied her parents, snuck out in the middle of the night, then gone to the Justice of the Peace.

"With Dad." Her own personal code for, "nobody knows."

Mama squeezed Patrice's wrist as she slipped her feet out of the bed. "Don't say that. You don't know what it means."

Patrice swallowed, surprised at Mama's admission, a situation the older woman almost never acknowledged. "I'll fill you in as soon as I know something."

Mama's toes touched the floor.

"Stay in bed."

"No. I'm up now."

No use arguing with Mama. Patrice patted her on the arm, then gave her a quick kiss on the forehead. "Go back to sleep."

Guilt slammed her as she left Mama's room, guilt that she had not given the older woman the grandchildren she'd wanted, that she had not embarked on a safer career, like medical doctor or even veterinarian, even nurse for heaven's sake, something to do with the biology Patrice had studied in college. "Why the army?" Mama had groused. And now, she was abandoning her mother again, just like Dad had done.

No, damn it. She'd warmed Mama. She'd said goodbye. More than he had ever deigned to do.

Patrice reached the front door and grabbed the duffle, grunting as she heaved it onto her back.

Mama chuckled, walking bent-armed down the hall, frilly nightgown billowing around her thin legs. "Your father would be so proud."

Patrice forced a smile over the glower that mention of that man brought on. But she knew better than to show her anger to Mom. The older woman would defend him to the end.

"Call Steve."

"I can take care of myself."

Yeah. Like when we were kids and you had to move in with your mother because you couldn't make enough money to keep the house.

Patrice jerked the front door open, let it slam into the doorstop and bounce back. Why was she doing this to herself? Damn it, Steve and his wife should have taken over care of Mama. So what if their situation was a little unpredictable? Hers was certainly the most unstable of the family.

She grabbed the door on its bounce back, then plunged outside. "See you later," she called over her shoulder, not waiting for a reply. A moment later, she was stuffing her duffle into the front trunk space of her little sports car, a spot supposedly big enough for a golf bag, but it wasn't going in. Damn it.

Through the front window, the light from the living room had turned from soft white to bluish. Crap. Mama had probably turned on the television. Sullivan had to get out of there now, before Mama figured out what was going on. She splayed her fingers across the rough canvas and jumped, pressing her entire body weight onto the bag. It popped into place, and she closed the lid.

The front door banged open. "Patrice!" Mama called, rushing outside, bare feet on the sidewalk, her frail form silhouetted by the nearby streetlamp. "You can't go! You can't!"

God, Patrice didn't have time for this. The clock had already started, and getting her whole unit in to work was now the most urgent priority.

Mama hurried toward her, arms outstretched.

Patrice pulled her car door open. "I don't have a choice, Mama."

Mama slammed into her, knocking her against the low-slung car, her back bending over the roof. Mama's arms grabbed Patrice around the waist. "No! No! I can't lose you, too."

Too? Had she just admitted her missing husband was never coming back?

But there was no time to check on Mama's grasp of reality. "I tell you what. I'll give Steve a call, tell him to check on you."

"The news says…" Mama's voice broke.

Crap. "Mama, I'll be fine," Patrice said, pulling Mama's arms away from her.

"You're sure?"

Patrice put one foot in the car, pushing Mom away so she could close the door. "Absolutely."

"But…"

"Have I ever lied to you?"

Mama shook her head, then took a step back, wrapping her arms around herself, then standing like a wraith in the fading headlights as Patrice backed out of the driveway.

God, she was going to have some serious penance to do when she got back home.

L. D. ROBINSON © 2022

But she couldn't allow herself to think about that, either.

Now headed to post, she kept her mind busy with her driving, until she found herself stopped at a red light. And then a wave of fear swallowed her. The road ahead looked covered with dark fog. The moon was gone.

"Please, God," she whispered, crossing herself the way her mother had taught her when she was a child, something she hadn't done in years. "Let this be a false alarm."

And inside her mind, another voice said, let the aliens come here. Come, you sons of bitches, and I'll show you what happens when you mess with the United States of America.

She shook her head. Did she really want the aliens to attack her country? Did she really want to have to send her soldiers out to be killed by them? What kind of nutty person was she, anyway? What kind of distorted assessment did she have of how well she could do against these advanced creatures? Sure, it was a fun fantasy, but realistically? More unlikely than not.

But if she could… a success in this kind of mission would assure her promotion.

She pulled her corvette into her reserved parking space, her car lights blazing even after she'd turned the engine off.

She glanced around. Dozens of soldiers trudged toward the headquarters building from the barracks, a few dragging their duffle bags over the sidewalks and through the round pools of light cast by scattered streetlamps. Other cars moved slowly through the parking lot, wives kissing their husbands goodbye and then driving away.

A twinge of regret pinched her chest. She didn't have anyone like that to kiss goodbye.

Not a concern she was *even* going to entertain. She wrenched her duffle from the truck, jaw muscles twitching, then bolted toward the safety of her office.

Chapter 4 — Hiding

Beyond the transparent bubble of the bridge, a jagged piece of rubble slowly spun, blotches of mottled snow creeping across the shadowed face, barely visible in the feeble light of the tiny yellow star which sat at the center of the target system.

Five other men stood in the invisible room, looking like they lived in space, without the need for air or heat or gravity, denizens of the darkness, clutching their foot-sized control pads, commanding the ship with light touches.

"Status?" Beglash said, letting his own pad rest against his thigh. Its displays of ship condition and personnel readiness didn't matter to him. It was the enemy ship out there he cared about, and an hour had passed since he'd last heard what they were doing.

"No change," Tordag, the second in command, answered, looking up at the captain with annoyance. "The Enforcers are patient."

"Stupid," Beglash corrected him. "If they want to catch us, then *they* should be hiding, not us."

Tordag smiled and nodded.

"You want to keep us stuck out here forever," Galth said, stepping toward the far end of the invisible bridge, waving his empty hand at someone Beglash couldn't see, someone Tordag kept out of Beglash's line of sight behind the other bridge officers.

And for a glorious moment, Beglash had almost forgotten the man was there.

"Get off the bridge," Beglash said, pointing his finger at Galth.

"What are you saying?" Galth said, now gesturing toward the other while staring at the captain. "You trust him? He says there's no change, and you take his word for it?"

Beglash didn't need to explain himself to this lowly transplant. Galth had arrived acting like he thought he should be the captain, like he thought he was better than any of the other officers, simply because of his former ship. It was time to teach the man a lesson in obedience. "Tordag, call security."

Galth clapped his hands onto his chest. "What? Now you're taking his side against me? You're going to defend an unspeakable, someone dressed in blue?"

A raging volcano exploded inside Beglash, spitting ash and molten rocks. The color of the bridge changed, bright red where shadowed scabs had been. And somewhere in the background, children's voices -- Ramed's boyhood voice -- chanted, "Beglash wears blue, Beglash wears blue!"

Two steps. A quick swing of a fist. Crack. Galth was down, slamming onto the transparent floor, thudding, blood and spittle spraying into a red doily. Breath whooshed between his split lips. Beglash kicked him, toes landing in the softness of an unprotected gut. Galth groaned.

"You will not speak to me like that!" Beglash bellowed. He looked around, saw the surprised expressions on the officers' faces, the fear in Tordag's eyes as he choreographed the movements of the others, keeping only a flicker of a blue shirt visible, and then it was gone again, hidden behind the dark red shadows of the Hhargashna uniforms.

The second in command rushed up to Galth, grabbing him by the shoulder and pulling him toward the exit. "Get out of here, before you get us *all* killed."

Beglash smiled, more to himself than to anyone else. It paid to have come by command in the traditional way, a bloodied dagger his instrument of promotion. The fear that fact created in his crew, the possibility of a shameful death, was one of his most powerful tools of control.

Beglash paced back to his original position, slowly enough that the remainder of the bridge crew could adjust their positions, blocking out the sight of the *Blood Fury's* greatest embarrassment, the worst insult to its captain.

Beglash's excitement was wearing off, leaving him with a dull ache in his knuckles. Well worth it.

Tordag strutted back onto the bridge, muttering something about Galth going to do performance checks on his shuttle.

"They're moving," the man in blue said from out of sight, directing his comments to Tordag.

"Captain--" Tordag began.

"I heard." Someday, after Beglash got used to his new sensor operator--Meliq, that was his name-- maybe after he got so he could trust the man, then perhaps he could stop pretending the unspeakable had never been assigned to his crew. And right now, he was anxious enough to want to hurry things up, get news that would allow him to take his ship out of this huge, spherical comet cloud and bring it closer to the target planet, down into the part of the system that formed a flat disk of planets and asteroids.

"Where are they going?" Tordag asked.

"Looks like the fourth planet."

"Sink it," Beglash muttered. Too close in, too likely the Enforcers were still watching for him.

"But don't they head to the outer planets before they get ready to leave the system?" Meliq asked.

"Sometimes," Tordag answered.

Beglash's fingers throbbed, red where they had made contact with Galth's face. Time for a little advancement on the target. He was so far out, and so far off from the angle of the system disk that the Enforcers were unlikely to spot him even if his ship exploded.

"Prepare to move to the outermost asteroid ring."

Chapter 5 — Plans and Preparations

As soon as she got to her office, she found Lieutenant Colonel Davis, the brigade executive officer, standing near the long conference table, his dark fingers wrapped around a stack of papers, the operations order, that he waved at her, held so that she could see the page with the words "to be determined" splashed across the emptiness, where their higher headquarters should have told them how to fight these bastards. And TBD was the most help they were probably going to get. "You got any ideas?"

She shrugged as she walked in, then closed the door and headed toward her desk. "Maybe we can take all the tension around here, suction it into some kind of weapon and shoot it at them."

Davis narrowed his eyes, like he'd taken her comment seriously. "What would that do?"

"Give them the heebie jeebies?" she said. "They'd head back to their own planet and never return."

Davis slowly lowered the order, then let it flop onto the long conference table at the far end of her office. "How the hell are *you* so calm?"

"It's my deception plan."

"It's a good one." He gave her a weak smile, one that seemed to say he was trying to keep his emotions under control. But it was harder than people realized. They had seen too much to think they could waltz into a battle with the Nabbers and win easily.

She slipped into her chair. "Status?"

Davis gave her a brief rundown of the assembling of her unit, of the little he knew so far. They hadn't gotten any word about meetings, or alien landing sites, or anything else they could act on. But it was still early, still dark outside.

"Okay, then," she said. "Send me Major Li."

"PIRs?" Davis asked. The priority information requirements were the questions Patrice had asked her intelligence officer to answer. It was a standard way to organize and analyze any intelligence they had, to make it useful for military planning, show how it applied to any particular operation.

She nodded and he left. A moment later, a trembling young major stood in front of her desk, a pad in hand, a look of hopelessness on his round face. "Ma'am," he said, "I've just been going over higher headquarters' intelligence briefing."

Oh, hell. He had nothing.

All the time they had spent going over the records of the previous attack, all the effort they'd expended, and they had nothing? Nothing but one soldier freaking out and another almost being killed? What kind of incompetent section was Major Li running?

She pressed her lips together. "I suppose they don't have anything, either."

"Their PIRs are very similar to yours."

Okay, now, he was buttering her up, trying to hint that she was thinking like the generals, that she was almost ready for that coveted promotion. She had no intention of letting Li off that easily.

"What weaknesses have you found?"

He swallowed. "They have shields, ma'am."

She didn't need him to tell her the obvious. "And does it have any seams? Is it stronger in some places than others?"

"We just don't have enough data--"

She jumped to her feet. "There are thousands of videos, bystanders with their cell phones recording every single move they made. How can you not have enough?"

"Ma'am, if the G-2 guys in the Pentagon and at Fort Huachuca can't come up with anything, how am I supposed to?"

She walked to the window, where the barest hints of light hugged the horizon, and the stars still sparkled. "You have a different way of looking at things. You should see something they don't."

At this point, she wasn't certain she believed that, but it was the line she had to tell him. He had to give her something to use in fighting these guys, or she and all her soldiers were dead.

Because she didn't think the infantry was going to succeed. And according to those orders Davis had left on the table, after the infantry was wiped out, she was supposed to take her unit in and do what they had been unable to do.

If only she had a clue how to fight them.

"I'm sorry, ma'am," Li said. "I'm not..."

She glared at him.

"I... I..." He closed his eyes. "No excuses. I know. But I just don't have any idea what to do next." His voice cracked.

She let out a long breath. The poor kid was giving it his all. And now he was asking for help.

Time to stop yelling.

She pointed to a chair at the conference table. As she walked there, she remembered how excited she'd been when she first saw it. Damn, an office big enough for her desk *and* a conference table. It really meant she'd come up in the world, she was important now. But sitting here with her S-2 almost in tears, facing an enemy no one knew how to beat, none of this pretentious office space really meant much. It was just a table and chairs, and she'd just become a teacher.

"Weaknesses," she said as she sat beside him, deliberately avoiding the head of the table, the place of power. "That's what I most need to know. Some way we can..."

"Override their superiority," he said.

Good. He understood. And it was time to give him a little empathy, an indication that she knew what he was going through. "But those weaknesses aren't always easy to find."

Relief washed over his face. "Tell me about it."

"So, what I think will work is for you to speculate. Brainstorm with your soldiers, make up some stuff."

His brows drew together over his nose. "Make up?"

"Like a scientific hypothesis," she said.

His eyes brightened. "Then all we have to do is see if we can disprove or verify."

"Right. So, suppose our theory is that there's a seam in their shields, and it's a softer target."

"I got it," Li said, starting to stand. "We should be able to test that."

She nodded. "Go." Then, as he reached the door, she added, "and remember to have new ideas in the queue for testing. That way, when you disprove one idea, you have another to start working on."

"Thank you," he said, then hurried toward the door, where he stopped, blocked by the bulky body of LTC Davis.

"Ma'am," Davis said, "we got information on the spaceship movements."

"Show me," she said.

"In the two shop."

She followed him to the intelligence area, where a television mounted on the wall showed a newscaster talking. The lieutenant had the remote control and was reversing the recording.

By now, several other people had entered the room, including Sergeant Clark from operations. Across the room, Sergeant Finley smiled at Patrice with a touch of bashfulness. Patrice motioned for her to approach. "How are you?"

"Good," Finley answered, "now Steed's gone."

"Okay, here it is," the lieutenant said. The television screen showed an image of the sky, black stars on a white background, and a line zigzagging from one side to the other.

That couldn't be right. It just didn't look like what an attacker would be doing, preparing to land shuttles on the Earth.

"Is that even the same aliens?" Davis asked.

L. D. ROBINSON © 2022

Oh, come on. Two different groups of aliens? That seemed like the least likely explanation.

Sergeant Clark took a step forward. "Looks like they're on patrol."

"But patrolling for what?" Patrice asked. Were they expecting the humans to have already put something in space to counter their efforts?

Clark shook his head.

Major Li put his hands on his hips. "Another mystery to solve."

The brigade sergeant-major entered the room and handed her a small paper. She glanced at it. Information about the commander's meeting. Looked like it was time to go.

She would get the latest intelligence there, and maybe even a few ideas about how to fight this foe. Or maybe not.

Chapter 6 — Moving In

"Synchronizing orbit now," the helmsman said.

Beglash let out a breath of relief. "Any sign we've been spotted?" Their last maneuver was one of the most dangerous, slipping from the comet cloud down to the plane of the system, to the outer ring.

A short silence followed the question, and then the man in blue shook his head. "The Enforcer ship's movements haven't changed."

Beglash stared at the large asteroid hovering outside his ship, which now served as a shield that would screen his ship, keep the Enforcers from knowing his whereabouts. As long as his crew maintained their patience, as long as no one did anything to alert the Enforcers, they would be okay. But the helmsman's finger kept moving over his control pad, then backing off.

"Maintain course." Beglash said.

"When are they going to leave?" the helmsman said.

Beglash rolled his eyes. "Just think of it as a game."

"And get your finger away from the engine controls," Tordag said.

The helmsman moved his right hand behind his back.

It didn't feel like their movement from the comet cloud to this ring of planetary debris was enough to make a lot of difference, but now the Enforcers could spot them much more easily. Now, they had to be ten times as careful.

Beglash rubbed a hand over his left sleeve to brush off a bit of dust from his dark red shirt. This was the color of his own caste, a color one could be proud to wear, the color of blood beginning to dry.

"The enemy is moving," Tordag said. He stared at his control pad with intensity. "Heading for the inner asteroid ring."

"Confirmed," Meliq said. He had positioned himself as far forward as possible, away from everyone else, now in full view of the captain, frantically punching on his control pad, as though he had something important to figure out. All that movement made Beglash nervous.

He turned to Tordag. "What is the sensor operator doing?"

"Looking for a better asteroid," Meliq said before the first officer had a chance to relay the question. "This one doesn't have enough iron.

Might not block Enforcer sensors as well as others."

Fathers and emperors, was that right? Or was Meliq trying to get them to move into view of the other ship, destroy Beglash's chances of success? How could he tell where this Unspeakable's loyalties lie? How would he *ever* know? Beglash turned back to Tordag. "Your opinion?"

Tordag glanced back at his pad. "This one has *some* iron."

"Some?"

Tordag lifted his shoulders. "Should be enough."

"They're headed in our direction." Beglash shouted. "Have they spotted us?"

"Not exactly in our direction," Tordag said. He held out his pad to show Beglash where the enemy was going, their angle of exit from the system off by fifteen degrees. It was enough that they would be millions - no billions - of *memgash* from the *Blood Fury*, should they get out this far, beyond the orbit of the blue ice planet, into a sparse rubble field that defined the outer edge of the system's flat disk.

But Beglash didn't want to take chances. "Can they see us?" he screeched.

Tordag huffed loudly. "There's no way to tell."

"Until they're on top of us," Beglash finished the thought. Not good enough. He spun around and looked at his natural shield again, glared at the rock in space as if he could get it to answer his questions through the emptiness. His hands wanted to reach out to it, choke it or slap it, get it to do better. Flying free through space, without walls to block your view, sometimes made you think you could do stuff like that.

"I think I spotted a good one," Meliq said, as though speaking to himself, his blue-covered shoulders hunching over the handheld pad. "Almost 78 percent iron."

"I suppose you want us to move there," Beglash growled, for once ignoring his rule about not speaking to the man.

"Too far away," Meliq said. "It would take too much propulsion. Leave too clear of a trail."

Sounded like the right answer. Sounded like exactly what Beglash would have decided, had it been left to his own discretion. But now he was doubting himself. When he got back to Dakhesh, he would have to demand that Meliq be assigned somewhere else. Either that, or he would have to send Meliq out an airlock, the consequences be damned. He couldn't deal with all this uncertainty.

"So, we just stay here? Wait for them to spot us?" He glanced again at Tordag. "You agree with that?"

"I... I don't know."

"Turn off our engines," Meliq said.

"You want to get us killed?" the helmsman barked.

Meliq just stood there, looking at Beglash, waiting.

"How will we get away if the Enforcers start to chase us?" the helmsman continued. He walked toward Meliq, looking like he owned space, one foot on a distant star here, another pressing against a blotch of a faraway comet, pushing on the blackness as though it were solid. "Huh? You know how long it takes to re-start the engines?"

Meliq rolled his eyes, then turned back to Beglash. "That's how I track the Enforcers when they're out of my line of sight. I follow their engine exhaust."

And it would be hours, if ever, before the Enforcers got anywhere close.

"Engines off," Beglash said.

"But--"

"*Off!*"

A moment later, the thrumming background of the engines faded into silence. All the lights and controls dimmed slightly, now running on stored energy. Now, all they had to do was wait and watch. He wouldn't venture nearer until the Enforcers were headed away. It wasn't just the prestige of this mission that was important. It was his son's life.

He didn't want to think about that, how he had only gotten his arrangement with the Minister of Ritual by agreeing that if he failed, Grelid would die in his victim's place. This mission demanded more caution than he had ever shown before.

Beglash let out an audible sigh. This could go on for days, the Enforcers moving around the system, trying to fake him out, get him to show them his position. He wouldn't fall for their tricks.

A spot on Beglash's control pad lit up. He pressed it, then frowned. It was a message from Zolbon, probably reiterating his offer to distract

L. D. ROBINSON © 2022

the Enforcers. Now the question was whether or not to even listen to it.

He turned off the light, then went back to watching Meliq. But a moment later, his curiosity forced a finger back on to the communications quadrant. The screen lit up with Zolbon's face, a big grin splitting the man's puffy cheeks. What was it now? Had Zolbon been promoted?

Beglash pressed the command to direct the sound into his earpiece. "Wonderful news," Zolbon said, that same happy tone that told him Beglash wasn't going to like the announcement. "Your son recently participated in a blaster competition, and damned if he didn't get first place!"

Beglash pulled his brows together. Well, that *was* good news.

"And he had major competition, including the previous champion. I tell you, Beglash, this kid is a crack shot. Amazing."

Beglash raised his brows. This wasn't anything like what he expected from his old rival.

"Of course, we know he got that from his mother's side of the family," Zolbon put in.

Okay, there it was. Now, Beglash just needed to come up with a similar insult to throw back at Zolbon. And he had plenty of time to think of one.

"So," Zolbon continued, "once Grelid becomes a man... I mean I assume you're going to be successful there... I want him posted to my ship. It'll give him a great start in the fleet. A lot better than if he got sent to the *Blood Fury*, don't you think?"

Beglash ground his teeth. When he got back to the empire, he was going to turn his weapons on Zolbon's ship, see if he could blast the entire thing into flotsam on the Night Sea.

"A large increase of output," Meliq said then, voice raised in what sounded like excitement. Didn't the man know what they were planning to do? Once he figured it out, he would never be allowed to speak to his people again.

Beglash walked toward the invisible wall, close enough that it made itself apparent by reflecting back his breath. "They're moving?"

"There they are." Meliq nodded with satisfaction, eyes squinting at his control pad.

"Engines on," Beglash said.

Tordag turned to the rest of the crew and started the process of reviving the ship's power source.

"The enforcers are moving outward," Meliq said. "Accelerating."

"Prepare to move into the inner system."

"Course already plotted."

Beglash lifted his brows. Evidently, the helmsman had kept himself busy by continually updating his course.

"Another large output," Meliq said, then grinned. "They just went into overspace."

"Move us in slowly," Beglash said. "We don't want any large engine outputs."

"All the way?" the helmsman asked.

"Only as far as the sixth planet."

"Complying," the helmsman said, and the stars began to move.

Beglash glanced around, still a little nervous. "Tordag, keep your sensors looking. They might come back into normal space."

"Understood."

The motions outside were slow, lazy. At this speed, it would take several hours to reach their destination. By then, they could be certain the Enforcers were gone. And then there would be no one to stop them from harvesting as many people as his ship could hold.

Chapter 7 — Re-Alert

Well, the commander's meeting had been a bust, everybody trying to sound important, trying to squeeze information out of turnips, trying to predict landing locations out of thin air. And in the end, the spaceship, or whatever it had been, left the system.

"It's possible they'll return, so we're not ending the alert yet," the senior officer had said. But the meeting had broken up.

Patrice had gotten a chance to exchange ideas and information with Colonel Barker, the infantry brigade commander she would support, should they ever be needed to fight aliens. And it had been useful. But not promising.

Now, back in her office, she put her phone to her cheek. Outside, the first glints of light were throwing long shadows over the dry grass. A lone fire hydrant and its dark shadow stretched over the sidewalk, looking like a drunken "L" laying on its side.

"Mama?"

"Oh, sweetheart, are you okay?"

Patrice blinked. Mama sounded like she was ready to worry herself into a major coronary infarction. "Hey, it's all good. Nothing to fret about."

Her office door opened, Major Li sticking his head inside. "Ma'am?"

Patrice stiffened. People didn't enter her office without an invitation unless it was serious. "Hold on, Mom." She nodded at her intelligence officer to give her his message.

"Another ship, ma'am," he said. "And this one's not dinking around the way the other one did."

"Tell Davis to call in the commanders and staff."

Li nodded and left.

"It's started again, hasn't it?" Mama said.

"I have to go now." Patrice tried to think of a better way to end the call, but she'd never been comfortable with phrases like "love you," or even "take care of yourself." She closed her eyes and tried to see her mother standing there but couldn't conjure the picture in her mind. "I'll talk to you later." Then she pressed the off button and stuffed the phone into her cargo pocket.

The first of her commanders walked through the door, and her chest constricted, like she was out of breath, like she'd been running full-out for five miles, like they were already on top of her unit, firing down at her. She pressed her eyes closed, then pushed the fears to the back of her mind.

In a few moments, all her battalion commanders and her senior staff gathered around the conference table in her office, some with computers but most opting for the old-fashioned pen and paper, to keep them from accidentally committing classified information to a non-secure digital device.

Major Li handed her a copy of the latest message about alien status. "No word yet on shuttle releases," she said as she sat at the head of the table.

The detention battalion commander, Lieutenant Colonel Palmer, folded his hands on the table. "Do we even know where we're going? I need to figure out where my unit will set up."

"Nothing is narrowed down yet," LTC Davis said. "Not even to the nearest hemisphere."

Palmer glared into the distance, and Patrice was certain he'd come close to rolling his eyes. She understood his frustration, but that didn't change anything.

And as if to make certain Palmer understood, they all understood, Davis added, "Nobody can plan nothing."

Patrice gave him a sharp look.

"'Cept the loggies." He motioned to the logistics officer, also known as the S-4. "Whadda you got?"

The S-4 ran through his coordination efforts, things like ammunition pick up; transportation, both air and ground; food and other supplies being dumped on the units in case their deployment lasted more than a few hours.

Once the S-4 finished, Davis turned to Major Li. "Anything new?"

"Yeah," Li said, a little smile quirking the edge of his mouth. "We've found a distance." He provided each officer a piece of paper with an icon in the center representing an alien shuttle, and a large circle drawn around it. "This is their engagement line. If you get inside that line, they will shoot at you."

"That doesn't do us a lot of good," Palmer groused.

"Sorry," Li said.

"Don't apologize," Patrice said. "Just keep working."

"Yes, ma'am."

"How is the deployment itself going to affect that?"

Li stared at her, as though he didn't understand the question.

"Once you're at the airfield, or on an aircraft, or a bus… can you keep doing this kind of analysis?"

"I don't think so."

"Then I want you and your people to stay back. Just send a couple of your soldiers to be liaisons."

For the first time since the original alert, Li looked relieved. "Yes, Ma'am. I think Sergeants Finley and Masters should be able to do that."

Patrice nodded. She wasn't certain Finley was going to be in any emotional condition to take on the stress level of a deployment, but at least in theory Li knew how she was doing. And it wasn't a good time to undermine her subordinate's decisions.

"Finley up to that?" Davis asked.

Thank God for subordinates who could almost read her mind.

"She's actually anxious to go," Li said. "Like she wants to prove what a woos Steed was." He smiled.

"Tough cookie," Davis said, a touch of admiration in his tone.

The door to the outer office opened, and Sergeant Clark stuck his head in. "Sorry to interrupt, ma'am."

"Yes?"

"Looks like three shuttles have separated from the spaceship, and they're headed for the east coast."

"*Our* east coast?" Palmer barked.

"Yes, sir. New York, Miami, Rio. That's the current best guess."

"New York," Davis said with a note of gusto. According to their orders, they were supposed to respond to attacks in the center of the country, not the east. That job was for the 82nd. "That means we'll live to fight another day."

Patrice let out a slow breath. At this moment, none of that mattered. "We're still on tap," she said. "And it's time to move." She stood. By now, most of her soldiers slated to deploy were already at the airfield, already getting ready to load. Now, the officers just had to catch up.

As her commanders scrambled out of the room, she swallowed. No time to text Mama and tell her plans had changed. Mama was just going to have to deal with it.

Chapter 8 — Flying Out

As Patrice stood on the tarmac watching her subordinate leaders supervise the loading of the aircraft, she remembered the chore she had forgotten to do. And as soon as she pulled her cell phone from her pocket, she realized that forgetfulness had been, on some level, deliberate.

But she'd promised Mama she would make this call. And for at least the next few moments she wouldn't have anything else to do.

She walked back through the terminal and out into the parking lot, where she could access a phone signal, then tapped in the command to call Steve.

"Don't tell me," he said. "You need me to fucking come and get Mama."

Patrice ran her fingers through her hair. "I don't even get a 'hello'?"

"I've been watching the news."

"Obviously."

"And I really don't appreciate that you think you can just drop one of these requirements on me any fucking time. I'm not on fucking call."

Damn it. Why did her brother have to be such an ass hole? No wonder Mama had not wanted to call him. No wonder she had been postponing the task as long as possible. "Look, I don't know how long I'm going to be gone."

"Like I said."

"It may be less than a couple of days."

"So you want me to drive all the way down there—"

"I want you to call her. On the telephone."

Silence. Well, good. At least he now realized that he had blown this whole thing out of proportion.

"Just check up on her once a day, make sure she's doing okay."

"And if she isn't?"

"She'll probably just want someone to talk to." Patrice covered her face with her free hand. That was a stupid thing to say. Why would Mama want to talk to Steve? Who in their right mind would want to talk to this man?

"Look, Pat, we've been through this a million times. The old lady needs to go into a home."

"Steve," Patrice said, "this is not the time." Mama had no pile of cash stashed away somewhere, no assets to sell, and only the meagerest of incomes. The type of "home" she could afford would be substandard, at best. Not to mention that Mama had objected to being put in a place where "people are just sitting around, waiting to die."

"You just don't want to spend any of your precious money," Steve said. "You can't be fucking bothered with helping her get a decent place."

"And how much did *you* offer to throw in?" she snapped.

"More than you!"

"Right. And as soon as she's in the home, then you'll withdraw your support."

"Look, you wanted to take her in. It's your problem."

The call clicked off.

Patrice stared at the phone, her hand trembling, rage pumping tears into her eyes. How had it happened that she came from a family so full of heartless people? Why did the men in her family treat her mother with so little respect or caring?

"Ma'am?" Lieutenant Colonel Davis called from the double glass doors of the terminal. "They're ready for you."

"Oh. Right." She stuffed her phone back in her pocket, then hurried back to the aircraft.

The roar of another take-off drowned out everything else. She caught a whiff of jet exhaust. Three more passenger planes lined up on the taxiway like quail chicks, small and vulnerable. Hers would be next.

"That was Barker, wasn't it?" she said, gesturing to the aircraft now arrowing toward the clouds. She wasn't certain how she felt about him now. Was he her competition, and did she hope he would fail, so she could be the hero? That was a terrible thing to think. It wasn't like she hated the guy or held something against all his soldiers. She should want them to succeed.

"Do they have our targets yet?" Davis asked.

She shook her head, then laughed with the kind of hopelessness soldiers often felt. "We'll probably be the last to know."

A call came through on Davis's hand-held radio, and he acknowledged it briskly. "Time to board."

She marched toward the metal bird, her face so stern it hurt, the extra work of carrying the bullet-proof vest around her torso making even the lifting of feet off the ground feel like an all-out run. She was about to embark on the worst part of the day—sitting inside an aircraft, not in charge of what was happening, no decisions to make. She wished she had something to distract her from having to surrender control, from having to become 150 pounds of helpless human cargo.

"How are the soldiers holding up?"

"Nervous," Davis answered. "I think they expect to be turned into red mist, just like all those police in the videos."

"Shit."

"I heard one say his only regret was he didn't have a chance to get drunk on the last night of his life."

Her stomach twisted uncomfortably. It was worse than she thought. But how could she rally them when she didn't have any bright ideas on how to make the mission anything *but* a bloodbath?

They reached the ramp to the aircraft door. Sullivan followed Davis up the ramp, as per protocol: the senior ranking person always boarded last.

Another plane rumbled down the runway, this one a commercial passenger jet pressed into military service. Another tranche of soldiers flying to their doom.

"We got the jump seats in the cockpit," Davis said.

Inside the plane, the stuffy air was filled with the low rumble of soldier's voices, the clicking of seat belts, and the occasional burst of laughter deep in the back of the cargo area. Soldiers struggled to fit themselves and all their armor into seats that were just a little too narrow, assault rifles pinned upright between their knees, barrels pointing toward the ceiling. Hydraulics whined as the rear cargo doors inched their way closed.

This was no Dreamliner. There were no windows, nor overhead bins, no interior walls—just exposed fuselage, wires and hydraulic lines.

Three steps more and she was at the stairway to the cockpit. Davis had already climbed up, but she knew she needed to talk to her soldiers first. She looked around, saw a veneer of calm, smiles and nods and confident expressions. Only a few of them showed any nerves.

She strode up to the center front, then gathered a deep breath and spoke with maximum volume. "We're going to win this one."

"Yeah," someone said, followed by a wave of assent.

"The Nabbers are making a big mistake if they think they can mess with the United States of America!"

"Hooah!" they shouted, pumping their fists in the air.

"We're going to kick some Nabber ass!"

The air erupted into a deafening roar, echoing off the sides of the fuselage, so loud her ears hurt. "Let's kill those bastards!" a soldier shouted.

She grinned, raising a fist above her head. "Let's *do* it!"

When the cheers died down, she gave them one last thumbs up, then walked toward the stairs to the cockpit. But the sight of General Turley standing in the doorway stopped her.

"You coming with us?" she said.

"I need to talk to you, outside."

Oh, great. She put on her best, bravest face as she stepped back down the ramp, a smile that should convey she was anxious to hear his words of advice, or whatever he was going to say to her.

"Nice pep-talk," he said.

"Thank you, sir."

Of course, that wasn't his main message. That was just a little nice thing people say to someone before they lower the hammer. She didn't like those kinds of delays, but she was in no position to tell him to get on with it.

"We just got an update from NASA. The shuttles have reached the stratosphere. Still too soon to know exactly where they're going."

"I see." She lifted her chin and threw her shoulders back, all with the hope it would make her look fearless. Turley probably saw through the entire smokescreen.

"Just be prepared for anything."

She swallowed. "We'll give it our all." She looked up into his grim face and wondered if the outcome of this battle would weigh on her next evaluation report, would finally get her a promotion. There was no way to tell. And no way to know if she would survive to *be* promoted.

"One other thing I need to emphasize," he said, his face gone even more stern. "If Barker's unit becomes ineffective, we still need you to pick up the ball. Get those civilians out of the alien shuttle."

She frowned. "If you can get us any more intelligence, Sir…"

He looked grim. "We may be asking you to help us on that," he said. "Try things out on them, see how they respond."

"Reconnaissance by fire," she said. "Not the way I like to do business."

"You have your orders, Colonel."

"Yes, sir. As I said, we'll give it our all."

"Good. I'll hold you to that." He turned and walked away.

She stomped back onto the plane, climbing the stairs to the cockpit like they were impossibly steep. It sounded like he *expected* Barker to fail, like he was certain she would end up shouldering the entire mission. Did he know something she didn't? Or did he think she would turn and run if the infantry failed?

Damn it, she had to prove her mettle.

The cockpit was claustrophobic, its curved walls covered with black control panels, its dashboard filled with flight instruments and indicators, seats jammed into tiny spaces. She flopped into the empty chair, mind grasping for new ideas, but delivering blanks. So frustrating.

"You okay?" Davis asked.

"How can we do it? If all Barker's men can't, how can we?"

"I don't know, ma'am."

"I feel like I'm being asked to shred the alien shuttle with my bare hands." She grabbed the ends of her five-point restraint harness and snapped it together.

"Maybe we can find some equipment there... welding lasers or something."

She gave him a sharp look. "We can't count on something like that."

"Right."

In the front of the cockpit, the two pilots worked through the last of their checklists. She expected her pilots to have streaks of gray in their hair, but these two looked like they'd just graduated from high school. She hoped the hell they knew what they were doing.

One of them popped his head up and looked at her. "Welcome aboard, ma'am. I'm Captain Angelo, and that's Captain Leighton."

She gave them a polite nod. They reminded her of her soldiers, down in the cargo bay -- young and hopeful, with their whole lives ahead of them, with everything in the world to lose.

And here she was, planning to lead them all into a death trap.

Chapter 9 — Approaching the Target

Galth smiled as the curvature of the planet below him seemed to straighten, and the thin veil of atmosphere grew in apparent size. His instruments told him the ship had already made contact with the air, and it was rushing by him at remarkable speed. But not so fast it created a fireball, the furnace older craft had to endure to enter a planet's domain. He had engines that directed his speed relative to the planet. He didn't need to rely on orbital mechanics to keep him aloft. That meant he could approach at a reasonable speed, a comfortable velocity.

It also meant it was going to take some time before they reached their chosen harvesting location.

He glanced down at his controller, debating an increase in speed.

"Time to target?" he said.

Kelm, his co-pilot, shook his head. "We've got problems."

Sink it. His first mission on this ship, and now Kelm was throwing problems at him? How was he supposed to impress his new commander and gain accolades if things didn't go according to plan?

"What is it?"

"Weather." Kelm shook his head. "The system was offshore before, and I expected it to move out to sea. But it's rolling inland."

Galth rolled his eyes. "We can handle a little weather." Clouds were of no consequence. Nobody needed a sunny day to do harvesting. Rain, or even snow, was no big deal. "Right?" Galth glanced at Reldak, who stood behind him in the control room. He had been assigned as the leader of the ground operations team, and he looked nervous.

"What kind of weather?" Reldak said.

Galth gritted his teeth. Why was this slime worm commander worried about a little storm? They could handle just about anything. Winds, even tornadoes, weren't going to present a problem.

"Fog."

Waves and foam. The one kind of weather they never wanted to encounter.

Galth glanced at the control pad, quickly fingering in queries to tell him how long it would take to go to his alternate target city. He didn't like the answer. "How thick is this fog? Can't we deal with it?"

Kelm shook his head. "My readings are level six."

"Fish bait," Reldak muttered.

Galth looked again at the time schedule, then grunted. "We've still got time. It'll burn off, won't it?"

"Could go to level seven."

Sink it, this could not be happening. Some cosmic misfortune, some angry god somewhere, was messing with everything Galth did. This was just not right, and Galth was not going to accept it.

"You need to turn to the alternate target," Kelm said.

Galth turned to Reldak. "You can deal with it, right? You can do everything inside. Don't worry about the outside."

"I have to have patrols."

Feces.

And every minute he delayed was going to take two minutes off his on-the-ground time. He needed to stop being petulant and just do the right thing. Galth put his finger on the controller, then finally, reluctantly, he forced his hand to move the virtual lever, and the shuttle began a slow turn. Another tap of his fingers sent a message to the *Blood Fury* of his change in destination.

Now he was going to be on the same kind of timetable as his fellow shuttle pilots. Now, he had lost his edge in his competition with them. It wasn't fair.

He slid the acceleration bar on his control pad up just slightly, but he knew he couldn't increase his speed too much, or he wouldn't have enough time to slow down for the landing.

"Wait a minute," Reldak said. "Why are we turning inland?"

Galth showed him the information on his control pad. "The alternate target is by a lake."

"Lake?" Reldak spit. "What kind of commands is Beglash giving us?"

Galth took a deep breath. In the short time he'd been assigned to this ship he had not been impressed with the commander, but this was his first hint others shared his disgust. Still, this particular command looked reasonable. "The lake is big enough to work just fine."

"Yeah," Kelm said, "probably even better than an ocean, since it's not gonna have a navy prowling around in it."

Galth nodded. Good point.

"Yeah, well..." Reldak looked to the side, brows still crumpled into angry knots.

Sink it, what kind of incompetent ground leader had he been assigned? All his capabilities would be wasted if his ground crew couldn't take advantage of their landing spot. Galth handed the controller to Reldak. "Pick a couple of good spots."

He may or may not land where Reldak picked, but at least it would get the ground leader to stop complaining.

Reldak took the controller and buried his nose in it.

They were getting closer. Time to ratchet down the speed, begin lowering altitude. "Don't take too long," he said.

Reldak let out a loud huff. "Lots of tall buildings."

"Find ones that line up against the lake."

"I know the criteria." A target building needed to be close enough to the water that any force attempting to stop them couldn't come at them from that direction, at least not in any large formations.

"Good," Galth said. Then he didn't need to enumerate any other specifications. The ease of the harvest always depended on the buildings selected, and Galth wanted to make certain their harvest was the best of the three shuttles heading toward the ground.

He eyed Reldak, watching the ground commander's reflection in his viewscreen. The kid bit his lip, let his finger hover over the surface for several seconds, concentration knotting his features.

"How many harvests have you done?" Galth asked.

"Suck water!" Reldak barked. "How many do you think?"

Well, okay, that was a stupid question. Nobody had gotten to harvest anything for years, ever since the last Dakh Hhargashian equivalent from Kalmon had been scooped up from that planet. And that had been decades ago, well before anyone on this ship was old enough to be in the fleet. That was why everyone was so excited about Zolbon's planet. You just didn't find Dakh Hhargashian equivalents on every planet that supported life. In fact, they were extremely rare in this part of the galaxy.

The communication signal on Galth's control pad flashed yellow. He touched the virtual button, and Beglash's face appeared on the screen. "There's a whole flock of aircraft flying toward your target," he said. "Some of them look military, probably carrying defenders."

"Easy as strangling a baby," Galth said.

"You can't take them out from orbit?" Reldak said from behind Galth.

"I've got other things to take care of," Beglash answered with an annoyed huff.

Galth grinned. "No problem. We'll blow them out of the sky."

"But that'll take time away from the harvest!"

Galth turned off his communications with the captain, then grabbed Reldak by the front of his shirt. "We have a can-do attitude in my crew. Got that?"

Reldak glared at him for several seconds, then finally nodded. "No problem."

Galth released his hand, then looked down at the controller Reldak held. "Does that one do weapons?"

"No."

"Take that one and step up front."

Reldak snatched a controller from the wall mount, then glared into the distance of the view screen. "Now, all you gotta do is get me to the aircraft."

"Right." With that Galth turned south. Time to deal some death and destruction. Harvesting was fun, of course, but nothing beat turning flying quivs into miniature supernovas.

Chapter 10 — Mid-Air Attack

Once they had achieved altitude, the pilots leaned back in their chairs, smiling. Angelo looked at her over his shoulder, his expression like someone who was out sightseeing. Patrice couldn't bring herself to smile back.

"Hey, ma'am," Angelo said, "I don't think you have anything to worry about."

She lifted her brows in a challenging expression. "Oh?"

"Air Force G2 got it figured out. We are going to take them out before they ever land, and then you won't have anything to do."

That all sounded a little too good to be true, but it deserved at least an attempt at a smile. "Hadn't heard anything about that."

"It's brilliant," Leighton added.

"Care to fill me in?"

Angelo looked at Leighton, a touch of doubt on his face. "You think we can tell her?"

"She's probably got a better security clearance than you."

Angelo gave her a nod. "They had the video from when the Indian fighter shot a missile at the shuttle."

"And it didn't make a dent," Davis said.

"No," Angelo said, "but when G2 ran the video in slow motion, they saw it did something."

Patrice leaned forward, a twinge of excitement in her gut. Her hands landed on her thighs, fingers draped over her knees, squeezing her legs softly. "But there was so much smoke and debris at the impact site…"

"Right," Angelo said. "But one of the cameras just happened to pick up infrared."

"So?"

"That's a frequency of light that *will* go through smoke and dust."

"And?"

Angelo's eyes lit up. "And the hull, right there at the contact point, collapsed inward for just a fraction of the second."

Patrice exchanged glances with Davis. Her area of study in college had been biology, not physics, and she wasn't certain she saw the significance in what had just been explained to her.

"They think that collapsing function is part of the shield system of the shuttle," Leighton said, as if he had intuited her confusion and knew she needed an explanation.

"Yeah," Angelo said. "So, if they can get two or three or more missiles to hit the same spot within a half a second of each other, they can cause an explosion while the hull is already collapsed, and that just might get through."

That sounded like a good possibility. Now, the only question was why hadn't the Air Force shared that intelligence with the Army? Or, worse, some idiot at the Army might've decided the information didn't apply to them. Either way, someone had screwed up. But it wasn't anything she needed to yell at the pilots about. She folded her hands on her lap and frowned. "Good information."

She slipped the headset onto her ears, so she could listen to the chatter, as someone with the call sign bandsaw—sounded like it was the AWACS controller—warned them that the alien craft was on an intercept course.

"So," Angelo said with a grin, "I think you're going to have the best seats in the house."

"What's our callsign?" she asked the pilots.

"Thug two – four," Angelo said, then squinted through the windshield. "There," he said, pointing to the right. "The alien shuttle. See it?"

Patrice spotted a tiny speck, at this distance looking like nothing more than a hyphen, silhouetted against the hazy blue.

To the far left, three Boeing 777s hung in the air, each at a different altitude, each going in the same direction. Beyond them, Barker's C-17 looked like a speck in the distance. To the right, a C-5 floated eerily above the clouds.

"Demon five-one," another voice said on the radio, "a flight of seven aircraft."

"Seven!" Leighton said. He looked like he wanted to give Captain Angelo a high-five, as if this was a time to celebrate.

"Who?" Patrice asked.

"Fighters," Angelo said with enthusiasm. "Seven of them!"

"They'll get 'em for sure!" Leighton added.

"And we'll be able to see everything!"

Patrice frowned. She'd rather be as far away as possible. "Can you see them?"

"There!" Leighton said, pointing to the left. Patrice spotted them, seven little dots, gnats hovering above the clouds. And now, the alien craft headed in their direction.

Patrice gripped her armrests, knuckles turning white, the pit in her stomach growing. Breathe, she told herself. Just relax and let them do their job.

The swarm approached from the west, then sparkled briefly.

"Fox one, seven missiles."

A trail of white, multiple lines of smoke cabled together, stretched between the fighters and the shuttle. When it reached the black alien ship, smoke billowed all around it, enveloping it. The swarm scattered, flying away from the enemy in all directions.

"Hell yes!" Leighton shouted. "Did you see that?"

Patrice leaned forward. What she'd thought she'd seen was blue light, little sparks and soft glows mostly hidden behind the darker wads of smoke. And a voice inside her head growled. That didn't look right. No explosion, no sudden outpouring of debris and destroyed craft. It just all hung together like wool on a sheep.

"Demon five-five," another voice said, "I thought I saw a dent."

"Hot damn! Rejoin, and we'll hit 'em again!"

"Let's get the hell out of here," Patrice said, even though she knew she had no authority to command the pilots. Outside, tiny dark flecks in the sky, growing larger by the second, whipped around into another formation, while the smoke obscuring the alien ship slowly sluffed off as it sped across the sky.

Angelo laughed. "Look at it. They got it on the run!"

And then, for a second, it looked like the alien craft split in two. But no, it was just the remaining whiffs of smoke continuing in one direction while the shuttle made an unreasonably tight turn, back around to face its attackers.

Sparks shimmered underneath the fighter aircraft and a second round of missiles sped toward their target.

Their apparently undamaged target.

The alien vessel spat out multiple beams of blue light, and the oncoming missiles disintegrated in puny dots. A microsecond later, another volley of blasts shattered the sky. An aircraft exploded, bits of fuselage racing away from a central fireball. Then a second and a third burst into fireworks.

"Evasive!" someone shouted on the radio.

"We need to get out of here," Sullivan said as the remaining fighter aircraft turned away.

More spears of light flashed from the surface of the space craft, reaching out to the scattered fighters, zapping them like a morbid fireworks display. One puff of smoke pin wheeled, leaving a spiral headed downward, out of control.

"Falcon five-one is gone," a woman said on the radio, her voice breaking.

"Damn," Angelo whispered. "Only three left."

"Rejoin," another voice on the radio said, "maneuver beta."

Sullivan tried to lean forward, but the safety restraints held her against the chair. "It's not working. What in the hell are they doing?"

Angelo looked straight ahead, face sagging, voice gone monotone. "I think they're going to ram it."

Patrice gasped, almost swallowed her tongue.

A beam of light from the alien ship slashed the air, and at the other end a puff of smoke bloomed.

"Evade, evade," Bandsaw said.

Two more flashes of light shot out, each one hitting its target, fire and debris spewing into the sky.

All Sullivan's internal organs jerked upward, blocking her throat and making it hard to breathe. She strained to see anything—a parachute, a pilot floating to safety. But they were too far away.

"This ain't good," Davis said.

"We need to get out of here," Patrice said again. "Turn around."

The pilots shared a quick look, then Angelo started a request for a new course.

"Just turn!" Patrice shouted. Lumbering passenger planes weren't made to fly into a dog fight. They had no armor, no weapons, and very little maneuverability, not to mention they had no fighter escorts—not that escorts would have done them any good.

"Ma'am," Leighton said, "we're doing everything we--"

"Thug two-four, Bandsaw one-three, change course..."

Finally, the AWACS was re-directing the cargo jets.

The alien shuttle pivoted, and now it was a circle, and she couldn't tell if it was coming toward them or going away from them, but she wasn't willing to bet on the latter.

Bandsaw came back on the radio, his pitch higher than it had been. "All passenger aircraft, the bogey is heading straight for you. Take all possible evasive maneuvers!"

Damn it. If they were going to get into a battle with aliens, why couldn't it be on the ground, where she had some authority, where she could direct her troops and have an influence on the battle? She didn't want to die just a target, a nameless blob the enemy fired on just to see if it could hit them.

"I gotta go to the baffroom," Davis said.

"This isn't a good time," Leighton snapped. He pressed on the controls and the plane banked sharply.

Sullivan threw her head against the back of her seat, hands gripping the arm rests, muscles stiff and trembling from the exertion. From the cargo bay, shouts of dismay floated up, punctuated by terrified screams and the occasional curse. Clouds spun in the pilot's window.

The most galling thing wasn't that they were going to die, but that she couldn't do anything to help. It was up to the pilots, these young kids who looked like they were barely out of diapers.

They had to know what they were doing.

They had to get her unit out of this.

Damn, she hated being so helpless.

The pilots seemed calm. "This is the kind of maneuver we used when we'd fly into Baghdad during the war," Angelo said over his shoulder. Maybe they would be okay. Or maybe he was just trying to make her feel better.

How many degrees had they turned? Where were they pointing? Dizzy and about to lose her lunch, Sullivan could no longer look at the spinning puffs.

Leighton pulled his controls in another direction, and the craft seemed to level out, although it still circled, from the way the clouds were acting. Then, a huge gray cloud panned across the windshield, spewing streaks of red.

"That's not a cloud, is it?" she said.

Leighton nosed the aircraft down. "That was one of the 777s."

Oh, god. That might have been one of her battalions.

"Which one? Do you know which one?"

"No, ma'am."

She saw another billowing explosion in the distance, and then after more spinning, a third.

"How many?" She'd lost track. Was that last one the same as the first explosion? Or had the aliens blown up three aircraft?

"The rest of the planes have split up," Angelo said over his shoulder. "Now, the aliens gotta choose who they go after."

Sullivan held her breath.

"Thug two-four," the control voice said, "he's coming after you."

Angelo crossed himself.

"Your airspace is clear," Bandsaw said.

"You want us to evade?" Leighton shouted. He slammed the controls to the side and the ship spun. "This is all we can do! He's faster than us, he's more maneuverable than us. And we're unarmed. Tell him we're unarmed!"

"Thug two-four, we don't have comms with the bogey."

Leighton straightened out the craft and turned the nose down. "Let's see if we can get more speed."

"I don't need to go to the baffroom anymore," Davis mumbled.

"There's no way we can get away from that thing." Leighton said. "It's coming at us too fast."

L. D. ROBINSON © 2022

A light glowed in one of the cup-like divots on the alien ship's surface.

"They're getting ready to fire," Sullivan shouted. "Do something!"

"This is it," Angelo said, his face grim.

The light on the spaceship flared, and the world turned white.

Sullivan grabbed her seat's arms, fingers pressing into the hard plastic, her restraint system pulling her tight against the seat back. A loud booming crack rent the air, and a blinding explosion lit the left side of the aircraft. The cockpit rattled, the fuselage groaned, and waves of heat made her cry out. She pulled against the seat restraints. If the plane was on fire, she had to get out of there!

Then her stomach rose into her chest, and blood exploded into her head. Her pen lifted off her lap, weightless. They were falling, the aircraft out of control and plummeting. And there was no place to escape to.

"Jesus, God!" Angelo shouted.

"Hold on!" Leighton groaned, wrestling with the controls as the cloud deck below raced toward them.

Bam!

A sudden downforce crushed Sullivan's torso and forced her head forward. The world went gray. She sucked in a desperate breath, and her vision slowly returned. The cloud bank cut a diagonal line across the front windows, and the pilots wrestled with the controls and cursed. She looked out her window, where half the wing was gone, shredded metal bent away from the direction of travel like palm leaves in a hurricane. Part of an engine cowling rattled.

"What the hell just happened?" Davis said with a groan.

"We lost an engine," she said. But at least they were still alive. For now. She took a deep breath of the odorless, processed air. "Can we still land?"

Leighton grimaced. "I've done this in a simulator before..."

Davis gave her a worried look.

Leighton adjusted the controls, and the plane righted itself, but only somewhat. Beads of sweat appeared on Angelo's forehead, while the plane rattled and bucked.

"Damn," Davis said.

"We've still got three engines," Angelo said with a forced smile. Yeah, he wasn't any more confident than she.

L. D. ROBINSON © 2022

Chapter 11 — A Fine Man

"This is the opportunity of a lifetime," Roland Craddock said, then stared at himself in the bathroom mirror. Not quite right, that expression. And the tone didn't sound confident enough. He lifted his chin. Better. That reduced the look of his jowls, gave him a slightly younger appearance. "This is the opportunity--"

The phone rang. Who would be calling at this time of day? The conference wasn't supposed to start for several more hours, and he needed the time to practice.

Maybe he should just ignore it.

"... the opportunity of a lifetime. And I really mean that. You need to invest now, get in on the ground floor."

Three more rings. It sounded like whoever was calling didn't want to give up.

Let it ring.

He needed to do that ground floor line a little better. He smiled as he rehearsed the words. Oh, hell, that was awful. Maybe grand gestures would work better.

Tap. Tap. Tap.

Damn it! Now someone was at the door. Right now, he needed to practice, uninterrupted. This was his first time running a business like this, and he had to get it right.

Not that he didn't have plenty of other money and assets to fall back on, but this was the best thing he'd ever come up with, and he intended to make millions with it.

Tap. Tap.

"Mr. Craddock?" a wavering voice said.

Oh, hell. Mrs. Steiner.

For a moment, he wondered why he'd even brought her. Such a sweet little old lady, with so little sales potential, she was only succeeding in this multi-level marketing business because of his help. But no one else had to know that. She made it all look easy.

And he had to keep her happy.

He tugged the tie on his bathrobe and walked to the door. "What can I do for you, sweetheart?"

"Didn't you get the phone call?" Her already wrinkled face puckered with concern, her hands gripped the front of her pink cardigan, and her eyes, enlarged by those ridiculous glasses, blinked at him with puppy-dog sincerity.

He ran his hand over his chest, over the plushness of the bathrobe fabric that was closer to fur than terrycloth. "I'm right in the middle of something here."

Mrs. Steiner grabbed him by the wrist, her skin as thin as tracing paper, soft and delicate. "We've got to go. The mayor ordered an evacuation."

"Evacuation?"

"Aliens," she said. "They might be coming here."

"Well, damn," he said, then walked across the room, grabbed the remote and turned on the television. Mrs. Steiner stayed in the hall, hand on her chest.

It didn't take long for the news to gel. Aliens were somewhere south of Chicago, still flying around, duking it out with military aircraft. Nothing that was going to affect him. He turned the volume to low. "I don't see what the problem is."

"They might come here," she said.

He smiled, trying not to look too condescending as he walked back to the door. "Even if they do, do you know how many high-rises there are in this town? What are the chances this is the one they'll attack?"

She brought her other hand up to pat his closed fist. "Better safe than sorry."

He sighed. Wasn't much chance he could talk her out of it, and maybe he could use a break, anyway. "All right. Just let me get a shirt on." He gestured for her to enter, offering the chair in the corner by the east-facing window with its fabulous view of the lake.

A police siren wailed in the background.

"Sounds like they're getting ready," he said from the closet as he ran his fingers over the shirts hung there.

Mrs. Steiner stood by the window, hand pulling the gauzy curtains back, staring down at the street level. "My goodness, there's a lot of activity out there."

Craddock walked to the window, slipping his hands into the pockets of his beige slacks. Highway 41 was a parking lot. "Look at that," he said, pointing to the cars stopped on a road wide enough to be an interstate.

"Oh, my."

"I don't want to get caught in that. And ninety-five is probably rush-hour on steroids." Stayin put was much better, with room service and a place to relax.

Steiner stood like a frightened cat, big blue eyes staring without comprehension.

"Look," Craddock said, "we're not in any danger here. I say we just shelter in place until this whole thing blows over."

Mrs. Steiner shrugged. "If you think so." She sunk into the chair, gnarled fingertips clasping each other in her lap.

"You just relax. Everything'll be fine. You'll see."

Chapter 12 — Shuttle Lands

The city was now in sight, towering buildings piercing the clouds. Dozens of them. No, hundreds, all clumped together in a jagged skyline, close to the water, reflecting the sun in their smooth glassy surfaces. "Approaching our target now," Galth said.

"We're ready Sir," Reldak, the leader of his ground team, answered.

This was always the trickiest part of the operation, maneuvering between the tall buildings without hitting something. Other shuttle pilots complained about it, but Galth just grinned. This was his specialty, and the reason he could boast about making more runs than the more junior pilots. Just before he entered the metallic canyon, he moved the controls so that the restraining fields held a little tighter than normal.

They were inside now, following a straight road, ducking lower and lower. He used his control pad to yank the shuttle to the right, then again to the left, switching roads, and then he slammed on the acceleration, while the buildings flew past on both sides so fast they were mere blurs in the windows.

The faces of his crewmen reflected in the front viewscreen, Reldak with his eyelids drooping, like he was about to fall asleep. Sink it, why weren't they all gasping in terror? He was going to have to switch out a few of them. Doing dangerous things like this wasn't any fun if you couldn't scare the life out of someone. And he couldn't think of any way to make it more frightening.

Double sink it! He'd just missed his mark, the building he'd previously lined up as his target.

He pulled back on his speed, then looked over the area ahead. Another tall building loomed on the left, just over the river, on a nice short street that would limit defender's access. He dropped altitude, skimmed over the intervening structures, down to the level of the trees. The building backed onto a narrow road, but his shuttle was thin enough to fit nicely. He wouldn't even have to smash any ground vehicles. But on the other hand, the shorter the tunnel, the easier harvesting would be. He dropped altitude again, now skimming the pavement just a few feet up.

A white car blocked his path, first small in the view screen, then ballooning to fill the view. The shuttle shivered on contact, engaging the sparkling shields, and making enough racket to rival a hailstorm on Mount Grovlach. The mass of metal whirled into the air, then tumbled onto the dark pavement, parts exploding, smashing into a wall of red brick.

He was now half a foot off the ground. His shuttle's nose plowed into a second car, bumping it forward and onto its side with a screech of metal. He hardly felt the impact.

Contact. A landing so soft it made no sound. Right next to a double glass door. You couldn't park any better than this.

The only disappointing thing about it was that there had been no pedestrians on the street. No carnage from the shrapnel, no blood spatters on the stone walls.

"Ground team, go," he said.

Reldak bolted out the control-room door, and seconds later the sound of the shuttle's outside door opening told him they were on their way. It would take them a minute to deploy the gangway and wrap the building to block off all but the designated exits. And any enemy defenders wouldn't be here for a while. That gave him a few minutes to relax. He leaned against the wall and let out a satisfied breath.

"The door doesn't open!" Reldak bellowed into the communications pad.

Galth frowned, glancing at Kelm, his co-pilot. "Is he really that incompetent?"

"Just a complainer," Kelm said.

Good. That meant he could ignore most of Reldak's transmissions.

A loud boom rattled the shuttle, and a light flashed in the corner of the viewscreen, where it seemed Reldak had solved the door problem with a blaster bolt. Galth soaked in the energy of the shuddering walls, smiling lazily at Kelm. Outside, more crewmen accompanied the building wrap down the street, toward a gaping concrete opening in the side of the building where the street turned in, a gap in the sidewalk, as though they drove their ground vehicles right in there.

"We're in the main building," Reldak's voice came through the communications pad. Screams sounded in the background. "Starting the evacuation now."

Galth grinned. Time to encourage the quivs to exit the building. He pressed the link on his communications pad. "Galth to *Blood Fury*. We're ready for ignition."

"Targeting now," someone from the ship in orbit said.

A moment later, a blue light flashed in the sky, visible only at the edges of Galth's viewscreen. In a moment, their shuttle would be flooded with refugees from the flames.

"I think I want to see this," Galth said. He walked out of the control room, down the short hall to the perpendicular corridor that led to the gangway and the shattered building door. Quivs in black uniforms stood at the doorway, where the leader, an overweight woman with exceptionally dark skin, had stopped.

"Come on in, quiv," Galth said. "We're not going to hurt you."

The quiv glanced back at her companions.

"Unless you jam up the process."

"Where are you taking us?"

"Just move!" one of Galth's brown-shirted crewmen said from behind the group. The quiv leader stepped into the gangway.

"Sink it!" Reldak's voice came through the pad again. "It's another building."

Galth rolled his eyes at the pad. He didn't need to listen to all this chafing. Maybe he should just turn the link off.

"Galth," Reldak said, "this place is crazy. It's a maze!"

"Just get the quivs in here and stop crying like an unspeakable."

"There are too many places for quivs to hide!"

"You have most of the crew. Deal with it!"

"And tell *Blood Fury* we need fire on the other roofs. They don't all go to the same building!"

Galth let out a frustrated breath. That concern sounded valid, unlike all Reldak's other complaints. He hurried back into the control room and sent Reldak's request to the ship.

That taken care of, he keyed up a report of quivs captured so far. Less than 10 in the cargo hold. This was going more slowly than he'd expected. He needed to do something to get things moving faster. He glanced out the viewscreen, where a lone crewman paced along the sidewalk, blaster in hand, ready to stop any defenders coming to destroy the building wrap. But there weren't any quivs around. The street was deserted. Perhaps he could send this crewman inside to help Reldak herd the quivs, to help locate hiding victims and force them into the shuttle.

Bam.

The crewmen crumpled onto the ground right where the street turned into the building.

Galth grabbed a control pad, his excitement surging as he fingered the systems to give him weapons control. "Did you see where the shot came from?" he asked Kelm.

"Incoming defenders!" Reldak shouted through the communications pad.

Galth scanned the area. The building across the street was nothing but a solid wall of red bricks. Maybe the shots had come from a window in one of the more distant buildings. But that was too many places to scan, too many places for the enemy to hide.

And all the windows on the left side looked like they didn't even open.

On the right side, though, there were lots of possibilities. He smiled as he aimed his shuttle's energy weapon at a set of balconies on the corner of a building just down the street, then shot a line of blaster energy from bottom to top. Metal grates sprayed into the air, twisted and broken, while glass shattered with a loud bang, spraying out onto the white walkway and dull gray street, the pieces landing with crisp reverberations, all too far away for any of them to reach the shuttle.

And anybody who'd been inside there was dead. He let out a satisfied breath, then looked at the motionless corpse and felt a pang of jealousy. No wonder the brown-shirts fought to be on building wrap duty. That guy was already in the arms of the Eternal Mother, soaking in the joy of a mission well done.

"I see a heat signature in a window," Kelm said, waving his controller in front of Galth.

Galth adjusted his targeting to zero in on the anomaly, someone peering out from the seventh floor of the nearer building. The angle was too acute for his front blaster. He switched to the top-mounted weapon, enabling the targeting reticle and panning across the face of the building, its ruddy exterior scrolling by until he found the window in question. Now, he could see it as though he were only a few feet away, a man just inside the room, and a long-barreled gun resting on the bottom windowsill. "Got you."

Now, there was only one issue left to resolve: should he target the whole side of the building? Or should he just wipe the sniper off the face of the planet?

A part of him wanted to leave the shuttle and go stalk the man on foot. That way, he would get to see the blood. Or maybe the look on the man's face when he realized he was about to die.

But it was a luxury he knew he didn't have time for. Back to remote killing, even though it was less satisfying.

Another shot rang out, and the muzzle blast momentarily blanked out the view in his control pad. But it didn't matter. The target was already locked in. And this defender was about to have his blood and brains sprayed onto the walls of his hiding place.

Chapter 13 — Escape Into Darkness

"My God," Mrs. Steiner whispered. "They shot him."

Craddock had never heard Mrs. Steiner swear before and it amused him. As for the police sniper whom the aliens had just taken out, well, it was unfortunate, since the guy had been trying to protect Craddock and people like him. But then again, the guy had been incompetent enough to get himself killed, so he probably wouldn't have been much protection for Craddock anyway.

The important thing was the decision on what to do next. And it wasn't running into an alien shuttle.

"We've got to get out of here," Mrs. Steiner said, grabbing his arm and heading toward the door.

"No, no," he said, hands around her shoulders. He walked her back to the chair and pushed her into it. "We can't. They'll be waiting for us down there."

Her eyes enlarged. "Oh! Then what do we do?"

"We'll just have to wait it out." He patted her hand. "Still lots of interesting stuff on the news."

He glanced at the television, where a reporter covered the clogged highways as the town tried to evacuate. Then he turned to the window. Out toward the lake, the highway was jammed with slow moving traffic. A flash of anger hit him. Those idiots had gotten the word in time. They were safe. But Craddock, stuck in this hotel, was in danger. The mayor should have made sure all the important people had been notified, not the riff-raff clogging up the freeway. What was the matter with those politicians?

"We should have left," Mrs. Steiner said, blinking back tears.

"This isn't my fault," he snapped.

She looked at him with a pitiful expression. "Oh, I'm not blaming you."

Better. Much better. There was no one to blame, anyway. "We'll be fine. As long as we don't go downstairs..."

Mrs. Steiner gazed at him with a look of trust. Damn, she was so naive for such an old lady. "What if the aliens send search parties up here, go room by room?"

"I don't think so," he said, then sat on the end of the bed. They waited in silence for several minutes, and he started to wonder if he should resume practicing his speech. Probably not. The conference wasn't going to happen as scheduled. "I hope my insurance covers my losses on this," he muttered.

"I'm sure you--"

A boom drowned out the last word of her sentence and she grabbed the arms of the chair. The floor rumbled beneath him, and the walls blurred for a split second. And then a loud alarm jangled his nerves. The television went dark.

"Oh, hell," Craddock said, running a hand over his face. He'd forgotten about the aliens setting the building on fire.

Mrs. Steiner was on her feet again. "We've got to get out of here!"

He grabbed her by the shoulders. "Relax. The sprinklers will put out the fire and we'll be okay." In fact, it was almost funny. The aliens must not have known how well protected American buildings were. Otherwise, they would never have come here.

Hell, there was a lot the aliens didn't know, and that was all going to come back around and bite them in the butts, if they had such things. Stupid creatures had picked the wrong country to mess with this time.

Mrs. Steiner shook her head, pointing to the sprinkler head just above the bed. "But they haven't come on."

"They're heat activated," he said. "They'll only get triggered in the rooms where there's actually a fire."

She nodded nervously, then dropped back into the chair. Craddock glanced up. They were on a floor near the top. The fire might get to them before the aliens decided they had enough kidnap victims and left. He stood. "Listen, maybe we should go to a lower floor."

She nodded, looking energized. "The gym is on the second floor."

"Gym?" He smiled at the unexpected location. "You spend a lot of time there?" he said as he escorted her to the door. He patted his pocket to assure himself he still had his key, then checked his pocket for his wallet and his wrist, to make certain he hadn't left his

Rolex by the sink. The rest of his belongings could be easily replaced.

The hall was dark, and three other guests walked in the shadows, one with a phone-powered flashlight pointed toward the end of the hall. Another person seemed to be watching him from the corner of his eye. Craddock put his hand on Mrs. Steiner's arm and guided her to follow them, feeling the frailty of her muscles and how they trembled beneath her calm looking exterior. He knew she didn't need the help, but the others would be impressed with his chivalry.

She glanced up at him with a look of admiration. If she had been a lot younger, he would've seduced her already.

"You're such a good man," she said.

Another boom shook the building, and their steps veered to the right. Mrs. Steiner hit the wall with a thud, then bounced back.

"You okay?"

She nodded, hand on the wall to steady herself, eyes locked on the exit sign. "Hurry!"

He rushed ahead of her and held the door open.

As he entered the stairwell, he caught his first whiff of smoke. Nothing visible, but the danger was growing. And the lights were out. Damn, why didn't architects think about how these things would be used during an emergency?

He made his way down between pools of light from the occasional emergency fixtures, one hand on the handrail to steady him whenever the building shook. Mrs. Steiner clung onto him with her gnarly fingers gripping the cloth of his shirt, making little grunts and whimpering noises.

For the first few floors, the stairs were only partially full, but with each floor the crowd got larger.

By the seventh floor, he needed to extend his free hand to keep from running into the bodies below. The air was suffocating. A woman farther down the stairwell sobbed loudly, howling like an injured coyote. Curse words littered the atmosphere.

These people just need to get out of his way.

They pressed on, down another flight of stairs, nearing another door, another entrance to the stairwell from the hallways, where a gaggle of people stood like idiots waiting for an opening, being polite of all things, like this was just a normal fire drill, like their lives weren't in danger. He couldn't deal with this anymore.

Fifth floor. Had they descended far enough? Yeah, the fire wouldn't get to this level for maybe an hour or more. By then, the aliens would be gone. This was the perfect place to hide out.

"Excuse me," Craddock said, more out of habit than sincerity, as he pushed the mob aside and forced his way into the hall. His shirt pulled backwards, and he remembered Mrs. Steiner, still clinging to him, stuck behind the other people, only her arm poking through the bodies standing in the door. She was going to slow him down. He grabbed her and pulled her through. That was easier than loosening the death grip she had on his shirt.

He slipped into the hallway, past the confused faces.

"Where are we going?" Mrs. Steiner said.

"Sh." He stopped several feet down, looking at the people trying to exit. So much the better. With their compliance, they would fill the alien shuttle and satisfy the kidnapper's desires for bodies. And with them leaving the floor, they would make more room, more space for Craddock to hide. This was all working out quite well.

More doors opened, and people dutifully moved to the stairwell. He hurried toward a recently opened door, stopping it from closing with an outstretched hand, while the people who'd just left the room continued toward the exit, their backs toward him. He invited Mrs. Steiner in.

"Are you sure?" she asked. "It's not our room."

"Only if you don't want to sit on the floor," he said. This was a narrower room than his, with two queen-sized beds, and he sat on the first, letting her walk past him to the second.

Another boom shook the building. This time, bits of debris and ash floated past the window like black snow, while more compact items plummeted through the air in smoky streaks of black. It looked like the top several floors had been disintegrated. Good thing they had left.

"We'll be okay here," he said, to fill the awkward silence. He checked his diamond-studded watch. Another half an hour should be long enough for the aliens to get everything they wanted, and he made a note of when to check, when to attempt a final exit of the building.

Mrs. Steiner made whimpering noises. Damn it, things would have been so much easier if she hadn't tagged along. How could he get her to shut up?

A *thump* coming from the hallway caught his attention.

"Who is that?" Mrs. Steiner said.

Like he would know. "Quiet," he whispered. If it was the aliens, and they could hear her... she might have just given them away.

The door exploded, and Mrs. Steiner screamed, falling back onto the bed, then rolling to the floor.

"You two," someone at the door said, "out. Now."

Craddock stood, gazing into eyes that glowed, like a cat in a dark alley, narrowed into a threatening squint, full of angry determination. Somewhere in the back of his mind, Craddock knew he should be terrified. But all that registered was inconvenience. Who the hell did these aliens think they were? Just when he was about to start the biggest money-making operation of his life...

But the pistol-like object the alien pointed at him looked deadly enough, and even though he didn't tremble, he knew, on an intellectual level, that he wasn't ready to die. He lifted his hands.

"Don't make that obscene gesture!" the alien snapped.

Craddock dropped his hands.

"Stupid quivs," a second alien muttered. This one, standing in the door frame, had dark, greasy hair that stuck out in all directions. His nose looked like it had been flattened in a fist fight when the man was only a kid.

"You boys in the military?" Craddock asked. After all, they were dressed identically. The plain brown shirts didn't look particularly martial, but the tight-fitting slacks and heavy boots would work well as part of any soldierly attire.

"Out!" the first alien said again.

Conversation didn't seem to be working as a delaying tactic. And fighting his way out didn't look like an option, either. He'd been a defensive linebacker in college, but these guys looked bigger than any offensive tackle he'd ever faced, shoulders so wide they barely fit through the narrow hotel room doors.

But Craddock thought of himself as a creative thinker. Maybe he could come up with something else.

He smiled beneficently, pointing to Mrs. Steiner. "Let me help her up."

The alien gave him one nod.

Craddock reached his hand over to her. By now, she was sitting on the carpet, legs akimbo, skirt hiked halfway up her boney, sagging left thigh. She didn't move for two or three seconds, just stared at the aliens with her mouth open, as if she couldn't comprehend what was happening. Finally, she put her hand in his. "Oh, thank you, dear."

He lifted her nearly weightless body to its feet.

No place to hide, no way to get around the aliens, no weapons to subdue them. He wasn't coming up with any ideas. And all too soon, his time was up. Mrs. Steiner walked obediently toward the hall, and he couldn't think of anything to do but follow.

In the hallway, another pair of aliens stood guarding four other people who'd been hiding, and a third alien stood with some sort of ipad-looking thing, pointing to a door just down the hall. "Three in here," he said.

Some kind of sensor apparatus, then. That completely ruled out any attempts to hide. He huffed in frustration. There had to be another way out.

But now he was in a little herd of people, being goaded down the stairwell, like livestock pressed into stunned obedience. His fingers twitched. Damn it, he didn't belong here.

Five flights of stairs later, they reached the lobby, where the furniture had been rearranged to create a little path directing foot traffic toward a door marked for maintenance personnel. That would lead to the back of the building, and then the alien shuttle. Across the lobby, the front doors, small as they were, invited him. Beyond them lay a circular driveway, and pillars, all surrounded by a ten-foot-tall wall of what looked like Saran Wrap. No problem. He could break through that easily enough... if he could get to it.

This was his last chance. He broke from the group, shoulder slamming into the nearby alien, knocking him onto his butt. Craddock dashed toward a dull dark couch, stepped on the cushion, and with his hands grasping the top of the overstuffed back, he vaulted over it, then dashed across the tiles. Brought back his days on the college football team, chasing after the running back, head down, steaming forward. A twinge of pain shot through his left knee, but there wasn't even time to wince. He stuck out his arm, ready grab the door.

"Hey you!" One of the aliens shouted. Craddock caught his reflection in the front windows, springing over the makeshift barrier and landing with a thud.

Craddock plunged ahead. But another alien ran toward him from the side. Craddock only had a few more steps to freedom, if he could keep his body, deteriorated far more than he had realized, going. Determined to outrun these kidnappers, Craddock bent his head forward and tried to increase his speed. His knee shot an electric bolt up his thigh.

And then, fingertips touched the back of his neck, warm yet prickly, and slipped under his collar. The knot of his tie dug into his neck, like it was going to break all the cartilage in the front of his throat. And his feet were still running, quickly moving out from under his center of balance. But the second alien grabbed his arm before he landed on his butt. They yanked him to his feet, then spun him around, toward their shuttle.

"Look," he said, putting a hand on one of the alien's shoulders, "you can keep all these other people, but you need to let me go."

The alien's eyes narrowed, and he pulled a large dagger from his belt. "You can get into the shuttle, or I can kill you right now."

Craddock stared into the man's eyes, then shuddered as the realization hit him that he was talking to creatures just like him.

"Mr. Craddock!" Mrs. Steiner screamed as another of the aliens pushed her toward the gangway. Her hands reached out to him, pleading.

Craddock glanced again at the front door, then saw the alien barrier stretched across the escape route, cutting off all hope. His shoulders sagged.

The alien moved his dagger in the air, then gave Craddock a cold smile. "It would make quite an impression on everyone else. Don't you agree?"

Not the impression he wanted to make. He exhaled loudly, then turned toward the alien shuttle and followed the others.

Chapter 14 — Landing

Off in the hazy distance, a black plume of smoke pillowed its way into the clear blue sky, marking the Chicago skyline, now barely peeking over the tops of masses of deciduous trees spread out over the countryside. The fiery orange base flickered, threads of flames occasionally leaping into the ebony balls of cotton.

"That's it, isn't it?" Davis said, his voice barely audible.

She glanced over at her executive officer, whose face sagged, as though all the muscles in his head had gone limp. "We shouldn't have to get too close."

He nodded, but his heavy exhale indicated he didn't believe her.

A large piece of the broken wing tore partly away, then flapped against the fuselage in fitful rage.

"We're losing oil in engine number two," Angelo said.

"Shit." Leighton glanced backward at the damaged wing, then shook his head. "I can't turn it off."

Colonel Sullivan gulped. Given how hard Leighton was already struggling, he couldn't handle yet another thing going wrong. Leighton's hair had gone shiny, sweat wicking into his collar, turning it dark.

"Stand on the rudders," Leighton said. Angelo nodded, then stretched out a leg, pressing his back into the seat, gritting his teeth.

The engines whined, the roads and isolated houses below steadily growing larger. They passed another small town, its grid of roads barely visible beneath the canopy of green. Crop fields spread out from each side of the town, the green beginning to turn yellow.

A flash of light caught her eyes, and she looked up just in time to see an orange streak blazing from above, appearing to strike the source of all the smoke.

The inferno erupted with flames lapping at the sky. The aliens were well into their operation. They probably had several hundred people already ensconced in their shuttle. And probably dozens of first responders had been killed. The grim reality of what was happening seeped into her bones, tightening her hands into fists. Somehow, she had to end this.

If she survived the landing.

The ground was getting close, a long runway directly ahead, four more all going in the same direction. She leaned forward. "This doesn't look like Midway." That had been the designated airport because it was twice as close to downtown.

"O'Hare," Angelo grunted through gritted teeth. "Longer runway. We'll need…" He took a quick breath. "…every inch."

The plane rattled again, riveting her attention on the rapidly approaching ground. Leighton leaned to the right, pressing all his weight against the yoke, grunting, while Angelo spoke into his mike. Red lights flashed on the distant taxiway, fire trucks and ambulances positioning themselves for the upcoming crash.

The thumping piece of wing slammed into the aircraft with a *bang* that echoed through the cockpit. Her seat rattled and she grabbed the arm rests, squeezing them tightly.

"Mother, mother, mother…" Davis whispered.

The end of the runway where all the tire streaks had colored it with a huge black patch loomed ahead of them, coming closer, growing larger. The plane rocked, shaking her from side to side. The horizon tilted. "Pull the circuit breakers on the left-wing spoilers," Leighton yelled. Angelo's hands darted to the breakers. The plane righted itself again.

"All right," Leighton said. They were over the end of the runway, now so close they had to be just inches from the ground. Leighton moved the throttle back. The engines still hummed, but Patrice's body moved forward, pressing against her harness.

Whump. She jerked. Tires screeched.

A loud cheer rose from the cargo area, clapping and whooping. But it wasn't over yet. They were still careening down the runway. Leighton moved the throttle into reverse on two of the engines and the backward thrust pressed Sullivan against her harness. More cheers from below.

The pilots grunted with effort. Brakes. The nose of the plane dipped a little, while the light fixtures on the side of the runway raced past. It didn't look like the speed reduction was going to be enough.

The plane hurtled past the gaggle of emergency vehicles, then over the white lines of the distant end of the runway, only a little concrete left, a grassy field growing closer.

"Come on, come on!" Leighton grunted.

Sullivan pressed her back into her chair, as though she could help stop the plane. Silly, those instinctive reactions. But she couldn't help herself.

The edge of the concrete slid under the nose of the plane. The cockpit dropped several inches, then Sullivan was thrown forward again. The ground outside finally came to a stop.

Leighton collapsed in his seat. "Damn."

Sullivan lifted her head, then released a long breath as relief washed over her. Now, finally, the cheering in the cargo hold made sense.

"Can we get out?" Davis asked.

Angelo shook his head. "Got to wait for clearance."

Bam! Blam! The fuselage rattled, and her seat sunk a few inches.

"What the hell?" Davis said.

"Tires," Leighton said. "The breaks had to be red-hot."

Finally, the ground rescue personnel approached.

Well, it was just as well they were staying put for a while. There was no one outside to greet them, no transportation to take them where they needed to go. All that was probably still at Midway.

This mission couldn't get any more messed up.

Chapter 15 — Into the City

As the engines of her plane wound down, the whine of hydraulics lowering the loading ramps filled the sonic void. She climbed down the steps from the cockpit, her feet heavy, fear shuddering through her. She needed to get her mind back on task before she lost her nerve and broke into a run to nowhere in particular.

She stepped into the cargo area, where the pungent odor of urine and feces assaulted her. That was what real fear smelled like. She quickly stepped through the open door, only to be slammed by the humid air and the heat of the afternoon sun.

Her body armor pulled down on her shoulders, and an invisible hand wrapped itself around her chest, so tight she could hardly breathe. All those soldiers… shot into oblivion, their body parts scattered over hundreds of square miles, most charred until they were unrecognizable, bits of blackened bone.

Can't think about that.

Behind her was a whole plane full of soldiers, still alive and with a mission. She had to keep herself functioning. For them. To keep more soldiers from dying.

She thumped down the steps to the concrete landing surface. In the distance, a camouflage-painted HMMWV drove up the taxiway, lights flashing, followed by a train of five commercial buses. Once they arrived, a young Army Captain got out of the truck and approached her, stuffing his hat into his cargo pocket, a manila envelope tucked under his arm.

Behind her, CSM Jabronsky's voice rang out as he organized the masses into chalks for the ride into the city.

Her stomach vibrated, shot through with tiny bolts of electricity. She needed some valium.

"Captain Hunter," the soldier said, offering a salute. "I'm your escort," He handed her the envelope, raising his voice to carry over the sound of the other aircraft approaching. "You'll need this," he said. "Suspension of posse comitatus."

"Good." That gave her people authority to perform law enforcement tasks with U.S. civilians. She hoped they wouldn't need it, and she didn't plan to tell the rest of her brigade about it until they absolutely did. She folded the paper and stuck it into her cargo pocket.

Captain Hunter gestured to the HMMWV, and she followed him there, noting that her brigade's first bus full of soldiers was already on its way. That would be Lieutenant Colonel Davis with the advanced party, assigned to get things set up before her arrival. They weren't going to have a lot of time.

She jumped into the right rear seat, and Captain Hunter sat behind the driver. "The first army elements to arrive at the scene was the National Guard," Captain Hunter said.

"That was pretty fast."

"The governor activated us even before he knew Chicago was going to be a target."

Colonel Sullivan nodded, impressed. "Infantry?"

"Straight leg."

Well, that wasn't as much help as it could have been, a bunch of soldiers with rifles and mortars, but not much else, dependent on trucks or helicopters when the distances were too far for their "leather personnel carriers," a nickname for boots.

"They took over from the local police," Hunter said. "It looks like the police had tried to fight them, but they gave up pretty quickly."

"Do your soldiers have mortars?"

"Haven't arrived yet. Best we've got are grenade launchers and antitank weapons."

"At least that's something."

"The antitank weapons don't make a dent."

She closed her eyes. Damn it, a few dents would have been nice, would have given her some hope. And if anti-tank missiles did nothing, grenade launchers were about as effective as fly swatters. "So what are they doing?"

Captain Hunter shrugged. "The active-duty battalion commander's been there about a half hour," he said.

"What about the tracks?" she asked. The infantry brigade had brought some serious armor with them, infantry fighting vehicles and tanks, but she'd not been given a run-down on which planes had survived.

"Shot down," Hunter said.

"Damn." This newly arrived unit of mechanized infantry was no better off than the straight legs. On the other hand, she wasn't too sure the armored infantry would've done any better.

"They've got more coming," Hunter added. "Don't know when they'll get here. Commander's name is Cooper. He's already run several operations," Hunter said, sounding hopeful, even though that statement rang negative to Sullivan's ears.

"Tell me about them."

The truck slipped through the airport exit, now on the interstate, the road headed into the city holding very few vehicles. The engine screamed as the driver pushed the speed. She frowned. It would certainly top off her day if her ride broke down on the way to the battle.

"First thing Cooper did was attach the National Guard unit to his brigade."

Colonel Sullivan wasn't sure how legal the move was, since it didn't sound like the National Guard had been federalized, but that was Cooper's problem.

With Barker dead, where did that put her in the hierarchy? One part of her said she should assume command, but it sounded like this Cooper guy was enough of a hotshot that he would try to fight her on it. And probably the bigwigs back home would give Cooper the command because he was, after all, a combat arms officer, trained in all the tactics and techniques of taking on belligerents. She on the other hand merely dabbled in combat, while missions like traffic control and detention of prisoners of war were more central concerns.

She looked out the window. They were in the outskirts of the city, but the freeway was jammed, all three lanes on the other side, and two of the three going into town were filled with desperate people trying to get out. Horns honked, and then an eighteen-wheeler pulled into her lane ahead. Her driver slammed on his breaks, then swerved onto the shoulder, bumping up a short curb onto a strip of grass. The truck zoomed past, horn blasting, the rush of air slamming into her vehicle, rattling it with a loud howl.

"Jesus!" Hunter said.

Patrice crossed herself, hand still shaking as the semi pulled back into its own lane of traffic with another wave of honking, vehicles weaving to avoid collisions.

Hunter stared out the left window, shoulders twisted, back to her, head bent forward. "What an ass hole."

"So, what has Cooper done so far?"

Hunter swung back around, then cleared his throat. "First thing they tried was a thermite grenade. Launched it from a drone, set it right on the shuttle roof."

Sullivan nodded, impressed. That was an option Barker hadn't mentioned, and it sounded like a good tactic. Those grenades could burn through almost anything.

"But their shields puffed up, and the grenade rolled onto the road."

"Puffed up?" That wasn't a description she'd ever heard for spaceship shields.

"Yeah. Just sort of a... like, a..." He made gestures like he was drawing clouds in the air. "A layer of sparkles or something."

The bottom dropped out of her stomach. Such a good idea, and it had amounted to nothing. Just a hole in the asphalt that road maintenance personnel would have to patch up.

"They've hit it with other weapons, too. And made several incursions on foot. Tried to get in the building through the entrance on the other street, but the aliens are patrolling around the whole block. Anybody tries to cut through that stuff they have wrapped around the building gets vaporized."

"How many casualties?" Patrice asked.

"I don't know," Hunter answered. "But from the sounds of it, I'd say a lot." He heaved a loud sigh. "Fire trucks were on the scene early, but they were… obliterated. Now, they're just hanging back, waiting."

Hunter's electronic device beeped, and he glanced at his screen. "Looks like the mortars have arrived."

She nodded, but by now she didn't have any positive expectations for the latest weapons to get there. "Is he even going to use them?"

Hunter shrugged. The road turned, opposing traffic now lighter, the buildings higher and closer to the highway. "Not much farther."

Finally, they reached downtown. The roads were clear, and they drove through a steep canyon of buildings, shadows over the streets in the late afternoon, but golden light from a fire reflected in the windows several blocks away. The smell of smoke drifted inside the vehicle, with a tinge of metal that pricked the skin around Sullivan's nostrils, and a sniff of odd chemicals burning, waxy, like a plastic container thrown into the fireplace by mistake.

A loud boom shook the vehicle, and Sullivan gripped the edge of her seat. Another blast, and then three more.

"That's gotta be the mortars," Hunter said.

Sullivan wanted to curse the infantry commander. He was probably killing more civilians than aliens. He was probably expending a lot of effort and getting nothing in return.

They were almost to the edge of the water. They turned right, then a couple of blocks farther south the driver pulled up to the curb in front of a drugstore whose windows glowed from the nearby fire.

"The operations center is there," Hunter said, pointing to the drug store. "Over there is New street, where the shuttle is parked."

Colonel Sullivan thanked her escort, then got out of the truck. Except for the flickering of the reflected flames, the scene was bucolic, the road lined with old trees, meters marking now empty parallel parking spaces. Down the street, a bowling alley sign butted into the crown of a deep green tree, and somewhere nearby, a single bird chirped insistently, like someone or something had strayed into its territory.

The shuttle wasn't quite in view from here, and she walked the few steps required to get a view down the street.

The shuttle looked smaller and farther away than she had expected. But that was a good thing. It certainly put her outside the area where the aliens would shoot. Still, the alien vehicle exuded menace, hunkered against the sidewalk, spanning half the road, with a tube running from the shuttle to the back door, just like in the videos from the previous attacks. The craft seemed to glare at her, without anything that looked like a windshield or a front viewing screen. Her stomach shivered.

Scattered across the road in front of the shuttle were random car parts, many burned around the edges, bumpers and hoods dismembered and crumpled. A lone steering wheel tottered a few dozen yards from the operations center. Farther down the road, a burnt-out car frame lay against the brick wall, clumps of broken windshield dangling from the front edge of the roof like glass backsplash tiles blowing in the breeze.

She closed her eyes and a new vision appeared in the darkness.

The car she rode in spun in a strange slow motion, throwing her hard against the seat belt, squeezing her gut and cutting into her thighs. The windshield turned into thousands of tiny squares, all reflecting light in different directions, and a branch crashed through the side window.

Not today.

She willed her eyes to open, forced her mind to the present. The glass still hung there, but she wasn't going to let it send her into the past. That was over with. No point thinking about it.

She gave the scene one last review. It was hard to tell how much of the damage had been done by the shuttle, and how much was due to mortar explosions or other attacks against the aliens. Either way, some poor insurance companies were going to be paying out a lot of money.

A screech of brakes sounded behind her. A large bus stopped at the corner, door opening. The first soldier off was LTC Davis.

Time to get to work.

Chapter 16 – Headquarters

She hurried to the drug store, meeting Davis at the front door. "Interesting place for an operations center," Davis quipped.

Inside, rows of merchandise shelves had been pulled from their normal resting spots, forming a zig-zag path designed to slow any enemy intrusion. Like that was going to help anything.

They snaked their way through the maze, and once she'd negotiated several turns, Patrice shrugged off her body armor with a sigh. Even though she couldn't see her t-shirt because of the uniform blouse she wore, she could feel the sweat hanging in round puddles under her arms and making smile lines under her boobs. She wanted to pull the undergarments away from her skin but restrained herself.

In the back, Cooper's soldiers had set up their main operations area behind the counters where the cash registers stood idle. In front of those, they'd opened up enough space for tables, easels and the few computers that had survived the air battle. She looked around, not certain which of the soldiers standing around was the acting brigade commander. But at that moment, it didn't matter.

Lieutenant Colonel Palmer, the commander of the Detention Battalion, had begun setting up a brigade command post at the back of the store, near the chilled drinks cabinet. He motioned her to an easel with a roughly drawn map of the area.

"Most of the civilians have already cleared out," Palmer said, pointing to the butcher paper. Behind him, a trickle of newly arrived soldiers wandered into the operations center, while Davis directed them into tentative working locations.

"The local police have set up a limit of military operations here," Palmer continued. He pointed at a large black rectangle on the map. "We've also coordinated locations for our two battalions, the medical unit, and the infantry units."

She nodded. Not much traffic control was going to be necessary. And nobody was going to have to go through buildings and force people to evacuate. They had underestimated the civilians this time.

"Good job," she told Palmer. "You can get back to your battalion."

Once he was gone, Colonel Sullivan paced through the area. They were too close to the infantry's operations center, and too vulnerable, in her opinion. "Move our operations center over there," she said, pointing to the pharmacy area.

"Right away," Davis said. He motioned to a couple of enlisted personnel, who picked up the few pieces of furniture they had and carried them through a door.

"I'll take this as my office," she added, pointing to a small room whose sign indicated it was for private consultations. "And leave the chairs in the waiting area free."

"Yes, ma'am."

"Not much space in here," someone said.

They were just going to have to make it work. It had an extra wall between them and the alien shuttle, and that could make all the difference.

She dropped her equipment in her "office," then made a reconnaissance of the entire location. The windows at the front of the store were all blocked with shelving and dividers, except at the right end, farthest from the doors. Here, all the material had been roughly pulled away, leaving windows overlooking the road the aliens had landed on. She walked up to it. The shuttle straddled the road several blocks down, facing her. Maybe looking at her. Her stomach did a cartwheel.

Damn, if Cooper thought this was a good spot because he could see most of the action, then he was an idiot.

A blue bolt of energy leapt from the front of the shuttle, angled steeply upward. *Bam.* She jerked backwards, dropping to her knees, her stomach skittering down the cosmetics aisle, completely disembodied. Damn it, there was no way to respond fast enough. If that bolt had been aimed at her, she would be dead.

"Sir," someone in the combat area said, "we just lost another sniper."

"Dammit," came the muttered reply. It had to be Colonel Cooper. "Instruct them to move after every shot."

Sullivan pulled herself off of the floor. Time to find out who this Cooper guy was. She probably needed to take command from him. But God, she wasn't looking forward to that confrontation.

"They are, sir," a sergeant standing at the front counter said, directing his voice into the photo processing nook in the back. "But the shuttle gun is too quick."

Cooper stood near the break in the counter, tapping his fingers on the melamine top, lips moving like he was trying to come up with something to say and failing.

The part of Colonel Sullivan that had wanted to take command stepped back. Over on the far wall, the personnel officer had a casualty list posted, numbers of killed, of wounded, of missing, and a footnote that indicated none of the above numbers included losses from the air battle. She stared at it, blinking a couple of times, trying to get the amounts to come into focus. Those numbers couldn't possibly be right. It was almost half a brigade's worth. It was... Cooper's brigade was already combat ineffective.

A little voice in her head wanted to gloat. *Hate to say it, but now I'm glad it's your responsibility, not mine.*

But she did have some information for him. She approached and introduced herself, and he invited her into his "office area." Once seated, she shared the information she'd learned from the Air Force pilots.

Cooper's expression came close to an eyeroll. It was a reaction she often got from men who still inhabited all-male units, who weren't used to dealing with women. She debated calling him on his near insubordination, then decided to ignore it. Cooper had enough on his mind. He didn't need to deal with a persnickety fellow officer.

Besides, from what she could tell of him, his cocky manner and down-the-nose stare, he was past saving, anyway.

"Yeah, interesting," Cooper said. "I'll see if I can use that info."

She didn't think he was going to give it a second thought. But she had done her duty.

"In the meantime," Cooper added, "we'll need a battle captain from your unit."

She stood, glaring at him with as much rancor as she could put in her face. "I know how to liaise with a supported headquarters."

His smile was less apologetic than condescending. Or at least that was how it looked to her. Son of a bitch, there wasn't a man in the universe she could trust.

She marched out of his office. Back in the MP Operations Center, her soldiers were busy moving shelves of medications out of the way. It looked like chaos, bottles of pills falling on the floor, wooden shelves scraping on the concrete. She walked up to her executive officer, her teeth pressing into her lip. She didn't need to take her anger out on her own soldiers. Still, right now she wanted to bite someone's head off.

"Battle captain?" she asked Davis.

"I sent Staff Sergeant Clark," he answered. "We're kind of short on officers." That last comment had sounded conciliatory, like he knew she was in a bad mood.

She needed to get over it. Men like Cooper were everywhere, but she had surrounded herself with good people who respected her and followed her lead, and she'd be dammed if Cooper's ass-holery was going to spill over into her unit. "Good choice," she forced herself to say.

He looked relieved.

L. D. ROBINSON © 2022

Then, SSG Clark appeared in the doorway to the MP Ops Center. "The press just arrived."

Oh, shit. Sullivan should have known they would be here sooner rather than later. And Clark was probably telling her this because her unit was going to be saddled with babysitting them. Not a duty she relished.

She poked her head out of the pharmacy area. Three men stood at the near end of the maze, just behind an MP escort. The tallest of the three, black and battered looking, reached his lean arms into the remnants of a pocket and pulled out his credentials. "I'd like to get an interview with the commander."

"Sir?" a nearby NCO said, looking at Cooper.

Patrice slipped into her little office cubicle. The reporters had likely not spotted her yet, and she wanted it to stay like that. She needed to spend her time figuring out how to fight aliens, not look good to the public.

In the meantime, Cooper let out an exasperated sigh. "Carve out an area for the press," he said. "I'll talk to them when I get a chance."

Patrice smiled to herself, then sat back at her "desk," a small table in a nook not much bigger than a latrine stall. But it was all hers, with a little privacy, even.

"Right over here," a voice said from over the wall. Damn. It wasn't much of a sound barrier after all, just a thin slab of plywood separating her from the pharmacy waiting area, now the temporary hub of the press corps. Maybe she should move. Or maybe she should tell Cooper to put the press someplace else.

But right now she didn't see a lot of better options.

"Fucking asshole," a man said from the other side of the wall. From the timbre of his voice, she figured it had been the black man, the actual reporter. "How long's he gonna leave us here?"

Great. Just great. Now she was going to have to listen to everything that happened in the press area. The need to move her office space took on a new urgency. She ran a hand through her hair. Then, the door to her little cubbyhole popped open. Cooper stood in the doorway.

"Listen," he said, "there are going to be more press here soon, and we can't handle all of them in here."

No shit, she wanted to say. But the politician inside her kept her response more business-like. "You want me to round them up?"

Cooper nodded. "We need to find a better work area for them... Can't let them stay inside here." He glanced over his shoulder, where his operations officer still stood at the easel, still monitoring the operation.

"Agreed."

"And see if you can find a PAO to work with them."

Sullivan stifled a growl. "I don't have a public affairs officer."

"Mine were on the plane with Barker," Cooper said. "And so was most of the brigade staff. I got nobody to spare."

More angry complaints rushed into her mind, but Sullivan bit them back. Operations were always like this, undermanned as if by design. Like it or not, she was going to have to suck it up. Or delegate the requirement to LTC Palmer's battalion. It wasn't like he was going to have a lot to do if things kept going the way they were.

"I'll see what I can do."

"Thank you, uh, Ma'am."

Chapter 17 — Interview

"Okay to film this?" a voice said from the other side of Patrice's wall. It was the cameraman for that reporter.

Damn it, Cooper had barely closed the door, and now, it sounded like they were setting up in the pharmacy waiting room, right next to her office. Clearly, Sullivan was not going to get much done for the next few minutes.

She closed her eyes and huffed out a little frustration. Maybe she could find some earplugs. Heck, there should be some for sale out in the drug store.

As if that would actually block out the sound.

"Okay," another voice came from behind the wall. "I'm Lieutenant Colonel Cooper, temporary commander of the brigade here."

Patrice ran her fingers over her closed eyes. Cooper still sounded so cock sure of himself, in spite of all his failures. Full of himself. Enjoying all the attention, all the cache this kind of publicity would get him for the next promotion board. What a jerk.

Worse, she couldn't see anything that was happening in the operations center. Her secure text application was all she had connecting her to the outside of this tiny room. Maybe she just needed to walk out and start doing the old "management by walking around."

But that might draw the attention of the reporter.

Would that be so bad? If the mission went well, notoriety in connection with the operation could actually help *her* get a promotion. Maybe she should be jealous of Cooper. Maybe she should elbow her way into the interview.

Or maybe not. She had other work to do. She looked back at a report just sent to her by text.

"What kinds of plans you got for this enemy?" the reporter said.

Patrice smiled. That was a stupid question, and if the situation hadn't been so serious, it would have been funny. This reporter obviously didn't understand anything about military security, and Cooper was unlikely to give any kind of direct answer.

Someone tapped on her door. "Come," she said. The door popped open, and Finley stood there. Patrice gestured for the sergeant to sit and close the door.

"We're looking for a way to render the shuttle un-spaceworthy," Cooper said. "Anything we can do to poke a hole in it." He sounded so confident. Where did people get this unreal sense of competency, especially after so much had gone wrong? Was the man delusional?

"Like what?" the reporter asked.

"We've got something coming," he said. "That's all I can tell you."

Patrice puckered her lips, like she'd just sucked on a rotten lemon, and it took all her self-control not to shudder. Sounded like Cooper had something else up his sleeve, and he hadn't said a word to her about it. She needed to be in on these things, damn it! What was the matter with him?

Finley sat across from Patrice, her face contorted into a look of concern. "Ma'am, I think we got a problem."

Yeah, no shit, Patrice wanted to say. Cooper was screwing everything up. But that wasn't something she could say to Finley, so she just put her finger to her lips, then gestured with her head to indicate the other conversation.

"Okay. What can you tell us, then?" the reporter asked.

Finley rolled her eyes, and that made Patrice chuckle. "What problem?" Patrice whispered, while Cooper waxed eloquent about the importance of his mission, and how he had "no intention of failing."

"That shuttle," Finley said, pointing through the walls with her thumb. "It ain't the same size as in the previous attack."

"So," Patrice said, "your engagement distance may be off?"

Finley nodded. "I gotta do another calculation, only I don't got as much data to work with."

"Do what you can."

Speaking of shuttle size, the reporter's words broke through to Patrice's awareness. "We estimate they can kidnap about a thousand people with the size of the shuttle there. How many of your soldiers have died already trying to rescue them?"

"This is not a numbers game," Cooper snapped. "This is about people." Now, he went off on another rant, talking about relationships and how all that made us human. Patrice wanted to roll her eyes, but Finley was still there, watching her, and the gesture didn't seem appropriate.

"Anything else from the rear?" Patrice asked.

Finley leaned toward Sullivan. "Major Li seem to think there's something about this shuttle being diverted from New York to here," she whispered. "But he don't know what."

She nodded. "Okay. Keep me informed."

Finley nodded and rose, while over the partition, Cooper had ended his diatribe on relationships. "Tell me about your own family," the reporter asked.

Patrice grabbed a pen, bracing herself for another long sermon on human connection.

"I have a wife and two boys," Cooper said. "They're my reason for being here, the thing that gives my life meaning."

Patrice shook her head. He wasn't here because of them, he was here because he had orders, just like all the other military in this fight. But now, he'd found the right sound bite, the story to make all the public worship him, the claim that having family somehow made his sacrifice all the more meaningful, made him more of a hero than any of the other soldiers here.

"What do *they* think about you being here?" the reporter asked.

"My beautiful wife has always been supportive," Cooper said.

Now, Patrice wanted to gag.

"Even if it means…" the reporter asked.

"Let's not go there, okay?"

A sigh of relief fell out of Patrice's mouth. Good. At least he wasn't going to wallow in all that gloom.

"So, what will happen if you can't accomplish this mission?"

"Okay, gentlemen," Cooper said, and Patrice could tell by his tone that he'd come to his feet, "I have a lot of work to do, so this interview is over."

Chapter 18 — No Good Solution

Not long after the interview ended, LTC Palmer and his soldiers escorted the press to a new location, the bowling alley down the street. None of the reporters were happy with it, but Palmer assured them they'd get all the information as soon as it was cleared for public release.

That left the operations centers to function a little more openly. Additionally, more of her soldiers arrived, and with each group, her headquarters felt more functional, more capable. And they were getting orders and passing along assignments, making things happen.

Slowly, chaos was giving way to order.

And Cooper was doing nothing. What was he waiting for?

"Sir!" one of the sergeants shouted. "A couple of planes landed with tanks on board."

Cooper straightened with a jerk, then punched his left palm with his right fist. "How many?"

"Two."

"How long before they get here?"

"I'll ask," the sergeant said turning back to his equipment. He typed a query into his computer, then watched the screen.

Cooper turned to his operations officer. "Already on it," the operations man said as he gathered a small team around an easel in the corner. He wrote "COA" on top of the paper with a squeaky black marker, indicating they would be brainstorming possible courses of action, a quick and dirty military decision-making process. SSG Clark joined them, his paper notebook on his knee. He thumbed the corner of the booklet, making the pages flip with a soft buzz and a thump as the last page landed. Then he did it again. And again.

Colonel Sullivan wiped her hands on the side of her uniform blouse, then walked up to Cooper. "Is there anything I can do to help?"

"We got this," Cooper said.

Son of a bitch. She wanted to help, damn it. Did he have to elbow her out, like he thought her contribution wasn't worth anything?

She held her breath to keep back the anger at being dismissed. After all this time in the military, working with all these men, she should be used to it by now. More importantly, arguing with the commander would just distract him, make things worse.

"Okay. Let me know if things change."

"About 15 minutes, sir," the radio operator called out. "They still have to fuel up."

"No more fuel than they need," Cooper said.

L. D. ROBINSON © 2022

She glanced back at the decision-making working group. They already had two COAs on the board and were arguing about a third. SSG Clark leaned forward, elbows on his knees, brow knotted.

Had Cooper even given them any guidance? Commander's guidance was the first step of the decision-making process, and it looked like he was leaving everything to his subordinates. Maybe she needed to step in, take command.

Maybe Cooper wasn't up to the job.

Maybe he was going to throw another slap-happy plan together and fail everyone in the process. Like her father had done when she was only eight, ignoring her pleas not to get behind the wheel, pretending everything was okay even though he was so drunk he could barely stand. "I'm fine," he had told her. "No problem."

"But Dad..."

"Get in."

Pain shattered her cheek and she rubbed it with her fingertips. That was a long time ago. It shouldn't still hurt.

She just had to get away from this craziness, stop watching this self-destruct in slow motion. But another part of her mind demanded she stay, do whatever she could to help. She shifted her weight to her right foot, then back again. God, when had she ever been so indecisive?

"Alien casualties," the intelligence representative at the easel said. "Three, at most."

The operations officer let his shoulders drop, like a balloon deflating. "What does that tell me?"

Sullivan smiled. Exactly the question she would have asked. Without information on how many aliens there were total, casualty numbers didn't amount to diddly squat.

L. D. ROBINSON © 2022

"They don't hang around where we can shoot at them much,"

God damn, why was this always so hard? If this was what they meant when they referred to the fog of war... Hell, that expression didn't describe the half of it.

She shook her head. Nothing to see here. With that, she turned back to her tiny office, then sat at her desk, looking over the various status reports from the battalions. The downed aircraft had cost her unit a lot. Technically, she was combat ineffective, too.

She ran her hands over her eyes, as LTC Cooper's words to the reporter came back to her. She didn't know why it bothered her, him going on about his wife and children, how they were what made his life worth living, and how, in the end, they were who he was fighting for. She had never felt that way about anybody. And what if she died here, today? Besides her mother, who would mourn her passing? Who even cared?

"Ma'am," LTC Davis said, "Colonel Cooper's briefing the next mission."

She grabbed a notebook, then stood. "I'll cover it."

"Give 'em hell."

Cooper was in mid-brief when she arrived, a small gaggle of personnel standing around a map hung on the wall and the easel with scribbled courses of action. The operations sergeant had dark circles under his eyes, and the rest of the personnel sat quietly at their tables, heads down like they were working, but not a pen or pencil moved. No tapping on computer keyboards.

She walked to the side of the group, where she could see the faces of the two company commanders, two earnest young white guys who looked like they should still be second lieutenants. One had his foot on a chair, helmet resting on his thigh.

Cooper pointed to the map with his finger. "Alpha, you're going to head this way." He drew a line along the street. "Bravo, you're over here."

The young captains scribbled in their notebooks.

"Get as close to the shuttle as you can. But try to stay out of sight."

The commanders nodded, both looking confident.

Idiots. They should be scared out of their gourds.

"Once you're in position, you're going to wait until the tanks have disabled the shuttle. You'll get your go-ahead to approach from this headquarters. Understand?"

The two nodded.

"One tank will approach from the front. That's where we figure the control room, the bridge if you will, of the vessel is."

Sullivan creased her brows. Where had they come up with control room placement? There was nothing on the outside of the vessel to indicate anything about the layout of the interior.

"The second will come at it from this direction, and will fire at the rear, where we think the engines are." He smiled at everyone, clearly an attempt to project confidence. She understood the gesture, but she also knew it was a lie.

When the briefing was over, Colonel Sullivan walked up to Cooper, who now stood in the corner, by his desk. That was good. Out of earshot of the others.

"How did you find out where the engines are?"

He glared at her. "We didn't."

"You're just assuming?"

"Have you seen their handguns?" he said. "Shaped just like pistols. Form follows function."

"But what if their detention area is in the rear? The overpressure from the tank rounds could kill all the civilians we're supposed to rescue."

"I have to make assumptions," Cooper said. "Deal with it." He turned and walked away.

Damned son of a bitch. Fucking Colonel High and Mighty, talking about how important people were in his life, now casually throwing away other's lives based on untested assumptions. It wasn't right.

But damn, she didn't see an alternative. It was the nature of the job, risking one life to save another. She'd never seen the paradox of it all before, never wondered why one life was more important than another, only that some had agreed to do this, some had agreed to serve, to sacrifice everything, if necessary, to protect others.

She didn't like it. She didn't like Cooper.

Damn, she didn't like anybody.

So why was she even here, ready to sacrifice her own life?

Good question. Besides orders, of course.

And her career.

Yeah, that was it. The chance to be a leader, the chance to be in control of the situation, the chance to bend others' wills to her own. That was what had brought her into the military. Not some fabled desire to serve mankind, some noble willingness to sacrifice her own good for the benefit of others. All that was poppycock. When people thanked her for her "service," she just had to smile and nod and laugh on the inside. It was more self-serving than anything else.

So now, how was she supposed to even like herself, with her cold-hearted desires for aggrandizement, with her ambition that seemed to make her willing to step on anyone in her way.

Including herself. She had forgone a romantic relationship for her career. A man in her life would have gotten in the way of her success. He would have put demands on her time that would take away from her ability to put her all into the job. And friendships had, for the most part, also been burned on the altar of single-minded devotion to her duties. It was the only way to compete successfully.

She headed back to her own headquarters, walking past the little desk where SSG Clark sat making notes, busy doing all the myriad things he did to make her look good. Back at her command post, Davis stood at a status board, going over numbers with the logistics officer. And Finley, toward the back, took notes as she talked to someone on the phone.

Did Sullivan see all these people as tools for her to use? Did she think she could abuse them or take credit for their ideas and work, and throw them under any oncoming bus just so she could get ahead? Actually, no.

That was a definite no.

She blinked with surprise. Maybe she wasn't such a bad person after all.

She wasn't willing to step on any of them. In fact, she was trying to save them, plus all the civilians in the alien shuttle. She was trying to do the right thing. In spite of how easy it was to dismiss people, to decide she disdained them, there were at least some she cared about.

At least, she thought she did. True, she would send them into harm's way if that was required, but she would also do her damnedest to make sure they had the best chance to succeed, to survive. That was a form of caring, wasn't it? She could still like herself, couldn't she?

She walked to her desk, then dropped into the chair. She didn't know how to give her people an edge in their fight with the aliens. She didn't have the foggiest notion of what would enable them to succeed. And if she couldn't come up with something like that, what was she worth? What was the point of her even being here?

The whine of jet engines told her the tanks had arrived. This, she had to watch.

"Finley," she called out. The sergeant jumped from her chair and followed as Sullivan made her way to the front of the store, then along the windows until she'd reached the place where she could see the action.

"Is this safe?" Finley asked.

Patrice pulled a mirror off a shelf and positioned it to look out the window. "Now, we'll just hide behind the wall."

That wouldn't protect them from a large blast, but the aliens were less likely to see them. That was the best she could do.

Finley settled onto the floor, eyes trained on the mirror, notebook in hand. Sullivan pressed herself into the corner.

Treads grinding the pavement, the first tank trundled past the drug store, its engine sounding more like a jet than a ground vehicle, wheels squeaking like it needed a little WD-40. Sullivan narrowed her eyes as it passed, all buttoned up, no one to man the 50-cal machine gun. Just as well. That weapon would probably be ineffective.

The tank stopped at the intersection, then made a slow turn, neutral steer, until its front faced the shuttle. Waves of heat shimmered off the back. and the angular turret swiveled atop the chassis, motors whirring. The main gun lowering into position to shoot. God, what a beautiful piece of machinery. Sleek. Sassy. Stunning.

She knew from the briefings she'd heard that the other tank had turned on another road and would come at the shuttle from the side. It would only be a few moments before they were both in place.

She slid down off her perch and sat beside Finley, smiling. "This is going to be good."

"Remind the tanks," Colonel Cooper said, his voice loud enough she could hear him without strain, "they are to shoot to disable."

"So they don't kill civilians?" Finley asked.

Sullivan nodded.

A moment later, another voice came from the operations center. "Sir, the tankers are not sure what that means."

"It means disable," Cooper said, his voice rising.

Sullivan and Finley exchanged glances. It felt strangely intimate then, sitting in a corner so close together, sharing their contempt at the commander's ineptness with raised brows and rolled eyes, voiceless acknowledgement nobody else could seem to get it right.

"They know how to disable a ground vehicle, sir," the radio operator continued. "Or even an aircraft. But what does this thing use to fly?"

Colonel Cooper huffed. "Just blow a hole in the damned thing."

"Roger," the radioman said.

"That ain't gonna be easy," Finley whispered.

Sullivan pulled her knees to her chest and wrapped her arms around her legs. "Just pray," she whispered.

"Dear Lord," Finley said, her voice low and grim, "give us this victory. Please, Lord. Please."

"All units are in place," another person said.

Colonel Cooper's voice sounded cocky. "Commence the operation."

Sullivan bit her lip. It still didn't sound like Cooper understood how badly this could all go, how horribly the aliens could react now that they'd brought in the big guns. They could all be just minutes from total annihilation.

Chapter 19 — Call For Help

"What are those things?" Galth said, staring at the strange vehicle that rode on drive belts and had stopped several hundred yards in front of the shuttle.

"Some kind of robot?" Kelm said.

"Yeah." Galth narrowed his eyes as though that would give him a better look, more detail. He didn't get any new information.

"There's a second one to the side," Kelm continued. "They're both pointing their guns at us."

It was the largest gun he had seen these quivs brandish, wider than his arm, its metallic shaft polished and straight. Looking down the borehole gave his stomach a jolt, an unfamiliar sensation of dread, like it could really do some damage, in spite of his shields.

Assuming the shields could hold out against this monstrosity.

He didn't need to take any chances. "Hand me the targeting pad," he said.

The quiv gun barrel jerked, a large flame bursting from the front like the blooming of a solar flare. The room jolted. He was thrown off the floor, feet in the air, and then his back slammed against the wall, forcing the air out of his lungs. The control pad flew from his fingers and slammed against the wall beside him.

Kelm landed on his butt and slid into the corner, control pad still in his hands. "They're preparing to fire again!"

Galth dove to the floor and grabbed the control pad. But before he could see the screen, he was thrown again, this time by rocking in the other direction. "Turn on the restraining fields!" Galth shouted.

"I'm trying!" Kelm said, fumbling with his control pad.

A second later, a soft force field enveloped Galth and he scrambled back to his feet with satisfaction. Those robots could hit them all they wanted now, and he wouldn't be hurt.

"Damage report."

"Shields down to 73%."

Feces. That was worse than he'd expected. "Transfer auxiliary power to the shields."

"That won't be enough."

"Do what I tell you!" Galth said, as he ran his fingers over the screen of the targeting control pad. Then he chuckled deep in this throat. "Let's see what they think of this."

He had a weapons lock on both robots--though it would be hard to miss at this range. A last touch to the control pad, and the satisfying orange fingers of his energy weapons leapt out at the robots with a thunderous crack. The shot lasted for less than half a second, a beam he'd been told was hotter than the surface of the sun, one end dancing on the robots' outer hull. In a moment, they would melt.

They just sat there.

He stared at the enemy machine, brow creasing. "Am I seeing that right?"

Kelm had his eyes fixed on his control pad. "The body absorbed some of the heat, but--"

"That should have blown a hole right through…" But all he could see was a dark smudge where his weapon had hit.

"We've got to recall the ground crew," Kelm said. "Pick another target."

Galth glanced out the side-facing part of his viewscreen, but all he could see there was the tunnel. A running tally of captured victims scrolled at the bottom of the screen. They were still adding more bodies at a satisfying rate, and if he stopped the operation now, he probably wouldn't have time to do all the set-up required to get to this point at another building before the defenders were on him again.

"Not so fast," Galth muttered, then sent another energy beam to bore into the enemy robot. Maybe this immunity to energy weapons only lasted for a little while. Maybe he would break through to destroy the robots sooner than he expected.

The beam hit the same spot as before. The blackened circle enlarged, but he couldn't see any evidence of breaking through. If they kept this up…

"He's getting ready to fire again!" Kelm shouted.

Galth slammed the firing pad into Kelm's hands. "Fire back!" Then, he grabbed communications and punched in the code to call Beglash's ship.

"Tordag here," a voice answered, his tone leisurely, like they were on shore leave.

"Two robots attacking us!" Galth said. "Fire on them now!"

"We're not even on your side of the planet," Tordag answered. Now, he sounded exasperated, as if Galth's call was interrupting his entertainment.

"Then get over here, now!"

Tordag breathed a long noisy puff of air into the communications pad. He sounded exasperated, like he didn't understand the level of the emergency. "If they hit you, the hull will heal itself."

"This is not small arms fire," Galth barked back. "We're not talking about holes the size of your thumb."

"Galth..."

"This is going to put a hole in my ship as big as your head. Can it heal from that?"

Another puff of air. "I don't think so."

"Where is Captain Beglash?"

The robot spit another flash of light, and the shuttle rocked, the viewscreen clouded in smoke.

"Shields 49%!" Kelm called.

"Beglash here. What's the problem?"

"Get over here now or you're going to lose an entire shuttle."

Galth looked back up at the robot, right into the blackness of the long muzzle. One more hit and he would be vulnerable. Two and he would be dead.

Chapter 20 — Big Blast

"Something's gotta give soon," Colonel Sullivan said, kneeling in front of the window as the tank fired its third round. The muzzle flash lit up the street, and the boom rattled the glass, prompting her to drop to the floor. She'd had glass blown into her face once already in her life. She didn't need that a second time.

The mirror she had set up would have to do.

Sergeant Finley sat beside her, head was below window height, watching the mirror intently, making notes.

"Looks like the shield's glow is getting softer," Sullivan said hopefully.

"I don know."

"Why do you say that?"

Finley paused, then let out a breath. "Eyes can trick you. We need a light meter to be show."

"Yeah," Sullivan said, then shook her head with disappointment. She wanted to see diminishing shields so badly, was she just deluding herself? Was she capable of such self-deception?

"DARPA need to invent a shield meter," Finley added.

Smart kid. She was going to do well in her career. "Hey, Finley, you ever thought about becoming an officer?"

Finley responded with a blank look, a slight crease of the brow. But a second later, she looked at the wall and her eyes fluttered, like she needed to clear out the dust in the air with her eyelashes or wash away a little mote that had gotten onto her eyeball. "Woah," she said under her breath. "Maybe a warrant."

"That would be good, too." Getting a commission was a long path for someone like Finley to take, since the sergeant hadn't a single college credit to her name. But Finley had the smarts to do it if she wanted. Sullivan resisted the urge to smile. "Let's talk about this when we get back to base."

"Um... sure, ma'am."

A sense of satisfaction nestled into Sullivan's gut. Something good might come out of this crazy operation.

Another boom sounded, bringing Patrice back to the current situation. She glanced out the window, saw the sputtering of the blue glow dying.

A brief rush of excitement washed over Sullivan. If they were really wearing down the shield, they might be about to finish off the aliens. Wouldn't that be something?

But if Finley was right, the tank might simply be hammering the shuttle in total futility. The creatures inside could be laughing at the puny human efforts to thwart them.

Her stomach twisted. She shouldn't be standing here, watching like she thought she was invulnerable. But she couldn't think of much more important things to do right now.

"They keep aiming for different spots on the tank," Finley commented. "Like they're trying to find its weakness."

"Show me," Sullivan said, slipping down to sit beside Finley, whose crude drawing of a tank had x's marked along the front side.

The world turned white, followed by a thunderous boom, so loud it seemed solid, slamming her head toward the floor, while the window above her exploded, glass spraying into the open air followed by smoke and flames. She wrapped her arms around her head to protect her exposed skin from the searing heat, which bored into her, suffocating, as though it sucked all the air from the room. She held her breath as shattered glass tinkled to the floor a few feet away. Then there was the sound of pebbles clacking against the far wall and onto the floor. Screams rent the air, driving icepicks through her ears.

"Medic!" someone in the operations center yelled.

"Finley!" Sullivan shouted, her heart pounding like a bass drummer. Everything had gone dark, damned pupils reacting to the bright light, and only shadows weaved in front of her, most of them probably not real. She patted the floor, moving her hand outward until she found Finley, curled into a ball on the floor, arms wrapped around her head.

"I'm okay," Finley said softly.

Beyond them, the sounds of whimpering filled the air.

Sullivan's eyes had begun to adjust. Finley moved, looked up, her face gaunt and frightened. The mirror was gone, and the shelves looked like an otherworldly cactus, slivers of glassy spines warning you not to touch it. All around her, shards of glass penetrated the shelves, the pill bottles and boxes of bandages, the plastic containers of cough syrup, now dripping red onto the tile floor.

But nothing had ricocheted off, nothing had bounced back at them. God, she couldn't believe how lucky she was. If she hadn't gotten curious about Finley's observations, she would now be a pincushion.

"Clark?" Finley said.

"Shit!" Sullivan said, jumping up again. She had to get back to the combat operations center and find him.

"Ow, damn!" someone else shouted in the darkness.

"What the hell was that?" another voice said.

She moved along the cosmetics display on the side wall, reaching out to touch it to keep her bearings, since her eyes still had not fully recovered. Something stung her finger and she jerked it back. More tiny glass slivers. Nothing was safe anymore.

As she got a few feet closer to the back, a lump came into view on the floor in front of her, motionless. A body. A fallen soldier. She swallowed her fear and pressed forward, then saw a glint of light poking up from the folds of his shirt. God, it was glass, sticking out of the sides of his arms and legs. Dozens of pieces, jutting up from pools of bloodied uniform fabric, a glassy porcupine.

She retched, throwing a hand over her mouth. A vision of her father, stumbling drunk and uninjured from the crash flashed through her mind. And the pain in her cheek, where something sharp had shredded the skin...

She blinked herself back to the present.

Across the room, Cooper had risen from his desk in the shadows and walked into the barely perceptible light. He stopped to stare out the window. "Jesus H. Christ," he said.

She could see enough now. She walked up to the soldier on the floor and felt his neck for a pulse. The skin had an odd, plastic feel to it. No heartbeat.

"Obliterated," Cooper said.

"What?" She stood again, turning toward his voice. He had walked over to her former observation spot, staring out what used to be a window, now a gaping hole, only tiny bits of glass still clinging around the edges.

"Look." He pointed down the street, then dropped his hand to his side like it was weighted down by an anvil.

The smoke was still settling, but she could see enough. The tanks were darkened lumps, their tracks ripped away from the road wheels and shredded, and their main gun tubes sagging.

"That blast didn't come from the shuttle," someone else muttered.

Cooper stumbled back to the main operations center, glass crunching under his feet, face like a mask, mouth partly open. He gestured to an NCO who looked uninjured "Take care of the wounded," he said, his voice a monotone.

She still hadn't found Clark. She hurried into the open area, scanning for her battle captain. Where? Where? Oh, damn it, had she killed him by putting him in this room?

Cooper turned to the communications NCO. "Get on the radio and see if anybody's still alive out there."

Sullivan's stomach fell. None of the soldiers outside would have survived. The blazing heat from the blast would have melted flesh right off the bones.

Which meant all Cooper had left was a few companies in reserve, if that.

"Ma'am?" a familiar voice said.

Sullivan turned around. Staff Sergeant Clark stood nearby, blood smeared across his forehead, another small laceration on the edge of his jaw. A line of blood ran out his ear.

But he was alive, and relief washed over her. "You're injured."

"I'm okay," he said. "The glass was big enough, I could pull it out."

She shuddered. "I want you to get checked out."

He acknowledged with a nod.

Behind him, Cooper was calling for status. Soldiers hurried from one spot to another, helping wounded, calling on the radio, trying to get an idea of what they had left to fight with.

Colonel Cooper's face was ashen, and Colonel Sullivan hurried around the corner, back to her own operations center. It had fared better since it had been shielded by the structure of the pharmacy.

LTC Davis set down the headset from the radio, his frown deeper than normal. "Ma'am, I think that last attack took out some of our detention battalion."

"Palmer?"

Davis shook his head. "Nobody in the battalion HQ has heard from him."

She nodded, eyes burning.

"We'll get you exact numbers as they come in."

"Casualties are pouring into the medic station," someone else reported.

"Where are my reinforcements?" Cooper asked, his voice soft in the distance.

"Checking," someone answered.

She leaned her head against the wall and closed her eyes. The last thing she needed was Colonel Cooper attaching her soldiers to his unit so that he would get them killed as well.

Not that she wouldn't be required to do the same if he failed.

Chapter 21 — Last Gasp

Sullivan hurried back to the combat operations center. Whatever Cooper had planned, she needed to know about it. She stood in the back, behind a clump of leaders from one of the only remaining units, a lieutenant whose pale face was bleached to white, his light red hair standing on end, a blank-faced first sergeant, and a couple of fidgeting non-commissioned officers.

"Okay," Cooper said, "let's at least stop them from getting any more people."

Sullivan swallowed. The brass at home wouldn't be pleased that Cooper had lowered the bar. Still, it was probably the right move.

"We need to get inside the building, stop the aliens."

The lieutenant nodded, pen hovering over a page in his little green notebook, but his hand didn't move.

"My thinking is that inside, you have more places to take cover, and you can then start shooting those bastards one by one."

"Hooah," one of the sergeants whispered. It was the weakest cheer Sullivan had ever heard.

"See if you can separate them from each other, give yourselves better odds." Cooper turned to a major named Rogers. "You got anything?"

Major Rogers stood. "Sir, we think, based on what we saw from the videos in Mumbai, that the wrapping thing around the building can be cut. But we also know there are aliens patrolling the outside, specifically to protect the barrier."

"Yeah," the first sergeant muttered. "That's why that police officer's head got turned to red mist."

The lieutenant standing beside him looked like he was going to puke.

"If you head up to this street," Major Rogers said, pointing to a nearby map, "then you can enter the near parking garage. We think that is the shortest length of barrier, so the place you're least likely to run into enemy."

Cooper stared at Rogers for a few seconds, then turned back to the lieutenant. "Any questions?"

"What if there's another one of those big blasts?" the lieutenant said.

Cooper's cheeks sagged. "Son, I wish I could tell you it won't happen."

Sullivan bit her lip. Would it be any consolation to know that if such an attack occurred, the lieutenant would die instantly? Would it make him feel better if she said that? Or would that make the entire endeavor too frightening to carry out?

L. D. ROBINSON © 2022

"Now," Cooper said, "once you get inside, and we've taken out most of the aliens, if at all possible, you need to try to get into the shuttle. Rescue all the people who've been captured."

"I understand," the lieutenant said. He sounded like a robot, a person who'd had to push his fear so far inside that there was no feeling left. Sullivan ached for him.

A few more final coordinating orders were discussed, and then the lieutenant left, a trail of soldiers following, out onto the sidewalk and up the street. Sullivan stepped out the door and watched them trudge into the distance, past the flower-filled planters on the edges of the broad sidewalk, ducking low so their heads stayed below the tops of the parking meters, behind the thin tree trunks, moving toward the big sign marking the bowling alley.

They were the last effort, and they knew it.

Back inside, she found herself a chair in the back of the room, her back butted up against the glass doors of the chilled beverage refrigerator. Cooper sat at his desk behind the counter of the photo processing lab, and the operations NCO scratched notes on an easel, the marker squeaking as he drew it over the paper.

The radioman stared at his equipment, situated next to the cash register, tapping a pencil against the countertop.

"We're across the street from the parking garage," a voice said over the radio.

Heads lifted. SSG Clark leaned forward, head tilted to keep his ear facing the loudspeakers.

Sullivan looked down, realizing that her fingernails had dug into the heels of her hands, the pain only now reaching her awareness. She straightened her fingers and shook her hands.

"Man down," the voice in the radio blurted.

LTC Cooper stood, took a few steps toward the radio, his skin pale under the fluorescent lights.

Popping noises stuttered in the distance, the distinct sound of military weapons spitting out three-round bursts.

"We got one!"

Everyone came to their feet, cheering, clapping, hollering loudly. Major Rogers high-fived a nearby NCO, and the command sergeant major hopped with excitement. Even SSG Clark joined the celebration, slamming his palm onto the table with a resounding, "Yes!"

But the commotion quickly died down, everyone there seeming to realize what Sullivan already thought. One alien down didn't mean that much in the overall scheme of things.

Cooper took another step towards the radio operator, as if that could give the operation some additional support. As if he could somehow pull good news from the speakers everyone listened to.

But there was only silence.

Several minutes passed. Colonel Cooper paced across the room, occasionally rubbing his hands over his face. The only sounds were murmurs of staff sharing information in cautious whispers, everyone afraid to interrupt the old man.

"How long has it been since their last call?" Cooper said.

"Five minutes."

Cooper screwed up his face, and Sullivan knew what he had to be thinking. As the commander, it seemed like a need, an imperative, to know what was going on, how the operation was proceeding. And yet calling them, asking someone to talk out loud when silence was required could undermine the entire undertaking.

She leaned forward, elbows on her knees, hands wrapped around her cheeks. Normally, at least some of the soldiers would have worn tracking devices, and all that would have been displayed on some fancy computer in the operations center. That was the level of detail people like Cooper were used to. But the major components of those tracking systems had been destroyed when Barker's plane went down. Now, they were back in the last century in terms of technology.

And it was eating away at her gut.

Static burst over the radio speaker and Sullivan straightened.

"We're in the parking garage," the Lieutenant reported. "It looks like we can cut through the barrier here and get into the building."

"Yes," Cooper whispered, the first look of hope lighting his eyes. He looked around the room, gazing at all the concerned faces, then gave them a slight nod. "I think those guys could use all your prayers."

Sullivan's mouth went dry. In her experience, God rarely intervened in things like this. Asking for prayers sounded like the commander had lost hope, like he was grasping at clouds, like he was throwing in the last shot of adrenaline to start the patient's unresponsive heart. Like he knew what they had put together wasn't going to be enough.

But it was the least she could do. She brought her hand to her forehead, her other hand reaching for a rosary that wasn't there.

Damn.

"We're inside," the lieutenant's voice said.

Sullivan looked at her watch. It was 1535, well into the afternoon of what was already a long day, over 12 hours from when she'd first gotten out of bed. And it didn't look like things were going to wrap up any time soon. "I need some coffee," she said to no one in particular. She walked to the pharmacy area and downed a cup, heavy with sugar to keep her energy levels up.

When she returned to the main operations center, LTC Cooper was standing by the front door, one ear facing the street as though he could hear what was going on in another building, on another road. Impossible. But she couldn't blame him.

And everyone else stared at the radio speakers, silent, grim.

"Anything happen while I was gone?" she whispered to SSG Clark as she sat beside him.

"No, ma'am."

She nodded, shifting in her chair.

"If they all get killed," Clark continued, "how will we even know?"

"Good question."

"Or if they get taken prisoner..."

Sullivan took a deep breath and let it out noisily. "That would be even worse."

"Yeah."

Cooper turned away from the door and paced across the open area, shoving his hands in his pockets. Sullivan could see his fingers moving beneath the cloth, as though he were trying to make a fist, then pry his hands back open again, like he had pocketed the hands lest they independently do something unauthorized.

Her own fingers wanted to fidget. Her feet wanted to start tapping, heels moving back and forth in a nervous dance. Seven minutes had passed since the last transmission. God, how much longer would they need to wait?

L. D. ROBINSON © 2022

"Get on the radio and call them," Cooper said.

Sullivan let out a relieved sigh.

The radio operator nodded, his face still as though he didn't want to acknowledge either hope or concern, then began his pleading over the radio. "Team Omega, ops."

Colonel Sullivan stared at him, waiting, listening, the hole in her gut stretching, deepening, turning black. Reflexively, she crossed herself again, then closed her eyes and tried to come up with a good prayer for this effort. But she didn't know many of them, didn't even know who the patron saint of warriors was. She'd just not paid enough attention.

"Team Omega, ops," the radio operator called again. Then he waited. And called again.

Nothing.

A rock had started growing in Sullivan's throat. Felt like she had just been garroted.

Colonel Cooper hissed a loud breath, then walked back toward the door, growling under his breath.

When he reached it, he turned back to the radio operator. "Call them again."

The radioman repeated the same call three more times. But there was no reply.

Colonel McFarlane stepped softly over to the commander, shaking his head. "We can't beat these guys."

"We don't have the option to give up," Cooper barked. "People's lives depend on what we do!"

"We can't keep sending guys out there," McFarlane argued, arms out and palms up in a pleading gesture. "They just get killed."

"We are trying to save these people!" Cooper stood stiffly, pointing toward the shuttle with an outstretched arm.

The vein above McFarlane's temple throbbed. "You've gotten more than half of my battalion killed, and you're no closer to victory than when you first got here."

"Back off."

"I'm not letting you send any more of my men to their death."

Cooper pointed a finger at McFarlane. "You make a move like that, and I will have you arrested."

Colonel Sullivan stood, breath coming in tight stutters. She didn't want to get in the middle of this argument, especially since she agreed with McFarland. Fucking Cooper was worried about saving people? Hell, all those dead soldiers, weren't they people, too? But if Cooper called on the MPs to apprehend another officer, those would be her soldiers. She would be forced to mediate this disagreement.

McFarlane took a step back. Confrontation averted.

Sullivan sank back into her chair.

And then the personnel officer stepped grimly to his easel. He stared at it, swallowed, then added twenty-five to the column labeled missing in action. Twenty-five. The whole little platoon they'd lost contact with. Once he dropped his hand to his side, he turned and looked at the commander, as though looking for a response, as though asking what the commander was going to do now, now that his last gasp mission had failed.

Cooper stared at it, and it looked for a moment like all the fight went out of him. He couldn't face it, couldn't stare down the personnel officer, couldn't accept his own defeat. He looked away, eyes searching the room like he could find some answer there on the shelves of candy and bakery products. Like he thought some superhero would pop out of thin air and rescue him.

But no, there was nothing left.

Finally, he understood. Finally, he was going to stop sending soldiers to their deaths.

His hands hung at his side, limp, flaccid. And slowly, his chest collapsed, and his face sagged, and it seemed that on the inside, Lieutenant Colonel Cooper, acting brigade commander, died.

Cooper's eyes closed. And then, when they opened, a strange determination sparkled there. His fingers twitched. His shoulders squared up. His chest lifted.

Oh my God. What was he planning now?

Chapter 22 — Change Of Command

"Maybe they'll take me," Cooper said softly.

Every person in the operations room not already looking at Cooper lifted their head and stared at him. "Sir," the Command Sergeant Major said, "what the hell are you planning?"

Without saying another word, Cooper walked toward the door.

Colonel Sullivan rushed over to him. "Colonel Cooper," she said, embarrassed now that she didn't know his first name. "We need you here."

He smiled at her but shook his head. "If I can talk to them, if I can come to an understanding of what they want, maybe we can figure out how to work this out."

"I don't think so," Colonel Sullivan said. "What they want is not something we're going to be able to offer them."

"Just let me give it a try." He slapped her on the side of the arm, then did an about-face, turning toward the door again. Only now, the command sergeant major stood in front of the revolving glass portal.

"I can't let you do this, sir," the senior brigade NCO said.

"You can't stop me."

"You don't have to do this," Sullivan said, grateful for the support the CSM was giving her.

He let out a frustrated breath, then looked her directly in the eye. "This is the only thing I have left."

"Not true. We can come up with something else."

"Yeah," the CSM said. "We'll get busy brainstorming. We'll think of…"

Cooper shook his head. "Direct contact. That's what we need. I talk to their commander. We come to an understanding."

"Sir, I don't think they… they don't… sir!"

"Step aside," Cooper said.

The CSM straightened his shoulders. "I can't."

"Fine." Cooper did a quick sidestep to the hinged door.

Sullivan stepped in his direction, but barely got a shoulder between him and the door. Remembering his words to the reporter, she put a hand on his arm. "What about your wife and children?" Her voice broke and her chest tightened, like she was being crushed by a boa. That surprised her. Did she really care that much about these people she'd never even met? But it didn't matter. They needed Cooper alive. She needed him in command.

Cooper glanced back into the center of the drug store, and for a second his resolve cracked. His eyes glistened with moisture, with a look of longing and painful denial. Then he blinked.

"Tell them I love them."

"Shit," the CSM whispered.

Cooper leaned forward and pushed the door open. Then he was gone.

"Sir!"

Colonel Sullivan slipped out of the door, leaving the stunned CSM behind. Cooper was across the street, halfway to the corner, passing all the gaudy billboards pasted to the side of the building hawking all the liquors sold inside.

She hurried after him, trying to think of something more to say, hoping when he reached the intersection, when he saw all the destruction there, he would hesitate, and she could escort him back inside. But as soon as he reached the end of the building, he slipped around the corner, out of sight.

Damn it.

She sped up, reached the cross street, and peered around the brick structure. Cooper was working his way around bits of brick and crumpled fenders, veering to the left to move around the disabled tank, stepping over trackpads that lay scattered across the pavement. Glass crunched under his boots, and the smell of a thousand burning chemicals filled the air. Once he'd gotten past the sagging gun barrel of the tank, Cooper lifted his hands in what any human would recognize as a symbol of surrender. No one knew if the aliens would interpret the gesture the same way.

"We need to talk," Cooper said to the faceless shuttle.

Then nothing happened. No response, no glowing lights, no alien stepping out to welcome him into their lair.

L. D. ROBINSON © 2022

Sullivan measured the distance between Cooper and the shuttle, trying to compare it to the circle Finley had drawn around the alien craft. He'd not quite gotten there, best she could tell. He could still back off and survive.

"Don't get any closer!" she shouted.

He stiffened, back still toward her, arms ramrod straight, shoulders hunched. Then, he took another.

She took in a deep breath and held it. He might actually make it. He might actually get to talk to one of the aliens. He was so close, in fact, that she was expecting one of those creatures to reach an arm through the door and grab him, pulling him into the shuttle.

Another foot forward.

Something moved on the front of the shuttle--a short metal tube no wider around than a drinking straw. Its tip turned red, and it slewed toward the center until it pointed directly at Cooper.

"Get out of there!" Sullivan shouted.

Cooper dropped his hands, put one foot behind himself.

"Now!"

He swung his shoulders around, ready to dive away from the threat.

A blue light enveloped him. His form disappeared in the brightness, fingertips first, then moving inward to the center, until only a ball of blue plasma shimmered in the distance.

Then it was gone, and only a black lump lay on the pavement where he had stood.

She trembled, spinning around to brace herself, back against the solidness of a brick building, eyes closed. Nothing she'd just seen even seemed real. It had happened too quickly, too quietly, and without any warning. He had surrendered, and they had shown no mercy. The enemy had turned him to charcoal in less than a second. Their weapons were too efficient. How could she possibly...

"Ma'am?" the CSM said, now standing outside, just in front of the drug store. "Ma'am, you need to get back inside."

Her knees didn't want to move. If she unlocked them, she might tumble to the ground. She slapped her palms against the wall behind her and took a deep breath. "Right."

In a moment, she had herself back under control, and she hurried back into the headquarters. On the other side of the door, Major Rogers stood at attention, eyes locked onto hers. "Ma'am?" he said.

He didn't look dismayed or horrified. Rather, his expression was, maybe, a little hopeful. What could he be thinking?

"Yes, major?"

"The brigade is now combat ineffective. So, according to the operations order, all soldiers in the brigade, including the remaining staff in the combat operations center, are now attached to your brigade."

She swallowed. This was the official hand over of the mission, and she had no idea what to have them do.

The major waited a moment, while Sullivan just stood there like an idiot with nothing to say, gazing into his hopeful expression, which only added to the pressure of her new position. Finally, he raised his brows. "What are your orders?"

Chapter 23 — An Idea

Colonel Sullivan rubbed her hand over her face, numbness descended over her as the terror overwhelmed her mind. She couldn't function in such a state of fear. She had to tamp it all down, just do what she needed to do--like a robot, no feelings, no emotions, no reason to surrender.

It didn't matter that she was without ideas. There was no time to waste thinking and mulling over various options. She had to get a plan in motion.

This must've been what Colonel Cooper had felt. And now it was her turn to get a lot of people killed.

She gathered Lieutenant Colonels Davis and MacFarland, the sergeant major and Sergeant Finley into a small conversation circle in the pharmacy waiting area. "There's gotta be a better idea," she said. "We can't just keep throwing spaghetti at the wall."

Colonel MacFarland shrugged. "At least something better than lining up and saying, 'okay, shoot me.'"

That was a grave summary of the previous commander's regime. And how long would it be before her own leadership earned her similar rancor? Not that it would stop her from doing what she knew needed to be done. This wasn't a popularity contest. But respect mattered. And good decisions usually got more respect than not.

"Okay then," she said. "Ideas?"

"Distractions don't seem to be enough," Davis said. "They got all directions covered."

"And their weapons are way more powerful than ours," McFarland added. "The tanks didn't do jack shit." He sat for a second of silence, then looked at his hands. "Pardon my French."

Colonel Sullivan glared at him.

"She speaks fluent Cursive," Davis said.

Sullivan let out a frustrated breath. "We need better intel."

"We're hosed," the sergeant major whispered.

"Finley," Sullivan said, "get me Major Li on the phone."

Finley nodded and left the group.

Davis frowned. "Wouldn't he have called if he had something important?"

"Yeah," she admitted.

A moment later, Finley returned, handing her a small phone. She put it on speaker, so everyone else there could hear.

"Li, what do you have for me?" she said, deliberately sounding hopeful, expectant.

"Ma'am, I, uh..."

She needed to get him warmed up, talking. Giving him someone else to blame would be a good start. "Anything from higher?"

"They're all wondering why the shuttle diverted from New York," Li said. "But they got nothing on weapons or shields—"

"They have a theory on the diversion?"

"Well…" Li seemed to hesitate. "Yeah, but… is that relevant?"

"I won't know until I hear their ideas."

"It doesn't answer any of your PIRs."

She pressed her lips together, holding back a loud huff.

"And anyway, it's just a theory."

"Major," she said, "what do they think?"

"Um… well the only difference between New York and the other landing spots seems to be that New York is socked in."

"Fog?" She hadn't intended it, but her incredulity clearly registered in her voice. "Seriously?"

"Sorry."

"Okay, they're saying that we have aliens with superior weapons, strong invisible shields, and space flight technology that can enable interstellar travel, and yet they can't navigate in the fog?"

"I know. Crazy, huh?"

"Strange," McFarland agreed.

"They gotta have better sensors than that," Davis said, nodding vigorously.

Sullivan shook her head. "They didn't even seem to care how accurate their landing was," she said. "They crashed into all kinds of stuff."

"It doesn't make sense," McFarland said.

She glanced around the room, a sudden sensation that she was living in an echo chamber.

Time to think outside the target reticle. "Would the fog disrupt them in some other way?"

"Yeah," Finley said, sitting forward. "Like, if their patrols can't see."

Sullivan gazed at her, a sense that something, some idea, was right on the cusp of her awareness. "You suppose particles of water in the air would disrupt their... weapons?"

Finley's eyes grew for a second, but she shrugged.

Davis shook his head. "Those energy bolts would just burn right through the fog, wouldn't they?"

"Depends on how heavy the clouds are," McFarland said.

"Really?" Finley said.

McFarland glanced around the group. "They're energy weapons. Water in the air will absorb some of the beam or, depending on the frequency, it'll at least deflect it. Just like a laser. The only reason you can see a laser beam is the parts of it that got reflected by dust in the air."

"No shit," Davis said.

"Then suppose you put a *lot* of dust in the air?" Sullivan said. "How much would you need to block it entirely?"

McFarland blinked. "I'm not sure."

"But even a little might help," Finley said. "I mean--"

"Those beams are pretty strong," Davis said.

She turned to McFarland. "Can you get us smoke pots?"

"Damn," McFarland said, then broke into a grin. "That would be better than fog."

"Better?" Davis asked.

"Fog is just water droplets in the air," Sullivan said. "Smoke's going to be particles of soot jamming the atmosphere. Bigger than water molecules, and able to absorb or deflect more frequencies."

"And you know what?" McFarland said, slapping a palm on his knee, "I can do better than smoke pots. How does a smoke generator sound?"

"Get me everything you have."

Chapter 24 — Smoke And Mirrors

Things were moving now. McFarland was on the phone, a moment ago coordinating the arrival of a smoke generation company. Now, he had the nearest ammunition supply point on the line and was asking for smoke pots, smoke grenades, and anything else they could think of.

She forced herself to move away, satisfied that McFarland knew what he was doing and understood the vision of the operation, yet itching to jump in and take over. What if he made a mistake somewhere down the line? What if he didn't get them as much as they needed?

She'd had her fingers in almost everything back in garrison. That's how she made certain things were done right. She did them herself.

Fine time to have to learn to delegate.

She went to the operations officer. "What do we have in terms of units?"

"Just scattered personnel. Nothing organized." He handed her a chart showing the remains of the infantry brigade, plus what little remained of her own. It was worse than she'd thought.

"Mostly just the staff we have here," the personnel officer added, stepping up beside them.

"We need to get everyone organized," she said, "back into units with chains of command."

"Right."

"I need three teams. Two to enter the shuttle and rescue the victims."

SSG Clark, who had been sitting at a nearby table, stood and leaned into the group. "I'll put those teams together."

"Good," she said.

"I'll lead one team. SGT Harvey for the other."

"Sounds good." Two highly competent military policemen, they would know what to do. "Then I need a third team to clear the buildings and the parking garage. Make sure there aren't any aliens shooting us in the back when we're entering the shuttle."

"I've got one company commander left," the operations officer said. "We can put all the rest of the people under him."

"We'll need medics in that group, too."

"Right."

She stepped back as the officers and NCOs began their reorganization efforts, a flurry of activity, phone and radio calls and more scribbles on charts. Her job now was to review the plan, figure out if she had forgotten anything, and try to guess how the enemy would react. She sat at Cooper's former desk, pen in hand, jotting down what was called the "warfighting functions," something the constituted a pretty good checklist of things to consider when planning an operation.

"Ma'am?" a female voice said from the other side of the counter. She lifted her head. Sergeant Finley stood in the opening to her little office, hands folded in front of her, determination in her eyes.

"What is it?"

"I want to go in the group that enters the shuttle."

Sullivan shook her head. "You're not an MP. This is a clearing operation, and we don't need hangers on there."

"Ma'am," Finley said, this time louder, "you're going to need an intelligence presence there. I know you'd take Major Li if he was with us..."

"I'll need..." she began, then closed her mouth. Somehow, the thought of sending Finley into that shuttle filled her with dread. No, she'd worked to hard to keep this kid alive. "You'll be in the way."

"But—"

She raised her hand and Finley closed her mouth. "I need you to stay with me," Sullivan said then. "Wherever I go, I want you right behind me."

Finley's face fell just a fraction, but then she nodded, looking resigned, accepting. "Yes, ma'am."

"The truck with the smoke pots just arrived," one of the operations NCOs informed her. "Offloading now."

"Good," she said. "You have a plan for how they'll be laid out?"

They showed her a diagram, with successive rows of smoke pots, each laid closer to the shuttle than the last. By the time a person got to the shuttle, the smoke would be so thick it would choke them. That was just what they needed.

The NCO indicated the alternate smoke pot deposition sites, marked with dotted lines. "Weather guy is monitoring the wind direction," he said. "These'll go down as soon as the main ones have been laid.

"Excellent." A change of wind wouldn't suddenly leave her without cover. This was a good staff. They had thought through most of the possibilities. Anything they hadn't foreseen… well, she wasn't aware of it, either.

Colonel Sullivan glanced out the far window, the only place in the drug store where a person could see the shuttle. Thick, white, heavy smoke, billowed into low lying clouds, hugging the ground. She'd seen these things used before. They would keep spewing out the smoke for hours.

And all that smoke would keep the enemy's energy weapons from doing any damage.

At least that was what she hoped. It would be just their luck that the beams would burn right through any particles in the air. But it was all she had.

She gave more orders, additional guidance. The teams were to assemble at the intersection, just this side of where the smoke curtain started. The non-rescue element needed to start cutting away the saran wrap from the building, allowing as many entry points as possible. Someone was to contact the local fire department to let them know when the aliens were cleared away, so firefighting operations could resume.

"Everyone's assembled," Davis said. "I'll give them the word to commence the operations."

"No," she said. "I'll do it."

With that, she started for the door.

"Where you going?" Davis said.

"To give them little pep talk," she said,

thumb pointing toward the street.

"But you ain't going with them."

"Not my plan," she said. She knew better than to get into her subordinates' business, and especially to try to do jobs the NCOs had been trained for. As an officer, she'd had an entirely different type of education, which mean she knew *what* they did, but not *how*, at least not in enough detail to be able to do it herself.

LTC Davis looked relieved.

With that, Sullivan headed outside, Sgt Finley right behind her.

The teams stood in a gaggle a few feet away from the corner, just close enough they didn't need to put on their gas masks. She glanced over the group, all of them staring at her, evidently as nervous as she, but also, strangely, finding comfort in her presence. She filled her lungs, lifted her chest.

"All present," a tall young captain said, dark skin glistening with sweat. "Ready to begin operations."

She looked them over. Both SSG Clark and SGT Harvey stood with small teams, and the remainder of the soldiers, maybe thirty in total, massed together in a third group.

"Anybody test the smoke screen yet?" she said.

The captain shook his head.

"I'll go," Sergeant Harvey said, lifting his chin.

Sullivan nodded in appreciation. A part of her wanted to do the job herself. Seemed like the leaderly thing to do. But she knew better. The last thing her now tiny unit needed, given the possibility that this wasn't going to work, was to lose its leadership.

But damn it, what if it wasn't done right?

Sergeant Harvey already had his gas mask out, ready to put it on.

Hell, what were they even testing here? Did she want him to get close enough for them to try to shoot him, see how poorly the enemy's weapons functioned?

She swallowed. "No heroics. Just see if you can get close enough without them spotting you."

"Right," he said as he inserted his chin into the bottom of the mask, then slipped it over his face, dark fingers dancing over the straps as he adjusted everything. He slapped his right palm over the air intake on the front of the mask, then breathed in. The mask collapsed against his cheeks, confirming that the mask was sealed. He gave them a thumbs up. "All right," he said. "Don't do nothin' until I get back."

She grabbed a hand-held radio and pressed it into his palm. He nodded, hanging it from a strap on his body armor, then headed into the swirling smoke. Before he'd taken three steps, he disappeared. As long as the smoke screen was this thick throughout, they would have little problem approaching the shuttle.

Another set of footfalls sounded, and she turned to see that tall reporter who had interviewed Cooper now standing a few feet away from her, his cameraman and sound guy standing behind him. "We're going, too," he said.

She shook her head, then walked toward him. He stiffened visibly, evidently concerned she was going to deny them access to the scene. The two standing behind him folded arms across their chests, the cameraman clutching his equipment like it was body armor, or like he thought she was going to confiscate it.

"What's the point of the camera?" she said. "You're not going to be able to see anything."

"We'll make do."

She looked them over again. Were they a threat? Was operational security going to be compromised with these guys tagging along? Probably not. The aliens already knew about the smoke screen and could well anticipate what was to follow. These newsmen weren't going to give anything away.

In fact, they might just give her efforts more visibility. Make her look like a hero.

"You're going to need a mask," she said.

"Huh?"

She indicated the smoke with her head. "Unless you want to cough your lungs out."

The reporter glanced around. "Yeah, but…"

"Ask inside. There should be some… extras." Sullivan looked away, not wanting to bring up the reason so many soldiers no longer needed the masks they'd been issued.

The reporter turned back to the drug store.

"Have them show you how to check it," Finley called out. "Make sure you got a good seal."

The reporter waved at her, then he and his small team went inside.

"He's back," SSG Clark said.

Sullivan spun around. Sergeant Harvey appeared out of the fog like a phantom from a nightmare, bits of white smoke coating his uniform. He took off his mask and gave them a thumbs up. "That smoke so thick it be like walking through molasses."

Sullivan sighed with relief.

"How close you get?" Finley asked.

Harvey smiled, cocky. "Close enough to touch it."

Finley gasped. "Did you?"

"Yup."

Damn it. That hadn't been such a good idea. That close, the aliens might have seen him. Now, they would not merely suspect an attack, they would know it was coming. Shit. Maybe she *should* have been the one to do this reconnaissance.

But there was no time to dwell on that. The smoke pots wouldn't continue belching soot forever. It was time to move.

She turned back to the group. "All right. Lock and load."

A cacophony of clicks and clanks echoed off the buildings as every person in the group chambered a round. Her arm muscles tightened. Her toes wanted to tap away the nervousness. She twitched her calves.

When all the soldiers looked up at her again, she continued. "It's going to be hard to navigate in this smoke, so stay close together. And make sure of your target before you shoot. I don't want friendly casualties."

The crowd murmured agreement.

"But when you see one of those bastards…" She took another breath, taking in the anticipation growing in the eyes of her soldiers. "You just blow a hole in their gut."

"Yeah!" SGT Harvey called out.

"Blast them into oblivion," she continued. "Let them have a taste of what they've done to us!"

"Hooah!" several other soldiers shouted. One pumped his fist, and another waved his free hand in the air.

"Make this so painful, they'll never want to come back!"

A cheer rose from the group, loud, excited. Soldiers smiled, gave each other high-fives.

She let out a relieved breath. They were ready now, full of adrenaline, mission clear in their minds. She turned to the commander. "Give them hell."

He nodded. "Let's go."

L. D. ROBINSON © 2022

Chapter 25 – Approaching The Shuttle

Everyone slipped their gas masks on, and once that was done the commander walked past Sullivan and Finley, the three teams following. One by one they disappeared into the sooty darkness. The last soldier was SSG Clark. He stopped, just before he made the transition to invisibility, then looked at Sullivan over his shoulder. She could barely see his eyes through the gas mask lenses and the smoke wafting around him. But it looked to her like a request, like concern, like he thought they needed more. They needed help. They needed her.

Damn. She was supposed to go back into the drug store and listen to the reports, monitor the battle from there. She was a colonel, for hell sakes, not a private first class. She was supposed to keep an eye on the bigger elements of the operation.

She turned to Finley, swallowing hard. "You got a radio?"

"No, ma'am."

"Wait here."

Back inside, she grabbed one of the hand-held radios from a shelf, then turned on the switch, just to make sure it had power.

LTC Davis hurried toward her. "Ma'am, what are you doing?"

"I'm going with them."

He covered his face with his right hand, massaging his eyes with thumb and forefinger. "Ma'am, I don't think that's a good idea."

"I know," she said. "But my instincts are telling me otherwise."

"Oh, man." He looked away, then seemed to relent. "I just don't want you... don't want you to end up like Cooper."

"I'll be careful," she said, then gave him a friendly punch in the arm. "Wish me luck."

He shook his head, this time with a hint of a smile. "Ain't you been telling me..." He didn't have to finish the sentence. She'd always insisted she didn't believe in luck.

"Yeah." She gave him a half-hearted smile, an admission that she was still scared, still not sure if this was a good idea. "But right now, I can use all the help I can get."

He lifted his hands, fingers crossed. "Go get 'em."

Back outside, she slipped on her mask and stepped into the gloom, Finley right at her heels.

God, she hated these masks. If the smoke wasn't bad enough, the lenses reduced her peripheral vision, and her breathing sounded like Vader. The plastic touched her nose with claustrophobia inducing pressure, and the hood draped over her head and skimming her shoulders kept all the heat of the summer afternoon in.

And she couldn't see a thing.

She took a deep breath, pushed her emotions away with the hard hand of authority. Finley walked beside her, reached out a dark hand to touch her, keep in contact with her.

The cloud was too good. The enemy could be anywhere. Aliens could jump out and strangle her from any direction. She drew her pistol, pulled back the slide and chambered a round. Holding the gun high, scanning the billowing smoke, she stepped forward again. The soldiers she'd sent in here earlier were long gone, too far away to follow. The buildings were invisible. She looked at the ground, but even the pavement faded behind swirling wads if cotton.

She needed to cross the street, get to the building. Then she could follow it down the street, keep from getting lost. Another step, shards of glass crunching beneath her boots, and then another. But this time, her foot stopped too soon, rammed against something large and heavy and hard, and her shoulders kept moving. She reached out her arms, tried to twist her body, bend her knees, roll as she landed. The elbow of her weapon arm slammed onto the pavement. Her hip connected next, then thigh, then butt... not the best parachute landing fall, but at least she hadn't broken her arm.

"Ma'am, you alright?" Finley's muffled voice said.

Her elbow screamed as electric shocks jolted her arm. So hard to ignore, but she had to. She forced herself back up, then waved at Finley. "I got it," she said. Her new technique for walking would be more of a foot drag, scanning each step forward with her toes before she leaned her weight into it.

A brief gust of wind cleared a pocket in the air, and the building loomed ahead. They weren't even close yet.

She took a deep breath, then plunged forward.

God, they'd be lucky to get to the shuttle alive.

Chapter 26 — Alien Reaction

Galth squinted out the front viewscreen, now surrounded by swirling smoke that rivaled the storms on Miovion. "What in the Night Sea is this?" he muttered.

Kelm let out a grumbling breath. "We can't operate in this… whatever it is."

Galth glared at him. "What are you saying?"

Kelm winced. "I'm getting interference on all my sensors. Communications is compromised."

"You think we should just leave?" Galth made the question sound like an accusation, like he thought Kelm was a quitter, a weakling who would run away at the slightest difficulty. Galth had the authority to execute cowardice on the spot, and he wasn't about to tolerate any of it.

"You're the commander," Kelm said.

Stupid *wilp* wouldn't even stand up for what he believed in.

Galth looked back at the street. Well, he looked where the street had been, but now he could see nothing. And if sensors weren't working, the enemy could creep up on them at any moment. "You got nothing?"

"Possible movements... but I can't tell."

Galth clamped his teeth together, jaw muscle pulsing. Incompetent. Everyone was so sinking... He had to see this for himself. He snatched the sensor pad from Kelm's fingers, then studied it. A row of heat signatures, dark blobs on the infrared sensor screen, lined the end of the road, the bowl-like objects they'd seen enemy soldiers deploying and lighting, which then spewed out this cloud. And every once in a while, other, smaller blobs, possibly enemies, appeared in the haze and then vanished.

If the enemy was coming, he couldn't tell.

He closed his eyes, trying to imagine himself the commander of the enemy soldiers. What would he be doing now? How would he take advantage of this obscuring fog? A claw grabbed at his gut and twisted.

He turned to his Sigali crewman, Abgoth. "How many quivs have we got now?"

Abgoth glanced at a small data pad in one hand, rubbing the other hand on his brown shirt, a symbol of his low status. "Less than 300."

Feces. Galth had bragged about his ability to fly in fast and make a quick harvest, and here he was without even a full cargo hold. If he left now, he would be mocked at best, transferred to an office job on Dakhesh at worst.

But the enemy, those who were trying to stop him, were much more clever than when Captain Zolbon had made the attempt, and they had deployed better weapons against him than they had against any of Zolbon's shuttles. The only thing that could possibly redeem him was if the other two shuttle pilots, making their harvest in other distant cities, had had equally adept opponents.

And considering how long it had taken this commander to come up with the winning tactic, likely the other shuttles were raking in quivs without effective opposition.

It wasn't fair that he was facing the most competent enemy commander. But he also knew that neither Beglash nor any other commander would consider how smart each shuttle pilot's foe had been. Galth needed to do something to even the game, make himself as successful as the others.

He needed to take out the enemy commander, destroy the architect of this attack.

Handing the sensor pad back to Kelm, Galth noticed a smile on his face. He could see his hands wrapped around the enemy leader's neck, see the terror on the man's face as he squeezed the life from him, see his regret as he realized he'd been just a little too smart for his own good.

"Orders?" Kelm asked.

Always good to answer a question with another. "Status of the approaching enemy?"

Kelm huffed. "I told you... wait. I think I see something." He pointed, not to his control pad, but to the viewscreen, where a shadow appeared in the smoke, the shape of a quiv soldier, or something that looked like a quiv. The ghostly form pointed his handgun towards the shuttle. Another ball of smoke drifted across his field of view, obscuring everything.

"Where'd he go?" Kelm gasped.

"Shoot him!" Galth barked.

"I can't see him!"

"Shoot where he was!"

Kelm tapped his control pad. A blue light emerged from the front of the shuttle, but in less than a foot it swelled into a balloon of glowing azure.

"Feces!" Galth slammed his fist against the wall.

"I don't think that got anybody," Abgoth muttered.

"Shut up!" Galth snapped, glaring at the brown-shirted idiot. He really didn't need some Sigali rubbing his failures in his face.

Kelm's skin had gone several shades paler. "We need to bring everyone back into the shuttle."

That claw that had recently grabbed his gut now jerked, ripping his entire abdomen in two. At least it felt like that. "Get on the coms, tell Reldak," Galth said.

"But the enemy is probably headed for the building," Abgoth said. "They'll be easy to pick off in there."

Galth took a deep breath to calm himself, to put his viewpoint back into the mind of the enemy commander. The answer was obvious.

"Some of them are coming here."

"Here?"

"They'll want to rescue the other quivs."

"Then we have to go," Kelm said.

"That's not an option," Galth said. "We have less than three hundred." The low number of captives would brand him a failure. He needed a way to get more.

L. D. ROBINSON © 2022

Kelm drew his brows into a confused expression. "They have projectile weapons. The fog won't stop them."

"We could target another building," Abgoth suggested. "Go to some other place in the city where we don't have to deal with this fog."

Kelm huffed a frustrated breath. "That would take too long to set up."

"Yeah," Galth said. Before they even got a second harvesting operation going, his enemy would have followed him, and he would have the same problem he had now. Not to mention, he wasn't even sure he could fly in air like this. "We need to do away with these defenders."

Kelm frowned. "How are we supposed to do that?"

"Call the ship in orbit," Abgoth said earnestly. "They can blow up everything on the street, like they did to the robots."

"It looks like they have an endless supply of this... cloud," Kelm said. "Enough to stop all our weapons."

Galth shook his head. "No, the quivs will become vulnerable, once they get close enough..." He turned around and opened up a storage compartment in the back wall, where the weapons of last resort hung from leather loops points dangling, blades smooth and sharp.

"You want us to use daggers?" Kelm said with a gasp.

"Reldak," he said into his communications pad, "Meet me at the entrance with your entire team." Then he turned to Kelm. "Keep watch here." Kelm nodded, and then Galth grabbed a handful of the weapons, motioning for Abgoth to gather up the remainder.

His heart pounded as he stepped out of the control room, excitement flooding him, drowning out any sense of fear. This was going to be his moment to prove himself as a combat commander, as someone worthy of promotion, as a leader with potential to overcome any obstacles. This would be his moment of glory.

His fingers tightened around the handle of his dagger. *Oh, spirit of war, grant us the embrace of your destructive powers!*

At the mouth of the gangway, he met Reldak, his men escorting six more quivs into the shuttle. And the edge of the tube on the side facing away from the enemy had been pulled away from the door, requiring someone to stay there, keep quivs from escaping through the opening. "Why isn't this closed?" he said.

"This door," Reldak said, pointing to the entrance Galth had selected, "only goes to a small part of the building. The people escaping from the tallest part come through here."

Galth's fingers tightened around the handle of his dagger. Didn't Reldak know that had been a rhetorical question? He hadn't wanted a sinking *answer*.

A popping noise outside brought his attention back to the situation. His conflict with Reldak was going to have to wait. Right now, he had quiv soldiers to deal with.

He handed each of the soldiers a shiny blade. Most wore brown shirts, not well educated, but all very expendable. He pointed to the disconnected side of the tube. "You three, head out to the other side. Use the overturned car for cover. And put your blasters away."

"But..." one of the crewmen said, "won't they shoot us?"

"Not if they can't see you. Use their own cloud against them."

The man nodded uneasily. "Maybe we should just shoot from in here."

"That kind of attitude will *not* get you to the great embrace," he snapped. "Now, do as you're told."

"Yes, commander."

"When you fire your blaster," Galth said, "that will tell the enemy where you are. You'll be a target. So, only use your blaster if the enemy is close enough to touch. Understand?"

The brown-shirted soldiers creased their brows but nodded. Sinking idiots were too frightened to admit their confusion. Well, let them die, then.

"Go!" he shouted.

The three men slipped out of the tunnel, tiptoeing nervously into the mist. One of them coughed and another complained. "I can't breathe!" But they kept going. Galth watched them until they were out of sight, hoping they were going all the way around the shuttle, around to where they could target the enemy.

"Now, you three go back inside the building and see if you can find out how to get to the door just down the street."

The soldier he spoke to nodded, but he didn't look like he understood.

"Hit them from the side," Galth said.

The soldier grinned. "Yes, sir! It'll be very effective."

Those three soldiers scurried into the building.

Galth looked at his remaining soldiers, seven brown-clad men and one in red, Reldak the complainer. "You," he said, pointing to Reldak, "This is your opportunity to redeem yourself."

Reldak's eyes burned with anger. "You never listened to anything I said. You didn't give me what I needed. And now, you think *I* am the one who requires redemption?"

"Take three more soldiers—" Galth stopped, now staring into the business end of a blaster. And for just this one moment, he wanted the enemy's fog to penetrate the gangway. "Reldak, what do you think you're doing?"

Chapter 27 - Mutiny

"This place was impossible," Reldak said, spit flying through the air. A nearby Sigali winced, then wiped the wetness from his cheek.

"There are no easy buildings," Galth said.

"Hallways to nowhere," Reldak ranted, "layers of underground caverns, exits we couldn't find..."

Galth glanced at the men surrounding Reldak. They looked restless, nervous, but he couldn't tell their mood, or their loyalty to Reldak. Clearly, Reldak felt no loyalty to him.

Outside, someone screamed. Sounded like a quiv, but Galth wasn't sure.

He looked at the other men again. "Are we just going to stand here while our comrades out there are laying down their lives?"

Reldak lifted the blaster. "Call everyone back in, and let's just leave."

Galth bit his lip. Somehow, he needed to appeal to the Sigali men beside Reldak, needed to get them on his side. But he hardly knew them. What were they willing to fight for? Where were their loyalties? "You agree with that?" he asked the nearest brown-shirt.

"Yeah," the man said. "Get everybody back in."

"How about we just leave without the guys out there?"

Anger darkened the face of the nearest man. Several others frowned. But then Reldak spoke. "Yeah. No time to get the others. Everybody back into the shuttle."

Galth stepped backwards. "I think we should get the others."

"Just *move!*" Reldak's face had gone red with anger, his cheek muscles twitching.

Galth nodded at the man just behind Reldak. He made a quick move.

The complainer stiffened with a gasp. Someone knocked the blaster from his hand, while the man behind him twisted the dagger, then ripped it away, flinging blood and bits of skin against the gangway walls. Reldak dropped to his knees, then his face slammed into the floor.

"Good work," Galth said. "You two," he pointed to the men who had taken down Reldak, "go back inside and keep guard on the quivs we have."

"Yes, sir," they said, hurrying back into the shuttle.

He had five soldiers left. "The rest of you, out the front. Don't let them reach the shuttle."

"The front?" one of them said, looking horrified.

But another tapped him on the arm. "Come on."

Galth pressed the opening of the tunnel away from the front side, while the last of his soldiers barreled into the swirls of smoke, waving their hands in front of their noses, coughing, hacking. Galth stepped out, then glanced around. Someone needed to remain here, at the opening, guarding the shuttle. Someone needed to be the last line of defense.

One of the soldiers, only a few steps away, grabbed his blaster and pointed it into the cloud.

"No!" Galth shouted.

But it was too late. The soldier fired his weapon. A burst of energy leapt from the pistol, then fizzled, the light spreading into benign nothingness, heat turning the smoke particles into sparkling lines of light, then ash falling to the ground.

And the response from the enemy was immediate. Sharp, percussive pops, blasts of fire spewing from the muzzles of their pistols, sounds cracking open the shroud of dust.

The brown shirted soldier plunged face first onto the pavement, and Galth dashed back into the protective cocoon of the tube.

More gunfire, loud, chaotic. People rushing around. His soldiers charging the enemy valiantly. Quivs shouting. Footsteps banging on the ground, desperate cries for help.

What else could he do? There had to be something. He couldn't just stand there, frozen, while his soldiers died all around him. He stuck his head back through the opening, waving his blaster at the swirls of cotton, waiting for someone to come into range.

Something whizzed by his ear.

Feces! A projectile, way too close!

He pulled his head back inside the tube, then squatted, breathing hard. Another gunshot rang out, and a hole exploded in the fabric of the tunnel wall just above his head. Demons of the Night Sea, they could have killed him. And this tube provided no protection at all.

He gritted his teeth, tried to remind himself that such a death would be glorious, it would usher him directly to the Great Embrace. He had to be brave, fearless, and so terrifying to the enemy that they would run in terror.

"They're right on top of us!" Kelm called through his radio attached to Galth's belt.

He needed something to tell himself he was doing the right thing. Something to get him back into motion. Then, it came to him.

"Now they're close enough to shoot!" Galth shouted. He pressed his weapon through the opening again. A dark outline approached, a monstrous form, fog swirling around the grotesquely shaped head, a black striated snout, like a wild animal, a demon from the depths. But not a monster. Just a quiv, wearing so much equipment his form was almost unrecognizable.

Oh, how Galth wanted to grab the man and pull him into the shuttle, secure just one more victim for the harvest. But the quiv had his hand up, pistol scanning for something to shoot at.

Galth angled his blaster upward, then thumbed his firing button.

Black plastic shrapnel. A splash of red and a pinging sound, followed by splats and taps as bits of the shredded head slapped against the sides of the gangway.

A low chuckle rumbled in his gut. *You thought you were so clever, enemy commander, but now there is a soldier standing here without a head. Now, look who has gotten the upper hand.*

The remains of the body stood stiffly, waiting a couple of heartbeats before it toppled sideways to the ground.

Galth scanned the area. No other enemy in view. But four Dakh Hhargashian bodies lay in the street, motionless, slowly turning white as the particles from the smoke cloud descended on them. How many others had fallen out of sight, behind the shuttle or too deep into the smoke to be detected? A quick calculation told him if he didn't leave now, he wouldn't have enough soldiers left to even guard the few victims they'd already captured.

Sinking enemy leader! Where was he? Why was he hiding in this miasma like a coward? Why didn't he come out and fight?

Galth slammed his fist against the wall of the tube.

Another scream rent the air.

Feces! He had to act now. "Everyone back inside!" Galth called out, then rushed into the shuttle, back to the control room.

Kelm frowned at him. "At least seven dead."

Waves and foam. He couldn't take any more losses. "Get inside!" he called into his communications module. "Now! As soon as everyone's back, seal up the gangway!"

A second later, Abgoth arrived at the control room. "Just two more of our crew out there."

Galth swallowed, handing Kelm the weapons controller. "Give them some cover."

Kelm nodded, firing the shuttle's front-facing weapons randomly. The energy beams couldn't do much, couldn't reach far, but they could at least keep the humans from getting too close while the rest of the crew returned to the ship.

"All on board," Abgoth reported.

That was all he needed to hear. It was time to get out of this accursed place.

"Retract the gangway," Kelm commanded.

Yes, get the ship ready to take off, ready to slip away from this evil enemy, to present to the empire their glorious harvest.

Except it was a pittance. Everyone he knew would laugh at him for the small number of humans he'd retrieved. It would be a humiliation beyond anything he could countenance.

Galth stared out the front, saw the shadows of enemy soldiers skirting around the front of the shuttle, moving to where the tube met the building. No point trying to fire on them. The quivs knew exactly how close they could get. "Wait," he said. Maybe Galth could turn the enemy commander's plan against the quivs. Because that same quiv leader had achieved enough success he was probably getting over-confident. Just the state of mind Galth could exploit.

"We need to get out of here!" Kelm shouted, "before the quiv soldiers break into the shuttle and rescue what few victims we have!"

"That's stupid," Abgoth said.

"They're looking at the gangway," Kelm said, pointing at the indistinct shapes creeping across the viewscreen.

Galth looked at Kelm and smiled. "We need more victims."

"Sir?"

Galth pointed a finger at Abgoth. "Get all the rest of the crew up here to the control room."

The Sigali crewman nodded and dashed through the door.

Kelm shook his head. "What are you planning?"

"Prepare the intruder control system."

Kelm stared at him uncomprehendingly. Then, after another second hesitation, he nodded, thumbing his control pad. "System armed."

Galth smiled with satisfaction as the last three crewmen piled into the bridge. Now they were standing shoulder to shoulder in the small space, but at least Abgoth knew how to follow orders.

"Lock the door," Galth whispered, then looked at Kelm. "But don't retract the gangway until I tell you."

Chapter 28 — First Success

Sullivan put her hand on the top of the still warm engine compartment of the burnt-out tank, now a grim gray coffin, with its track twisted like a pretzel, scraps blackened and jutting into the smoke-filled air. It meant she was only half-way there, still many more treacherous yards to go.

She needed to move faster. The gunfire had finally died down, only an occasional pop. Shit. She was clueless here. Should have stayed back in the drug store.

"Status?" she said into the radio hanging from a strap on her body armor.

"We're in the building," the commander said. "Looks like... looks like a hotel lobby."

"Any aliens there?"

"All gone. Just a bunch of civilians."

"Roger," she said, now winding around the track pads scattered on the pavement.

"Soldier down," a voice came over the radio. Sounded like SGT Harvey.

"You need a medic?" the commander asked.

"Jus a minute. Let me che--Oh, hell!"

"Harvey?"

"Just... what's it called? Graves registration?"

"Understood."

Sullivan let out a disappointed breath. She'd known this operation would probably have casualties, but that hadn't stopped a part of her from hoping. "Damn it," she whispered, then stepped past the tank's sagging main gun barrel. The end of the barrel was only a few inches from the pavement. That energy burst must have been incredibly hot. Behind her, Finley grunted. "Geez."

It wouldn't be the last time one of them tripped. They just had to keep going.

"I got a dead alien here," another voice said over the radio. "What do you want us to do with him?"

Sullivan keyed her press-to-talk switch. "Leave him for now." They could clean up the battlefield once the fighting was over.

"Okay, we've reached the tube," Harvey's voice said. "It ain't sealed like I 'spected."

Her stomach clenched. "No escaping civilians?" She had expected a flood of them, just like those people who'd gotten away in Mumbai.

"Nobody at all."

She swallowed. Something unexpected usually meant something was going wrong. She needed to figure out what that was. "Clear the area," she said. "Then hold there."

She moved closer. Finley was in front now, picking her way through the rubble.

Then Sullivan heard footfalls behind her. Damn! She spun around, pointed her pistol at the interlopers.

The reporter, alone and masked up, camera on his shoulder, walked toward her, then flinched, ducking and pointing the camera toward the ground. "Hey, man, don't shoot!"

She bent her elbows, drawing the weapon away from him. "Sorry."

"Sure," he said, voice barely registering.

"Clear!" a soldier yelled somewhere in the distance. They were in the building. Still no alien resistance.

But the shuttle was still there. She could occasionally get snatches of it through the smoke. Where were the aliens? What were they up to?

She continued her march to the shuttle. Off to the side lay a body, face down, unarmored, hand clasped around a large knife. An alien. It took all her willpower not to go over to him, turn him onto his back and give him a thorough examination. In spite of her college training, she was a military commander, not a scientist. The question of alien biology would have to wait for some other time.

A few more steps and a line of soldiers came into view, forming a semi-circle around the entrance to the tube, which was separated from the building by only a few feet.

The shuttle's dark form loomed ahead of her. She was almost there. And damn, it was a lot bigger than she'd realized.

Now she was close enough to the entrance, and to the tunnel, that she could see it was only about eighteen inches from the brick wall. No one had fired a shot. The aliens were hiding, or they had set up an interior ambush. She bit her lip, grinding the soft flesh between her teeth, then stopped when she tasted blood. Damn it.

She just had to trust that her MP soldiers knew how to clear a room.

She hurried to the gap, the doorframe blackened, shattered glass and melted metal that opened into a large room filled with industrial laundry equipment. SSG Clark and his rescue team stood behind a sheet folding machine, while SGT Harvey's team clustered on the other side of a blue recycle bin.

Sullivan slipped off her mask and stowed it, then scanned the area. Still no sign of the enemy. And no excuse not to make the next move.

She looked down the gangway, the accordion-like tube that led to the shuttle, the door still open. She expected the inside of the shuttle to be an open room, but there was only a straight hallway, an extension of the tube into the interior, intersected by another hallway which ran the length of the shuttle.

What was she waiting for? She lifted her hand to signal SSG Clark to go, but something inside her pulled the gesture back. Something wasn't right.

But their mission was to rescue. And she could see her two NCOs starting to wonder what she was waiting for.

"Go," she said to Clark.

SSG Clark slipped past her, his team hugging the walls of the gangway, carefully working their way into the alien craft. Sergeant Clark stopped about five to seven feet in, where it looked like the hallway ended in a T.

SGT Harvey lined his team up near the entrance, waiting for their turn to move into the shuttle. SGT Finley took up a position just behind the last member of his team.

Still no sounds, no resistance. No firefight.

"Ma'am?"

She turned toward the sound, and found the young commander striding in her direction, still halfway across the cavernous laundry room. She walked toward him, around the bulky sheet folding apparatus, but just as she slipped past it something crunched, and she felt a lump under her boot. She stopped.

A small red glob lay by her toes, and another nearby. Dozens, no hundreds, all radiating out in a circle. And there, splayed across the tiles, lay a woman's body, short and plump and headless, her hand still clutching a white sheet. Sullivan retched.

"Damn," Sergeant Harvey said behind her. "I seen a lot a shit, but I ain't never seen nothin' like that."

"What is it?" a female soldier said. Her name tag read "Francisco."

"Brains," Mendez said. The kid smiled, like this was all normal. "Some skull, char-grilled skin, and maybe a little snot."

"Ew."

Sullivan trained her eyes toward the commander, so she didn't have to see the horror before her, so she could pretend it hadn't been a person there, someone's aunt, someone's mother.

Continue the mission. Keep moving.

Sullivan walked around the majority of the blobs. It seemed somehow wrong to purposely step on them.

The commander stopped a few feet from her, then pulled out a note pad and gave her a quick rundown on his operations. He'd already summoned more help, more medical personnel, more intelligence agents. He seemed to have everything well in hand.

"Any aliens?"

He shook his head. "Cleared out, ma'am."

"Carry on," she said. Now she could turn her attention back to the main mission. The more difficult mission.

She hurried back to the darkened shuttle entrance. There, Finley waited, pistol still in her hand. Beside her, the reporter leaned against the door, peering through the eyepiece of his camera.

She looked down the tube. Both her teams were now out of sight, and all she could do was wonder what had happened to them.

"You rescuing the people inside?" the reporter asked, pointing a thumb at the shuttle.

She didn't want to talk to him right now. She needed to hear from Clark and Harvey. Her hand went to her radio, hung from her body armor over her heart. But she couldn't call them. They knew to report, as soon as they had something, and if they weren't calling her, it was probably because they were practicing noise discipline.

Sergeant Finley walked up next to Sullivan, shaking her head. "Clark and Harvey turned toward the back of the shuttle."

Sullivan nodded. That was the direction they suspected the prisoners would be found in. Nothing surprising there.

"Nobody went for the front."

"Front?" The tension pulled on the skin of Patrice's cheek. "You think that's where the aliens are hiding?"

Finley drew her brows together. "That's where the bridge is."

"Damn." Sullivan nodded. The aliens could still do something unpredictable from there. The two teams she'd just sent in could be sitting ducks. There could be blast doors the aliens would lower, or forcefields they could turn on that would trap her soldiers, and no one would be rescuing anyone.

This is about to turn into a pile of shit.

"We've got to take the Nabbers out," Sullivan muttered.

She lifted her hand-held radio and keyed it to the channel the combat operations center would be monitoring. "You got any more soldiers you can send me?"

"Wait one," the voice of the radio operator said. In a moment, he came back. "Negative on additional soldiers."

It didn't really matter. They wouldn't be able to get here in time. "I'm going in."

"Don't you dare," Lieutenant Colonel Davis's voice came from the other side. He must have grabbed the mic from the radio operator.

Sullivan smiled, and even considered thanking him for caring. But radio communication always had to be terse. Nothing left to say.

She pulled out her weapon, then looked at Finley. "Follow me."

L. D. ROBINSON © 2022

Chapter 29 — Gone

Sullivan pressed forward, scanning the area with her pistol, teeth closed hard to keep any pesky feeling from coming up, to remind her of her determination, and stop her mind from questioning her decision. Darkness closed in as she moved farther into the tunnel, the floor rising beneath her feet, making a seamless transition into the shuttle.

Where were the damned aliens? Why weren't they challenging her incursion into their space?

Got a bad feeling about this.

She pointed her pistol at the entrance of the forward-facing hallway, the one they thought led to the bridge, then gestured with her head to Finley. "Check that hallway," she whispered. "See where it goes."

Finley nodded and slipped past her.

Sullivan took another step forward, then heard metal moaning, that strange hollow sound of straining parts. Hydraulics whined.

My God!

Sullivan spun toward the door, where the reporter stood with his camera pointing at her. "Something's happening here," he said. But he was rapidly disappearing behind a door flap that had lifted from the floor.

"Finley!" Sullivan called out as she dashed toward the doorway that was about to shut her in, slamming her shoulder against the metal slab. She bounced off, tumbled to the floor. "Shit!"

Finley dashed past her and pressed herself against the door as it closed with a pneumatic hiss.

Sullivan scrambled to her feet, still focused on the door, but then the tube floor puckered like a giant accordion. She lifted one boot while the other slipped between two puckers. "It's closing up!" she shouted, scrambling to get her foot out before it got wedged in.

"I can't open it," Finley huffed, still pushing against the end, trying to open the door.

"The tunnel!" Sullivan hollered. "Get out of the tunnel!"

As if she were on a conveyor belt, Finley slid toward Sullivan. The end of the tunnel screeched across the sidewalk. Sullivan grabbed Finley's arm, then dove into the shuttle, landing hard on the floor, the sergeant flopping atop her, then rolling to the side.

Clang. Another door slammed closed from a wall pocket. A loud *thrumb* made the whole shuttle shiver, shook her until the walls blurred and her teeth rattled.

Sullivan's mind screamed in panic. They were moving into space! How was she going to escape when the shuttle was surrounded by vacuum?

Sullivan moved to get up, pressing her hands into the floor pushup style, but her elbows gave way, and she plummeted back down like a lead weight, like someone trapped under barbells without a spotter.

How was she going to stop the aliens when she couldn't even move?

"What the hell?" Finley shouted.

She closed her eyes as the jittering walls smeared themselves in her vision, and the confusion from her senses worked its way into her stomach. And then, her surroundings stilled. The excess weight was still there, not so overwhelming as before but enough to make getting to her feet difficult.

Time to take stock of the situation.

She glanced around. Her pistol lay near the end of the exit hallway, right where the tube had folded itself back into the shuttle fuselage. She grabbed it and quickly checked it. Still a round in the chamber. She was ready for anything.

Finley still lay on the metal deck, grunting as she tried to lift her head off the floor, her eyes so wide the whites looked like a pair of full moons on a dark night. Her pistol lay beside her.

Sullivan crawled forward, the shoulder she'd used to ram the doorway now complaining under the body armor, the pistol still in her palm. She wasn't about to stick the weapon in her holster. Not when the enemy could appear at any moment.

She made it to the T in the hall. To the front was a short hallway, about five feet long, ending with another closed door. Sullivan looked behind her. This stretch of hallway was about twice as long, and there, all her other soldiers lay sprawled on the deck, still as corpses. Her heart thudded. Were they dead? There was breathing, soft and quiet. One of the soldiers snorted.

Thank God.

But it was a mess. Pistols lay strewn over the metal floor. Bodies heaped on top of each other. The sole of one soldier's boot had a dark smudge in the center, where a hole would soon form. Time to replace it. Maybe she should have the sergeant major order all the boots of all the soldiers to be inspect--

What was she thinking? This was no time to be worrying about footwear.

They had to get out of here.

The best time to escape was always as soon as possible after being captured. So, now was the time, before this infernal ship got so high in the atmosphere...

Think, Sullivan commanded herself. Think! What now? What was about to happen? And why hadn't she seen any aliens? Why were they still hiding?

Maybe she could smoke them out.

Finley was up now, wobbly but standing. Sullivan forced herself to her feet, then motioned to Finley. "Stand back."

Sullivan lifted her pistol and pointed it at the door behind which the enemy presumably waited, down the short hall. If she could force them to land again, and open the door...

Did she dare shoot? An explosive decompression out in space would mean death for everyone.

Another two labored breaths. Nothing happened. They probably couldn't see her, didn't even know she was pointing a weapon at them.

She had to come up with a way to prod them, coax them out of their hiding place. "What's the matter with you guys?" she said. No way to know if they could hear her, and even if they did, no way to know if they understood her. "You a bunch of cowards?"

That should get them roused. That always got under men's skin.

A mechanical hum buzzed to one side, followed by two popping noises.

Something smacked Sullivan on the upper arm. A slight pin prick. Her knees wavered.

"Oh, damn," Finley said. Sullivan turned to see Finley falling against the wall, then sliding to the floor. The sergeant's pistol clanged on the metal floor.

A drug. That was why her soldiers lay in a pile, motionless. And now Patrice had only seconds left. First priority: hide her pistol. Shaking, gasping for breath, she reached behind her to grab at her pant waist. The damned body armor was in the way. Her knees slammed onto the deck. She unsnapped the front of the vest with shaking hands, The walls smeared themselves in waves, eerie in their movements, fading in and out. Hand around to her back. Under the armor. Lift. The. Pistol.

Darkness closed in. The pistol slid into the small of her back. The heavy plates of her body armor smacked against it, slamming metal against her spine. She'd gotten the weapon hidden.

Unless she'd hallucinated it all.

She lifted a hand. Needed to check again.

But then the lights went out.

Chapter 30 — Captives

Colonel Sullivan awoke with a gasp and tried to sit up, but something heavy pressed on her rib cage. She blinked to try to clear her eyes, then realized it was one of her soldiers, Mendez, unconscious and sprawled over the floor, saliva dripping from his gaping mouth. It looked like someone else was positioned across his legs. The whole group, all her soldiers, had been dumped in an ungainly pile, weapons missing. She was sure they were all alive--a couple of them were snoring, and Mendez's body heat was a convincing sign that he was warm-blooded.

She grunted and tried to push Mendez off her. But he wasn't going to budge. She shook him by the shoulder. "Beauty sleep's over."

A little old lady leaned over the top of the pile. "Can I help you, deary?"

Colonel Sullivan grunted and pushed again.

The old lady looked in the opposite direction. "Have we got some strong men here that can give us a hand?"

In a minute, a young man in a suit and a stocky older gentleman in jeans and a plain white t-shirt pulled the soldiers off of each other. As soon as Colonel Sullivan could sit up, she sloughed off her body armor, then patted the small of her back. The gun was still there. She let out a sigh of relief, then slapped her hands against her left cargo pocket. Another magazine was tucked away inside, heavy with bullets. Thank God.

Her soldiers were coming around, muttering various expletives expressing their surprise and chagrin. "What the hell?" Sergeant Harvey said. "*We* s'posed to be helping *you*."

The floor beneath Sullivan shifted, like they were listing to port. She slammed her hand back onto the floor to keep from falling over. Others in the room protested loudly with grunts or ohs, and one person screamed. But just as quickly as it happened, everything stabilized.

She looked around the room to get her bearings. The walls were solid from floor to ceiling. One door, and no windows anywhere.

"Wish I had some smelling salts," the little old lady said.

Colonel Sullivan walked over to the woman, where she knelt beside one of the soldiers, fanning his face with a folded piece of paper. "I'm Colonel Sullivan," she said, holding out a hand to shake.

"Mrs. Steiner," the old woman said, taking Colonel Sullivan's hand by the fingertips and giving the gentlest of shakes. "Oh well, I suppose I should give you my first name."

"Not necessary," Colonel Sullivan said. "I'm used to last names."

Mrs. Steiner smiled, but then her worried look returned. "Do you know what's happening?"

Sullivan didn't want to say what she thought – that they were being taken to some barbaric alien slave market. "I'm afraid I don't know any more than you."

But she needed to figure out a lot, and fast. She still had her mission, to rescue all these civilians, even though now that included rescuing herself as well. No doubt about *what* she needed to do. The only question was how.

How in the hell?

She looked over the civilian crowd. In the far corner, a young girl who appeared to be barely eighteen leaned her head on a nearby man's shoulder, softly sobbing. Others looked dazed, and a number of the men had anger written on their faces. None of them were going to be any help.

The young girl sat up straight, looking directly at Colonel Sullivan, red circles around her eyes, wet streaks running down her cheeks. "We're doomed," she said.

Colonel Sullivan lifted her shoulders and brought her chin up. "Not if I can help it."

Heads rose, and people straightened. A woman clasped her hands together. "I have three children," she said. "They need their mother."

Sullivan's stomach shuddered. Children. Family. All the things she had never had, never thought she wanted. Yet these people acted like it was the most important thing in their lives. Just like with LTC Cooper, it was their reason for being.

Was she missing something?

No. Her soldiers were her family, the people she shepherded and protected. She had everything she needed, and she would get them all back to Earth, if it was the last thing she ever accomplished.

And she was going to bring *all* of them back, both the ones who had family, and the childless people. They all deserved that.

"I'll do everything I can."

"And we'll help in any way we can," a man with a booming voice said. He stood, brushing off his beige slacks and straightening his tall frame. There was something odd about him—a confidence that seemed somehow disingenuous, a charm that almost dripped syrup. But he was offering help. She'd take it.

Such as it was. This was a rag-tag band of misfits, most of whom probably didn't even know each other, had no military training and probably even less discipline.

But that was not the attitude she needed. To be a general, to get that promotion she so desperately wanted, she needed to learn to deal with civilians. The whole government was full of them, run by them. At the highest levels, even the military was run by them. And most strategic assignments, she had learned, were full of requirements to deal with people who were not obligated to obey, who had to be influenced and convinced.

That didn't mean she had to like it, though. She'd deal with all that when the time came. Right now, civilians were simply the personification of her military mission, her assigned objective.

She shook Craddock's hand, introducing herself. "I'll let you know if I need anything," she said.

"Roland Craddock," he said. "CEO of the investment firm Craddock and Miller. My friends call me Andy."

"Very nice," she said. It sounded like he meant to impress her.

"And one more thing," he continued. God, he sounded so full of himself, like he thought he was God's gift to kidnap victims everywhere. "I know you got your hands full with the soldiers you command here, so I'll take charge of the civilians."

She hesitated briefly, not sure of his qualifications. But on the other hand, it would get her out of having to babysit a bunch of civilians. It would solve her problem of having to deal with this motley band. Better to let him have that job, since he seemed to want it so badly. What an alpha-hotel.

She gave him a forced smile. "That does seem appropriate."

Craddock turned to the rest of the group. "Does everybody here agree with that? I mean, since you guys didn't really sign up for doing any military duties."

"Yeah," one of the men said, followed by a chorus of agreement.

Craddock beamed at her. "Looks like that's settled."

Colonel Sullivan turned back to her own soldiers, a group of people she felt comfortable with, people she knew would follow her orders. Dealing with the civilians was not something she was ready for.

She gathered the military into a small group by the door, glancing over them to make sure none were injured or in need of care. Most of them were people she already knew, though only distantly. Nothing personal. And she only had a minimal knowledge of their skills and abilities. "Any of you besides Finley have experience in military intelligence?"

They all shook their heads. "MPs," they muttered.

"Sorry," SSG Clark said.

"It's okay," she said. "But now we all have to start thinking broadly, taking in every piece of information we can get. The more we know, the better chance we have of succeeding."

"We'll do whatever it takes, ma'am," Clark said.

She nodded at him. She had confidence in this small group. For one thing, they were highly motivated. And they were fearless. Otherwise, they wouldn't have gotten this far.

She put a pen to a blank page in her green notebook. "Now, the first thing we need to do is list out everything we know about these aliens."

The soldiers exchanged glances, but no one said anything.

She needed to demonstrate. "They're humanoid," she said, writing quickly in her notebook, "and they can be killed by bullets."

"Isn't that obvious?" Mendez said.

She nodded. "Even the most obvious things need to be listed. Just so we don't miss anything."

"They're pretty strong," Finley said. "Like they have the shoulders from hell."

"Good," Sullivan said. She looked at the others.

A scream broke her concentration, echoing off the metal walls, making it hard to pinpoint where the sound had come from. Sullivan swiveled her torso to see Mrs. Steiner jumping to her feet and backing away from the corner.

Damn. The civilians were supposed to be just neutral objects in her life, but if they got out of control, they could become impediments to her mission accomplishment.

She had to figure out what was going on.

Colonel Sullivan handed Sergeant Clark her notebook. "Keep going," she said, then walked over to the civilian side of the room.

Mrs. Steiner looked relieved as Sullivan approached, her arm reaching out like she would grab Sullivan and never let go. God, this level of neediness sent chills over her skin.

"What happened?" Sullivan asked.

"It was a little creature," Steiner said, clasping her palms together, fingers intertwined, almost like a prayer. "Shiny, beady eyes, staring at me from under the wall."

Colonel Sullivan creased her brow. *Under* the wall? Had Steiner been so stressed out that she was hallucinating? Then again, this was an alien ship, and probably an alien animal. In that case, anything was possible. "Where was it?"

The old woman pointed to the corner, to a spot where the floor and the wall separated, leaving no more than an eighth inch of space. Sullivan added "small" and "flexible" to the list of traits this alien animal possessed.

"What did it look like?" Mr. Craddock said.

"I don't know. I don't know," Steiner said, her gnarled fingers curled up against her chin. "It was furry, and it had a long snout and a black nose, like some kind of rat thing."

"That makes sense," the man said behind her. "Don't most ships have rats?"

Oh, God, this was just a big misunderstanding. This old housewife had seen something in the shadows and assumed it was like a terrestrial animal, a rodent of all things. A mouse, something to make the typical female jump onto a table and act like an idiot.

Still, there was a chance the creature had been real. Not enough evidence to know, either way. "Whatever it is," Colonel Sullivan said, "it's probably alien. I recommend you don't mess with it."

"The Colonel is right," Mr. Craddock said, voice booming. Then he turned to Mrs. Steiner. "It's probably just as afraid of you as you are of it."

Colonel Sullivan frowned. They didn't really know that, either. But if it would keep the civilians calm, she was not going to argue with Mr. Craddock. "If anybody sees it again," she said, "pay attention so you can give me a thorough description." If it *was* an alien creature, then, she could use her knowledge of biology to classify it or make assumptions about it.

Not that that would help them out. But it would be interesting.

"Good idea," Craddock said. "Everybody keep your eyes open."

She gave Craddock a weary smile. So far, his brilliant leadership had consisted of parroting her commands. Not that she wanted him to take a lot of initiative. God, she didn't know what she wanted from him. But she was starting to feel certain that, whatever it was, he wasn't going to be able to measure up.

She returned to her soldiers. As she took her seat, she realized that Mrs. Steiner had followed her, gnarly hands outstretched like she wanted to cling to something.

"You don't mind if I join, do you?" Mrs. Steiner said as she sat beside Sullivan.

God, was this old woman about to become her new shadow? Sullivan had thought the civilian problem was solved, and now, she had become someone's security blanket. "We're gathering military intelligence," she said, hoping her tone would communicate that this was not a job for civilians.

"Maybe I can help, then," Steiner said, her face brightening.

"You been around the aliens?" Finley asked before Sullivan could rebut the suggestion.

"Oh, definitely," the old woman said, nodding for emphasis. "Right up close."

Well, now Sullivan would look stupid shooing Mrs. Steiner away. Stifling a sigh, she turned to Clark. "What have you gotten?"

"Okay," Sergeant Clark said, glancing at the paper. "They shoot energy weapons, which don't seem to work in foggy conditions."

Colonel Sullivan nodded at them.

"Yeah," Sergeant Harvey said, "they got hand-held weapons, and great big mother fuckers they shoot from their ships."

Mrs. Steiner let out a soft gasp.

"That's a good way to describe them," Colonel Sullivan said with a smile. Maybe a little harsh language would scare away the civilian interloper. "Anything else?"

The soldiers looked at each other, then shrugged.

"They seem to have translator capability," Mrs. Steiner offered.

Sullivan looked at her with surprise. "They spoke to you?"

"Yes." The old woman chuckled. "It looked like they were in a badly dubbed foreign film."

OMG. Sullivan had badly underestimated Mrs. Steiner's ability to contribute. What else had she missed? She glanced at the other civilians, then dismissed the thought. This had to be a one off.

L. D. ROBINSON © 2022

"I saw dead people in the laundry room," SSG Clark said. "Did they kill a lot of people?"

"Oh, they were very careful," Mrs. Steiner said. "It was like they were trying to keep us alive."

Sullivan stared at her. "Can you give us an example?"

"When Mr. Craddock tried to escape," Steiner went on, "they chased him down and threatened him, talked about how killing him would make an impression on the others, but it sure looked to me like they didn't want him dead."

"Thank you." That validated her suspicion about people being taken to be sold as slaves. Her stomach twisted. She turned back to her soldiers. "Anything else?"

Heads shook.

"Okay. So, this is what we know. Now, let's brainstorm what can we do. Any ideas?"

The soldiers stared at her silently.

"Anything you can come up with," she said. "You know. This is brainstorming. Crazy ideas are welcome."

More silence.

"Stupid ideas. Impossible ideas. Anything."

The soldiers' expressions were blank, vacant, confused.

Mrs. Steiner patted Sullivan on the hand. "Oh, sweetie, I don't think they have the vaguest idea."

Chapter 31 — Cargo

The shuttle floor rocked again, not the spongy sinking and rising of a ship in motion, but jerks accompanied by bangs. Colonel Sullivan flattened her hands on the floor and closed her eyes. It sounded like they had crashed into something. But the shuttle stabilized, and all that remained was whirring, and the soprano sounds of hydraulics.

Then, the entire back wall of the room they were in fell away, opening into a room four times as large as where they had been staying. It had to be the main ship. Colonel Sullivan slowly rose to her feet, knees fluttering. Behind her, hinges creaked as the door from the shuttle opened.

"Move in there," a commanding voice shouted.

She looked over her shoulder. The alien standing in the back door was a brutish looking creature, dressed in a dull red shirt and black pants.

He had the build of a Neanderthal, broad and stocky, a heavy bone structure and muscles to match. If it came to hand-to-hand combat, neither she nor the strongest of her soldiers stood a chance against this man.

All around her, people shuffled where they were directed. Or more like they were backing away from the alien. And her instincts screamed at her to do the same. But she needed to get a better look at him.

She stepped toward him, lifting her chin, making her stance as confident as she could. He sneered at her, and then his eyes moved. He was looking at her scar. She thought she saw a flicker of respect there. Yeah. You see it, don't you? I've seen some action!

She pointed to the larger room with her thumb. "Is this the main ship?"

"Just move." He tucked his chin into his throat, scowling.

"I was only curious." She stood with her feet shoulder width apart, hands resting on her hips and elbows out, though in reality she didn't think it would intimidate him. He was almost a head taller than her, and twice as wide.

"Get going."

"Sure," she said. She wasn't certain how far she could push him, but she needed to find out. "We are at the main ship, right?"

He grabbed something at his belt, tassels, one brown and two green. He shook them at her, like he was pointing a gun, making a threat, but that was the weirdest threat she'd ever seen.

"You see these?" He shook them one more time, as if to emphasize what he was saying. "I'll kill you if you don't go now."

Weird. Was she supposed to be scared of some pom poms?

He stepped toward her, brows knitted, his neon green eyes glowing with rage, then shoved her, one beefy hand slamming against her shoulder.

She took a few steps backwards to keep from falling. He still had his hand out, ready to push her again. "Okay, I'm going."

"Hey look, man," a tenor voice said from inside the room. "Windows."

"Hanging, dude," someone else responded.

"Oh, wow, I can't believe this," said a third. "We're in friggin' outer space."

Sullivan rolled her eyes as she stepped into the main ship. Hanging? Like, being a kidnap victim in space was a good thing? Or like they'd missed "windows" so much they were thrilled?

The three young men stood by the side wall, where a window maybe four feet wide and three high, trimmed in metal braid, looked out into space.

"Man, I don't care what happens to us now," one of them said. "Whatever it is, this makes it all worth it."

"I'm a friggin' astronaut," the shortest one said with a grin.

God, what idiots.

Well, okay, it was pretty amazing. The stars shown steady and colorful against the blackness, many glowing with a reddish hue, a few orange or white, and a solitary blue diamond in the corner.

But she couldn't dwell on that. She had her priorities, knew what she needed to do first—evaluate her surroundings, see what she had to work with here.

The larger room had ten long, rickety tables, at most 18 inches wide, made of knotty wood that she would've assumed was pine had the ship come from

Earth. Along each side of the tables ran a bench made of similar material, roughhewn and full of splinters.

Despite the risk of being stabbed by wooden slivers, some of the people lowered their butts onto the benches. Tired elbows plunked onto the tables, cheeks resting in hands. Others moved into the corners, or sat on the floor against the walls, knees pulled to their chest and arms wrapped around their legs. She wanted to join them, lower her head to her knees and surrender to exhaustion after a long a trying day. But she had to keep going, keep looking for ways to get out.

On the far side of the room was one small door which led to the rest of the ship, trimmed in a braid made of hundreds of thin black wires. The top of the door had a square opening, like a little security window with no glass, big enough to put your hand through. She motioned for Sergeant Finley to check it out.

SSG Clark walked up to her.

The wall-sized door to the shuttle closed with an echoing *clang*. The alien who had directed them into this room now stood by the recently closed door, one of three similar doors lining the back of the room. Three fellow aliens surrounded him, weapons in hand, facing the humans in threatening poses. These guards, she noted, wore brown shirts, not the dark red of the first man, and their eyes were dim, lacking the spark of intelligence she would've expected in a space faring species. But then, maybe they didn't need to be particularly bright. They could just be the grunts, the poor bastards who were stuck with doing all the unpleasant labor.

The first alien stuck his fingers into a pouch that hung on his belt, right next to those harmless-looking tassels, then pulled out a thin, crooked metal rod. He lifted a lever by the door, stopping when the mechanism clicked, which appeared to move the door into a tight seal. The alien then pressed the small object into a slot and turned it.

She leaned her mouth toward Staff Sergeant Clark's ear. "Is that what I think it is? And old-fashioned key?"

"That's a little disappointing," Clark said.

"Yeah." Sullivan squinted at the alien as he pulled the key from the lock, then walked to the edge of the door. Was that another door? An entrance to this room from another shuttle?

"You'd think they'd at least have electronic keys," Clark said. "Something they could just wave at the door."

"Maybe there's some tech in the key we can't see," Sullivan offered.

The second door dropped, and a new, slightly smaller group of civilians reluctantly moved into the space. And finally, the third door opened, and the process was repeated. And each of these doors was sealed and locked by the first alien.

Sullivan watched the new arrivals carefully, waiting for the military captives the other aliens should have also taken on board. But there was not a military uniform in sight.

Evidently, her people had made more progress against these aliens than any of the other defenders. She let herself feel a moment of pride in that accomplishment, then brushed it away. Getting herself captured was not going to help her in the promotion arena.

And the room they were in was now crowded, loud with meaningless chatter and cluttered with movement.

L. D. ROBINSON © 2022

She looked back at her small group of soldiers. Only seven of them, not enough to overpower their captors. But somehow, she was going to have to make do.

"Make way," the alien shouted as his brown-shirted guards pressed toward the door to the main ship, pushing a person here, jabbing their weapons at another there, menacing a route through the throng of humans. The man in red strutted in the cleared path, satisfaction draping his face with a look of superiority. Then, when he'd almost reached the door, he stopped, staring at one of the humans.

Francisco.

His eyes got large, iridescent green irises darkening, eyes moving up and down over her body. *Oh, shit. Please tell me that look isn't what I think it is.*

Francisco stepped backwards, then to the side, behind SGT Harvey. Yup, she saw it, too. And Harvey had his fists planted on his hips as he glared at the space creature.

The alien chuckled, then turned to one of his guards. "This is going to be fun."

The man in brown laughed, but it looked like a nervous response, not the sharing of some pleasant anticipation.

Colonel Sullivan trembled. She couldn't just stand there and watch. But what was the alternative? How could she protect her soldiers, when the enemy so outgunned her, when they were so much stronger than any of her soldiers?

"See you soon," the red-shirted alien said, peering around Harvey to give Francisco a glint-eyed last glance. And then they all left, the door slamming behind them, key rattling in the lock.

Sullivan breathed out a sigh of relief. For the moment, she had a reprieve.

Across the room, Craddock had positioned himself in front of the newcomers, announcing the decisions about chains of command. She walked up to him.

"Listen," she said, "maybe you can find out if we have some veterans in the group. Or off-duty police or something."

He nodded, then began what sounded like a prepared speech to the crowd.

She wandered back to the window, around tables scattered in her way, people sitting on the floor with their legs straddling the aisles, friends huddled together and crying. Then, someone touched her arm.

"Yes?"

"You look tired, dearie," Mrs. Steiner said.

Damn, what a sweet little old lady. Reminded her, in a way, of her own mother, someone who acted like she cared. Tears welled up in Sullivan's eyes, and she bit them back, looking away to keep the tell-tale moisture out of sight. "I'm fine. Thank you."

"You need some rest," Steiner insisted. "A good leader knows to take care of herself."

"But—"

"How can you make good decisions if your brain is exhausted?" Steiner held out her hands in a shrug.

Sullivan sighed. "You're right. Just let me get a few things taken care of, and then, I promise..."

"Good girl." Steiner patted her on the arm, then walked away.

Sullivan blew out a relieved breath. Enough with the civilians trying to butt into her affairs.

But then a tall frail man with wire-rimmed glasses stepped in her path, a guy with a face so tense his lips were pressed into oblivion. "Excuse me," he said, pointing at Craddock, "but that man over there said you're in charge."

Damn. Thanks a lot, Craddock. I thought you were going to deal with these guys, answer all their stupid questions. She didn't have time for this.

Well, she had to say something. But what? She finally settled on a question. "What do you need?"

He shook his head, his face suddenly sagging, lips turned down. "My name is Andrew Dajos, and I work as an actuary."

She squinted at him, not certain how much help he could be, unless he thought he could assist with intelligence analysis. But even that seemed doubtful. "What do you need?"

Dajos shook his head. "I only want to warn you. If you try to escape, you will anger the aliens. And then they will punish us."

She tried not to roll her eyes but wasn't certain she'd succeeded. "It's my duty to try to escape."

"According to my estimates, you have a five percent chance of success. But if you fail, you endanger us all."

She frowned. "Thank you, Mr. Spock."

"Dajos."

"Right. And I don't need you to tell me the odds."

"You haven't been elected," Dajos said. "What gives you the right—"

"Mr. Dajos," she snapped, "you haven't been elected, either."

He huffed, folding his arms over his chest.

"Look," she continued, "I'm well aware of the problems. But I also have information you don't."

"Really?" He raised his brows.

"Not to mention, I don't think you've done any kind of psychological or sociological study on these creatures. Nobody knows how they'll react."

"I can make an educated guess."

She nodded. "Thank you for acknowledging that your estimate is just a guess. My guess is our chances are much better than you think."

Dajos stiffened. "This is my job, to estimate the probabilities of certain outcomes."

"And what actuarial tables do you have on alien activities?" She gave him a smile that she hoped he took to be dismissive.

"Well, I…"

"Thank you for your input. Now if you will excuse me."

She made her way across the room, between benches and around huddled bodies, stepping over legs sprawled across the walkway. Finley, still at the door, had brought a bench up to the thing so she could see through the small opening. "I can see down the hall," she reported. "Nabbers sometimes pass by. They're always armed."

"Good observations," she said. "But we can't have a bench in front of the door. Get Mendez over here 'cause he's tall enough.."

Once Mendez was in position, Sullivan said, "Let me explain what we need." She ripped a couple of pages from her notepad and handed them to Mendez. "I want to see if you can find identifying characteristics on each individual Nabber."

Mendez looked confused. "Like what?"

"Just like you would do with people. Maybe one has a big nose, and another has a scar. Some are tall and others are short."

"Oh," he said, his face brightening. "Sort of like a description of the suspect."

She chuckled. "Of course. I was going to say like the way biologists count animal populations, but that's even better."

Mendez snorted, motioning out the door with his head. "Hell, that's the way I've been looking at them."

"Like animals?"

"Sure as hell not humans," Mendez said, brows rising in earnestness.

"Give them made-up names if that'll help," she added. "In the end, I want to have the best estimate possible how many crewmen work on this ship."

Once she was satisfied that he was doing his job correctly, she moved over to the other soldiers, who had gathered in a circle near the back corner. "Okay, guys," she said, "the next thing we need to figure out is the layout of this ship. I'll take any ideas anybody's got for how to do that."

"I guess," Finley said with a shrug, "we can look out the window."

"That'll be a start. Then try to think of excuses for the Nabbers to take us to other rooms."

"Maybe we need to go to the baffroom," Harvey suggested.

"That's a start."

"How about somebody is sick?" Finley offered. "An they gotta take that person to the doctor."

Sullivan swallowed, not wanting to express her reaction to that thought. Would the Nabbers even care if someone were ill?

"Any other ideas?"

She waited, but no one offered anything else. And they weren't just low on ideas. Morale was flagging, hope of getting out of this mess slowly circling the drain, ready to slip into the sewer of despair. Sullivan needed to come up with something to give them confidence, some idea for them all to work on. But her mind was equally blank.

They settled into a dull conversation, and Sullivan sat on the floor, resting her head against the wall. Her eyes were about to close.

She shouldn't go to sleep.

But it had been a long day. She glanced at her watch. It was almost midnight, Chicago time. No wonder she was sleepy. She closed her eyes.

Got to escape before we get too far out into space, a voice in her head muttered.

And then another voice laughed. Too late for that.

Chapter 32 – Asteroid Belt

Sullivan awoke to a shrill scream echoing off the metallic walls. Around her, the sounds of awakening humans filled the air, groans and mutters of confusion, and chirps of protest from frightened women. God, sounded like another rat-thing had made its appearance.

She sat up and looked at her watch. Seven in the morning. Guess she'd been really tired.

Another scream pierced the air, this one higher pitched, more grating, painful for her ears.

"Look out!" a man shouted, and a clump of bodies moved on the other side of the room.

"More of those friggin' rat things," SGT Harvey said with a wry smile. He lay on his side, propped up on an elbow.

She walked past a woman who had climbed onto one of the benches. Another, wearing the dark uniform of a hotel restaurant, stood on her knees atop the table. Both stared into the far corner, where an impenetrable wall of humans blocked the view of what was happening.

"Get back!" somebody shouted.

Colonel Sullivan strode to the side wall, then shouldered her way through the crowd. Finally, she got a glimpse of a small creature, sitting on its haunches, its front paws clasped together like little hands. A bald man with olive skin stood in front of it, holding out his hands like he expected to be handed something. "Gimme a club! A weapon," he shouted in a slight Italian accent.

The rat-thing hissed like a cat, showing off long canine teeth. Not actually a rodent, then. It was no larger than the hated animal, with bulging black eyes and dark fur. Its snout was long and thin, and its cheeks looked like a chipmunk with a mouth full of nuts, which gave the entire head a decidedly triangular shape.

Oh my God.

"Get away from that animal now!" she shouted. "It could be venomous."

"Oh yeah, like you know all about this thing," Dajos said, arms folded over his chest.

"Look at the shape of the head. Weren't any of you in the boy scouts?"

"She's right," another man in the group said, this one wearing the uniform of a maintenance man. "Those ain't regular teeth. Those are fangs. That thing's poisonous."

The entire crowd suddenly backed away, the man who had been calling for a club forcing his way through the group. The rat thing turned, skittering through the crack where the wall met the floor, its long, wiry tail following in eerie S shapes.

She let out a disgusted breath. All this time, she thought she knew how to speak with authority, but none of the civilians believed her until a man corroborated her idea. Dammit, what was she doing wrong? What did she have to do to be taken seriously?

Maybe she just wouldn't rescue all these mansplainers.

That would show them.

She turned back to the other side of the room, shoulders sagging. Of course, the whole idea of only saving some and not others was ridiculous. It was like deciding to take half the objective and leave the enemy in possession of valuable ground. Not really an option.

And there was no point getting annoyed about how the civilians treated her. She had much bigger problems to solve.

She passed the side window on her way to rejoin her soldiers. The three young men stood there, gazing out like they were on a drug trip, like they'd never even gone to sleep.

"Hey lady," one of them said.

"Come on, Kyle," his friend said, nudging him in the arm, "she's got more important things to do."

Well, at least *some* civilians were giving her respect.

She turned to Kyle. "Yes?"

The young man pointed out the window. "Does it look to you like we're not moving?"

She studied the scene through the window, where a distant asteroid, which looked like a gray potato pocked with craters, appeared to be about the size of her fist. "I don't know," she said. "The stars don't seem to be moving, either."

"Yeah," one of the other young men said. "It's just too far away for us to see it moving."

Kyle shook his head. "It's close enough."

"Yeah," Sullivan put in, for some reason wanting to defend Kyle. "Look at all the detail of the craters."

Kyle's expression turned strained. "You can't tell closeness that way."

She blinked. "Really?"

"The surface of an asteroid like that is fractal." He must have seen the confused look on her face because he continued. "That means it looks pretty much the same from any distance, any scale."

Sullivan glanced back at the asteroid, nodding. "So, it could be hundreds of miles wide, but just too far away to look that big."

"You got it." He smiled, then stopped himself, shaking his head. "Thing is, it's close. Close enough, if we were moving, it would have slid out of our field of vision just in the time we've been talking."

Okay, that didn't sound like the kind of sentence that came out of the mouth of a high school dropout. "How can you tell?"

"Parallax."

"Para what?"

He pointed back out the window. "Look at the asteroid."

"Okay."

"Now, close one eye, and then switch eyes."

She followed his instructions.

"Did you see it jump?"

She tried it again, this time paying more attention to the apparent location of the space object. "Only slightly."

"Right. Which means it's close enough you can detect parallax with your naked eye."

She squinted at Kyle. "Are you an astronomer?"

"Software engineer."

"Programmer," his friend said. "*Game* programmer."

The third young man shook his head, laughing. "Yeah, ask him about his master's degree thesis on the 'Science of Robert A. Heinlein'."

The friends giggled and punched each other in the arms.

Kyle gave them an indulgent look. "With the asteroid this close, we should be able to detect relative motion."

That was the second time he'd used the word "detect" in almost as many sentences. Nerd was probably a good way to describe him. Educated and knowledgeable were equally good descriptions. He might be of some use to the operation.

"So, I was thinking," Kyle went on, "that if we're not going anywhere right now... I mean we're not getting farther away from Earth..."

She nodded. "This is the time to escape."

"Right."

She looked up, into his face. He was taller than her, and that made it difficult to look directly into his eyes. "I need you to keep an eye out, let me know if anything changes."

"Right." His chest appeared to puff out slightly, and a smile broke out on his face.

She returned to her soldiers, and they began another brainstorming session. "Remember," she said, "no criticism of any idea, no matter how bizarre or unworkable. Just throw out your most ridiculous solutions."

"But if they no good..." Finley started, clearly confused.

"Something may spark another idea," she said, "and eventually, one of those ideas might spark a viable option."

But before they could start, Mendez hurried over. "Bill and Joe are coming," he said.

"Who?" Colonel Sullivan said.

"I was going to name them Rover and Spot, but then I didn't have enough dog names."

"You mean the aliens," she said, jumping to her feet.

Rattling at the door got everyone's attention, and the muted conversations of the captives died away.

Everyone stared as the door opened and two aliens stepped in, their energy weapons scanning the room.

"Which one is which?" she whispered.

"That's Joe," Mendez said, pointing to the alien wearing a deep red shirt trimmed in gold, the same man who had forced all the people out of the shuttle. The way he swaggered into the room indicated he was trying to impress people as he slipped the metal key into his belt pouch. Bill, wearing the brown shirt of those who were more subservient, had stood guard last time she'd seen him.

This was the moment she had been waiting for. She hurried over to the aliens, not certain which to address. Her gut told her to go with the cocky guy, the man in red. She reached out her hand as an offer to shake but the alien just stared at it, sneering.

Well, that was awkward. She withdrew the hand.

"My name is Colonel Sullivan, and I'm the senior ranking officer here."

"None of you has any rank anymore," Joe said. "You are all cargo."

That wasn't good. She needed to try to get him to think of her and the others as people, not just objects to be bought and sold. "What's your name?"

The alien lifted is chin and looked over her head. "Everyone sit on the benches, and spread your hands over the table top."

Damn it, maybe she just needed to go to the top. Colonel Sullivan took a deep breath. "I need to speak to your commander."

Joe threw his head back and laughed. Then, when he had a chance to turn his expression serious again, he growled at her. "Sit with the others."

She stood her ground, hands on hips. "Since you don't seem to want to talk…"

Behind Joe, Bill pulled something through the door, a large tray on wheels, topped with five metal vases about as tall as her forearm was long. He stopped the cart and closed the door.

Joe slapped a hand on Sullivan's shoulder and pushed down until her she collapsed onto one of the benches.

Bill pulled the cart to the head of each table and set a vase on each.

"What is this?" Craddock said.

"Water," Joe said. "Take a drink and pass it along."

"What?" Mr. Craddock said, coming to his feet. "That's terribly unsanitary. I demand you bring cups so we can each have our own."

Voices in the group murmured assent. One of the men in the back shouted, "Yeah, I ain't drinking out of no vase that everybody else has had their mouths on."

Joe shrugged. "Fine. Die of thirst." He chuckled as though the idea of someone dying was a form of entertainment.

Colonel Sullivan's stomach twisted. Maybe they weren't going to be slaves at all. Maybe they were going to be gladiators. The idea made her shiver, especially when she thought about people like Mrs. Steiner, who wouldn't last even a few minutes in the ring.

Bill pushed the cart back into the hallway, and Joe turned to leave as well.

"One more thing," Sullivan said, hoping to find some topic she could get him to talk about. "Where are the... latrines?"

He stopped, turning back to the group, and a frisson of triumph rushed through her. It was all she could do to keep from grinning.

"That corner," he said, pointing to the opposite side of the room. "Lift up the lid for solid waste."

She'd seen the spot, just a slanting floor, leading to a drain grate, and a covered hole no bigger around than her palm. No privacy, no toilet paper...

"I don't think that's going to work."

"Then you can hold it." He turned again to leave.

"And what about... We've been seeing a small animal on the ship."

"So?" he said, sounding annoyed.

Okay, what exactly was her question? What would get him to tell them more, stay here longer while she attempted to figure out what was going on? "Um, I'm surprised you haven't been able to exterminate them. Assuming you would want to do that."

He gave her an eye roll. "They're tougher than other animals. So, we've learned to live with them."

"Anything we should know?"

Joe appeared to think for a moment, then nodded at her. "The animal is called a *theet*. It's very dangerous, so I suggest if you see it, you avoid it."

She stared at him. Where was this concern coming from? Warning them about dangerous animals and providing them water confirmed what the civilians had told her earlier: the Nabbers wanted to keep as many people as possible alive. But why? If she could figure that out, maybe she could use it to her advantage.

"It won't attack us, will it?"

He let out a loud sigh. "If you have food, it'll try to get that from you."

"Oh. I guess we should share, then, huh?"

"And also use the latrine. That'll keep them from getting so hungry they want to eat *you*."

"They eat that, huh?"

"They can get extremely aggressive when they're hungry," Joe said. He looked over the crowd one more time. Most of the people sitting at the tables had started drinking from the metal containers. Just watching them made Colonel Sullivan's mouth water. But she had to try to engage Joe one more time. "I would really like to know your name," she said. "Otherwise, we'll have to keep calling you 'Joe,' and I don't know if you'd like that."

He stopped, giving her an icy stare. "What kind of a name is that?"

"What do you think?"

He paused, eyes moving to indicate a brief moment of thought. "I think it's an insult."

"You might be right."

He nodded with a little laugh, then slapped her on the shoulder, pushing her off balance. "I think I'm going to ask the captain for permission to kill you."

Chapter 33 — Crew Shortage

His duty to the prisoners completed, Galth headed for his quarters, hoping for a well-deserved rest. This particular harvest had been more difficult than he had expected, and he was exhausted.

"Galth to the bridge," a voice said over his personal intercom.

Sink it. He rubbed his face briskly, trying to get his alertness back, then stomped his way to the bridge. This ship was so poorly run, how had he been assigned here? He needed to ask for a transfer, preferably back to *The Bone Stripper*, Zolbon's ship. Or better yet, he needed to take command himself.

Once he stepped into the transparent bubble, he glanced at the stagnant view, stars stuck in their places, and planetesimals suspended all around them. Sink it, he would never get off this ship if they just stayed here, never got back to *Dakhesh*. "Why have we stopped again in the comet cloud?"

Captain Beglash looked up from the control pad he had been studying, his eyes a little redder than normal, and the skin underneath them sagging. The man was getting too old to be a captain. He should just get out of the way and let someone competent take over.

"First of all, this is not the comet cloud. These are just big rocks."

Galth's fingers twitched, ready to wrap themselves around Beglash's scrawny neck, moving as if by their own will, demanding revenge for this latest insult. Just to be on this ship was bad enough, but now the incompetent were insulting him?

"Yes," Meliq added. "It's the inner asteroid ring."

Well? Are you going to allow this unspeakable to talk down to me, too?

"Secondly," Beglash continued, "there are Enforcers patrolling around the orbit of the third planet. "I think they're looking for us."

Demons of the Night Sea, Enforcers were no threat, as long as your engines could give you enough speed. And once your ship had crossed over into Dakh Hhargashian space, those self-appointed protectors of undeveloped planets would never pursue. Did Beglash think he couldn't outrun them?

"So, you're just hiding from them behind this big rock?"

"They'll leave the system eventually, when they decide we're not here."

"But not before your whole crew decides you're a coward."

Beglash lowered his chin, staring at Galth with disdain. "My crew understands what we're doing. All except for you." He paused then, not taking his eyes off Galth, as if he thought he could somehow intimidate with his stare. Not going to work.

Then, Beglash chuckled, lifting his brows. "But, if you're so brave, I'll let you take a shuttle and distract the Enforcers while we get our precious cargo back home."

"I'm not stupid," Galth said. A ship could outrun the Enforcers, but a shuttle would leave him open to capture and imprisonment.

Galth paced for a moment, wondering what the captain had wanted him for. He'd only recently been informed that Reldak the Complainer, his now-deceased ground team leader, also had the duty of Custodian of Victims on the ship. But Reldak and most of his ship-board team were... enjoying the Great Embrace. So now Galth was probably going to be assigned that duty. It was the last thing he needed.

"Speaking of stupid," Beglash said, "I have an assignment for you."

Sinking flotsam, this didn't sound like it was going to be good news. "I'm already very busy," he said. "The shuttles took a lot of hits while we were down there."

Beglash rolled his eyes. "Shuttle maintenance can wait."

"But—"

"Shuttles won't help us escape the Enforcers."

Galth puckered his lips to keep from spitting out an enraged shout that the captain didn't need to tell him stuff he already knew.

"On the other hand," Beglash continued, "if the Enforcers stop us and try to board the ship, we'll need all our weapons, won't we?"

"You don't have to lecture me."

"Good." Beglash smiled with satisfaction. "Then you'll understand that I want you to head down to the armory and help with weapons maintenance."

Galth straightened himself to his full height. "I will not." How dare the captain assign him a task that was meant for the brown-clad lower echelons?

"How many soldiers did you lose on the planet?"

"We always expect to take losses on the ground," Galth objected. "Crewmen fight to be on the ground teams."

"Maybe you should have been one of the casualties."

Right about now, Galth wished he had been. Even floating stranded in the Night Sea would be preferable to serving under this inept commander.

"I was up against a formidable foe," Galth said. With an incompetent ground commander, he wanted to add, but since he didn't know what the relationship had been between Beglash and Reldak, he decided to leave that complaint out of his litany.

"We have a small ship," Beglash said. "Your dead soldiers would now be working on the weapons if they were still alive. You, on the other hand, have little important to do right now, and I need those weapons tuned up."

Galth stared at the man for several minutes, uncertain how to parry the argument, but unable to absorb the idea that he had lost the debate. "I, uh… It's been so long since I've done that, I don't remember how."

"The armorer will help refresh your memory."

Feces, he hated being on this stupid little ship. He hated the captain. He just needed to kill the man and take his place. Well, he'd also have to kill Tordag, but that wouldn't be an issue. Or maybe he should talk to Tordag, get the second in command to cooperate with a coups, get him to help separate Beglash from his bodyguards.

Beglash pulled his brows together. "Why haven't you left yet?"

Galth tapped his thighs with his fingertips. Any way he could get out of this? Anything he could say?

Probably not. Beglash already looked perturbed. More arguments would just get him thrown in the brig, a fate worse than death. So, what Galth needed to do now was make some long-term plans to deal with the captain. He wasn't about to drop this little scuffle. It would just add to the long list of reasons to do away with Beglash.

Galth turned to exit the bridge, then remembered one more thing he needed to bring up. "By the way, one of the humans wants to speak to you."

Beglash heaved a weary sigh. "Someone claiming to be their leader, I suppose."

"Which is pretty stupid," Galth said with a laugh.

"Well, you know what to tell him."

"Right. Only one thing." Galth smiled inwardly, relishing the affliction he was about to lay on the captain. His revenge for being put on maintenance duty would be to force Beglash into having to deal with a female as an equal. "This was a woman."

Beglash's brows rose almost halfway up his forehead. "They let women hold positions of leadership?"

Hm. Beglash hadn't quite gotten the point here. Galth needed to make it clear. "She said something about being an officer."

"Puh! You can't be serious."

Galth shrugged.

Beglash ran his hands over his face, as if he were trying to remove the grogginess from his mind. "Very strange."

Then, Galth had another idea. Maybe this woman was the person who had led the soldiers on the ground. Could that be? No. Not even possible. Not a woman. But if she had been, then Galth's two worst enemies could torture each other, while Galth sat back and watched with glee.

"Well, I was thinking, since we usually enjoy some of the female victims before we deliver them home, you might be in the mood."

Now, it looked like Beglash was thinking about it. This just might work.

Except he wasn't taking the bait. "Unless you're too tired."

Beglash heaved a deep sigh and dropped his hands to his side. The gesture looked like the movement of someone too exhausted to function anymore. "Sounds like… a good plan." Beglash's smile looked weak, like the ghost of an old man, gray and haggard.

"Shall I go get her?"

He nodded. "That way, I can show her what women are meant for."

Galth laughed. "Show her what a real man is like."

"Captain," Meliq broke in on the conversation. "The Enforcers are scanning the asteroid ring."

Startled, Galth looked through the transparent walls, in the direction he thought the Enforcer ship lay, though he wasn't certain. "I don't see it."

"Right there," Meliq said with a tap on his control pad. A small circle appeared around a tiny dot, smaller than the dimmest star.

A cold finger slithered its way down Galth's back. Nobody wanted to deal with the Enforcers. The kinds of things they did to a person were unimaginably horrible.

Beglash gestured to the helmsman. "Just a gentle nudge on the thrusters," he said. "Put us behind that big rock over there."

"Why move the ship?" Galth said, alarm bells ringing in his head. "They'll spot us for sure."

"If they're using active sensors," Beglash explained, "they already know we're here somewhere."

Tordag nodded. "We just need to keep them from zeroing in on us."

Galth's thigh muscles twitched, an almost uncontrollable urge to run. And now his stomach cramped. He was going to vomit all over the transparent floor. "But if they know we're here..."

"Relax," Meliq said, like he thought he'd seen fear on Galth's face. "Even if they've found our exhaust trail, by now the particles have been scattered by the solar wind. They won't be able to narrow down our location well enough to see a thruster blast."

Galth gritted his teeth. He wasn't going to let an Unspeakable see fear. He would die first.

Then, as if summoned by Meliq's statement, a puff of flame shot from the starboard thruster, and the *Blood Fury* drifted toward the lumpy brown object.

"Slowly," Beglash said.

The helmsman nodded, but he looked unsure of himself. He was a junior pilot, without Galth's experience. "Want me to take the helm?" Galth asked.

Beglash glared at him. "Why are you still here?"

"I'll go get the woman," Galth said. That would at least bring him back to the bridge where he could see what was happening, maybe take over the helm.

"Later. I'll let you know when."

Galth stared into the captain's steely eyes for another moment before it dawned on him why the little red veins on Beglash's eyeballs had expanded. The man probably hadn't slept in several shifts. There weren't enough crew on board anymore to do everything that needed to be done. Well, at least the captain had not sent him to the galley, where everyone would see him preparing food. At least no one would see him in the arms room.

Who was he kidding? He was going to be down there taking instructions from a brown-shirted Sigali.

He stepped backward with a curt nod to the captain. "As you wish." Then, he exited the bridge, but stopped just as the ship appeared around him, at the top of the three steps down into the main corridor. He needed to figure out which of the alien creatures was responsible for the death of so many of his crewmen. He needed to know if it had been that woman, as improbable as it seemed.

And if it turned out it was her, well then, she was about to learn a new meaning of the word rage.

Chapter 34 — Small Problems

"Hey, lady," Kyle Smith called out, his hand resting on the window frame.

Before Colonel Sullivan could respond, Sergeant Harvey jumped up and ran over to the window. "You call her 'ma'am', chicken head."

She hurried over to the window, looking at her soldier. "Thank you, Sergeant," she said. "But be nice to them. They haven't been through basic."

"Of course, ma'am," the sergeant said, giving the young men one last stern look before he left the area.

Once he was gone, she smiled apologetically at Kyle. "You have to understand, they take a lot of pride in their commander being treated with respect."

"No problem, ma'am," he said, but he looked uncomfortable, maybe a little intimidated, like he hadn't realized before how high ranking she was. "Um, we think we're moving now."

"Show me."

They huddled up to the window, and Kyle pointed to a potato shaped asteroid just coming into view from below.

"It's hard to see it at first, but the asteroid is getting bigger."

She nodded. She had a sense that it was still quite a ways away, and that it must be enormous.

"It almost looks like we're heading straight for it," Kyle continued.

"Why would we be doing that?" Sullivan said.

"Maybe to use its gravity to gain speed?" his friend suggested.

Kyle shook his head.

"Yeah," the friend continued. "You know how NASA uses gravity assist to speed up their spacecraft."

That sounded sensible to her, but Kyle's headshaking became more forceful. "That thing doesn't have enough gravity to accelerate a pebble."

Colonel Sullivan's face fell, then she forced her expression into something more neutral. "Well, knowing why probably doesn't matter, and there's no telling you'll be able to figure it out."

"Yeah," Kyle said.

"What is important is that you guys keep me up to date. This could be vital." Knowing where they were, especially once they got control of the ship, would be essential to their ability to return to Earth.

Another high-pitched scream pierced her ears. Colonel Sullivan closed her eyes for a moment, gritting her teeth. These people needed to get a grip, get some perspective. They'd been kidnapped by aliens, for heaven's sake. Those stupid little rat-things were the last problem they needed to get hysterical about

"Get it out of here," one of the women said.

Maybe Craddock would handle it. She looked at him, but he was backing away just like everyone else. So much for the great leader of the civilians.

That same bald Italian who'd been calling for a weapon before stepped in front of the rat-thing, then picked up one of the shorter benches, swinging it over his head. "I'll-a show you how to handle this," he said.

"Stay away from it," Colonel Sullivan called out.

"Stupid little vermin," the man said.

"*Vermiglio.*"

"Don't do it!" Colonel Sullivan shouted.

The bench came back down in an arcing swing, and then it was chaos. Several women screamed, people climbed over each other to get away, and the man who had wielded the bench—weapon now lay on the floor, writhing and screaming, his pant leg shredded, blood spattered onto the metal floor. The rat thing had vanished.

"Where did it go?" someone asked.

"He's hurt!" someone else called out.

Colonel Sullivan gulped, then turned to Mendez, still standing at the door. "Call for help." Then she rushed over to the man and knelt beside him. The skin on his calf looked like it'd been chewed. This was going to take better first aid than anything she had learned.

A brown-skinned man with streaks of gray in his black hair took to his knee beside her, a calmness on his face that told her he knew what he was doing. "I'm Doctor Samra," he said. He grabbed the pant leg and tore it away from the wound. "This kind of injury is not my specialty…"

"What is?"

"Oncology."

Shoot. That was way off from emergency medicine. But in the end it didn't matter. A cancer doctor was still a doctor, and that was what they needed.

The injured man trembled as Doctor Samra unbuckled the man's belt, then tugged on it. "Help me with this," Samra said. Patrice grabbed the end and the belt slipped out. Samra quickly wrapped the belt around the man's leg, just above the wound, cinching it tight.

The man groaned, closing his eyes.

"Keep him awake," Samra said as he pulled a knife from his pocket and examined the wound, a mass of flesh that looked more like hamburger than leg.

Patrice shook the bite victim's shoulder. "Hey. What's your name?"

The victim turned his dark eyes on her, whites showing beneath the irises, nostrils of his outsized nose flaring. "Carlo. Carlo Lorenzo."

"Italian?"

He tried to smile, gave out a little puff of air. "How you know?"

"Good guess."

"No," Lorenzo said. "Too much macho." His eyes rolled upwards.

"Hey, stay with me, Carlo." She squeezed her hand around his shoulder. Damn, a little humility from the man, and suddenly she was frantic to keep him alive. She looked up at the doctor, hoping for guidance.

Samra shook his head, his expression grave. "That animal got the venom in very deep."

Lorenzo's face had gone pale. He shuddered.

"Keep your eyes open," Samra said. "Stay with us."

Lorenzo groaned.

It wasn't working. Nothing was working, and they were about to lose the first civilian since they'd taken off. She couldn't let that happen. But what could she do? How could she arouse this man's attention?

Arouse? Patrice smiled then. Too easy. "Carlo," she said. "You know that's a sexy name?"

The man's mouth perked up, one corner moving into a half smile. "Bella, bella."

It was working. If he'd had more energy, she imagined he would have reached out to pinch her on the butt. And though she didn't want to admit it, damn, he was just a little charming.

"Bill and Joe are coming," Mendez called out.

Finally! Patrice nodded appreciatively at Mendez, then patted Lorenzo on the arm. "Okay, Carlo, we got help on the way."

"It was so fast," Lorenzo said. "So fast."

She looked back to Samra, who had gotten the last of the water and was pouring it over the wound. "Listen, I need you to go with him, then, you know, give us an idea of how the ship is laid out."

Samra glanced up, at first surprised, but then confident. "I can do that."

"Get out of the way," Joe barked from the other side of the door.

Patrice shook her head. She'd never thought she would be glad to see that asshole again. Of course, she couldn't rule out that they would simply come into the room to watch Lorenzo die as though it were entertainment.

After what seemed like an eternity of noises that sounded like fumbling with the key, the door slammed opened, and Joe loomed in doorway, scanning the crowd with his pistol. "What's the problem?"

"Over here," Colonel Sullivan called. "He got bit by one of those... What did you call them?"

Joe frowned, then stepped into the room. Bill stood behind him, arms hanging limply beside his body. "Get him," Joe commanded.

Bill hurried into the room, picked up Lorenzo and threw the injured man over his shoulder with a grunt. He marched back to the door, grumbling under his breath.

"Our doctor should go with him," Colonel Sullivan said, rushing up behind Bill. They'd reached the door, and Joe stepped aside to let Bill through.

"Not necessary," Joe said, turning away from them, his hand on the door handle, pulling it closed.

"I know we look a lot alike," Doctor Samra said, "but there may be some subtle differences, and I should be there to advise your doctor."

That was if they were actually taking him to a doctor.

Joe appeared to think about it, then finally nodded. Doctor Samra hurried toward the door, looking back at Colonel Sullivan for just an instant, and giving her a nod and a smile. Colonel Sullivan clutched her hands together. Suddenly, it seemed their entire operation depended on Dr. Samra. She hated feeling so dependent on someone else. She hated not being the one to go with them.

In a moment, Joe and his party were gone, the door locked behind them.

Colonel Sullivan stared at the door for a moment, her mind churning. Perhaps this whole event could be the template for an escape attempt. Call for help, overwhelm the two aliens who arrive, then slip out the door before it could be locked again. It just might work.

Her soldiers huddled in a corner, shoulders slumped, heads bowed. Everyone seemed depressed, hopeless, eyes glazed and cheeks wet with tears. Sergeant Mendez leaned his head against the wall. "Man, I'm glad my family can't see this mess."

"Why?" Francisco asked, her voice lower than Patrice expected.

"It's so damned embarrassing."

"I miss my family," Francisco said. "My mom, you know, she gives the best hugs."

Wow, Patrice thought, this was really getting heavy. She had to pull everyone out of the dumps before they all wasted away from helplessness.

"Hey, lady... I mean ma'am," Kyle Smith said. "Check this out."

Colonel Sullivan hurried back to the window. The view was now filled with something that looked like a pile of rubble and dirt. Straining hard to look upward, she could see a sliver of black space, and maybe one or two stars.

"We're right up next to this asteroid," Kyle said. "I don't think we're moving relative to it, not even an inch."

She stared out the window, looking at a large crater just off to the left. She closed one eye and then the other, and the crater seemed to bounce back and forth. "We're really close."

So, why were they stopped? Perhaps they had a maintenance problem, but that didn't explain why they were up against an asteroid, so close it seemed you could open the window and reach out and touch it. It didn't make sense.

But it did mean one thing. If it was true that they were in the asteroid belt between Mars and

Jupiter, they hadn't left the solar system. If they were going to attempt an escape, this was the time to do it.

L. D. ROBINSON © 2022

Chapter 35 — A Plan of Action

"All right," Colonel Sullivan said, motioning for her soldiers to gather. "Over there," she said, pointing to the corner of the room farthest from the door. There, they had less chance of being overheard.

Mr. Craddock walked up beside them, an Asian looking woman trailing behind him, looking for spots on the floor where they could sit, join in the meeting. Sullivan frowned. She hadn't invited them, and it was pretty presumptuous of Craddock to invite himself. On the other hand, that seemed to be part of Craddock's personality. Maybe she needed to have found someone else to "be in charge" of the civilians.

On the other hand, they needed to know what was being planned, if they were to be any help. They needed to be part of the meeting if they were going to be part of the solution. She just had to keep reminding herself of that, keep her gut from rejecting their participation.

As long as they stayed in their lane.

And as long as these two were part of the group, there were others who needed to join. She motioned to Kyle, who quickly sat in the circle.

"Colonel," Craddock said, his smile giving her a chill, a reaction she didn't understand, "This is Emily Chiharu." He gestured to the woman as he sat beside SGT Harvey. "She's a linguist."

Sullivan raised her brows. That was unexpected. "Welcome to the team," she said, extending a hand for a quick shake. Emily's response was strong and confident.

"I was just thinking," Emily said as she sat beside Craddock, pulling a writing pad from her pocket, "that once we get out of this room... onto a bridge or something, we're going to need to read their language before we can operate their ship."

"Makes sense," Sullivan said.

Emily nodded. "So, I've been looking at all the little signs around."

"Signs?"

She pointed toward one of the walls, where a small metal plate had been rivetted to the wall, with something scrawled on it. "There are several of them," she said. "Some over by the doors from the shuttle, one by the main door."

"Oh." Sullivan smiled sheepishly. Why hadn't she noticed them? Probably because she hadn't thought they would be of any use. But to someone like Emily, they could be a gold mine of information. "Can you actually tell anything from them?"

"Just that it appears their writing system is alphabetic," she said.

"I see." That was a little disappointing. Not that Sullivan expected Emily to have deciphered their entire language. "Well, keep at it."

Emily nodded, her smile weak, like she knew she'd not really added anything useful to the group.

Sullivan turned to Craddock. "Let me know if you find anyone else in the group who could help."

Craddock lifted his chest, looking a little too satisfied. "Will do."

Damn, why did every move he made set off alarms in her mind?

But there was no time to dwell on that little mystery. Sullivan turned to the rest of the group. Finley sat with her hands tapping softly on her thighs, teeth worrying her lower lip. Clark stared at the floor, looking like he'd lost hope. She gave them a confident nod, put some self-assurance into her voice. "I think we can pull this off. Here's what I've come up with."

Clark's head came up. Harvey leaned forward, and Finley stilled her hands.

"So here's what I've been thinking. We have to figure out a way so that next time some aliens enter the room, we can overwhelm them."

"Hand to hand combat," Harvey said, nodding. "Get them in a choke hold, then rip out their throats."

"Something like that," Sullivan said with a smile.

"And we got those water containers," Harvey said. "Look to me like we can smash them on the aliens' heads. That'll do them."

"They were awfully light," Kyle said. "Like, maybe aluminum."

Harvey blinked. "So?"

"I think you'll just put a dent in the metal," Kyle said, "but not on the aliens' hard heads."

Harvey grinned, and the other soldiers laughed.

Sullivan looked at SSG Clark. "What do you think?"

He nodded, his expression pensive. "Sounds like something that would work," he said, "at least for getting out of here. After that, I'm not so sure."

"Hell," Sergeant Harvey said, "once we disable the bastards, we take their weapons. With a couple of them friggin' ray guns, we can jack them chicken heads hard."

Sergeant Clark's hard expression softened into the ghost of a smile. "Two guns against the whole ship aren't very good odds."

"Not to mention we don't know how to use them," Private Francisco said. She picked up a long strand of black hair that had fallen out of its bindings, gave it a little twirl and then re-pinned it to her head.

"We'll figure it out," Sergeant Clark said. He looked over at Colonel Sullivan. "Maybe we can use one of those rat things to test them on."

"Besides," Colonel Sullivan said, pulling her pistol out of the small her back, "at that point, we'll have three guns."

Craddock's eyes enlarged. Finley grinned.

"No shit," Harvey said, a note of admiration in his voice.

"Well, if you've had that all this time," Craddock said, "why haven't you used it already?"

Sullivan slipped the weapon back in its hiding place. "It makes a lot of noise," she said, "and that's going to draw more enemy to us."

Everyone nodded, though Craddock still looked a little perturbed. But that didn't matter. Everyone else had lifted their heads just a little higher, and some even had hints of smiles at the corners of their mouths.

"Now," Sullivan continued, "we just need to come up with a reason to get the aliens back in here."

"Well," Finley said, "they came in here to give us water. What about we ask for some food?"

"I think they'll give us food on their own schedule," Craddock said. "No point in asking."

"We can have a fight start," Mendez suggested. "Lot a yelling and screaming."

"You think they'll even care?" Craddock said.

"Mr. Craddock," Sullivan said, "can you treat this like a brainstorming session?"

He frowned at her. "Those are bad ideas."

"They're ideas. They might help us think of better ideas. But if you immediately shut everything down, no one will be willing to offer what else they've thought of."

"Fine," he said, leaning back, like he'd just decided to take himself out of the conversation. Sullivan stared at him for a second. Should she replace him with someone else? Maybe put Emily in charge of the civilians? Or Kyle?

"Maybe we get sick," Clark offered. "I mean, pretend to be sick."

"Wait a damn minute," Sergeant Harvey said. "What we thinking? They gonna be coming back any time with Doctor Samra and that skeezer who don't know how to follow orders."

Colonel Sullivan sat up a little straighter. "Can we be ready that soon?"

"Harvey," SSG Clark said, gesturing to the other NCO, "Bill will probably be escorting the guy back in, so you take him out."

"Right," Harvey said. "Mendez, you work with me."

Clark nodded. "I'll handle Joe."

It seemed to make sense. Joe was taller than Bill, Clark taller than Harvey. Only one problem. "How are you going to jump Joe if he's got a weapon?"

Clark shrugged. "I grab him from behind."

"That means he's got to be inside the room," Sullivan said.

"Yeah," Finley muttered as she pointed toward the door. "He always keep his back to the hallway out there."

Clark stared at her for several seconds, then his skin blanched. "You're right. I didn't think of that." He turned back to Sullivan. "Sorry, ma'am. Looks like I'm not on my game."

"We're all a little off," she said. "Blood sugar's getting low."

"No excuse," he said.

She smiled then, almost got up and gave him a hug. Except that was not the way military commanders heaped appreciation on their subordinates. Best to just continue on with the discussion, pretend that the little mess-up hadn't even happened. "So," she said, "what's the solution?"

Francisco looked at Sullivan, a little smile quirking the corner of her mouth. "I think they might be easily distracted," she said, "with the right stimulus. I mean, who knows how long it's been since they had any?"

An invisible hand reached in and grabbed Sullivan's gut, twisting it sharply. "I don't like what you're suggesting."

"All I gotta do is lure him into the room just a few steps."

Bad idea. Really bad… it could get them into a situation so much worse than what they were already experiencing. They had to think of something else, and she had to come up with a good reason to stop Francisco. "It's too risky."

Francisco looked her straight in the eye. "Ma'am, I was ready to give my life when I got on that plane. And even more when I ran up the ramp into that shuttle. I'm going to do whatever it takes."

God bless her soldiers.

"That's fine for you to say," Craddock blurted, "but how can you make that choice for all the other women here?"

Francisco glared at him. "Look, pervert, we're escaping. Not opening the door for all the aliens to get their kicks. Got it?"

Before Sullivan could say anything, Craddock threw his hands into the air. "Okay, okay. I didn't mean it that way."

"All right," Colonel Sullivan said. She needed to get everyone back on task. "Now, we need to talk about what we're going to do once we get out of this room."

"It's simple," Craddock said. "After we take over the ship, we fly it back to Earth. Right?"

"Who's going to fly it?" Sullivan said. "Do we have any pilots here?"

Emily leaned forward. "Unfortunately, I think the guy who got bit was a retired pilot."

"Shit," Harvey muttered. "What if he don't survive?"

Damn, why did it seem fate was trying its hardest to mess up her plans? What other things were going to happen to destroy everyone's chances of escaping?

Chapter 36 — Taking Action

This was the first time in over a day that Colonel Sullivan had felt anything positive. Just the idea that they could end this ordeal gave her a little spring in her step, helped her stand a little straighter, walk a little prouder.

For the last 15 minutes or so, she had watched Sergeant Clark rehearse the takedown of the aliens, using a couple of the young men as stand ins for Bill and Joe. He had Sergeant Harvey follow Bill, while he waited for Francisco to lure Joe into the room. Joe only had to lean in just slightly, and Clark would be on top of him. To make that happen, they worked out that Francisco should stand on the other side of the open door.

For her part, Francisco had gotten so far into her preparations that Sullivan wanted to look the other way. Francisco had taken her T-shirt off, then replaced her uniform blouse, the top two buttons undone, displaying the top of her breasts. "What do you think?" she said to Harvey. "This enough?"

"You got *my* attention," he said.

Colonel Sullivan took a few more steps. It was her habit to pace while she reviewed a plan in her mind, but her feet hurt. Not only that, but her stomach had started complaining loudly. That little sip of water everyone had been given was just not enough keep her going, not when she was expending so much mental energy.

She sat on a bench that had been pulled up to the wall, leaning her back against the cold metal bulkhead. This was just taking too long, but she didn't dare try to get any sleep. Those aliens could return any moment.

Oh, but her eyelids were so heavy. She would just close them. Not go to sleep, just rest her eyeballs.

"Ma'am," someone said. Finley, hand on Sullivan's shoulder, shaking her. "Ma'am, Mendez says they're coming."

Colonel Sullivan jerked her eyes open, then realized a line of drool snaked out of the corner of her mouth and down her neck. Damn. She wiped the wetness on her sleeve, then glanced around to see if anyone else had noticed.

Clark and Harvey hurried to their positions as Joe fussed with the lock, while Finley wrung her hands.

"Just look normal," Sullivan said.

"Normal?" Finley clapped her hands onto her cheeks. "If they're unlocking the door, normal is terrified, isn't it?"

Sullivan let a choked chuckle puff through her mouth. "Yeah."

The lock turned over with a loud *clunk*. The shiny black handle moved downward, and the door swung open.

As expected, Bill entered the room with Lorenzo riding over his shoulder, still unconscious, Doctor Samra walking beside him.

In the meantime, Joe stood just on the other side of the threshold, pistol ready, watchful. Francisco sauntered up to him, one hand on her hip, the other on the narrow side of the door. "Hey, man," Francisco whispered, "you never came back."

Joe sucked in a quick breath, staring at her with surprise. But he didn't move.

Sullivan wanted to close her eyes, block out the image of what might happen next, but she had to know if it was going to work. By now, Bill and the patient had reached an open spot in the center of the room. Bill stopped, then motioned for Samra to help him lower the patient to the floor.

And Joe, still standing in the doorway, appeared to be frozen. Come on. Take the bait. Take it.

"I've always wanted to have sex with an alien," Francisco whispered. "What do you think?"

Joe's eyes opened wide, moving up and down as he took in the view Francisco offered. Even his breathing sped up. "Come with me," he said. But he wasn't taking a step into the room. He hadn't even leaned forward.

Francisco inched sideways, toward the back of the door, just enough to be out of reach. "Tell me what you want to do."

Joe rolled his eyes. "Not here."

"Will you be rough?" Francisco said.

Lust swept over Joe's face and he looked like he was going to swoon.

Francisco inched around the door, now almost out of Joe's sight.

Keeping his weapon trained on his captives, Joe reached around the door, hand probing for Francisco, but grasping only air. He stretched his arm, but still got nothing. He huffed.

Come on. Step in. Just one step. Just do it.

Joe eyed Clark, who stood nearby, watching Bill and Dr. Samra get Mr. Lorenzo settled in. "Move back," Joe said.

Clark looked surprised, but then he shrugged and stepped away. One step. Would that be enough?

It was like being back at the S-2 shop, watching Clark try to position himself to disarm Steed, while simultaneously keeping the later from suspecting. He even stepped away from the wall a little, moving toward Bill and his helpers, as though he was paying no attention to Joe.

Step in now. Do it.

Joe glared at Clark's back. He still hadn't moved. Bill was almost ready to leave the room. Something had to give, or this wasn't going to work.

Francisco brought a hand to her chest. Sullivan couldn't see exactly what the young soldier was doing, but it looked like Francisco had brushed a hand over the tops of her breasts.

Joe reached out again. One step.

Clark spun around. He leapt on Joe's back, wrapping his wrists around Joe's neck and jamming his knuckles into Joe's Adam's apple. The alien grunted loudly, face turning red. He straightened, first slamming his weapon against his chest, where it stuck, then grabbing at Clark's hands.

In the center of the room, Harvey mowed Bill to the floor. Mendez joined them, holding Bill's right arm behind his back.

L. D. ROBINSON © 2022

Francisco slammed the door shut.

Colonel Sullivan bit her lip. What Clark had done to Joe would have rendered any human unconscious, but Joe was still on his feet, reeling.

Joe growled.

Clark's team member, Sanders, followed them around with a water jug, trying to hit Joe in the head. But Joe swung around madly, growling and fuming, fists darting in threatening jabs while Sanders jumped away, then turned back, waving the jug, trying to get a lock on his target.

Sullivan nudged Finley. "Get the weapon," she said, rushing them, reaching toward the pistol still attached to Joe's shirt. Joe swung around, flinging Clark's legs at her, tossing her to the floor. Joe finished the circle, then jumped backward, slamming Clark into the bulkhead.

Pain ripped its way across Clark's face.

Joe kicked and the water jug flew over Sullivan's head, landing and bouncing across the room. Another kick, and Sanders doubled over, then fell to his knees. Sullivan tried to get back up, but Joe's heel slammed into her shoulder, while Joe seemed to use the recoil to thrust himself against the wall again.

Clark cried out in agony. Sullivan scrambled to her feet, then grabbed Joe by the arm. Hell, what was she trying to do? He flung her away like she was nothing to him, then slammed into the wall a third time, even harder.

Clark's eyes rolled into the back of his head. "No!" Sullivan screamed, climbing to her feet again. Joe grabbed Clark's arms and threw him on the floor. Clark bounced, then lay still like a corpse, while Joe snatched his weapon off his chest and pointed it at

Sullivan. "Back off, you whore, or you're going to be dead."

Sullivan backed away, a slight pain in her hip as she shifted her weight.

"Now tell the others to let Abgoth go."

Sullivan turned to Harvey and his team, who had wrestled Bill/Abgoth to the ground and had his wrists cuffed behind his back. She could let Joe kill her, but that wouldn't disarm him. Nothing she could do now would make this end well.

"Harvey, let him go," she said.

Harvey hesitated, but he had probably made the same calculations as she. He grabbed the keys to the cuffs, unlocked them and let them fall on the floor, then stepped back. Abgoth clamored to his feet, rubbing his wrists.

"Don't leave those there," Joe said, pointing to the silver handcuffs now decorating the metal deck.

Abgoth grabbed them, stuffing them into one of the pouches on his belt.

"And get the rest of those," Joe said.

Abgoth walked around to each of the soldiers, examining his or her belt, removing handcuffs wherever he found them. And then Joe and Abgoth were gone. The door slammed, echo taunting her. She'd failed. And trembles washed over her, sudden pains from her multiple falls, from kicks and hits.

And Clark still hadn't moved. She hurried over to him, crouching in spite of her complaining knees. His eyes were still closed.

Samra knelt beside her, lifting Clark's eyelids, staring into his eyes.

"Well?" she said.

Clark's hand came up, brushed the doctor's arm away.

"Do you have any pain?" Samra asked in his soothing voice.

Clark's eyelids fluttered, then his hand went to his ribs. "I'm okay."

"Can you get up?"

Clark started to sit, but quickly fell to the floor again. "Ow. I think I got a broken rib."

Samra nodded, looking at Sullivan. "No sign of concussion yet, but that may take some time to manifest."

She nodded, then looked back at Clark. "Next time, we gotta do better."

Clark smiled through his pain. "Next time, I think I'll kill that son of a bitch."

Chapter 37 — Summons

Beglash hurried through the door, heart pounding, fear and confusion throbbing through his mind, terror softening his knees. The sight of Abgoth sitting on the treatment chair, blood trickling over his cheek, the doctor wanding away the cut with his healer-rod, thrust away any hope the reports were exaggerated. He had a rebellion on his hands.

He gathered his anger as he came to a halt in front of Galth. All the better to keep his fear from showing. "What happened?" he said.

The shuttle pilot gave him a laconic glance, then went back to dabbing a de-clotter wad over the dark bruise on his cheek. "Could be they were trying to escape."

"Escape?" The idea didn't even make sense. "Where were they going to escape to?"

Galth shrugged. "I don't know what else they would have had in mind."

"Maybe they wanted to eat us," Abgoth said.

Beglash rolled his eyes. Why did he even listen to one of these lowly Sigali, poorly educated and not read in to the intelligence they had on humans.

"Stop moving," the doctor said, clamping a hand on top of Abgoth's head.

"And anyway," Beglash continued, still glaring at Galth, "no victims have ever tried to escape before."

"At least that we know about," Galth said.

Water and drowning, that couldn't be right. "No captain would dare hide such a thing," Beglash said.

Galth raised his brows. "Are you going to report it?"

Point taken. It certainly didn't sound like he had things under control. He could lose his entire command. "The problem here," Beglash said, putting a growl into his voice, "is that the victims are not being properly supervised."

"Supervised? You sent me down to weapons maintenance. Now you're blaming me for not supervising them?"

"You're the one who got Reldak killed," Beglash said. If Galth's ground commander during the attack were still alive, he would be overseeing the victims, but Galth's leadership, or lack thereof, had ensured more than half his crew never returned from Earth.

Galth threw up his hands, like he thought this was all too much. "How was I supposed to cope with the humans when you didn't give me enough crew and enough information?"

"You're saying it was *my* fault?" Beglash bellowed.

Galth took a step back, swallowing. Finally, it seemed, he realized he was crossing a line. "No. I mean, those victims have been nothing but trouble, right from the start."

"Then you're off weapons' maintenance," Beglash said. "Now, you can deal with the troublemakers yourself."

Galth blinked, then smiled. That hadn't been the reaction Beglash was looking for, but it didn't matter. As long as Galth did his job. "How many will be in my team?" Galth asked.

Beglash wanted to sigh, but he held his breath. Just like Galth to want to see how grand his new assignment could be, how much power he would wield. And Beglash was happy to disappoint. "Three. Including you."

"What?" Galth said, his hand with the de-clotter dropping to his side. "I need five times that many."

"Reldak did just fine with only three," Beglash said, then turned toward the door. But then a stab of fear shot through him. He was, after all, the prime target for assassination on his ship, even without giving someone an excuse to be angry with him. But Galth was clearly upset.

Beglash really needed to get rid of this over-confident pretender before Galth decided to take command of the *Blood Fury*. The man wasn't even ready to be second in command.

"Yes," Galth said, "three Sigali. But you've only given me two."

"You can do double duty. With your great capabilities, I'm sure you can manage it easily."

Galth's expression turned dark. "I'm not a sinking Sigali."

Beglash raised his brows, annoyance itching his insides, like something he needed to scratch but couldn't reach. What was the matter with Galth? Didn't he realize that Beglash was about to punish him?

"Perhaps I should request that you be reassigned to the Ministry of War." That would be the worst fate. Most of the men there died of old age. The chance for death in combat was almost zero.

Galth stiffened and swallowed hard. Good. About time. "Not necessary," Galth said.

"I'm glad you finally understand," Beglash said, then slipped out the door.

"Sinking worm carcasses," Galth muttered, loud enough Beglash could still hear him even in the hallway. "I'll show those prisoners what happens when they get out of control."

Beglash stopped, fingers flexing. That kind of attitude might lead to unauthorized actions, things that would diminish Beglash's haul. He already wasn't certain he had enough victims to meet the expectations of the Ministry of Ritual. If Galth started killing the leaders, he would have even less. He had to ensure that Galth didn't take his reprisals too far.

He stepped back into sickbay and smiled at Galth, just enough pleasantness to keep Galth from knowing Beglash had heard his comment. "When are the prisoners due to be fed?"

Galth dabbed the wad against his cheek, checking himself in the mirror. "Probably soon. I'll have to check the instructions." Then he glared at Beglash over his shoulder, layering a smile over the angry look. "Not my normal job, you know. So, I don't have the routines memorized."

"Good idea to read the instructions carefully," Beglash said. "Oh, and I have a few more instructions for you to add to your list."

Galth's stare turned cold. Yeah, he knew what was coming, and he wasn't going to like it.

"No 'enjoying' of the victims."

"But—"

"Not only don't we have enough crew to allow that kind of diversion, but any of the victims who fight it could be injured in the process."

Galth puckered his lips. "So?"

"If she is injured, and especially if she has lost hope, such a victim could die."

"We're going to kill them all eventually, anyway. What does it matter?"

Beglash lowered his chin, giving Galth his most stern expression. "I don't want any victim deaths. None. Understand?"

Galth's lower lip trembled. It looked to be involuntary, because the man quickly stiffened his entire face. "Got it. And if someone dies... accidentally?"

"I'll send you out the airlock."

Abgoth gasped, and even the doctor stared, but only for a moment. Then, he went back to his final healing motions. And Galth, suitably horrified, because that was not the kind of death that would get you to the Great Embrace, nodded wordlessly.

Beglash stared at Galth for another moment, unsure he had made his requirements clear enough. And there was always a chance things could get so out of control that Galth would not be able to handle it.

Clearly, Beglash needed to do one more thing. And in fact, he would combine this one action into two, let Galth understand where he was in the hierarchy, and what he had yet to achieve before he let his ambitions get ahead of his training.

Beglash tapped his hand against the door jam, hoping to look contemplative, wise. "So tell me, then, Galth," he said. "Is there anything else you should do?"

Galth's mouth opened, but no words came out. His eyes bulged and his brows drew into a tight knot.

Beglash couldn't help but roll his eyes. "Clearly, you are not ready for promotion if you can't even come up with what needs to be done next."

"I, uh..." Galth's eyes danced, as though he were looking first at one ear and then the other. Then he smiled, like he thought he had figured it out. "I should find out who is behind the escape, who organized it."

"I think you already know who that person is."

"Yes, Captain. The woman who said she was an officer."

"Very good. And now, you should bring her to me."

Galth sneered. "So *you* can enjoy her?"

"Don't be ridiculous," Beglash said. There was no time for frivolous activities like that. Too many things to do, and not enough crewmen to accomplish them. But he did need to make certain this leader of the humans understood where she fit in the scheme of things. He needed to deliver the message that escape attempts would be severely punished.

And if it took torture to get that message across, so be it.

Chapter 38 — Meeting

This was Sullivan's big chance. As the swaggering alien directed her through the corridors, she reached a hand toward her back, toward the pistol hidden there, for a moment just like this. Once she had blasted his head off, she would grab the keys and his pistol, and rush back to the others.

But the noise would be horrendous, drawing attention from other nearby aliens. They would descend on her in a hoard, and she would probably be captured or killed before she could get back to the cargo hold.

She brought her hand back around to her front. Better to use this trip as an information gathering foray. Better to plan things out and have everyone prepared for action.

She tried to construct a map of the ship in her mind. Occasional signs adorned the walls, but they were in an unknown script, and Joe had never been one to explain much.

With every step, the deck rattled, and Joe--she didn't know what else to call him--grinned, like he took delight in making as much noise as he could. It was like a rickety scaffolding, and she could see parallel hallways running on the floors above.

But there were weirder things. The light, what little there was, shone so diffusely that neither she nor Joe cast a shadow on the bulkheads. Pockets of darkness cowered in every corner, sometimes extending from the deck above them. Shortly, they came to a break in the hall, and Joe grabbed her arm and turned right heading up a flight of stairs. So far, they had followed the path Doctor Samra had described in his account of going to whatever passed for sick bay. At the next deck up, Doctor Samra had turned left, but Joe continued climbing up the zigzagging stairs. One more flight up and the stairs ended.

They turned right, walking down a new hallway. This was good. She was building a map of the ship. Doctor Samra had told her that engineering was just down the hall from sick bay. He had thought it odd, because an engine room was not the most sanitary of places, and sick bay would have never been put to so close to such a place in a human designed ship.

The hallway they were on now was short, and it ended with another staircase, only three steps before the pathway met a thick black curtain covering the way forward. Joe stomped his way up, then held the curtain aside and motioned for Colonel Sullivan to pass through.

Colonel Sullivan ascended the stairway, put both feet on the top level, and then froze. There was nothing there. No floor, no walls. Just the un-ending depth of space, stars below her, stars to the right, into the front... And men there, most in red or brown, but one of them in sky blue, standing as though they were hovering upright in the vacuum.

It had to be okay. But her legs refused to move. Maybe this was an optical illusion, or maybe she would fall into space and freeze instantly.

Something touched her back... five little spots, fingers splayed across her lats. She looked over her shoulder. Joe gave her an evil smile as he pushed.

She hopped forward, each step landing on something as solid as any floor or deck she had ever trod. She turned around to see Joe, but there was only more space, more polka-dotted black, more nothingness. The only thing that didn't look like it was in space was a small red blinking light.

A second later, Joe stepped through, chuckling as he gazed at her. "It's a test of bravery," he said. "You failed."

She gave him her best insincere smile. She wasn't in a mood to play any mind games with him, wasn't going to tell him all the things she had done that required a great deal of courage. She didn't have anything to prove. "Where's your captain?"

Joe gestured to a man standing a few yards away. "Captain Beglash."

The captain crept up to her, his eyes roving over her body, face, chest, hips and down to the boots. He was ugly, his eyebrow hairs extra-long and hanging down over his eyes, his head covered with straight, stiff hair, poking up in all directions.

By the time he stood toe to toe with her, his eyes had risen back up to her breasts, and the neon green of his irises had almost disappeared, his pupils had gotten so dilated. Then he lifted his eyes to her face and grimaced. "What is that scar?"

Relief washed over her. Her scar had saved her again, kept some awful man from wanting her, controlling her. Now, if she could just get his reaction to notch up one more bit, get him to find the whole thing intimidating…

"It was a knife fight, against a man as tall as him," she said, pointing to Joe with her thumb.

"It doesn't matter," Beglash said with a sigh that sounded disappointed. "You're too ugly to enjoy anyway."

"Oh, but it does matter. When he slashed me, it made me so angry I killed him with my bare hands."

Beglash looked her over again, this time without the lustful intent. When he finished his analysis, he grabbed her hand, dangled it by her index finger. "These little things?"

She jerked her hand away. "I'm warning you—"

"Warning?" His grin broadened, then he gestured toward his neck. "Why don't you show me how you did that, how you killed a man with nothing but those scrawny fingers?"

Damn it, he'd called her bluff. No way she could take him on, even if he was all alone. But she couldn't back down either, couldn't admit to her lie. "Return this ship to Earth and let all the captives go."

Beglash threw his head back with a hearty laugh. Joe joined in, as did several other crewmen on the bridge. That gave her another chance to look around, see what she could figure out. There were no consoles anywhere, no buttons or controls, or at least anything that looked like controls. Did they use a mental link to operate the ship? Did they have implants to transmit their commands? If that was the case, her people had no chance to figure out how to drive this thing once they took over the ship.

Then the crewman in blue lifted an object that looked a lot like an iPad and pressed his finger on a couple of spots on the screen.

She wanted to sigh with relief but held her breath so she wouldn't give away any of her feelings.

"So," Beglash said, looking delighted, though she wasn't certain why, "that's what you call your planet? Earth?"

That seemed like an innocuous piece of information, but her instincts started yelling at her not to answer the question. Can't give the enemy any intelligence. Can't.

Beglash didn't appear to mind. "And yes," he said, "we *should* go back to Earth. There's plenty more space in the cargo hold. What do you say?" He looked at Joe and a couple of the others on the bridge. "Shall we go get more?"

"Yes," Joe said, lifting his brows and grinning.

Beglash looked directly into her eyes and laughed like he was enjoying her discomfort at the idea they would pile even more victims into his ship. Make her even more of a failure as a leader. But then his expression turned grim. "Now, about the reason I called you here."

Colonel Sullivan lifted her brows. She'd thought she was here because she'd asked for an audience with him. It hadn't occurred to her that he had his own motivations. A trickle of fear carved a spiraling path through her gut.

"You and your people attacked my guards," he said. "We assume it was an attempt to escape."

The blood drained from her face, and damned if her kidneys weren't over-reacting. Worse, the look on Beglash's face told her she'd been unable to hide her fear. "That's kind of crazy, don't you think?" she said. Damn it, her voice had gone a couple of decibels softer, not the kind of confidence she had wanted to project. Time to change the subject. "By the way, it looks like you're not moving anywhere."

"You," Beglash said, stabbing a finger on her collarbone, "can go swim in the Night Sea."

Oh, sounded like she hit a nerve there. She wasn't certain what that meant, but it sounded close enough to "go to hell," that she decided that would be her interpretation. "I'd love to, if you'll come with me."

He twisted his mouth in an expression of disgust. "Why would I want to spend any time with you, when there are much more attractive women available?"

"Yeah," Joe said, "like that little temptress that tried to get my attention."

"Good," Beglash said with an evil grin. "Bring her to me."

"She has a sexually transmitted disease," Colonel Sullivan said.

Beglash scoffed. "You think I want to... soil myself with your filth?"

Yeah, she thought that, and nothing he said was convincing her otherwise.

"She's coming here to be my insurance," Beglash said. "You try another escape, and I will strip her naked, give her to every member of my crew, and when they are all done, I will kill her."

Sullivan's arm muscles twitched. Now he was talking hostages, threats to the well-being of her soldiers, actions so fowl she couldn't contemplate them. This bastard needed to be taught a lesson. "Your stupid threats won't get you anything. I don't negotiate with scum suckers."

L. D. ROBINSON © 2022

Beglash jerked forward. A loud cracking sound reverberated through the bridge, and Patrice's cheek stung like it had been pierced by a thousand small needles. The captain stepped back, returning his arm to his side, fingers still flexing.

Okay, she chided herself. Insulting him was probably not such a good idea.

"You think this is funny?" he shouted. "You think her torture… and I can tell you, some of my crew are frustrated enough they will be very inventive in how they torture… you think that is nothing to concern you?"

Such a strange question from her captor. He was appealing to her humanity for God's sake. It just didn't make sense.

A little huff escaped her lips. Damn it, again. She'd been going about this all wrong. Intimidation wasn't the answer. Instructions on how to respond if you're a hostage were to get the captors to see you as a human, maybe even develop a relationship with them. That would make it harder for the captors to kill you. And that, she realized, was something she was poorly equipped to do. Develop a relationship? She couldn't even do that with her own mother.

But she had to try. "So, Beglash… that was your name, right? Beglash?"

He blinked.

"Do you have a family back at your home planet?"

Beglash narrowed his eyes. "You're no threat to them."

"Oh, no threat here. Obviously." She shrugged. "I just wondered if *you* have people who… 'concern' you."

"That is why I am here," he said. "That is my mission."

Okay, sounded like family was important to these creatures. Maybe this was something she could work with. "You know, all of us have family, too."

Beglash ran his eyes over her. "Hah. You have a husband?"

Oh, so that was his next move. But she couldn't tell him the truth. "Of course, I do."

He stepped closer to her, then grabbed her by the chin. "Why don't I believe that?" Another pause as he gazed into her eyes. "No, you're much too cold to have a family."

"You don't know anything," she said.

"It doesn't matter." He smiled serenely as he let her go. "The needs of my family will take precedence over those of yours." He patted her cheek with his open palm, then took a step back. "Time for you to return to the cargo hold."

No, she couldn't leave yet. She didn't know enough about the ship and how to operate it. But what could she say to get him to allow her to remain?

And then, as if in answer to her unspoken prayer, another crewman, this one wearing a brown top, stepped forward and handed one of the pads to Beglash. The captain grabbed it impatiently, then glanced at the screen. His eyes opened wider for just a micro-second, just long enough to tell Patrice he hadn't liked what he saw. A moment passed, him just staring at the thing, the crewman waiting for a response. Finally, he let out a long breath, then ran his fingers through his hair.

Patrice's leg muscles tensed as she suddenly wanted to step away. Something about this captain was so… so… *creepy*.

Beglash handed the control pad back to his crewman. "You think they've spotted us?"

"You mean the Enforcers?" the brown-shirted one said.

Beglash stiffened to the point of shaking, then shouted. "Who else would I be talking about?"

Colonel Sullivan looked back at Beglash, one brow raised. "Are these enforcers giving you problems?" Damn, now she sounded condescending. That hadn't been her intent, either.

"You don't need to worry about that," the captain snapped. Then he turned to Joe. "I told you to get her out of here."

"One last thing," she said. If she could get him to start talking about himself, bragging, he might decide to leave her here a little longer, give her just those few more minutes she needed to figure things out. "I notice your shirt is red. Is that what people in command wear?"

Beglash rolled his eyes. "It doesn't matter to you."

"Of course, it does. That helps me know how to interact with your crew."

Behind her, Joe laughed.

"Or is red for officers, and brown is for enlisted? Something like that?"

"Get her out of here," Beglash said to Joe, waving a hand toward the door, his tone low and threatening.

Joe's fingers wrapped around her arm and pulled her toward the blinking red light that marked the exit.

She dug her feet into the invisible floor. "I mean, I get that red is very prestigious. What do you have to do to earn that color?" Joe tugged harder and her feet slipped across the deck. "Is blue for the science officer?"

Beglash's face turned red, and he shouted, "Get out, now! Before I kill you!"

Woah. What had she said wrong? What had set him off like that?

Her arm jerked back, almost pulling her off her feet. She scrambled to keep up, feet pumping, boot treads slipping on the invisible floor. And then, she was back in the solid ship, tripping down the short staircase, still off balance.

Joe stopped, giving her a chance to catch up, right herself. She tossed him a nod of appreciation. At least he wasn't going to drag her all the way back to the hold.

"Okay," she said.

As they walked down the hallway, Colonel Sullivan reviewed what she'd learned. She'd probably gotten way more information than the aliens would've liked. And those enforcers out there, whoever they were, sounded like space police trying to apprehend these aliens who had committed a criminal act. And maybe they could rescue all the humans.

The presence of these other aliens created a lot of questions. She turned to Joe, who walked beside her. "What happened to the captives from the first ship that came to Earth?"

Joe smiled, his expression serene, like he was in the middle of a tantric meditation. "They're all dead."

She wanted to stop walking, maybe even throw up, something to express how awful that seemed. But she didn't have the luxury to do that. She had an important mission to accomplish. "So, the enforcers never stopped that other ship?"

"We Dakh Hhargash know how to deal with Enforcers."

"Dahh what?"

"Just keep walking."

They reached the staircase and started climbing down. Colonel Sullivan reached her hand out, but then she remembered there was no handrail. Her palm pressed against the smooth, black, metallic wall and she stopped. "Are the enforcers looking for you guys?"

"Keep going."

"That's why you're hiding behind this rock, isn't it?"

"You are about to be dropped into the waves," Joe growled.

"Too many questions?"

"You are a prisoner, not a fact finder."

"Okay. Right." She continued in silence to the bottom of the stairs, and when they made the left turn toward the cargo hold, she knew her time out in the ship, and her ability to get more information, were almost over. "What about you? Do you have a family back on your planet? Children?"

"You don't need to worry about anything," Joe said with a sneer. "We will keep you all alive until we reach our planet."

"And then what happens?"

"You all die."

Chapter 39 — Small Death

The door to the cargo hold loomed ahead. Was there any more information she could get before she walked through that awful portal?

"The people on that first ship," she said, wishing she had known one of them, wishing she could speak about someone specific, "they were good people."

He nodded, like this was not anything to feel guilty about. "And they all died well."

She rolled her eyes. "Most of them were too young to die."

"They died with a purpose. Isn't that what you want?"

She glared at him. "If it's something I think is worth dying for, maybe."

He nodded. "Good."

"No. Not good. None of us are ready to just roll over and kick the bucket for any old purpose. It needs to be a purpose we believe in, something worth dying for."

His smile grew. "And you think our purpose would not fit that criteria."

"Maybe you can convince me otherwise."

They reached the door, and Joe stared at her pensively, like maybe he would consider it. Not that knowing why they were about to be killed was going to help her in any future escape attempts. Why had she allowed him to take the conversation in this direction?

But after a few seconds of thought, Joe put the key in the lock, and when he'd gotten the door open, he gestured for her to enter. She gave him one last look, afraid her feelings were all over her face, a pleading desire for someone to help them. She was starting to think she wasn't up to the task.

Remember. Friendly. Build relationships.

"So, I'll see you around, Joe," she said as she stepped through the door.

"It's Galth."

"Oh. Well, then, thank you, Galth."

A scream echoed off the walls, and Colonel Sullivan could tell just by the shrillness of the sound that another rat thing had made an appearance. Galth pulled his pistol from his belt and swung it around the room. "Everybody against the wall."

Most of the people were already standing on benches or tables scattered throughout the room. A lot of the benches were already right next to the wall, and those were full. The rat thing was on its haunches, reaching up and nipping at the edges of the bench in the corner, as though it wanted to get a bite of one of the people, but was too small to make the jump.

Galth stepped in, closing the door behind him, his gun still panning around the cargo hold. The rat thing got back on all fours, looking around. When it spotted her, it dashed forward.

"You," he said, pointing his weapon at Colonel Sullivan. "It's about to bite you. Get up on that bench."

Colonel Sullivan took two steps back, bumping into one of the tables.

"Get up there now!"

Colonel Sullivan jumped, landing her butt on the table and swinging her legs around, out of range of the rat thing.

The rat thing made a squeak of protest. Now the only remaining target was Galth. Sullivan looked at the pistol in Galth's hand, determined to learn how he fired the thing, since there was obviously no trigger like in a human weapon.

But he just stood there somberly while the rat thing slowly approached him. Then he caught Colonel Sullivan's eye. "This is how you deal with a sinking *theet*." As the rat thing sniffed his boot, he lifted his other foot and stomped it on the rat thing's tail. The animal screeched, then spun around and viciously attacked Galth's boot, teeth embedded in the leather, head moving as if it was trying to tear his flesh apart.

With his other foot, Galth tapped the top of the rat thing's head. As it started to turn toward his boot, he pressed down, smashing the tiny cranium against the hard metal floor. Bones crunched. Venom squirted from the fangs. The feet thrashed for a few more seconds, then went limp.

Galth backed away, then lifted the animal by the tail, opened a small door that had been hidden in the wall, and dropped the carcass into what looked like a tube moving downward. The door snapped shut, followed by a whooshing sound.

He scanned the room once again with his weapon, probably making sure that no one was close enough to get the jump on him, then quickly opened the door. Just before he closed it behind him, he pushed his head into the opening and looked at Colonel Sullivan with a wicked smile, like he'd just enjoyed ending some creature's life. "You're welcome."

Chapter 40 — Hunger

Colonel Sullivan climbed down from her perch. Time to get back to the business of planning an escape. She gathered her soldiers together again, allowing the civilians who had joined her before to listen in. Lorenzo sat beside Francisco and gave her a flirtatious grin. Sullivan was going to have to keep her eye on that man. Next to him, Kyle and Emily filled in the side of the circle.

Craddock sat next to her, then leaned forward, hands clasped together like he was anticipating some reward, or something he could use to his advantage. "So, what have you learned?"

She gritted her teeth and forced a smile, certain he had not intended it to sound like he was in charge, like she was reporting to him. Of course, he wasn't. But suddenly her guard was up. She glanced back at the soldiers, huddled together, all still looking a little shell shocked. "Okay, let's start with the layout of the bridge." She described the look of the place with as much detail as she could remember, where everyone stood, and the handheld pads they seemed to use to control everything.

"So, they're like tricorders?" Kyle asked.

"Thin as an i-pad."

"Touch controls?" Finley said, moving her finger like she was punching a screen.

Sullivan nodded

"There are no sticks or levers on these controllers?" Mr. Lorenzo asked.

"No," Sullivan said.

Lorenzo threw his hands into the air in a gesture of frustration. "How am I supposed to fly this thing?"

"What?" Kyle asked with disbelief. "You think you can do that?"

Lorenzo's face turned angry, and his mouth opened, but Sullivan pre-empted his verbal response. "He's a retired pilot."

Kyle nodded, but his expression was exasperated. "That doesn't mean he can just start flying this."

"Yeah? And how many spaceships have *you* flown?" Lorenzo barked.

"This is not like on the sci-fi shows on tv," Kyle continued. "You can't just sit down to a totally alien helm and operate it like you've had years of training."

"Stop," Sullivan said, hands in the air. "We need to work together, not fight with each other."

"It's just not…" Kyle said, then let out a loud sigh. "Everything is going to be a lot harder than it seems."

"That's right," Lorenzo said, nodding like he was the one who'd just been proved right. "And you gonna need someone with flight experience to try to figure it out."

"This is not like flying in the air. There is no lift and drag. You have to know orbital mechanics."

Lorenzo's mouth formed the letter "o," but he said nothing.

"Listen," Sullivan said, "it does sound like there are some issues to work out. So, after our meeting, why don't you two get together and exchange information, see what you can come up with."

They turned to each other, still frowning. Lorenzo crossed his arms over his chest and Kyle rolled his eyes.

"Gentlemen?"

They both looked back at her, then nodded reluctantly. "Sure, we can exchange information," Kyle said, "as long as he'll listen."

"Whadda you take me for, some kind of idiot?" Lorenzo hollered. Damn, that man had a pair of lungs.

"You need to listen, too," Sullivan said, staring Kyle in the eye.

"Yes, ma'am," he said, then turned to Lorenzo. "I didn't mean it like that."

Lorenzo nodded, a begrudging acceptance of an apology without words.

That was all she could ask for. Civilians. Right now, it looked as likely they would mess things up as help.

"Okay," she said then, "there was something else that happened that I thought was interesting."

She then recounted the discussion between captain Beglash and one of the crewmen about the other aliens out there, the people he had referred to as the "enforcers."

SSG Clark leaned forward, brows lifting. "You think they might be able to rescue us?"

"I don't think we can count on it," Sullivan said. "But I'm not ruling it out, either."

"Maybe if we can do something to get their attention," Sgt Harvey said.

"Yeah," Finley said. "Since the captain of this ship doesn't want to be found… that was your impression, right? He's hiding?"

She nodded.

The soldiers looked at each other, but none spoke. Still, Sullivan could sense the thinking, the excitement of her soldiers at the news of these other aliens.

"There's something else we should consider," Kyle said. "It's possible these enforcers will be worse than our current captors."

"These guys are planning to kill us," Sullivan said. "Not much worse than that."

"We just have to be ready for the unexpected," Kyle said. "I mean, what if they rescue us, but then they never return us to Earth?"

"That would suck," Finley muttered.

"Why would they do that?" Clark asked.

"Maybe they have some kind of prime directive," Kyle said. "Maybe if we've seen their technology then they can't let us go back."

"Maybe they're slavers," Finley said.

Everyone in the circle looked at each other, all silent, like they'd just heard the death sentence pronounced on them.

Sullivan ran her hand over her face. It sounded like she needed another PIR. "Finley, I need you and Kyle to come up with some way to figure out what the enforcers are going to do."

Finley's eyes got big, but she said nothing.

Until they came up with anything else, Sullivan would have to go with the assumption that the enforcers would help them out. If she could signal these enforcers, let them know where Beglash's ship was...

"Clark and Harvey, I want you two to try to come up with some way to signal the enforcers."

"Right," Harvey said, nodding vigorously.

"We don't even know what types of communications the enforcers use," Kyle said. "Could be a technology we haven't even discovered yet."

Harvey rolled his eyes. Looked like he was getting as tired of Kyle's objections as she was.

"Hey man, no technology," Harvey said. "I'm thinkin' 'bout using smoke signals."

"Oh." Kyle looked surprised, maybe a little impressed, like he didn't know how often soldiers were called upon to make do with things that were not designed for the mission at hand.

"Field expedient communications," Sullivan said with a smile.

"Yeah. Good idea."

"But like I said, any help we get from the enforcers can't be counted on. We have to figure out how to do this by ourselves."

Nods all around. Good. At least there was something everyone agreed on.

"Okay, let's go over our plan. First, we have to get out of this room, then we have to take control of the ship from the aliens, and then we have to get the ship back to Earth."

"Woah, that sounds like a lot," Craddock said.

"Let's take it one step at a time," she said. "Has anyone come up with any other ideas of how to get out of this room, or do we still just need to get another alien in here, like we did with Galth and Abgoth?"

"Seems like our only option," Clark said.

"We'll make a lot of noise when you ready to shoot him," Harvey offered. "That way, they still going to be surprised."

"Okay, agreed," Sullivan said.

"I have my fingers crossed," Mr. Craddock said.

Colonel Sullivan looked at Sergeant Clark. "You'll get the first alien weapon. I want you to be the first to fire any time we come across one of the aliens. We'll continue policing up the weapons of the fallen aliens and we'll hand them out to the other soldiers in order of rank."

Sergeant Clark nodded.

"Once we have a couple of soldiers with weapons, we'll split up. I need a team to find engineering, make sure the aliens don't do any sabotage down there, and another group to go room by room."

"Sergeant Harvey," Sergeant Clark said, "you take the group to scour the ship."

"They won't get pass me," Harvey said.

She looked at Clark again. "Mr. Craddock will show you who are the veterans in the crowd. I want as many people on each team as possible."

"Right."

"We have twelve of them, I think," Craddock said.

"Good. Anything else?" she said. She looked at Kyle, ready for him to throw more water on the plans, ready for his anticipation of doom

Kyle shook his head, his frown deeper than ever. "None of that is going to do any good unless we get more information about everything," he said. "Otherwise, just getting rid of the aliens... we'll end up in a metal coffin, waiting for the energy to run out."

"Or the food," Finley said.

"Or the air," Harvey added.

Damn, they needed to be a little more optimistic. "We'll figure it out."

"Yeah, you can do that field expedient thing," Craddock said. "You'll get it."

She bit her tongue as she looked at Craddock. God, he made her want to shiver.

She closed her eyes, worried her thoughts were becoming muddled. Maybe it was just low blood sugar. They hadn't eaten since well before they were taken into space, and it was starting to show. Maybe she just needed to refuel.

"Can someone go to the door and ask for food?" she said. "I don't know about you, but I'm feeling like I need a little fuel to carry this out."

Sergeant Clark nodded. "We're all hungry."

Emily raised her hand. "I'll go ask."

Sergeant Harvey shook his head. "Too dangerous for civilians. I should axe them."

Emily lifted her chin. "I think after our last attempt, they'll be more amenable to talking with the civilians."

Sullivan looked over Emily, uncertain. She was pretty, at least by human standards, at least as attractive as Francisco. "You still might get more than you bargained for."

"I'm so hungry," Emily said, shaking her head, "I'll take whatever I can get."

"You're sure?"

"And talking to one of them, you know, it might help me with my efforts to understand their language."

Sullivan raised her brows. That sounded like a stretch, like something Kyle would object to just on the logic of how much you could accomplish with one brief conversation. But then her stomach growled. How much of a risk was it, after all? Maybe it was worth it. Sullivan nodded at Emily. "All right. You got yourself a job."

Emily grinned. "Now?"

"Five minutes ago," Sergeant Clark said, his smile broad.

Emily jumped up and ran to the window in the door, while Colonel Sullivan watched, her fingers crossed behind her back. She imagined what they would bring, freshly baked bread and a huge, tossed salad, filled with all kinds of wonderful vegetables and maybe even some fruit.

She knew all that wasn't likely, but it was fun to hope.

Emily pulled a bench up to the door and stood on it. "Hey, you guys," she shouted through the little window.

She waited a moment, and when no one arrived, she stuck her hand through the little opening and slapped it against the metallic door. Bam, Bam, Bam. "Somebody, come over here."

"Okay," Colonel Sullivan said, "while she's doing that, let's do a sand table on our plan." She turned to private Francisco. "Can you lend me the clips out of your hair?"

Francisco nodded, slipping three bobby pins from her tresses, which now fell over her shoulders in luxurious ebony waves. And then they just keep coming. By the time she was done, fifteen pins lay on the floor.

Colonel Sullivan took them and laid them out to represent the hallways of the ship. She asked to borrow Doctor Samra's knife and cut all the buttons off of her uniform blouse. Then she started narrating the plan. "This is my team," she said, holding her first button. "We're going to the bridge." Patrice moved the button as indicated. Then she stopped and stared. "Now, what?"

"We grab the control things," Lorenzo said. "And you," he said, pointing at Emily, "help us figure out what they say."

Emily shook her head. "I don't know what you think I can do here, but it would take me years to figure out their script."

"Years?" Sullivan's voice sounded more strained than she'd intended. But clearly, such a pace would not be helpful here.

Kyle nodded at Emily, a gesture of relief, like finally he wasn't the only one pointing out the problems. "We're going to need one of the aliens to help us."

Lorenzo nodded. "Definitely. I can start punching buttons, but we're right next to a big asteroid. If I accidently move us in the wrong direction..."

She looked around, at all the civilians laying around the room, most having fallen into a state of hopelessness. That first failed escape attempt had taken a huge toll on their emotional state.

"Mr. Craddock," she said, "do we have any police in here?" She might be able to get them to do some interrogations, pull information out of the aliens they didn't want to give.

Craddock, who'd also been surveying the crowd, jerked his head around to look at her. "Um, we have a lot of bankers and lawyers. A few MBAs."

"I see." Damn it. Policing expertise would have been very helpful. She could use a lot more civilians like Lorenzo. But not guys with master's in business administration. They would just get in the way. "What about prior military service?"

"Quiet," Emily said, the word spoken with lots of air and very little vocalization, what could only be called a loud whisper. "One of the aliens is coming."

Colonel Sullivan ran her hand over the metal floor, gathering the bobby pins and buttons into a single pile that wouldn't give away that any plans had been created. Then she leaned against one of the benches, ears toward the door, pretending she wasn't listening.

"What's the problem?" the alien said. It sounded like someone Colonel Sullivan hadn't dealt with.

"We need food," Emily said. "I'm starving."

The alien's laughter echoed off the walls, and Colonel Sullivan gritted her teeth, jaw muscle twitching. She turned her head to watch the action.

"Look at you," the alien said, his hand in the small opening.

"Get your hands off me," Emily said, yanking her arm away from the door.

"You have lots of fat left under that skin," the alien said. "Lots of muscle you can use, too."

"What the heck are you saying?"

"Just don't worry about it."

"No, please. I need something."

"You'll live."

"Wait! Come back! Please."

Footfalls sounded in the hall, growing more distant.

"I'll do anything."

Colonel Sullivan sucked in a gasp. If Emily had told her she was going to say that, Colonel Sullivan would never have agreed.

The steps stopped, like Emily had suddenly gotten his attention, like he was now considering the unthinkable. But then he spoke. "I don't have time for this."

Thank God.

"I can help with the cooking," Emily said.

The footsteps grew louder. "You'll help," the alien said, his tone now different, excited, expectant. "But not like that." Shit. Back to the worst-case scenario. Keys jangled, then clunked as they were shoved into the lock. Colonel Sullivan stood and moved into position to pull Emily away and refuse the alien's disgusting desires.

"What are you doing?" another voice bellowed in the hallway. This one sounded like Galth.

The alien at the door laughed again, but this time the cruel glee was gone, replaced by nervous tittering. "I was just--" The key made another clunking sound, like he had pulled it out of the lock.

"Get back to work," Galth said.

"No, no," Emily sobbed. "Please give us some food. We're in pain in here."

She was met with silence, the kind of thing Galth liked to do, keep you waiting and guessing. Colonel Sullivan wanted to go slap him, and she grabbed the cloth of her pant legs and squeezed hard.

"Fine," Galth said, letting out a disgusted huff. Then, after a pause, he continued. "Wait here while I go get something." Then he walked away, banging his feet on the rattling floor.

That reaction surprised Colonel Sullivan. In fact, it was totally out of character. She turned to Doctor Samra. "What are the chances we can safely eat their food?"

Samra shrugged. "The question is more can we use the nutrients?"

"I suppose," Sullivan said. "As long as the amino acids are left-handed…"

He pressed his lips together in an expression that said he was both surprised and impressed. "You know a little about nutrition."

"I majored in biology in college."

"Then, why are you in the Army?"

She laughed. "You sound like my mother."

Samra got a far-away look in his eye. "I keep trying to tell my wife she can't dictate the careers of her sons."

"They almost grown?"

"My oldest recently got his MD. Going to do plastic surgery."

"You sound proud."

"Momma doesn't think it's important, that it's helping enough." He smiled, then Patrice realized he was looking at her scar.

She touched her cheek with her hand. "I could have gotten it fixed," she said. "But I thought it made me look more menacing."

"Whatever works."

She nodded. She wouldn't tell him it also served to ward off unwanted suitors, men who thought they could run her life.

Heavy footsteps sounded in the hall, then Galth called out, "You want food?" Though he didn't laugh, there was definitely a note of cruelty in his tone. "Here you go."

He chunked a small object into the room, what looked like a crust of bread, not much bigger than someone's nose. It landed on the floor with a soft tap, crumbs breaking off in all directions. All the people in the room who'd been sitting suddenly stood, staring at the unappetizing looking morsel, everyone aware that this one tiny piece would give no one any relief.

Was she supposed to do something here? Did she need to take the piece and somehow divide it into microscopic portions for everyone to share? Or should she allocate it to the people about to do some hard work, thus angering a good portion of the rest of the group.

Or would Craddock be able to come up with something better?

But then, it no longer mattered, as a rat thing dashed out of the corner and clamped down on the crust with its mouth. It turned back in the direction it had come from, feet slipping a couple of times on the smooth floor before it scrambled back to its hiding place.

Emily slumped onto the bench, pulling her knees up to her chest and resting her head on them.

Mr. Craddock walked up to her, patting her on the shoulder. "It's not your fault, young lady. These aliens are just impossible to deal with."

Chapter 41 — Questions

Beglash sat back in his leaning chair, feet up, a good position to relax in, a privileged position since no other quarters on the ship was large enough to house a lounge chair. One of the perks of finally being captain.

    He looked at his communications pad, which displayed an image of his son at the end of his recent message, in which he had recounted the happenings at the shooting competition, and how jealous the former champion had been when he was unseated. A fight almost broke out, only the military leaders stopped the two from exchanging blows, because they didn't want any potential new recruits damaged.

    Beglash had done that once, back in upper school, after the teasing he'd endured from Ramed and his gang had been especially galling. Beglash had jumped Ramed when his school mate wasn't expecting it and rammed his face against the stone wall. Broke several bones in Ramed's skull, his nose and his sinuses.

Beglash smiled at the memory, at seeing his rival cupping a hand below his nostrils.

His door chime sounded and Beglash set his communications pad to the side. Someone was probably bringing him bad news. People didn't come to the captain's quarters for trivial things, or to have a friendly conversation. Questions or concerns could be handled over the ship's communications or discussed on the bridge. Sink it, why did these disruptions always come just when he was starting to enjoy himself? "Who is it?"

A pause. Even more ominous.

Beglash jumped up and walked to the door, letting it slide open as he reached it. Then he stopped, as if he had been hit in the face.

Blue. There was nothing there but blue, like the sky over the desert of Eastern Kalda, horizon to horizon, choking and hot. "What are you doing here?" Beglash barked.

Meliq swallowed, his expression cowering, his throat moving in a frightened swallow. "I need to talk to you."

"Need?" Beglash bellowed, then stopped himself from finishing his sentence, stopped himself from insisting that Meliq had no relevant needs. Meliq was his only qualified sensor operator, and the kid who worked sensors on the off shift just didn't have the mental capacity to really get it. Bridge operations would be severely degraded if he had those two switch places.

Ramed had put the *Blood Fury* in this untenable position, and it was time Beglash finish escorting Ramed to the Night Sea. But he would have to wait until they returned to Dakhesh for that. In the meantime, Beglash had to deal with the assets he'd been given.

He had to somehow appease Meliq without angering or alienating the unspeakable.

"I'm busy." Beglash waved a dismissive hand, hoping Meliq wouldn't realize this was a lie. He had plenty of time. Nothing to do but sit around while they waited for the Enforcers to leave.

"Please, sir."

Beglash coughed. "You're showing your unspeakable training, you know that?"

Meliq looked away, glancing down the hall as if there were something there to look at. "My mother was a strong teacher."

For a second, Beglash wondered how difficult this was for the man in the blue shirt, living in a culture he was unsuited for, hated by everyone, not certain how to act or how to respond to others. But that quickly passed, and Beglash returned to his normal attitude, pure contempt. "You're off shift now? Go back to your room and get some sleep." *And get away from me.*

Meliq swiveled his head back toward Beglash, then stared at him in the eyes, those dark brown circles more intense than he'd ever realized an unspeakable could be. "How can I do my job if I don't understand what's going on?"

Currents and undertows. Meliq's caste, the unspeakables... well they were important to the society, but they had to be kept in the dark, because they were, well, unspeakable. Kind and caring and soft. If they knew what this ship was out doing, what the entire imperial fleet was out doing, they would withdraw their support to the empire. All the scientific and technological advances the empire enjoyed from the caste would be lost forever. The fleet wouldn't be able to run.

And Meliq had never been on an actual mission like this. Previously they'd only gone on patrols, pretending the purpose of the fleet was to defend Dakh Hhargashian space from invaders. Nobody ever told Meliq the Enforcers never crossed into their space. So it had all been credible, and the unspeakable had never questioned anything. But now... Meliq must have aimed his sensors at the shuttles as they were returning from Zolbon's planet. He must have seen all the captives, realized they were stuffed into the cargo bay, and wondered why they had been kidnapped.

There was no way Beglash could explain it truthfully, and lying to an unspeakable could be... problematic. All Beglash could do was distract.

"And why are you even on my ship? Who assigned you here? This is no place for... someone of your caste." Best not use the word 'unspeakable,' since many Mindoval took offense at the nickname.

It was a stupid question, and he knew Meliq wasn't aware of the rivalry between Beglash and the chief of personnel for the imperial fleet.

"I don't know," Meliq said. "And is that even relevant to my question?"

"Stop with all your big words!" Beglash barked. "You people try to act like you're superior or something."

Meliq stepped back, then stood silently, and underneath the smooth cloth of his blue shirt, his arms trembled.

And that made Beglash smile. He may be forbidden from killing an unspeakable, but accidents could be arranged, and crewmen could become casualties during a battle, and Meliq knew that. He wasn't as safe as his protection should have made him.

"Now, go back to your quarters," Beglash said. "I'll see you at the beginning of our shift."

Meliq closed his eyes. "Why have we captured all those people?"

"Waves and foam!" Beglash said, throwing up his hands in a gesture of frustration. "You don't know? They are our enemy!"

"They have no space flight technology," Meliq retorted. "Even the Enforcers don't contact them."

He shouldn't have made that claim, that the victims were enemy. But it had been the only idea that seemed to make sense, and he had blurted it out before considering how Meliq would respond. Now, sink it, he was stuck with the idea. Now, he had to defend it. Because if he admitted he had lied, well, Meliq would never trust him again. And a captain needed a sensor operator who followed his lead without ever questioning.

"Oh, but you're wrong about that," Beglash said. He didn't dare elaborate. Anything he said that could be falsified would undermine his position. Repetition was now his friend. Keep saying it until it stuck. "They are a more serious enemy than the Enforcers."

"How can that be?"

"Look, there are secrets here, understand? I can't explain it to you. You'll just have to take my word."

Meliq looked aft again, and Beglash realized his gaze was in the direction of the cargo hold. Demons of the Night Sea, was he planning to help the captives? Was he about to betray his own captain? And if he did that, could he then be executed?

How was Beglash supposed to know what he could and couldn't do with this man? Why hadn't Ramed provided an instruction manual when he'd put Meliq on this ship? It had to have been Ramed who did that. No one else in the personnel directorate of the Admiralty hated Beglash the way Ramed did.

Maybe it hadn't been such a good idea to break Ramed's head open and render him unable to serve on a spaceship, due to the aftermath of his injuries. That had all but ensured that Ramed would never become a captain, never fight the enemy in battle, never die a glorious death.

Never go to the Great Embrace.

That delightful memory, a young Ramed bawling over the blood in his cupped hands, had come back to bite Beglash, had practically disabled his ship. Now, it wasn't so enjoyable after all.

"Well," Meliq said, proffering a weak smile, "I guess I shouldn't worry about it anymore."

Beglash nodded briskly. "Right. Nothing to lose any sleep over."

"Sorry to have bothered you, Captain."

Beglash watched Meliq walk away, and once Meliq was several doors down the hall Beglash closed his door. He had no good options now.

But an uncooperative Mindoval with control pads on the bridge was even worse.

Beglash picked up his communications pad and signaled his second in command.

"Tordag," the other answered.

Beglash frowned into the camera, just to make certain Tordag understood the gravity of his next command. Then he spoke the words that would possibly cripple his ship. "Arrest Meliq and put him in the brig."

L. D. ROBINSON © 2022

Chapter 42 — An Offer

Roland Craddock left the sniveling Emily after she'd seemed to cheer up. Some people needed so much coddling. At least she'd made Craddock look good for a few seconds.

But now it was time to do something with their captors that would actually work. Some negotiation, some compromise, some trade of favors. He wasn't certain what that would be, though he had some ideas. In any case, the aliens were easy to deal with. He could always tell exactly where they were in a bargaining situation. Unlike humans, the aliens didn't try to hide who they really were.

He spent a few moments rehearsing what he would say, and then coming up with a follow-up, should the alien not give him the right answer. Finally, he figured he was ready.

He walked to the door and hollered through the little window. "Hey! I need to talk to someone!"

No one came initially, and that was to be expected. But after several minutes, the alien who called himself Galth approached the door, looking annoyed. Upset or not, Galth was a good target, a good mark. Craddock would be able to deal with him easily.

"I suppose you want food," Galth said.

Craddock lifted his chest, presenting the aura of authority the aliens seemed to respond to. "I need to speak to the captain."

Craddock had expected Galth to throw back his head and laugh, like he had for Colonel Sullivan. Instead, the alien just rolled his eyes. Craddock smiled to himself. Obviously, Galth took him more seriously than that loser of a woman.

"The captain is busy," Galth said, his expression indolent.

"The captain was willing to see the military representative. But she doesn't represent the civilians. I do that."

"Seriously?" Galth sounded like he was about to laugh. "Nobody here cares who represents the others. You're just cargo, and the last time I checked, captains don't usually negotiate with their cargo."

Craddock nodded, then lowered his voice. "Look, it's not so much that I need to talk to your captain. It's more like he needs to talk to me."

Galth stared at him, and Craddock could see the thoughts churning, the possibilities presenting themselves in the alien's mind. But then his face hardened. "And if I don't take you to him?"

"I suspect he'll be very angry."

Galth shook his head, frowning dismissively. "I don't think so."

Craddock huffed in frustration. "Then, how about I just talk to you?" If Galth was smart, he would realize Craddock wanted to speak with a little more privacy.

"I can't do anything for you."

"Don't underestimate your power," Craddock said, trying to think of how he could butter up the alien. What would he respond to? "You can be very…"

"Stubborn?" Galth ventured, brows raised like he was be proud of his intransigence.

"Determined," Craddock said.

"Don't try to flatter me.."

"I can't seem to say anything to you at all," Craddock said, then turned his back on the man. Everything Craddock had come up with beforehand had failed, and he was going to need to rethink this whole effort, develop a better strategy.

Craddock sat on a bench and rested his head against the wall. He couldn't allow himself to go down this way. Colonel Sullivan had said the aliens claimed they killed all their captives once they reached their home planet, and if she was to be believed, he had to do something to avoid that fate. But what?

He could have handled slavery, be like Joseph in the Bible, sold into Egypt only to rise to the highest levels of government. That was totally possible. But to just be summarily killed?

Maybe he should go back to helping the military, do something to aide them in their next escape attempt. But he knew it wasn't going to work. In fact, it could get him killed. These aliens knew how to run a prison, and they weren't going to make the kinds of mistakes that could lead to the success of such a rag-tag group.

He looked out the window. That damned asteroid still sat there, meaning the ship hadn't gone anywhere. This was going to take forever.

It was almost an hour later when Galth returned, unlocking the door. Craddock watched with a detached feeling. This was going to be another water delivery or something like that. Right now, Craddock didn't care about water, or food. He needed to figure out how to avoid being killed.

Galth stuck his head into the room and looked around. He caught Craddock's eye, then motioned for him to come.

Come? Craddock jumped up, excitement swelling his breast. His chance had finally arrived, and now he had to make the most of it.

Craddock followed Galth to the end of the hall, to where the stairs headed up. Galth stopped, then turned to Craddock with a threateningly angry face. It was one of those moments when Craddock knew that most other people would be intimidated by such a look, yet Craddock had no fear. In fact, he couldn't even imagine what such an emotion would be like. "What's your problem?" he said.

"Tell me what you have to say to the captain is worth his time."

Craddock nodded. "You want the escape attempts to stop, don't you?"

Galth's eyes widened. "They're planning another?"

"She won't give up."

"Waves and foam," Galth muttered.

Craddock had never heard such an odd phrase, but based on the tone of voice, he was certain he had made the right impression on Galth.

"All right," Galth said, "Follow me."

They headed the way the military woman had described, and Craddock's confidence grew. He was about to be successful. And when he reached the bridge, it was just like she described it, totally transparent, giving the impression that if you stepped into it, you would fall forever.

He didn't even hesitate. Once they were both well onto the bridge, Craddock turned back to Galth.

The alien introduced the captain, who stared with arms crossed over his chest and eyes narrowed into slits.

"Good to see you," Craddock said, letting his voice boom. It tended to intimidate people sometimes, and the captain looked like he could use a little taste of awe.

But Beglash dropped his chin, so the angle of his eyes left rings of white around the bottoms of his irises. "You have something important to tell me?"

"You guys get right to the point, don't you?"

Beglash huffed, sounding disgusted. Guess these aliens weren't going to respond to charm. They would probably be more impressed with ruthlessness. He could do that, too.

"Listen," Craddock continued, "I can tell this ship is meant to hold a lot more people."

"What do you care?"

"I can help you. In exchange for some considerations."

"Look at me," Beglash said. "Do I look like I need help?"

"Of course, you don't," Craddock said, then pointed toward the aft of the ship. "But keeping that colonel in line could be a lot easier..."

Beglash rounded on Galth. "You don't have them under control yet?"

"They are cowed," Galth said, but everyone could tell he was just saying what he thought the captain wanted to hear.

"You're so sure?" Beglash shouted.

"We defeated her last attempt," Galth said. "They know another try is pointless."

Craddock shook his head. "Look, I hate to break it to you, but that woman's got some surprises up her sleeves, and I am telling you, if you don't make a deal with me, you're going to end up dead."

Beglash rolled his eyes, then turned to Galth. "Take him back to the cargo hold. I don't have time for this."

But Galth looked pale and worried. The alien guard turned back to the captain, a tremor in his voice. "Can we promise no one will kill him when we get back to the planet?"

Craddock sucked in a quick breath. That confirmed Colonel Sullivan's suspicions, and it meant that he, Craddock, was going to have to double down on his efforts to get on Beglash's good side. He'd won Galth over, but that wasn't going to be enough.

Beglash pointed angrily at Craddock, while addressing Galth. "You really think he's going to tell you something you don't already know?" He dropped his hand, letting out a weary breath. "Besides, we need all the victims we can get."

And there it was, the opportunity Craddock needed, handed to him on a plate. "I can help you with that, too," Craddock said, lifting his arms and spreading his hands apart, a satisfied grin puckering his cheeks.

"Really?" Beglash didn't sound like he believed that.

"And I can help you with those enforcers, too."

The captain stared at him, a hint of surprise on his face, an indication that he was considering Craddock's offer. "And what... considerations... do you want in return?"

"South America. Let me be the dictator, and then I can get you all the captives you need, and you won't have to face any military opposition to get them."

L. D. ROBINSON © 2022

Chapter 43 — Lost Hope

Colonel Sullivan looked at the door, wondering what Craddock thought he could say to the captain to get them all out of this mess. Perhaps it was something good. Craddock did have a way with people.

She shouldn't be so jealous of his charm.

She sighed, then called her soldiers together. "Are you ready to go?" she asked.

"Itchin' to do it!" Harvey said.

Sergeant Clark looked a little more serious. "I can't think of anything else we can do to be more prepared."

"All right, then. As soon as Mr. Craddock gets back, we'll launch."

"Aliens coming," Private Mendez said. "Looks like Galth and some other guy I've never seen." He paused. "Uh... and a bunch of other guys."

Other guys. Sullivan repeated the words in her mind. That couldn't be good. She walked to the door and peered through the little opening. "It's the captain," she said, her volume so low she wasn't certain anyone could hear her. And he looked gruff, angry. Her stomach churned. What in the hell had Craddock done?

As the aliens approached the door, Sullivan backed away, trying to reassure herself that this might be a normal thing, that the captain might make at least one trip to the cargo hold to evaluate the quality of his captives.

Or they might be here for... recreational purposes. She looked down at her shirt, its buttons gone. In spite of her t-shirt underneath, the aliens might get the wrong idea. She grabbed the bottom corners and tied them in a knot.

The key rattled in the lock, and then the door burst open, banging against the wall with a loud *thwack*. Five men dressed in brown scrambled inside, holding their weapons like they were ready to fire. Then Beglash strutted into the room, stopping within a circle made by his guards, like a quarterback in the pocket, looking around with an angry sneer.

Even though her legs felt like they were mere worms--no bones or joints--she forced herself to walk up to the captain.

The center of his lip curled upward, showing yellow teeth.

Behind him, Galth laughed. "You do realize that that's an obscene gesture," he said between cackles.

She dropped her hands quickly. God, was that right? She remembered LTC Cooper, way back there in Chicago, approaching the alien shuttle, thinking he was surrendering while giving them the equivalent of the finger. Now she understood why they shot him.

But it didn't matter. The captain's face had gone red and his eyes burned their way through her skin. She had to say something to calm him down. "I also want to thank you for providing medical care to our injured comrade. We know you didn't have to do that."

Beglash made a quiet chuckle, a brief little huff of air that was gone almost before it began, while the anger on his face never faltered.

"Is there anything you need?" she asked.

Beglash turned to Galth, giving him a look that was as threatening as what he had given her.

Then Galth stepped forward, grabbed her by the shoulders, and spun her around so that her back was facing him. He grabbed the hem of her uniform blouse and tugged on it, forcing the knot to unravel. As it lifted, cold air rushed up her back, and sweat shivered down her spine. The barrel of her pistol jerked, slid up a few inches, and then it was gone.

Oh, God! Oh, God! Her one ace in the hole was gone. How could this have happened?

How had Beglash known?

Craddock. God damned son of a bitch had bought his life with her pistol.

She spun back around, her horror at being disarmed replaced by an unquenchable anger. "Where is Mr. Craddock?"

"Dead," Beglash said. "He became a little too impertinent for my taste."

The heat drained out of her. At least she didn't have to worry about his disloyal ass anymore.

But on the other hand, Beglash's answer could be a lie.

Beglash held out his hand to Galth, and Galth turned Colonel Sullivan's pistol over to his captain. Beglash turned the weapon over in his hands while Colonel Sullivan held her breath. It would be too much to hope that the pistol would go off while Beglash had the barrel pointed toward himself, especially since she was certain the safety was on.

"What does this button do?" Beglash said, pointing to the magazine release.

She shrugged, not that he would believe she didn't know. But then again, he might not even understand the gesture.

Beglash's stare bored into her. Then, he pressed the button. The magazine dropped to the floor, clattering on the metal surface. Colonel Sullivan flinched, but not a muscle moved in Beglash's face.

One of the guards picked up the magazine and handed it to the captain, who examined it, and then tried to put it back into the weapon... backwards. When it refused to seat, at least Beglash was smart enough to turn it the other way, and this time it clicked into place.

He looked back at Colonel Sullivan and smiled menacingly. "You won't attempt another escape," Beglash said.

"You certainly put a big dent in our plans," she said with a forced laugh.

Beglash cocked his head, lips thinning as his grimace became more pronounced. He lifted the weapon and held it up to Colonel Sullivan's forehead. "Perhaps we should see how well this weapon works."

Colonel Sullivan looked into his eyes, refusing to let her gaze move to the weapon, to its safety, trying not to let her smile give away the fact that she knew he couldn't fire the weapon now.

He held the weapon up for several more seconds, seconds that felt more like hours. If he played around with the weapon long enough, he would figure it out, and she didn't want to be around when that happened.

Finally, he lowered the pistol, but his glare was still menacing. "I should just kill you now."

Colonel Sullivan's gut jerked like she'd been stabbed with a large dagger, and her bladder was suddenly so full it hurt. Now, if he did anything else that frightened her, she didn't know if she could hold it. That would be more embarrassing than anything she could imagine.

She lifted her chin, raised her chest and threw her shoulders back. "Do what you must." At least this way, her soldiers could see that she faced death bravely.

Beglash turned to Galth. "Take her away."

As Beglash spun around and exited the room, followed by his guards, Galth grabbed her by the arm and pulled on her to follow. "Where are we going?"

"Shut up." He dragged her out of the room, and one of the guards held her while he relocked the door. Then he marched her down the hall, turning left into a side hall, all the way to the end.

He worked the door lock with its old-fashioned key, while she had the chance to look around, get her bearings. The doors in this hall, just like everywhere else on this ship, came in pairs, each directly across the hall from the other. And like the door in the cargo hold, each had a little window toward the top. And the room opposite where they were going to put her was occupied, a face peering through the little hole in the door, watching everything with brows drawn together.

His face looked familiar. Of course, it did. All these Dakh Hhargash looked alike.

Except for those dark brown eyes. Everybody else had gray or neon green eyes. The only brown eyes she'd seen was that kid on the bridge in the blue shirt. Was that him? Why would he be down here? And was he locked in there, or was that just his quarters?

Galth swung the door open, then stepped back. "Your new home."

She glanced at the face in the opposite room but couldn't make eye contact. No way to tell what was going on with him.

As Galth pushed her inside, she grabbed the front of her uniform blouse and pulled it together. Damn, all this excitement about the gun and she'd almost forgotten her other vulnerability.

But Galth didn't even look at her. "You can do all the escape planning you want to in here," he said. The door slammed, echoing off the walls, sending a shuddering tremble through her. And then his footsteps sounded, growing distant.

Relief that he wasn't going to attack her lasted only a split second. No time for things like that. She had to come up with her next step.

Colonel Sullivan glanced around the dark room. The only furnishing was a small bench, maybe wide enough to seat three, complete with its splinter infested top and rickety legs. The corner floor slanted downwards just a bit, to a metal grate, all so any liquids on the floor would drain away. At least here, she had some privacy.

Once she'd relieved herself, she waited several more minutes, until she couldn't hear Galth anymore. Now, it was the time to make her move. If she could get this guy across the hall to help her... assuming he was a prisoner, too. It certainly seemed that way. None of the other doors in the ship had these little windows. Only the rooms where people were imprisoned.

Standing on tip toes, she looked through her door window, directly into the window across the hall. The man who had been there was gone.

Well, that made sense. Once Galth had closed her door, there was probably nothing left to see. The man with the blue shirt and brown eyes had probably sat down.

"Hey, you across the hall," she called in a loud whisper.

She waited, but nothing happened.

"Hey, come talk to me."

His bench creaked, responding to a shift in weight. She held her breath. And then his face appeared in the door, eyes angry. "I'm not a traitor." He spat the words at her, then turned away.

Well, so much for that idea. She was on her own.

Chapter 44 — Lies And Reassurances

"Of course, she wasn't afraid," the sinking human man said, standing on the bridge like he owned the place, like he was the captain as he pointed at the weapon Beglash now held in his hand. "The safety is still on."

Beglash really wanted to break his agreement with this Mr. Craddock, but he stood to gain too much by following through. Maybe he could just punch Craddock in the nose. That would give Beglash the satisfaction, while he could still garner all the prestige of his little coup.

"Are we clear about what's supposed to happen next?" Beglash said.

"I got the whole script memorized," Craddock said, giving Beglash a smile that did nothing to make the captain more comfortable.

And what was this script thing he was talking about?

"Helm," Beglash said, "move us out of this rock ring."

"It's called the asteroid belt," Craddock said.

"Do you think I care?"

"Sorry," Craddock said.

Time to just ignore the man. The *Blood Fury* was now heading out of the system, acting like they thought they could get away without the Enforcers spotting them, even though being spotted was exactly what they wanted. And in just a moment, the enemy ship made a quick turn and headed in their direction.

"The Enforcers are asking for communication," one of his crewmen said.

"Project it a few feet ahead."

The figure of an enforcer woman now sat facing him. He'd seen images of them, but this was his first live encounter with one. All the little frills around the edges of her ears were moving like they were being blown in a breeze. And of course, it had to be a woman. The sinking Enforcers did things like that just to annoy him. It somehow took all the glory out of the encounter.

"Dakh Hhargashian ship," the Enforcer woman said, her posture stiff and her tone formal. "You will immediately return your prisoners to Earth."

Beglash rolled his eyes. "You don't know what's going on."

"If you're trying to claim that you have no prisoners--"

"Not at all. But we have negotiated an agreement with Earth."

The Enforcer woman jerked back her head, as though she had been slapped. "I judge that to be very unlikely."

Beglash waved confidently at Craddock who stepped forward with a casual air. "Good morning, or evening... Whatever it is on your ship."

The Enforcer woman leaned forward, and the expression on her face turned puzzled, as though there was something she didn't understand. "Who are you?"

"Roland Craddock," he said. "I am a representative of Earth's governments and the agreement my dear Captain Beglash mentioned does in fact exist."

"That makes no sense," the Enforcer woman said. "We understood that the bulk of your government is centrally located. How would a representative of such a government just happen to be one of the people taken captive?"

This was an unexpected question, and Beglash held his breath to see how well Craddock could answer it.

"It's simple," Craddock said. "After the last attack, we were sure these aliens would return and attack again. So, several dozen men were designated to be representatives, and we were placed around the globe in locations we thought were likely to be attacked next time. And once the news came that the aliens were returning, I was able to make my way to the location of the attack and arrange to get myself taken captive."

The Enforcer woman's lips thinned as she pressed her mouth closed. "Why would you have allowed yourself to be captured? Isn't that a dangerous move?"

"Well the aliens never made any kind of contact with us in their previous attack. We figured the only way to get in touch with the leader from the alien's culture was to get onto one of their ships."

"I see." She didn't look convinced, but she was no longer arguing. "And now, what kind of agreement do you have? Is it an alliance?"

"Not exactly," Beglash broke in. They hadn't discussed this part either, and Beglash wanted to make certain Craddock didn't make claims they would be unable to fulfill.

One of the other Enforcers came up to the woman they were talking to and whispered in her ear. She frowned, eyebrows drawing together.

"So, what is your name?" Craddock said, a smile on his face that Beglash was certain wasn't sincere.

"The transmissions we're receiving from your planet don't include any information about an agreement."

Waves and foam. If the Enforcers were listening to the inhabitants of Earth, then it would be impossible for either he or Mr. Craddock to get anything by them.

"Of course!" Craddock said, raising his hands to his sides like he was about to hug someone. "The information about this agreement hasn't been provided to the media yet. You know how that is. You can't let the details out until the deal is finished. Otherwise, you may be giving away some of your advantage in the negotiation process."

"But they do not even indicate discussions going on."

"Right. Of course. Look, I don't know how reporters are on your planet, but on mine, once we let on to them that this is happening, they're going to have questions up the wazzoo."

"Up the what?"

Beglash chuckled to himself. Clearly the enforcers were prudes, because he could imagine several places to stuff things up that were unpleasant and to be avoided.

"But I can assure you the governments of Earth are very anxious to deal with our new friends. We have a lot of things we can accomplish together."

The Enforcer woman lifted her brows, then turned her stern gaze to Beglash. "You must not provide these creatures with any of your technology."

Beglash grinned. "Never been part of the deal."

Craddock stuck his thumbs into his belt, the smile on his face more confident than ever. "You can leave our solar system now."

"I want confirmation of this agreement."

"You'll get it. Don't worry."

The Enforcer woman shuddered, the frills on her ears stiffening, but then her image blinked out of existence. The other crewmen on the bridge cheered.

Beglash grinned. They had actually pulled it off, outwitted an Enforcer. Beglash's restraint in not killing Craddock had paid off, and now he had accomplished something no other Dakh Hhargashian captain had ever done. It was time for a small celebration. "You've done your part," Beglash said to Craddock. "Now, you shall receive your reward."

Chapter 45 — New Plan

Sullivan's eyes had finally adjusted to the dark, but there wasn't much to see, even then. She moved the little bench up against the wall, then dropped her butt onto the hard surface and closed her eyes. Continue to plan? With what? How?

Of course, Galth hadn't really meant that she should continue to plan, but she still needed to continue to do it. Not only that, but she needed to come up with side plans, for when things went wrong. But she didn't have a clue what any of that should be.

She leaned her head back and let out a frustrated breath. The only thing she could come up with now was still... still that man across the hall. That alien who knew all the information she needed, who knew she wanted to talk him into helping her, but who insisted he would never be a traitor. She needed him to show her how to read the alien's language and operate their equipment. God, she needed him, like she had never needed anyone else in her life.

No, she just needed to stop thinking of him in this way. The likelihood that she could get any alien to assist her, even under extreme duress, was so low it had run down the drain with her urine.

And even if he agreed to help, she still had to get them both out of their cells. Just exactly what plan did she have for that?

She brought her fingers to her nose, right between the eyes, where a headache threatened. Now, she didn't even have anyone to talk ideas over with.

She wrapped her arms around herself. She was so hungry. Mama would have cooked a scrumptious dinner when Patrice came home exhausted from a hard day's work. God, she missed that woman.

She missed people.

She'd never realized before how helpful it could be to have someone with whom to talk ideas through.

The room blurred and she blinked several times. Even an unimportant person would have been helpful.

Shit, solitary had gotten to her worse than she'd expected. She needed to get back to planning.

Planning? Right. Like that was going to work. These aliens were too competent. She could never beat them.

A rock materialized in her throat, cutting the cartilage right at the bend of her neck.

She had to stop thinking like this. She had to distract herself from her problems, at least until she got her emotions under control. But even that was hopeless. What was there here that she could use to distract herself with?

Well, there was the guy across the hall.

She walked to the door, then spoke in a loud whisper. "So, what are you in for?"

No response. That was probably just as well. She didn't need another man to betray her, like Craddock. Just thinking about him put the color back into her face. She needed a fan to cool her skin. If she saw him now, it would take all of her self-control not to kill him with her bare hands.

She leaned against the door and closed her eyes, and a part of her shuddered. Was she capable of killing someone? All this time in the military she'd trained with her pistol, shot targets on the range, even imagined what it would be like to point the thing at an enemy and pull the trigger, but she'd never done it personally. Never had to.

How hard could it be?

Her sister had jokingly called her a "trained killer" once. But did she have the guts to actually do it? Would her respect for life suddenly rear its head and make her hesitate when she was close enough to look her target in the eye? And would she feel wracked with guilt afterwards?

"Hey," she called out to him again. "You ever killed someone?"

The bench in his room scraped against the floor with a loud complaint, which probably meant he'd gotten up faster than normal. Then he was at the door, eyes burning. "What are you talking about?"

"Just a question."

"Never." He huffed, looking away.

His response didn't make sense. These guys were all like, you know, Klingons or Sardaukar, ruthless little killing machines with nothing else on their minds.

"Galth has," she said. "I'm pretty sure a lot of the others have, too."

"How do you know that?" He spit his words at her, like this was such a terrible accusation. His anger just didn't compute.

"I watched it," she said. "I saw them turn on their little energy weapon and burn one of my fellow officers to ash."

His eyes widened for a split second, a little micro-expression that she interpreted to mean he was surprised and didn't want to admit it. Not like the others at all. Maybe his shirt color did indicate something different about him. Maybe that was why Beglash had been so angry when she'd asked about the color blue.

Maybe she could talk this guy into something.

"And Galth keeps telling me that when we get to your planet, they're going to kill us all."

"No," the alien said. "That can't be right."

"Well, if you mean that's the wrong thing for them to do, I'll agree with you there."

"I mean he had to be lying to you."

"Why would he do that?"

The alien let out a little sigh, eyes cast downward. "I don't know."

Why were the aliens doing any of this? Why did they want a bunch of people, just to kill them? Why had they gone to so much effort, including sustaining casualties, for such an unfathomable reason? She leaned against the door, wanting to breathe out her exasperation. "Well, if they're not going to kill us," she said, "what have they kidnapped us for?

The only answer she got was silence.

"I mean," she tried again, "none of this makes any sense."

"Yeah."

Had he just agreed with her? She gave the air a celebratory fist bump. It might not be much, but this

L. D. ROBINSON © 2022

could be a turning point. "So, what's your name?" she asked.

Silence. Oh, great, he was going to be like Galth and not want to tell her anything. She scratched her fingers against the door like she was trying to dig her nails into the metal.

"Meliq," he said tentatively.

She gasped, straightening and lifting herself onto her toes. "Nice to meet you. I'm Patrice."

"I think I shouldn't be talking to you."

She nodded. She should probably give him a little time to get comfortable with what they had done so far. Or let him get uncomfortable with the silence. "I understand."

How long could she wait? She was running out of time. She needed to keep pushing this.

She didn't dare.

She didn't have a choice.

"Do you have a family?" she asked.

"I'm not a traitor," he said, followed by a loud bang. Sounded like the bottom of a boot slamming against the door.

"Sorry."

She let out the sigh she'd been holding. There had to be something else she could do. She was the commander, and it was up to her.

She closed her eyes again, trying to clear her mind, but all she could see were the desperate faces of the civilians in the cargo hold, people she was supposed to rescue. It didn't matter anymore, did it? She was going down with all of them, and that was going to be mission failure.

Damn. She was exhausted.

Maybe a little sleep would help her mind recover. She slipped off her uniform blouse and wadded it into a pillow. It wasn't doing much for her anyway, since all the buttons were missing.

Now, all she could hear was her own breathing. She let out a long sigh, an attempt to distract herself, to get herself to relax. Didn't seem to be working.

Scratch, scratch.

She straightened. There were rat things in her wall, and she had to be careful to avoid them. She would have to sleep on this awful, splinter filled bench, or she could end up dead.

A shivering thrill rushed through her arms. The rat things were a possible weapon. Venom. Deadly and quick acting, and if she could keep the aliens from accessing their own anti-venom, she could do away with several of them, and the others would have no idea. Unlike her pistol, injecting a little venom would be silent.

Now, all she needed to do was coax one of the rat things into her cell.

Chapter 46 - Fangs

She walked back to the door. "Hey, how often do we get fed in here?"

His response was a loud sigh. "I don't know."

Guess he hadn't been in here that long, either.

Well, if real food wasn't coming soon, maybe she could find something else to offer the *theets*, something that used to be alive. If the little animals were hungry enough… She pulled her wallet out and looked it over. It was made of eel skin, but it had probably been treated with so many chemicals that it would be unrecognizable as a biological object. The same was probably true of her leather holster. Still, she had to give them a try.

After placing these two items on the floor, she waited another half hour. There were no takers. Perhaps if she roughed up the leather a little bit, the odors of the leather's former biological identity would tempt the creatures.

She took out her small pocket-knife, once again amused that the aliens had never made a thorough search to dispose of any potential weapons. Perhaps that was because they usually kidnapped only civilians, people who didn't ordinarily carry anything dangerous.

She popped open the blade, then shook her head as she gazed at the tiny length of sharpness. This one was probably not lethal, anyway.

She ran the blade across the side of the holster, scraping away the beautiful finish and leaving crumbled leather in its wake.

The rat thing stuck its nose through a crack in the wall and sniffed. Then, the nose disappeared. She waited several more minutes, but nothing happened.

It was time to get serious.

Again, she took out her knife, then pressed the point to her thumb and gritted her teeth. A little pain now would be a lot better than dying later. She just had to remember that, so she wouldn't chicken out.

She pushed on the blade, and jagged spikes of pain shot through her. As she withdrew the blade, she beheld a satisfying amount of blood. Reaching her thumb out, she let it drip onto the floor, squeezing the appendage to force more blood out of the cut. The blood pooled, surface tension causing it to bead, the dim light reflecting off the surface in a bright slash.

Finally, she took a $20 bill out of her wallet and wrapped it around her wound, then lifted her boots back onto the bench, positioning herself to leap down as soon as the rat-thing was in place. Her thumb throbbed, demanding way more attention than it deserved.

L. D. ROBINSON © 2022

They better come this time, because I don't think I can cut a chunk of my skin out. She just had to remain still, so she wouldn't register in the creature's visual cortex. She would have to become a statue.

She waited. The muscles in her legs complained and her knees shuddered. Her back howled. She was probably dehydrated, very hungry, blood sugar definitely low. Having been very successful at keeping her body lean, she didn't have a lot of fat to burn in this kind of situation. But all those problems were no worse than the cut in her thumb, and she didn't want to have to do that again if the rat things decided dried blood wasn't to their taste.

Her eyelids were getting heavy. Sleep would feel so good. Yes, it was just what she needed. Darkness descended, until all that was visible was a blurry slit at the bottom of her vision. She put her hands against the cold metal wall, willing herself to remain standing.

The soft shuffle of tiny feet moving across the floor snapped her back to full attention. There it was, the biggest rat thing she had ever seen, calmly lapping at the blood.

In spite of its size, this rat thing looked very thin, though it was difficult to tell through all the dull gray fur.

Colonel Sullivan steadied herself, making careful note of the rat thing's position, and where her feet needed to land.

And she had to do it now. The rat thing had almost completed its meal.

She sprang off the bench. Her right foot landed just where it needed to, clamping the rat thing's tail to the floor. But her left foot slipped off the edge of the shoulders. The rat thing screeched, then spun around, it's spine curving unbelievably into a C shape, a level of flexibility that few earth animals had. The rat thing sunk its teeth into her boot, head writhing as if it was trying to tear the skin in multiple directions. So far, it hadn't gotten through the leather around her leg, but in another few seconds it would tear a hole in her boot.

She stuck the toe of her other boot between the rat thing's body and her leg, then pried the animal away. It made a strange growling sound, high-pitched, but clearly angry. She quickly turned her foot again then pressed down on the rib cage. Crunching sounds accompanied the collapse of the animal's torso, and legs flailed helplessly. A moment later, the rat thing's protruding eyes went from shiny to dull, then sunk into the skull.

She remained there for a moment, shaking from the adrenaline rush. She'd done it. But her feet were killing her, and she sat beside the dead creature.

Just a little bit more, she told herself. She needed to finish the job before the animal began to decompose. Plus, it would give her time to process the adrenaline. She certainly couldn't sleep in the condition she was in now.

Holding the carcass over the slit in the floor that passed for a toilet, she ran her pocketknife across the front of the neck, severing what should be the largest blood vessels easily accessible, assuming the similarity in the animal's physiology went all the way into the circulatory system. A satisfying flow of blood poured into the toilet.

Once that was finished, she lay the animal on the bench, then straddled the other end of the wooden seat. Just like back in her anatomy class, she cut open the skin underneath the jaw, carefully pulling it away until she found the sacks of venom. Now came the most delicate operation, removing the entire venom system. She grabbed one of the fangs and moved it from side to side, listening carefully as bones and cartilage cracked. In a moment the fang was loose. Now all she had to do was remove the gossamer tissue that held the tubing between the venom sack and the fang in place. She drew a line with the point of her knife backwards toward the venom sack, but then a little tremble twisted the knife and cut the duct.

She jerked her hands back, not certain if the venom could be absorbed through the skin, especially where her thumb had recently been cut.

She cut off a piece of fur and laid it over the leaking venom tube, wiping away the liquid. Now, she had to try again, but her hand was still shaking.

She closed her eyes. Maybe her problem wasn't adrenaline. Maybe it was hunger. The meat of this little rat thing was probably edible, even uncooked.

The thought made her stomach jerk and she popped her eyes open. She wasn't that hungry.

The glint of a dark eye flashed from the corner. Another rat thing. Maybe they were cannibals, especially considering how hungry they all seemed to be. If she messed up on cutting out this venom system, she could just leave a piece of rat thing meat on the floor and try again.

She let out a sigh of relief, then went to work. Her hands moved with precision, and in a moment, she had the entire apparatus removed, intact.

She dropped a glob of rat meat on the floor, then got herself back into position. In a moment, another rat thing ventured into her room. She repeated the entire process. Three complete venom systems were ready to go.

Now she just had to wait for an alien to come along, to give her water, or maybe food.

Chapter 47 — Attack

Colonel Sullivan placed the three venom injection systems on the end of the bench, then took off her uniform blouse and laid it over them. Now, she should be able to get some rest.

She positioned herself back on the bench, lowering her head next to the fabric, and as soon as she closed her eyes, she was out.

Keys rattling in the door startled her awake. She sat up, as something sharp stung her forearm. "Ow." A large splinter had lodged just under her skin. Better that than a rat-thing bite! And it was big enough she didn't need tweezers to grab hold of it. The spot bled for a moment. Damn, now that she didn't need any more blood to entice rat things in, she was bleeding all over the place.

The door popped open, and Beglash stepped into the room, hand at his belt and lustful grin on his face.

"What are you doing here?" Colonel Sullivan asked as she came to her feet.

He closed the door with a loud *clank*, then leaned against it, stuffing the keys back into a little bag that hung from his belt. "You know, I've been thinking."

"That would be a first," she said.

"I've come to realize how resourceful and clever you are," he said. "And for some strange reason... I just don't know why..."

She sidled up to the spot where her shirt lay on the bench, aware that he was staring right at her breasts. "If you think I'm so resourceful, you shouldn't be in here."

"Now, even that scar on your face is beautiful."

"You'd better leave, now."

"I will," he said, then grinned. "After I'm finished."

She grabbed her uniform blouse, grateful that she had placed everything just so, and now she had her fingers around one of the fangs, hard and cold as it curled around her skin. She held the blouse up to her chest.

Two steps and he had crossed the small room. He grabbed her head with both hands and pulled her toward him, then planted his lips on hers. This was gross, but that didn't matter. She moved her arm around to the side, then let the blouse drop, exposing her weapon. Arm sliding up his back, she carefully placed her fingers around the fang, the venom sac wrapped in her palm. He moaned and pressed himself closer to her. His hips gyrated. She moved her lips, nibbled at him to keep him distracted.

His hand slipped under her t-shirt, his warm flesh running up her back, thumb riding up her side, ready to slip around the front.

Don't flinch.

One last check to make certain her aim was good, she moved her hand until it rested at the meaty part of his shoulder, right where it met his neck. She plunged the fang into his skin, then squeezed the venom sack.

He jerked back with a yelp, then swatted at the back of his neck, hitting her hand with a sharp *smack*. The fang and venom sack dropped to the floor with a *tick*. He took two steps back, sucking in a breath.

"Demons of the Night Sea," he said under his breath, then looked at her angrily. "What are you..." The last word came out breathy, strained. He grabbed at his throat, his eyes grown wide as his mouth opened and closed, like a stranded fish searching for water, for breath, but unable to get anything. His eyes darted around the room and he lunged toward the door, cheeks red, hand shaking as he grasped the key.

It fell from his fingers, clattering on the floor, and then his knees buckled, and he leaned forward, cheek against the lock. She must've given him an extra-large dose. The venom was acting much more quickly than what she had seen before.

She kicked the key across the room.

"No," he wheezed, face plastered against the dark metal, lips now gone a faint blue color, fingernails scratching the wall like he would claw his way out of the cell.

Her stomach twisted and she took a step backwards as he toppled onto the floor, legs flailing, back arching. God, she was just standing there letting him die. Her own breath faltered, as if she were vicariously dying with him. This was worse than she had ever imagined it would be.

She turned her back, covering her ears with her hands, willing the struggle to be over. When she closed her eyes, a vision of his iridescent irises stared at her, pupils dilated, begging her for help.

Already, beady eyeballs peered out from under the walls.

She turned to look at him. He lay on his back, hand over his chest, mouth open, still alive. A tear slid down his cheek. "My son," he wheezed.

My son? Beglash was not simply her enemy. He was a father. Oh, god, a father, who was never going to return to his family, never again going to hold his son in his arms and play with him, never again going to teach important life lessons or joke with his child, never again going to admire his offspring or tell him how important the child was to him.

An image of her own father flashed in her mind, dim and uncertain, it'd been so long since she'd seen him, so many years of yearning for him to return, to play with his little daughter, to validate her worth, to tell her he loved her.

God, she had just killed some innocent child's dad. She had destroyed not just one life, but two.

She had to save him. She rushed to the corner where the keys lay, snatching them off the floor. But when she looked back at Beglash, his eyes had dried out, their sparkle now only a memory, the orb collapsed into his head. His skin had a strange sheen to it, like a plastic doll, and the expression of terror on his face had softened as muscles, sagged.

She drew her hands up to her chest, clutching her heart as her own pain squeezed her ribs. The keys dropped back to the floor, and tears streamed down her cheeks.

It only took a second, though, and her agony morphed into anger. She turned on him, face hot, huffing like her breath had turned to fire.

"How *could* you?" she said. How could he have been a better father than her own? How was it that his last thought was of his child, caring in a way that her father never did. There he lay, this alien, now suddenly an emblem of the importance of life, of people, of relationships.

Damn him!

She kicked the body, seeing her own father lying there, worthless and inattentive. "Son of a bitch!" she screamed, then slammed the tip of her boot into his ribs. He barely moved.

And that made her even more angry. "Fucking asshole!" she shouted, this time ramming his chest with the heel of her boot. His ribs crunched.

"Damned bastard! Damned!" she bellowed, screaming her frustration at the realizations she didn't want, the revelations she couldn't bear.

She lifted a trembling hand to her mouth as sobs formed there and all the pain of her abandonment rushed in at her. She wanted to cry out, beg her father to come back. And she wanted him to see her now, see how successful she was, see how proud of her he would be.

The emptiness of the room taunted her. She lifted her head, pressing lips together, and the steely edge of anger slipped back into her mind. No way she was going to let this dead captain stand in her way.

No way she was going to let her missing father ruin her life anymore.

No way she was going to let all that misery from the past distort her life, her very purpose, a purpose she could see clearly for the first time. She wasn't here on a faceless mission, to rescue nameless people, mere pieces on a life-sized chess board, objects to garner her a good grade, an outstanding evaluation report. God, they were all people, people who had relationships, who meant something to other people, who constituted someone's whole purpose in life.

And she loved them all.

Her heart ached for them, abandoned in the cargo hold without any hope, abandoned by her. Dear Mrs. Steiner with her gnarled fingers and her gray bun, Kyle with his cogent concerns about how to proceed, Mr. Lorenzo with his inappropriate lust. Yes, even Mr. Lorenzo. They were all worthy of rescue.

She had to get back there. She had a mission, a new mission, a much more important mission.

A rat-thing slipped out of its hiding place, hesitating as it seemed to look for a way to the feast without coming too near her. She stepped away from him, and the creature scurried up to Beglash's nearest arm and tore into the flesh.

She took a shuddering breath, then donned her uniform blouse, stuffing the three venom systems into her front pocket. She wasn't sure if the one she'd used still contained enough venom for a second strike, but she wasn't willing to leave it either. Then she retrieved the keys and snatched Beglash's weapon from its attachment strap. She pointed it at the rat-thing.

Feeling the weapon in her hand, she tried to imagine what the firing mechanism was. No trigger. In fact, the only time she'd seen the weapon used, she hadn't detected any motion of the man's hand. If this was somehow controlled by an implant in the mind, or telepathy, she was screwed.

But there was a button just above where her thumb rested. She eased her thumb up and pushed lightly. A blue beam of energy leapt from the weapon, frying the little creature mid bite.

Nice. These weapons weren't point weapons like what she had trained on, where you had to have a direct hit. The energy beam spread ever so slightly, meaning less accuracy was required. She could do this.

With a new sense of self-confidence, she left the room, locking the door behind her.

Chapter 48 — On the Offense

The side hall was short, and there were no aliens here now, but she could hear footfalls in the distance. Where could she hide? The doors were only recessed into the walls by a few inches. Maybe she should've taken Beglash's clothes and disguised herself as an alien. But stupid tricks like that only worked in the movies.

She got to the end of the hallway, where it T'd onto the main corridor. There, she stopped and listened, her back against the wall, energy weapon held up, ready to fire at the least provocation.

When there were no sounds, she slipped around the corner, then headed toward the cargo hold.

Hard, rattling footsteps echoed in the hallway behind her. They sounded close, and she needed to find a place to hide. Off to the side was a stairwell going down, and she crept into it then slipped down the stairs as softly as possible.

Once she'd hit the landing, she stopped and listened. Below her, there was nowhere to go. The stairwell ended at an airlock.

"No, they wouldn't dare," an alien said.

"I suspect that woman has trained her subjects well." It was Galth's voice, with a tone of respect Colonel Sullivan had not heard before. "She'll want them to continue their mission."

"Speaking of her, should we drop by her cell and give her some of this food?"

"We need to wait. I think Beglash plans to kill her."

Colonel Sullivan shuddered. It was good to know she had stopped those plans. But it also meant any other aliens who spotted her would think nothing of finishing the job.

"Get away from the door!" Galth shouted. Keys jangled as they turned in the lock.

"Food!" someone shouted. Sounded like Sergeant Clark.

"Not much here, so dole it out carefully."

People yelled, feet shuffled on the floor. "Stop pushing," one of the captives yelled.

"Stand back," Sergeant Clark shouted. "You'll all get your fair share."

Colonel Sullivan waited nervously, while the two aliens headed back down the hallway, until it sounded like they had turned up the stairwell.

Letting out another breath, she slipped around the corner of the bend in the stairs, then tiptoed up. She pulled the keys from her pocket, then realized there were six of them, all different. She would have to cycle through them all.

The first one wouldn't even go in. The second slipped in but wouldn't turn. Again, the third refused to enter the lock.

More footsteps.

Dammit. She grabbed the three keys she had already tried, then slipped back down the stairwell. These footfalls didn't sound like they were approaching, so Colonel Sullivan crept back up to the top step, then peeked around the wall. Two aliens sauntered down the hall, passing from one shadow to the next, then walked into a room.

Quickly back to the door, she took the fourth key and slid it in the lock. It turned.

She pushed the door with her shoulder and slipped inside, closing the door quietly and re-locking it. Her soldiers stood in a small circle, mouths agape.

"You got one of those blasters," Sergeant Harvey said.

"Quiet."

Mrs. Steiner walked up to her stiffly, as though it was hard to bend her knees. "What happened to Mr. Craddock?"

"I think he was the one who betrayed us."

Mrs. Steiner's brows pulled together, and she shook her head. "But he was such a nice man."

"In my experience, a sociopath can be very charming."

"That's not... not..." She looked so confused, Colonel Sullivan wanted desperately to explain things to her. But this wasn't the time.

"It doesn't matter. We've got to get out of here before they kill us all." She turned to Sergeant Clark. "Get the teams together."

"Right."

Then she turned to the mass of civilians. "I'm looking for people with prior military experience.

Preferably Army or Marines. Combat experience, infantry, anything like that."

Several men raised their hands, scruffy-looking guys, with beards and long hair, and guts hanging over their belts. But no, that wasn't the way to look at them. They were tough looking guys, with tattoos and leather jackets and solid determination in their eyes. Clark motioned for them to join him.

"Ma'am," Kyle said. He'd come up beside her so quietly she almost gasped at his approach.

"Yes?"

"The ship has left the asteroid belt. Looks like we're headed out of the solar system."

She looked out the window, where all she could see were distant stars. "Damn." Then she patted him on the arm. She needed to keep this guy beside her. He seemed to know what was going on more than anyone else. "Go tell SSG Clark you're on my team."

"Right."

Once the teams were assembled, Colonel Sullivan gave the soldiers a quick briefing on what she knew about the alien weapon. Then she gave the keys to Mrs. Steiner. "Keep it locked, so no aliens can get in. We'll come back and get you once the ship is secure."

Steiner nodded nervously, stuffing the keys down her blouse front until they settled between her breasts, resting on the bottom strap of her bra.

Colonel Sullivan smiled. "I like your hiding place."

"These things can come in handy sometimes," Steiner said with a wry smile.

"One more thing," Colonel Sullivan said, handing Mrs. Steiner a walkie-talkie. "I'm going to put you on channel three."

"Oh, gracious. What do I do with it?"

"Just keep an ear out. If something doesn't go the way we planned, I may need you to send me help."

Mrs. Steiner nodded, looking doubtful. "Whatever."

Colonel Sullivan turned to the little army she had formed, then gave Doctor Samra a smile. "Let's hope we don't need your services."

"Fingers crossed," he said.

"Let's go."

She stepped into the hall, then motioned for her team to run past her to the stairwell where she had hidden before. She ran there herself. And just in time. Footsteps ricocheted off the metal walls as someone entered from the opposite stairs and walked toward them. But before he'd reached them, the sounds changed. He had gone down one of the side halls. "Captain? Are you finished?" The alien's voice echoed in the short hallway.

He was about to discover his captain, deal. No more time to wait. Colonel Sullivan dashed out of her hiding place and sprinted to the side hall.

"Captain?"

She slid to a stop, then pointed her weapon and fired. The alien barely had a chance to look in her direction before he slammed into the wall, then slid his back against the smooth bulkhead and dropped into a clump on the floor, a giant blackened hole in his upper chest.

Damn, these weapons were efficient. And the results were... messy, awful.

"You killed him!" a voice said. It had to be Meliq, still locked in the cell opposite hers.

Damn. Now there was a witness, and she needed to figure a way to keep him from raising the alarm.

Assaulted by the smell of burning hair and oil, she had to force herself to run up to the dead alien. Many more killed and the entire ship would reek. The other aliens would quickly figure everything out. And she didn't even have keys anymore, so she couldn't lock the corpse in with the captain. If someone came across it, they would raise the alarm. Her only hope was that this deck had only a small amount of foot traffic.

She slipped the weapon from the alien's belt and hurried back to the group, meeting Sergeant Clark on the way. She slapped the pistol into his hand. "Your weapon. Now, I need you to go back to the cargo hold, get the key, and let this guy out." She pointed to Meliq.

He nodded but looked confused.

"Hide the corpse in his cell, then give the keys back to Mrs. Steiner, and bring him up to the bridge."

He nodded, then hurried away.

She bit her lip. Damn, things were already getting complicated, and Meliq was a wild card who could tip the balance in either direction. Still, she thought maybe she could get him to help. Especially since she'd just freed him.

And taken him prisoner. He wasn't likely to be grateful.

She let out a breath. No time to keep mulling this over. They needed to keep Meliq quiet, and so he was coming with them. That was the end of it.

She moved forward, weapon at the ready. Her heart pounded, and she tried to tell herself that it was because of the running. But dammit, she was in better shape than that.

Hell, it was hard to breathe, like her throat was closing in on itself. She pushed out a breath and forced herself onward, licking her dry lips.

On the next deck up, she stopped to survey the hallway, make certain there were no aliens about to attack them. The place was deserted.

By this time, Sergeant Clark had rejoined the group, a blue-clad alien under the control of one of those biker-dude looking veterans. "Meliq," she said. "How are you?"

He glared at her. "I told you. I'm not a traitor."

So much for the hope he would help them out. She turned to Sergeant Clark and his team. "Any questions?"

"We got it," he said, then headed aft, toward engineering, based on Doctor Samra's description of what he had seen.

"This way," she said to her team, with Sergeant Harvey's team following. Again, she headed up to the deck that held the bridge.

She stopped at the upper stair, where the stairwell met the corridor. The hallway reverberated with talking and laughter. Sounded like there were at least three aliens, getting closer, about to come around the corner. And there were probably more than she could handle with her one weapon. Leaning her back against the wall, she held her weapon up, steadying it with her second hand, searching the shiny bulkheads to see if she could get a glimpse of the enemy reflected on the metal, but she could only make out smudges.

But something about the images let her know they would be on her in an instant. And it told her where to aim.

She swung her weapon around the corner, getting herself a quick visual before she fired. She hit one of the aliens in the left shoulder, blood splatter arcing into the air. He dropped to his knees with a shout of dismay.

"Son of an unspeakable," the alien walking next to him said with a hiss. He reached for his weapon.

She pointed her pistol at him, then thumbed the button. But this time, nothing happened.

"Shit," she said, as the alien raised his weapon and pointed it at her head.

Chapter 49 – Casualty

She jumped back behind the cover of the wall. What was the deal here? Did the weapon need to recharge?

"Come back here, you mucus-filled piece of worm dung."

She made an inappropriate chuckle, since worm dung was the finest dirt a person could get, and people would pay good money for it. Her weapon vibrated. She glanced at it. *Hope that's the signal that it's recharged.*

The alien burst into view, and she fired on him, her shot landing in the center of his chest, a rainbow of blood and bone spraying over the stairway. But he still stood there, eyes bugged out, reeling, weapon moving in confused arcs, like he couldn't figure out where to shoot. And then the third alien presented himself, pistol aimed right between her eyes.

She dove at him, hitting him on the thighs with her head, knocking his butt onto the deck. She landed on top of him, grabbing for his weapon. The pistol went off, energy beam bouncing randomly.

"Get down!" Mendez shouted somewhere in the stairwell.

The alien lifted her off of him and threw her aside, like she was a mere wad of paper. She rolled a few feet, and her weight smashed her knuckles against the hard metal and her hand screamed. She clenched her fingers more tightly to keep from dropping the weapon.

Francisco rushed over and stomped on the man's knee. He howled, swinging his arms. Francisco went down.

But by then Patrice was up again. Her pistol buzzed. She pointed it at the alien's head, point blank range, then fired.

The air turned red. Blood splattered on her face. She closed her eyes and spun away, ducking.

"Colonel!" a voice called out. Sounded like SGT Harvey.

She forced her eyes open. Wiping the moisture from her face, she turned toward the stairs. The second alien's body had fallen into the stairwell, blocking her path to the rest of her team. She gestured to Francisco. "Help me with this." Francisco pulled the alien's leg while Sullivan tugged his arm. In a second, they had moved the corpse far enough for her to pass by.

She slipped through, started down the stairs, then stopped.

Mendez lay in the corner of the landing, his right arm gone. Dr. Samra leaned over him, pressing hard against Mendez's body, pushing Harvey's t-shirt into the gaping wound. Harvey stood behind them, his uniform blouse hanging limply in his hand, bare chest covered with nothing but a set of dog tags and a few tufts of tightly curled hair. God, what had she missed? Why hadn't she been able to prevent this?

"Mendez!" Francisco gasped, rushing past Sullivan. She knelt on the other side of the wounded soldier, wrapping her hands around the one he had left. "Mendez, man, come on. It's gonna be okay."

Samra grunted.

Mendez looked at Francisco, a flicker of a smile there, but then his eyes rolled.

Samra gestured to Sullivan with his head. "I need more weight. Lean on my shoulders."

Sullivan forced herself to move, to hurry up to them, stopping when she got to the large red puddle. She leaned over it, then put her hands on the doctor's shoulders, pressing as hard as she could.

"I'm losing him," Samra whispered.

"Come on," Francisco said, her voice breaking. "Hey man, hang in there."

Sullivan closed her eyes. She didn't need to see Mendez die. She'd seen it happen to someone else, seen the shine leave his skin, the soul depart his face. Once was enough.

"Mendez," Francisco cried. "No..."

Sullivan felt the tension in Samra's body release, and he pulled back. Sullivan opened her eyes, first spotting the red handprints she had left on the doctor's shirt, then the corpse of the soldier she had just lost. Francisco sat beside him, curled into a fetal position, sobbing quietly.

"Ma'am?" SGT Harvey said as he slipped his uniform blouse back on, now without the t-shirt.

Sullivan straightened. "What happened?"

"That alien you shot… the one that didn't die right away…" Harvey pointed at the creature who had blocked the stairwell.

"Hell." Next time she shot an alien, she needed to make certain he was completely dead.

"We can't stay here," Harvey said.

"Yeah." She took a breath to pull herself together, then hurried backup the stairs, where the alien dead lay in splatters of red. She gathered up the alien weapons, one still in the hands of its former owner, the other two several feet from the hands that had formerly wielded them.

Harvey came up the stairs, looking both ways. "For your team," Sullivan said, handing him two of the alien guns. He headed back down the stairs to join the other members of his team.

"Thanks."

"Finley," she called out, handing the last weapon to the intelligence specialist.

"You gonna be okay?" Harvey asked Francisco. The young woman came to her feet, knees wobbling visibly, her hand out to the wall to brace herself. Francisco sniffed. "I think so."

Harvey handed her a weapon. "You gonna make it," he said.

Francisco wrapped her hand about the pistol, then used the back of her wrist to wipe away the stray moisture on her cheek.

"Take point."

Francisco nodded and then marched up the stairs.

Sullivan put her hand on Francisco's shoulder as she passed. "I know this is tough," she said, "but right now, we gotta survive."

"I know," Francisco said. "Let's finish this."

Sullivan nodded, a lump forming in her throat. God, she loved these soldiers, their bravery, their tenacity. She would do whatever it took to get them home.

"Finley," Sullivan called out. "Ready?"

Finley swallowed but nodded.

Sullivan looked at Harvey and his team, and then at the body of Mendez, sprawled over the stairwell landing. She didn't want any more casualties, and that meant she needed to mass her forces, keep herself from being out-gunned again. "Sgt. Harvey, you and your team stay with me."

"Ma'am?"

"Once we've taken the bridge, you can start your sweep of the ship."

He nodded, then stepped beside her. "Let's do this, man."

Colonel Sullivan headed toward the bridge, while her soldiers followed her silently. When she got to the short stairway going up, she turned to Harvey. "Remember what I said about the bridge."

"It'll be like flyin'," Harvey said with a grin.

Sullivan nodded, pleased at his game attitude. She turned to the civilian members of the team. "You guys wait here until we've cleared the bridge."

"Right," Emily said. Lorenzo shifted beside her, and the biker-dude handling Meliq rolled his eyes.

Turning back to her objective, Sullivan stepped onto the bridge, onto the invisible floor, taking in the scene with surprise. It wasn't the half dozen men who'd been on the bridge when she'd last visited. Only three aliens stood there, control pads in hand, facing away from the humans and appearing to be engrossed in their work. This was going to be easier than she'd thought.

As soon as she sensed the rest of her soldiers behind her, she smiled. "All right, turn around and put your hands over your heads."

One of the aliens spun his head around, looking at her over his shoulder, his eyes enlarging with surprise. "What the…"

"That's right," Sullivan said. "Raise your hands. Give me that obscene gesture of yours."

The three bridge crewmen stood stiffly, backs still to her and the team. One of them moved his arm toward his weapon. "You don't wanna do that," SGT Harvey said. "We ain't afraid to use these weapons."

The alien chuckled, like this was something vaguely humorous. "Likewise, we're not afraid to die." Then he stepped toward Harvey.

The sergeant blasted the alien in the gut, his exploding abdomen virtually chopping him in half. The alien's expression bore out his claim. There was no surprise there, nor pain nor terror. Only peace. Relief. His body crumpled into the pool of his own blood and entrails, forming a small visible platform on the transparent deck.

"Diós," Francisco muttered. "Someone's gonna have to clean that up."

"Yeah," Harvey said. "And it'll probably be you."

Sullivan shook her head. Leave it to a private to start worrying about a GI party. But clean up wasn't the main problem here. Getting these guys to cooperate, that was going to be hard. The other two aliens had turned toward the invaders, both with pistols still stuck somehow to their Velcro-like belts, still holding their control pads. One alien eyed his dead comrade coolly, the other looked into Sullivan's eyes. "I told the captain he should have just killed you."

Sullivan narrowed her eyes at him. The captain had gone to great lengths to keep everyone alive, and Sullivan figured she knew why. But it would be good to hear that from one of the aliens, confirm her suspicion. And since he was talking, maybe she could get some more intelligence from him. "So, why didn't he?"

The alien shrugged.

"Your mission is to get us to your planet alive, isn't it?"

The man closed his mouth and just smiled.

"Drop your weapons," Harvey said. "Now."

They weren't going to comply. They weren't even going to give her their equivalent of the finger. And the longer they stood there, the more things could go wrong.

But she didn't want to just shoot them, especially since neither had made a move for his weapon. But she was certain they were just waiting until they saw a lapse in the humans' vigilance, and then they would shoot as many people as they could.

And anyway, she needed one of them to help pilot the ship.

Unexpected footsteps sounded behind her. She looked over her shoulders, where the civilians tromped warily onto the bridge.

Shit. Too soon. She needed to disarm the aliens before these potential hostages presented themselves to the enemy.

Only one thing left to do. "Drop your weapons," she said, repeating the command in a tone she hoped they took as threatening.

The first alien smiled, then stepped to the side, like he was heading for Mr. Lorenzo.

She lowered the aim of her weapon, then squeezed the trigger. The alien's knee exploded in a spray of florid color.

"Ow! Fathers!" the alien cried, tipping sideways and landing on outstretched hands. As soon as he landed, he reached for his weapon.

She blew his head off.

Then she turned her weapon to the last man. "Two down, one to go. What is your pleasure?" Her weapon vibrated.

The remaining alien looked at his fallen companions, then shrugged. "So, I have to reach for my weapon before you'll kill me?"

"How about I just blow your hands off?" It would have been better if they still had their handcuffs, but there was nothing she could do about that now.

The alien lunged at SGT Harvey, hand reaching around to draw.

She fired.

Harvey ducked, but not soon enough. The splatter drenched the side of his face and the backside of his arm. If only they still had their handcuffs, they could restrain these idiots without having to blow their heads off.

"Oh, shit," he said, brushing the liquid from beside his eye. "I think I just been baptized into combat."

Finley quickly walked around the fallen aliens, picking up their weapons, while Emily took the controllers, wiping them off against the dead aliens' shirts. She looked them over like she thought she could make out some kind of information there, know what functions they served.

"How we gonna know what to do now?" Lorenzo said.

"I got it," Emily said, handing one of the controls to Meliq. "Is this one yours?"

Meliq left his arms hanging by his side while he glared at her.

"Answer the question," Biker-Dude said as he slipped Meliq's arm around his back, then lifted it. Meliq's eyes bulged.

"Let him go," Sullivan said.

The biker-dude glared at her. "He needs to cooperate."

"No torture. Are we clear on that?"

The biker-dude curled his lips in a sneer, but then he pushed Meliq forward a few steps and out of his grasp.

Meliq rubbed his arm.

"Can you teach me how to read this?" Emily said.

"Please," Sullivan added.

Meliq took in a deep breath, then exhaled loudly. Looked like he was considering it.

"Which one of these does the pilot use?" Emily said, now holding the pads like playing cards arranged for him to pick.

He glanced at them, then turned back to Sullivan. "I'm sorry."

Emily closed her eyes.

"Looks like we'll have to do this the hard way," Sullivan said, grabbing two of the pads, then handing one to Kyle and one to Lorenzo. "Just start pressing buttons and see what happens."

Chapter 50 — Discovered

When Galth reached Craddock's room, he sat on the earth man's sleeping platform and leaned against the cold wall, smiling possessively.

"Excuse me?" Craddock said, gesturing for Galth to leave the room.

"You may be the dictator of South something or other, but you have no authority on this ship."

"We'll see what your captain says about that," Craddock said, lifting his nose like he thought he was somehow superior.

Galth smirked. "He's busy."

Craddock smiled at him, but Galth could tell he didn't mean it. The expression was something intended to give Galth the wrong idea. "You must not realize," Craddock said, "what a great asset you have here."

"Asset?" Galth scoffed. "There's nothing you can do for me." He lifted his knee and dropped his boot onto the bed with a thump.

"I don't know," Craddock said, ignoring Galth's boot and talking like he thought Galth was a child. "What would you like?"

"Besides being assigned to a different ship?" He wasn't certain why, but this conversation was making Galth frustrated.

"Perhaps becoming the commander of this ship."

"This is a piece of trash," Galth said, thumping a fist against the bulkhead. "The hull isn't even strong enough for us to hide in your gas giant planet. If we'd been able to do that, we could have gotten rid of the Enforcers a long time ago."

"They should've left by now," Craddock said. The arrogant *hiezul* was so clueless.

"Ha!" Galth said, jumping to his feet and pacing in the small space. "They haven't bought your stupid story, and they never will. We're going to run out of food long before we can ever get out of here."

For the first time, Craddock looked like he understood the gravity of the situation, but then he smiled again, like he thought he had the problems solved. "They must at least be confused. I mean, since they haven't attacked you…"

Galth wasn't going to admit that out loud, wasn't going to give Craddock credit for anything. Craddock was nothing but a tool to be used against the enforcers, and maybe the humans as well.

Galth spun around, glaring at the softness of Craddock's body, the disgusting fat that circled his waist. Nothing like the human military people. And speaking of military, there was one thing Galth wanted to know.

He sat forward, resting his elbows on his knees. "So, tell me," Galth said, "who would have been in charge of fighting my shuttle while we were still on your planet?"

"That was probably Colonel what's her name."

Galth straightened his back. Just as he'd suspected. But so very alien. Dakh Hhargashian women never did anything clever or important. "You think she figured out that blowing all that stuff in our way would disable our weapons?"

"She's pretty smart."

Galth huffed. "I should've known. Sink it." He dropped himself back onto the hard sleeping pallet, letting out a disappointed breath. Beglash had probably already killed her. Sink it, now that Galth knew who to exact his revenge on, he was being denied the opportunity.

But maybe Beglash was taking his time. Galth might still get there before the captain had finished.

He jumped off the bed then rushed down the hall, Mr. Craddock on his heels. "What are you going to do?" Craddock asked, his words sandwiched between loud exhales.

Galth ignored him, continuing to the side hall where her cell was. It was strangely silent, the only noise coming from Craddock's heavy footfalls.

Galth looked back at the human, who was smiling like he was looking forward to whatever he was about to see, like he was hoping to watch her being killed. He was more Dakh Hhargash than human, and someone who could betray Galth without a moment's hesitation.

Galth turned down the side hall. The far wall, darkly shadowed, shown with a glint of red, liquid splattered at head height. Galth stopped suddenly. Craddock bumped him from behind.

"Waves and foam," Galth muttered. He could smell it now. Blood. And there were drag marks leading into Meliq's cell. He hurried up to the door and tried the knob. Locked. He pounded on it. "Meliq," he called out. No response. Galth grabbed his keys and flung the door open. There lay the body of one of the crewmen. Meliq was gone.

"Colonel what's her name," he said, his voice turned into a growl, fingers curling into fists.

Craddock shook his head. "But she's still inside there. How could she have done something like this?"

Galth pulled the keys from Meliq's cell door and shoved one into the opposite lock. "You said she's smart."

While Galth worked on the door, Craddock bent over the body, his hand on the stump of a neck. "It's getting cold," he said. "This was done a while ago."

The door to Sullivan's cell swung open with the creak, revealing the captain laying face up, eyes wide with horror, but eyeballs sunken and dull.

Waves and foam. How could she have...

"Oh my god," Craddock said, now breathing over Galth's shoulder.

The cargo! The victims! They were getting away! And Craddock was just standing there in the hall, blocking Galth's way.

Galth shoved Craddock into the bulkhead, then ran to the cargo hold, shoving the key in the lock with shaking hands. There were still people in there. He could see them through the little window. He slammed the door open. "Where is Colonel what's her name?"

A hunched and wrinkled human woman approached him, hands clasped in front of her waist, innocent expression on her face. "I don't actually know."

Huffing, his breath coming quickly, he glanced around the room. She wasn't there. In fact, there wasn't a single victim in the room wearing a uniform.

Feces.

She had escaped, and who knew how many civilians went with her? Sink her, when he got his hands on her, he was going to strangle her.

Maybe he could strangle this little human woman first.

No. No time for that. He could come back to her later. He backed out of the cargo hold, then slammed the door shut, then pulled his communications device from its pouch. "Galth to bridge. Commander Tardag. " He waited for a moment, but no one answered.

"Tardag!"

Demons of the Night Sea, could she have already gotten to Tardag? Was the ship's second as incompetent as Beglash? And now, what was Galth going to do about it? Did this put him in command?

No time for doubts.

He changed his comms device to broadcast. "Attention on the ship. We are under attack. All crewmen are ordered to close on the enemy and kill them."

Predictably, someone came back on the radio. "Enforcers?"

"No, humans."

"Oh." Fathers, it sounded like a Sigali on the radio, someone too dim-witted to figure things out quickly. "Are you sure we should kill them? Shouldn't we just capture them?"

"They're too dangerous."

"If you're sure..."

L. D. ROBINSON © 2022

"Meet me on the bottom deck." He put his communicator away, letting out a breath to clear his mind. With a couple of crewmen at his side, he could retake the bridge. He could already hear footsteps coming down the stairs, ready to join his team.

He had the advantage now. And once he got everyone together, she didn't stand a chance.

Chapter 51 — Alien Ship

"This is not possible," Lorenzo said, turning to look at Colonel Sullivan with a confused expression.

She walked up to him, shaking her head in frustration. Back in the cargo hold, he had been full of confidence, but now... "You can't figure out anything?"

He threw out his arms in a gesture of exasperation. "I thought they would have a slider or a yoke or something I could operate. This is just..."

"Alien," she finished his thought for him. "Kyle, have you come up with anything?"

"I'm clueless, ma'am," Kyle said, sounding demoralized. "Not only can't we read the instructions, but there's no haptic feedback."

Damn it, couldn't they figure out anything? And now Kyle was speaking in a foreign language, some sort of engineering jargon she didn't understand. "Okay," she said, "let's take this one step at a time."

"Right," Kyle said, taking one of the control pads from Lorenzo. "There are five control pads."

Lorenzo lifted one of the aforementioned objects. "And they're all different."

Colonel Sullivan took one and looked it over, then turned to Emily. "Can you tell anything?"

Emily frowned. "Most of the control pads have twelve symbols on each pad, none of which repeat even between pads. That's a lot of letters for an alphabet, so my guess is icons."

"You're expecting miracles here," Lorenzo said, tapping his foot on the invisible floor.

"I'm expecting to get this pile of junk back to Earth," Colonel Sullivan snapped. "And I'm not used to taking 'no' for an answer."

"I wanna help," Lorenzo said, sounding a little indignant, like he thought he'd been falsely accused of sabotage. "But I don't even know what to do with these. You push them? Maybe slide them?"

"It's possible," Emily said, "that each control needs a different input."

Lorenzo groaned.

"Or maybe you push them in a certain order," Emily said.

Kyle nodded. "It'll take years to hack this."

"We don't have that much time," Sullivan snapped at Kyle, then she sighed, waving her hand at him and hoping he took it as an apology. "Fair enough. But how do hackers do it? They just keep trying until something works?"

Kyle's brows pulled together. "Basically."

Oh, lame, lame. But what else could they do? She nodded at Kyle, hoping it looked decisive and confident. "Then do that."

"I did something!" Lorenzo blurted from behind Kyle. "It worked!"

"What was that?" Colonel Sullivan asked, stepping toward him.

"When I pushed this button," Lorenzo said, pointing at his control pad, "it made a beep."

Colonel Sullivan swallowed a dry lump. If that was the best they could do, they were all dead.

Lorenzo dropped his finger back to the control pad. A sparkling glow flashed around the ship. Sullivan gasped, looking back at Lorenzo, who grinned broadly. "Maybe I turned on the shields?" He tapped the pad again and the glow died away. "But we don't need shields now, am I right?"

She nodded at the pilot, gave him a little thumbs up, then walked back to the alien in blue. "Meliq, please," she said. "I know you don't approve of what the others were doing. I know you think it's wrong to just kill."

Meliq glanced at the bodies of his dead crewmates, splattered over the deck, his frown darkening. "It's wrong to kill."

Her stomach clenched. "It was self-defense," she said. She gritted her teeth. Still no time to give up.

"I'm not a traitor."

"Meliq, listen, if you don't help us, if the others take over again, they're going to kill us."

He shook his head. "They won't do that. They can't."

"They will. And you're just going to let them?"

He gave her a mournful smile. "I would like to help you. But I can't."

Sullivan gestured to the civilians struggling to decipher the controls. "All you have to do is tell us—"

He lifted a hand. "They're holding my family," he said.

Her mind froze as she tried to visualize the unthinkable but couldn't. "Hostages?" she said. "They're forcing you to work for them?"

He closed his eyes as a grim reality seemed to descend on them all. "It may be too late for them already."

"I'm so sorry." The crack in her voice surprised her, the depth of her sorrow for this man both deep and unfamiliar.

And there was nothing left to say, no way she could cajole him into betraying his people, his family, now.

Chapter 52 — Rings of Saturn

Only five crewmen had made it to the bottom deck, all of them Sigali, but Galth was out of time. If he was going to re-take the ship, he needed to move now.

"Let's go," he said, feeling the heady excitement of leading men into battle. And since he was now in command, taking the ship back from the enemy would elevate him to a position he'd only dreamt of holding. And if it turned out that Tordag was still breathing, Galth could remedy that problem easily enough.

He headed toward the stairs, and when he was half-way up the first flight, Kelm came around the corner, descending two steps at a time.

"Galth!" Kelm said between gasps. "They've taken over engineering!"

Galth growled, looking back at his tiny fighting force. At every turn, the enemy was proving herself more dangerous. It was going to be a much harder fight than he had realized.

"They're going to kill us," one of his soldiers whispered to another, and now Galth felt the energy of fear clutching at the throats of his tiny force. If he didn't do something, they were going to turn and run.

Galth turned back to face his men. "A glorious thing," he said in a whisper with the tone of a rant, like a victory speech, a call to arms and to triumph. "Death at the hands of a competent enemy."

The men looked at each other, still doubt playing there.

"Yes!" Kelm said, grinning. "This is our moment, our offering to the eternal mother, our request to be welcomed into the Great Embrace!"

The Sigali soldiers' faces stiffened and they nodded to each other, while one man took out his weapon and shoved it into the air in a gesture of defiance. "The humans cannot frighten us!"

Galth gave them a nod of approval. But then another Sigali crewman stumbled down the stairs, the weapon on his hip missing, his expression like he had just been scooped up from the Night Sea. He stopped when he reached Galth, falling back against the bulkhead of the landing, hand grasping his chest.

"Where is your weapon?" Galth barked.

"They took it," the man said.

"Who?"

"Humans," he said between gasps. "On the third deck. Tying us up. Disarming us."

"Then the enemy has a lot of weapons," Kelm said.

"They're coming," the man said, pointing upwards.

"Son of Chavey," Galth muttered.

"Where can we go?" Kelm said, sounding like a frightened Sigali. "If they control the entire deck…"

Galth grabbed Kelm by the shirt, just below his neck, twisting the fabric to tighten it like he was going to choke the man. "Be a Hhargashna," he growled.

Kelm immediately straightened, then nodded, all confident again, at least on the outside. "Your orders, my commander?"

Galth released him, then looked around, evaluating the small number of crew he had, the lack of weapons, the possibility they could be walking into a trap. He had referred to Colonel what's-her-name as a competent enemy, and now he had to re-evaluate his position. Because even though death would be welcome, it wasn't the optimal result. He wanted to win.

There had to be some way to gain the advantage. And then, he remembered. There was a place the military woman didn't know about, and it was someplace where he could disable all the controls of the bridge and engineering, and anywhere else on the ship they might capture.

"Alternate control," Galth said, then smiled at his own cleverness. He hurried up to the second deck.

The forward part of this deck was mostly crew quarters, dozens of small rooms, most now vacant, formerly occupied by crewmates who had gone to the Great Embrace.

Beyond the last of the quarters, in a place no one would suspect, alternate control waited for a moment just like this. When he reached it, he input a secret code into a wall mounted keypad to unlock the door. Only the specially anointed could have access to this place.

He burst through, all his companions following, almost shoving in their anxiousness to get inside. "Shut the door," Craddock said in breathless desperation.

"No!" Galth shouted, but it was too late. The door closed with a decided thunk, and now they were locked inside. It was a good measure for a last stand, but that wasn't what Galth had intended.

"Sir," Kelm said, now standing beside the control panels embedded in old-fashioned countertops. "We've got a message coming in."

Galth tore his attention from the door and walked over to Kelm. "Who?"

Kelm looked desolate. "The Enforcers."

Galth's stomach sank. He keyed the receive button, then a hologram of an Enforcer woman appeared just above the array of controls, clad in her long gray robe, her face solemn, her size about one tenth actual. That made her look frail and easily defeated, and he wanted to reach out and swat her into the waves. But the technology she commanded made such a move, even in person, impossible.

"Dakh Hhargashian ship," the woman said, her voice grave, "You will return all your captives to Earth, and then you will be taken into custody."

"Custody?" Abgoth said. "What does that mean?"

Galth rolled his eyes at the idiot Sigali.

The Enforcer woman raised her brows, like she'd taken offense at the expression. He wasn't going to correct her assumption. And he wasn't going to allow himself or his crew to be captured.

He looked at Kelm. "Have you disabled engineering and bridge?"

Kelm nodded, his expression determined. "They can't do anything now."

Galth acknowledged the news with a nod. Then, he looked back at the Enforcer woman. What did he need to do about her?

It was possible the Enforcers were just sending out that message in the blind. It was possible they didn't even know if anyone on the ship was hearing them. If that was true, then he and his crew were okay. Now, he just had to determine what the enforcers knew.

He looked back at the controls, turning on passive sensors. The readout came on in an instant, and Galth's stomach fell. "They're heading straight for us."

"Are you sure?" Kelm said anxiously.

"Are you saying I don't know how to read sensors?"

Kelm shook his head, but he also stole a peek at the display, and his chest seemed to cave in. "What are you going to do?"

Galth stared at the readout for another minute, silent, thinking, There had to be some way to lose the enemy ship, maybe trick it into thinking his own ship had been destroyed. He scanned the map of the system.

The ringed gas giant. He had an idea about how to hide there without going too deep. If he could find a thick enough cloud... It just might work. It would only take a slight detour to reach it, and if he got there quickly enough, the Enforcers wouldn't know where he had gone. They would think he had gone into overspace inside the system, and they would leave then, too.

He smiled to himself as he fingered the controls, changing the ship destination, increasing speed, zigging a little here, zagging there, just to make his trail all the more difficult to follow. The planet already appeared in his viewscreen like a little star, too distant to make out the dozens of moons, a system of rings, and a whirling storm or two in the atmosphere that could confuse anyone.

"They're changing course," Kelm said.

Galth nodded. He would be sure to leave plenty of trail markers for them to follow. But the trick was going to be on them.

Once they'd gotten close enough to see the planet, he surveyed the system again, making certain he knew where all the important space bodies were. Then he checked the time for the Enforcer's ship to arrive. Perfect.

He adjusted his trajectory.

"Sir?" Kelm said, "you know this ship doesn't have the hull strength to hide inside a gas giant atmosphere."

"Yeah. You suppose the Enforcers know that, too?"

Kelm chuckled as understanding hit him. "That's why I enjoy working for you."

The planet filled their viewscreen, the soft orange atmosphere decorated with curls and striations. "Wow," Craddock said behind him, stepping closer. "Isn't it gorgeous?"

"Not every system has something quite so beautiful," Galth said, letting his admiration show.

"And if Sullivan is on the bridge," Craddock said, "she probably thinks we're about to crash into the thing."

Galth chuckled again. "I doubt they're spending a lot of time enjoying the sights."

"We're not... are we?"

"I wish I could see her fear," Galth said, smiling to himself at how nervous Craddock sounded. He changed the angle of approach, so he wouldn't hit the atmosphere so fast he would generate additional heat. That was not the idea.

Slower, he commanded the ship, tapping gently.

They skimmed the tops of the clouds, orange whiffs of gas licking at the bottom of the ship. He'd almost slowed enough to match the wind speed, give his ship just enough difference in velocity from the atmosphere that the *Blood Fury*'s hull would experience the air as a light, cooling breeze. That required extra care, additional lift, to keep him aloft. Otherwise, at this slow speed, the ship would plunge into the planet like a rock dropped from atop a cliff.

"How deep are we going to go?" Craddock asked.

Galth looked at Kelm. "Give me a running readout of hull pressure."

Kelm nodded, staring at his instruments.

The ship slid further down, and now clouds blocked all views of the stars, the dark expanse of space.

"Twenty-five percent," Kelm said.

Galth checked the readouts of the last known Enforcer location. Still far enough away that the *Blood Fury* would be almost on the other side of the planet by the time they arrived. This was going to work perfectly.

"Thirty percent."

Galth smiled. The hull temperature was falling, cooled by the enveloping clouds. It just needed to get a little colder.

Another several minutes passed, each bit of time seeing them deeper into the swirling storms, the heat of the ship dissipating into the planet's gasses. Just a little more.

"Fifty percent," Kelm said. "We don't want to go beyond seventy-five."

"Not even close," Galth said with satisfaction. He turned the ship up, almost straight out of the atmosphere. He needed time to transit the gap between the planet and the rings, and he didn't have a lot of time before the Enforcers arrived.

The ship popped out of the clouds, barreling towards the rings. He checked below to make certain his exit hadn't left a telltale blip in the movement of the clouds. Nothing he could detect.

Again, he adjusted the angle, then expertly slid into the system of rings, adjusting his orbit as he approached one of the embedded moons, a little glob of rock only a touch larger than his ship, but big enough to hide behind.

"Engines off. Everything off," he commanded.

Kelm nodded.

"Why are you turning things off?" Craddock asked. He looked worried.

Galth regarded him for a moment. He really didn't like having Craddock here. Too many questions. And if the human got too frightened, he might do something to cause problems.

"Maybe I should just kill you," Galth said.

"It was just a simple question," Craddock responded. "And anyway, you might still need me."

Unfortunately, that was true. Sink it.

"The hull is cold enough now that the Enforcers won't be able to detect our ship with their infrared sensors."

"Ah," Craddock said. "And you don't want to heat it up until they've gone."

"You'll make a pretty good Dakh Hhargash," Galth said. He turned back to the sensors, tracking the movements of the Enforcer ship. They were wandering, moving back and forth, active sensors penetrating the gaseous atmosphere.

"We've lost them," he said with satisfaction.

"Brilliant," Kelm added.

Galth grinned. There was nothing more delightful than a tactic well-executed. He had accomplished his mission.

He grabbed at the control panel, like he thought he could pick it up and walk across the room with it. Old habits, like he'd forgotten that he wasn't on the bridge. Sink it. He'd only accomplished the first step in the mission.

He let out a heavy sigh. "Now, we need to figure out how to take the ship back from Colonel what's her name."

Chapter 53 – Realizations

Sullivan had totally lost control. Only a few moments ago the civilians had been screaming and running around, the biker-dude rushing out of the bridge in terror as the invisible ship rammed itself into the planet, the creamy atmosphere swirling around them like they were immersed in a liquid.

And she had been unable to stop any of it. Frozen in fear, she'd just stood there while adrenaline pumped itself into her blood stream and everyone around her disintegrated into raving maniacs, so frightened most of them didn't notice when the ship then spiraled back out to join the rings.

She looked around the bridge. Was there anyone still in control of their faculties? Lorenzo sat on the deck, hands covering his face. Emily whimpered near the exit. Finley hadn't moved a muscle in over ten minutes, like she was catatonic or something.

"Finley?"

"I'm all right," Finley said, but her voice quavered.

Kyle picked himself up off the invisible deck, looking around like he was in a daze, walking to the front of the bridge, until he bumped into the transparent wall. "It's one of the shepherd moons," he said, staring at the large object the ship had settle behind. He turned back to look at Sullivan. "Interactions with its gravity help keep the ring material in place."

Interesting, Sullivan thought. But that wasn't going to get everyone else functioning again. "Everybody okay?" she said.

The biker-dude stumbled back through the entrance, now tapping his feet on the floor like he thought he would fall through with every step. And Lorenzo was slowly coming to his hands and knees, like he needed the extra step to get back on his feet. Emily was already up, but still looking unsteady.

And Meliq, damn him, just stood there smiling.

He'd been no help at all. Even when she'd gotten him to accept one of the control pads, punch some buttons on it, he refused to explain anything. And nothing he'd done seemed to affect the ship.

"You did this," Lorenzo shouted, pointing an accusing finger at Meliq. "You set up some kind of sequence."

"Yeah," the burley, tattooed biker-dude said, walking up to Lorenzo, flexing his fingers. "What the hell were you trying to do?"

Meliq looked back and forth between his two accusers, a glimmer of concern in his eyes. "I didn't bring us here." .

"Bullshit," Biker-dude answered with a growl.

"I swear," Meliq said, the pitch of his voice rising in alarm. "I don't even know how to work the helm."

"Let's punch his lights out." The biker-dude stepped toward Meliq.

Meliq swallowed, then glanced at Sullivan with a look that clearly said, "Please protect me."

"That's enough," Sullivan said. She stared at them, glowering, angry, ready to put herself between that tattooed behemoth and the alien. God, what had just happened here? Whose side was she on? She pointed at Meliq with her thumb. "We still need him."

Biker-dude pointed an accusing finger at Meliq. "You saw! He was smiling!"

"I don't think he did it," Kyle said.

Now, Biker-dude rounded on Kyle. "You little shit-face, what the hell do you know?"

Sullivan bit her lip. She needed to defuse this now, before the humans turned on each other, but realistically, she was in no shape to take on the tall, beefy man threatening everyone.

"Every ship has an auxiliary control," Kyle said. "Someone took command of the ship from there."

Sullivan looked at Meliq, and he nodded.

"You sure?" Biker-dude said, a note of doubt in his voice. But at least he appeared to be backing down.

"Try that shield control," Kyle said to Lorenzo. "See if it still works."

Lorenzo nodded his bald head, then lifted his control pad and pressed the appropriate button. Nothing happened.

So, that was it. She had taken over the bridge but had control of nothing. "Shit."

Emily rubbed her hands together. "Does it feel like it's getting cold up here?"

"Engines and environmental controls are off," Meliq said.

"Off?" Damn it the news just kept getting worse. "How long until we all die up here?"

"The air's still good," Meliq said, brows pulling together. "Whoever's controlling the ship must be turning it on from time to time."

"Is there anything we can do?" Sullivan asked. And maybe, just maybe he was starting to sense that they were all in this together.

"He's also disabled all these control pads," Meliq said. "I can read status on them, but they don't operate anything."

Sullivan rubbed her hands over her face.

"Can we use the control pads for communication, like to send a message to Earth?" Kyle asked.

Sullivan dropped her hands and took a breath, then looked at Meliq.

"Don't think so," Meliq said.

"Check everything," Sullivan said. "Do we have control over anything?"

Meliq swiveled his eyes to look into her face. "I told you, I'm not helping."

"You *are* helping," Sullivan said. "You need to face that, get over it."

Meliq dropped his hands to his side, his face gone solemn. "No."

He was protecting his family, she reminded herself. Or at least he thought he was. But given the violent tendencies of the other aliens she'd seen, she doubted anything Meliq did now would save them. "Look, what are the chances they already think you're helping?"

He appeared to consider that thought, but finally said, "I can't risk it."

Then, an unfamiliar female voice came from the control pad in Meliq's hand. "Dakh Hhargashian ship, it's time you come out of hiding."

Sullivan took in an excited breath. "That's the Enforcers, isn't it?"

Meliq swallowed, eyes filling with tears.

"They don't know where we are," Sullivan continued, "and we need to do something to help them spot us."

Meliq stared at the pad, motionless and somber. Maybe he was finally facing the facts, he would finally help them. Maybe. But she could no longer wait for him to finish sorting out the issue. She needed action now.

She walked over to Kyle, a vague plan forming in her mind. "Listen," she said, "we need something that will generate some light, or some heat."

Kyle glanced around, brows pulled together. "I don't know." Now he was looking straight up, at an unfamiliar star-scape. "You suppose the bridge transparency is one way or two?"

"I have no idea."

"Anybody have a cigarette lighter?"

Sullivan looked around the room, but it appeared everyone there was more health-minded than normal. No lighters.

"Oh, well," Kyle said. "It probably wouldn't have worked, anyway."

"We have to come up with something," Sullivan insisted. "Some way to signal them."

Kyle glanced at Meliq, then lowered his voice. "You think we still have weapons control?"

"I..." She huffed a breath of frustration. "Why would they leave that on?"

"They're not something we could use to steer the ship with," Kyle said, still whispering. "Maybe they thought we wouldn't use them."

She nodded. "But they would make a strong signal."

"Right."

"And how are we going to get Meliq to fire one?"

Kyle looked around, then eyed the moonlet, so close it seemed to press in on them, like it had lowered the ceiling. "Just give me a minute."

She understood the request. If he did anything while she was with him, it would sound more suspicious to Meliq.

Sullivan walked back to her spot near Meliq, allowing her disappointment to show. "We're going to come up with something," she said to the man in blue. "But it would be a lot easier of you would help us."

He gave her a strange smile, like he thought it was odd she was reassuring him this way.

A moment later, Kyle pointed into the ring, toward rocks that were well behind the ship. "That one," he said. "You see it?"

She turned and looked. "Which one?"

"It's tumbling," he said. "And it's getting closer." He stepped up to her, eyes narrowed as though that would help him discern the rock's action better. "Kind of yellowish, with one really bright spot."

"I see it." And indeed, it did appear to be approaching them.

"You think it'll hit us?" she said, voice gone soft, as though she didn't want the alien to hear.

"I don't know." He stepped closer to it, although in reality the distances were so vast that one step would make no difference. Still, she understood the instinct. "Yeah. Looks to me like it's coming straight at us."

She frowned, because it really did look like that, and it was strangely fortuitous that such a rock should appear. "Meliq?" she said. "Are we in any danger?"

He scanned the rock, then shook his head. "It's going to miss us by several hundred *memgash*."

Kyle gave Meliq a doubtful look. "Is that a lot?"

"Yes."

"Won't our gravity change its trajectory?"

Meliq looked like a zen monk, calm beyond reason. "This ship is mostly hollow. It's gravity, compared to all the other sources of gravity, is miniscule."

Kyle nodded and turned back to the rock. "True." Now, he looked disappointed. He'd almost come up with a reason to move the ship, or fire weapons at it, or something else that would call attention to their position.

But Meliq wasn't taking the bait.

And most certainly, whoever was piloting the ship down in auxiliary control would be aware of the same dangers they could see. And they would do whatever they needed to keep the ship safe without sabotaging their hiding spot.

"Dakh Hhargashian ship," the voice from the Enforcer ship said again, "we know you're still there. Come out now, and you will be treated with compassion."

Meliq stepped backwards, looking around, like he was suddenly afraid, like he didn't trust the enforcer woman's claim of humane treatment.

"What will they do to you?" she asked Meliq.

"I've just heard whispers," Meliq said. "Nothing specific."

"Maybe," she said, "if you help us, I can talk to them, get them to let you go."

Meliq stared at her for a moment. Looked like he was considering it, like he was weighing the pros and cons. But he said nothing.

"Dakh Hhargashian ship," the Enforcer voice said again, "we've spotted your exit point from the planet's atmosphere. Now, it's just a matter of time before we locate you."

"Is that true?" Sullivan looked back at Meliq. All around them, her soldiers and civilian helpers were coming to attention, looking hopeful again. She was feeling it, too, a warmth in her chest, an excitement that made her heart beat faster in spite of the chill in the air.

Meliq looked back at his pad. "Carbon di-oxide levels are rising."

"What does that mean?" the biker-dude asked nervously.

"It is getting a little stuffy," Kyle said.

"They trying to kill us?" Lorenzo barked.

Meliq shook his head. "There's only one environmental control system on the ship. Whoever's doing this can't isolate the bridge without messing up his own air, too."

"Then why is he doing this?" Sullivan asked.

Meliq's expression was inscrutable.

Kyle stepped toward them. "He wants to keep the machinery off because it creates heat."

Disappointment flashed on Meliq's face.

"Yeah, that's right," Kyle said, walking toward Meliq, his voice taunting. "Pretty soon the hull of this ship is going to warm up enough it'll stand out like a full moon on a cloudless night."

L. D. ROBINSON © 2022

"Dakh Hhargashian ship," the voice in Meliq's control pad said again, "time to give up. We've located you."

L. D. ROBINSON © 2022

Chapter 54 - Self Destruct

o," Galth said. He wasn't going to give up so quickly, so easily. They would never take him alive.

And the Enforcer could just stand there talking until she ran out of breath. He wasn't going to respond to her, either.

"They're heading toward us again," Kelm said, staring into the sensor panel and shaking his head. "You have to do something."

Galth nodded. He wished there were a priest here to advise him, but the fleet didn't think such a luxury was necessary.

"No!" Abgoth wailed in the back of the room. "I don't want to be a prisoner."

"Quiet," Galth barked. Nobody wanted that, a fate truly worse than torture. No, it *was* torture, and he was not about to let that happen to the warriors he led.

The Sigali closed his mouth, still frowning. "But what are you going to do?"

Galth gritted his teeth. He'd tried all the other actions he could think of, and no new ideas presented themselves. All that remained was the solution of last resort. "There is only one thing left to do."

Kelm stepped back, straightening his shoulders and lifting his chin. "I concur."

Then, Mr. Craddock stepped forward. Sink it, for a glorious moment, Galth had forgotten the man was still with him. He was going to be a problem.

Galth pressed buttons, inputting the code he had learned years ago, hoping he remembered it right.

"Code incorrect," the computer display said. Fortunately, Craddock didn't have a translator lens, and the computer wasn't vocalizing its responses, so the human wouldn't be able to figure out what was going on.

"What is he doing?" Craddock said to Kelm.

"He is giving us an honorable death," Kelm answered.

Galth rounded on Kelm. "What? Are you as stupid as a Sigali?"

"He's working for us, isn't he?" Kelm said.

"Death?" Craddock said, grabbing Kelm by the shoulder. "You mean, like, self-destruct?"

"Just get back," Galth commanded.

"Hey," Craddock said, sounding dismayed, "is that really necessary?"

Galth turned on Craddock. There was no time to coddle him or try to convince him. "They're coming for us!" He pointed at the screen above the control panels, where a distant ship made its way through the space between the planet and the ring, its nose pointed at them.

"Just let me talk to them again."

"They don't believe you."

"Galth," Craddock tried again, "there has to be another way. Some other solution we haven't thought of yet."

"Shut up." Galth tried his secret code again, fingers tapping at the control panel. "How long until the Enforcers get here?"

"If you just let me talk to them, I can explain the situation, and maybe they'll back off."

"I don't want them to back off," Galth said, lifting his fingers from the keypad for a second. "I want them to catch our explosion right in their bow."

"I get that," Craddock said. "But isn't there another way?"

Galth ignored him. He only had two digits left in the code. All he had to do was remember it correctly. He put his finger back down, pressed a number.

Craddock pressed against him, breathing heavily. "This is not necessary. Please let me try."

Last digit. Galth moved toward it, but then Craddock pushed Galth's hand away from the keypad.

Galth spun on him, shoving him back, slamming him into the bulkhead of the small room. Craddock landed with a thud, eyes ready to pop out of his skull. "You interfere one more time," Galth snarled, "and I will kill you personally."

A couple of Sigali crewmen grabbed Craddock by the arms and moved him toward the opposite wall, acting all tough, even though Craddock had stopped resisting.

One last digit on the code. If he'd gotten it wrong this time, maybe he would have to let Craddock talk to the Enforcers. He pressed the last digit.

The display screen went black, then came back on, displaying the text Galth had been waiting for. "Self-destruct activated. Ten-minute countdown begins now. Do you wish to change the countdown time?"

"Did you get that time on the Enforcer's arrival?" Galth asked.

Kelm sighed. "They're slowing down. And they keep varying their trajectory."

"Sink it," Galth said. Well, as long as he kept his own crew from the unbearable torture they would undergo as prisoners he would be okay with the outcome. He pushed the button, agreeing to the 10-minute time limit. Then he turned around and sat on the floor.

"What do you think the Eternal Mother looks like?" Kelm asked wistfully, still standing.

"She's beautiful," Galth said, feeling the peace of knowing he would soon meet her, fall into her warm arms. "More beautiful than *hgavidellum*."

Kelm sighed, but then he jerked. "Galth, the enforcers are speeding up."

Galth jumped back to his feet, taking in the new information coming at him from sensors. "Yes," he said with a grin. "The Eternal Mother has blessed us."

Kelm nodded, sharing Galth's excitement. "They'll be here before the ship blows. It'll tear their hull to shreds."

Chapter 55 — Shuttles

Sullivan was so pleased that the enforcers were coming that it took her several minutes to notice that Meliq was frantically tapping his control pad. Now, she knew that something had gone wrong.

"Meliq? What's up?"

He looked up at her, his face gone paler than the icy chunks outside. "Nothing."

She cocked her head. "Something bad, isn't it?"

He closed his eyes.

Damn him, she wasn't going to let him off that easily. She walked up to him and grabbed his arm. "Tell me."

He remained stiff, eyes shut tight, fingers gripping his pad until the tips had turned white.

She pulled the gadget out of his grasp, then looked at the read-out. A large, yellow icon flashed at her.

"Kyle?" she said, handing the pad to him. "What do you think?"

He looked at it, furrowing his brows. Then he blanched. "I... I think it's a self-destruct warning."

The entire bridge swayed.

"Say again?" Finley said, walking toward him, her expression one of disbelief.

"Well, I don't know for sure," Kyle said.

She turned back toward Meliq, who looked apologetic. "We only have nine minutes left."

"Shit!" Finley said.

Sullivan glanced at her watch, noting the time, seventeen minutes after. Then, she looked back at Meliq. "Can we turn it off from here?"

Meliq shook his head.

Colonel Sullivan grabbed her walkie-talkie as she took a step backwards. "Sergeant Harvey," she said, her voice gone several notes higher than its normal pitch, "get your team down to the cargo hold now!"

"We still got a couple of--"

"Immediately! And call Sergeant Clark's team and give him the same message."

"Wilco," Harvey said.

She switched channels to call the cargo hold. "Mrs. Steiner, are you there?"

No answer. And no time to wait for someone to get around to answering. "Let's go!" she shouted, then dashed toward the red light marking the exit from the bridge. Almost everyone rushed toward the exit. All but Meliq.

"Grab him, bring him with us," she said to the biker-dude.

"I'm staying," Meliq said.

"You'll die."

"I won't go with you. I won't help you."

"Let the son of a bitch die," Mr. Biker-dude said, walking out.

"Kyle? Lorenzo?"

Meliq stepped away again. Damn it, he was using up their precious time. They couldn't just saunter down to the shuttles. They had to get out of this ship well before it exploded, or the blast would take the shuttles with it. But she needed him to help pilot the damned things.

Kyle grabbed Meliq's arm. The alien seemed to relent, walking with the others, his control pad still clutched in his fingers.

Once they were halfway down the first flight of stairs, Mrs. Steiner's voice chirped over Sullivan's walkie-talkie. "What can I do for you, dearie?"

Oh, god, what a relief. "Take out the keys and see if you can open the hatches into the shuttles."

"Is there a problem?"

Sullivan stopped, her hand trembling, as she reached Mendez's body still sprawled across several steps, a black hole in his chest.

"Dearie?"

Sullivan shook herself. "No time to explain! Get someone to help you. Now!" She turned to the rest of the crew, all staring at her. "Grab the body," she said to one of her soldiers.

"Got it," he responded, and she continued down the stairs. Twenty-one minutes after. Five minutes left.

Meliq, still being dragged by Kyle, shook his arm loose and caught up to her. "Why are you taking a dead person?"

"We don't leave our people behind," she said.

He looked puzzled, and that made sense. The Dakh Hhargash had left a half-dozen fallen soldiers on Earth without any apparent issue. "I see."

They got to the bottom level and turned aft. At the end of the hallway, Sergeant Clark and his team were entering the cargo hold. "Leave the door open," she called out, breaking into a sprint.

She slid into the room, grabbing the doorframe to stop herself. "Self-destruct!" she shouted. "This ship is going to blow up!"

"Holy shit!" one of the men trying to open the shuttle ramps said. "Let's get this damned thing open!" All around him, people who had been sitting in sullen depression jumped up and started moving, frantic action without purpose.

"Pull on that thing!" another man at the ramps shouted.

"Get out of the way!" someone else hollered at the people now swarming under where the ramp would land.

"I think we'll only need two shuttles," Sullivan said to the man who seemed to be directing the opening of the third shuttle. "Help out the others."

He nodded and his helpers quickly joined the efforts to open the first two.

Emily hurried up to her, Lorenzo at her side. "We've only got one pilot," she said.

"He'll go in the first shuttle, and you and I will be in the second."

Lorenzo lifted his arms in a gesture of impotence. "But I still don't know how to fly these things," he said.

"You'll figure it out," she said, watching him frown in response.

The shuttle ramp cycled to the floor, and before it had bottomed out, frightened civilians clambered onto it and pushed their way inside. With a nod, she signaled Sergeant Clark and his team to go with them.

She glanced again at her watch. Three minutes to go.

Patrice turned to Meliq. "How do we fly the shuttles?"

He lifted the control pad, still in his hand. "This is what the helm icon looks like," he said, pointing to a circle in the upper left corner. "Hold it for three heartbeats, and the helm will open up."

"Got it," Lorenzo said.

"Then, you slide your finger from bottom to top to increase speed."

Lorenzo nodded enthusiastically. "Capisco."

"And how do you steer?" Patrice asked.

"By varying the direction of the upward slide," Meliq said, demonstrating on his pad.

"Grazie, grazie," Lorenzo said, then ran into the shuttle.

The second ramp slammed onto the floor with a loud thud, with a cloud of dust.

She watched as everyone entered, Sergeant Harvey and his team, Emily, even Doctor Samra, and all the other civilians, most of whom she still didn't even know.

Almost everyone was in the shuttles now. She and Meliq were the last people who needed to embark. She turned back to the large door, where one of the civilians stood at the entrance, looking into the far corner of the room. "Andy, come on!"

Damn it! An older man huddled in the corner of the cargo hold, his knees drawn to his chest and his arms around his legs. It was Dajos, that actuary who'd tried to convince her not to resist. And now, he looked paralyzed with fear, his eyes red and wet. She ran up to him. "Get up, Mr. Dajos."

"I can't go back in there." A movement of his head indicated the shuttle.

"You'll die if you stay here," Colonel Sullivan said.

He looked directly at her. "This is my choice. You can't force me."

She gritted her teeth. She could try to convince him, but there was no time for a debate. And she wasn't about to risk all these other lives for one man.

But he mattered as much as everyone else.

"Harvey!" she shouted. "Get somebody to help me!"

"No!" Dajos said. "I can't go in there!"

Sergeant Harvey and two other men quickly returned. The largest man grabbed Dajos by the hand, then threw him over the man's shoulder. In a second, they were all on the shuttle.

She turned to look at Meliq, then realized he was heading for the door going back into the ship.

"Meliq! Where are you going?"

He glanced at her over his shoulder, his lips pressed together with what looked like resolve. "You only have a few minutes left. And if you aren't far enough away before the explosion, none of this will matter."

"Then we need to hurry."

Meliq shook his head. "I'm going to alternate control to convince whoever's in charge to stop the explosion. That'll give you your best chance."

"But if you come with us, it won't matter."

He grabbed her arm. "If I go with you, they'll kill my family."

There it was again, the Dakh Hhargashian devotion to family. And how could she argue? She gave him a quick nod of understanding. "Good luck."

And with that, he was out the door, sprinting down the hallway.

She closed the shuttle ramp, listening for something to tell her the ramp had sealed, but heard nothing. Two minutes left.

She ran into the main part of the shuttle, a long corridor with doors on each side. The cockpit was at the frontmost part of the shuttle.

She rushed into the flight deck, where Francisco was handing out control pads to the other military in the room. But first priority was the release mechanism.

She looked up and was rewarded with the sight of a large black wheel, like those used to shut the hatch on a submarine. That would do nicely.

"Give me a lift," she said to Harvey. He knelt on one knee. She climbed onto his thigh, the nearest people holding their hands out to steady her. She grabbed the wheel and turned.

The entire shuttle rocked gently and started drifting slowly away from the ship. Everyone cheered, and one of the men held out his hand to help her down.

One minute left.

"Call the other shuttle and tell them what to do," she said to Francisco. Then, she took one of the control pads from Francisco and ran her eyes over the first one while Emily, now standing beside her, looked on. The oval surrounded by a circle sat in the center of the pad. "Shields?"

Emily nodded, pressing a button on her pad.

An unimpressive flash told Sullivan shields were active.

She engaged the helm, using the techniques Meliq had described. The small circle in the corner of the control pad snapped into a large balloon, and she zipped her finger over it. Her body slammed against the back wall of the control room, knocking the air from her lungs. Damn, that was some acceleration!

"We're out!" SGT Harvey shouted with a giddy laugh.

She glanced at her watch. Twenty-six after. Time was up. Had they made it far enough?

The viewscreen turned white and she rammed into the side wall, Emily and several others splatting beside or her jamming into her, crushing her ribs and squeezing her shoulders together. Ticks of debris hitting the shuttle drummed in her ear. Her eyes blurred, and every cell in her body screamed.

They were dead, she thought with despair. Frozen in space. Pulverized.

But her eyes continued to register, no matter how confused and blurred they were. Screams of agony assaulted her ears, and enough swearing to embarrass Sergeant Harvey.

As the bodies crushing her finally gave way, she took in a ragged breath, then gasped with pain. Must be a broken rib. If that was the worst of her injuries, she would be lucky. "Doctor, are you okay?" she called out, struggling to get to her feet. But every time she moved her head, the crowded compartment spun. But not the people. Dizziness, then. Brain damage.

Shit.

She didn't need that. She still had to lead.

Leaning forward, she put her hands on the deck and tried to steady herself. Then her elbows bent and she knew she was going to fall. The light faded for a moment, and then a hand rested on her shoulder, her cheek plastered against the cold floor. "Open your eyes, please," a male voice said.

It was Doctor Samra, bent over so his head was next to hers, gazing at her face, no, her eyes, like he could read her future in them. "Looks like you have mild TBI."

"Take care of the others," she croaked.

He quirked a smile. "I've got people helping each other, but we need you to be well first, don't we?"

She closed her eyes. She didn't have time to get well. There were things that had to be done.

"Here," Doctor Samra said, "let me help you up."

She sat, then rested her head against the wall, her eyes rolling involuntarily as the room slid in unpredictable ways. "Is there anyone uninjured?"

Sergeant Harvey appeared beside Doctor Samra. She moved her eyes to look at him, not wanting to turn her head. "I'm good," Harvey said.

Doctor Samra smiled ruefully. "Yeah, it looks like you and the three or four people stacked on top of you cushioned his landing."

"There are a few people in the back lucky like me," Harvey said. "Includin' him," he said, indicating Doctor Samra with a finger.

"Any serious injuries?" She smiled at the implication that her injuries weren't all that bad.

"We had one fatality," Doctor Samra said, sadness showing in his normally stoic face. "It was the old woman."

"Mrs. Steiner," Harvey added, his voice breaking.

The air went out of her lungs, and her shoulders bent forward. Her eyes burned, and the irony was that the extra liquid didn't reduce the heat. It just spilled out and drew wet lines over her cheeks. She wiped them away, careful not to move her head. This was ridiculous. She never cried. What was wrong with her?

"Don't be too hard on yourself," Doctor Samra said. "With injuries like these, you don't have enough mental resources left to hold in your emotions."

"Oh," she said, her voice cracking. She bit her lip, hard enough to bring pain, something that could bring her back to reality. And yet, she needed to know more detail about everything bad that had happened. "What's the status of the ship?"

"Shields bit the dust," Sergeant Harvey said.

"It's likely they saved our lives," Doctor Samra said.

She let out another heavy breath, grateful it wasn't all bad. "What about the shuttle's trajectory?"

Harvey studied the view screen.

"Tell me."

He gave her an apologetic brow raise. "I have good news and bad news."

"Shit."

"The good news is that we're moving at a pretty good clip."

Colonel Sullivan closed her eyes. "Do I want to hear the rest?"

"We're heading straight towards a big fucking wall of rocks."

Chapter 56 — Ring Moon

"Wall?" Colonel Sullivan croaked. Her head had suddenly cleared. She needed to figure something out while she still had the adrenaline. She reached out her hands. "Help me up."

Harvey and Doctor Samra lifted her by her arms, one hand on an elbow, the other around her upper arm. Once she was on her feet, she leaned against the control view port with a sigh. "Why don't they have chairs in this damned place?"

"Shoulda brought a couple a benches," Harvey said.

Outside, debris englobed the shuttle, rocks and dust and pieces of space vessels, all matching the shuttle in both speed and direction. It was like a cloud, and the largest items blocked much of the view.

But she could still see it, a flat expanse of boulders stretched out ahead of them.

"What in the hell?" She turned to Kyle. "Is that the ring?"

"Um, I think so."

"How is that possible?"

Kyle squirmed. "I'm not an expert on orbital mechanics," he said. "But this is what I think happened."

Sullivan swallowed, not sure she going to understand the explanation.

"We started out orbiting the planet, right along with the rings," Kyle said. "But then the explosion accelerated us, while also blowing us out of the equatorial plane of the planet." He held up his hands, one horizontal to represent the ring, the other moving vertically.

"Oh, geez," Sullivan said. "Just give me the bottom line."

Kyle looked into the viewscreen, then shrugged. "Depends on the relative velocity between us and whatever we hit."

"We got no shields," Harvey said.

"Then it won't take much," Kyle answered.

She looked back at the flat expanse of ring material, then shook her head. "How far away is it? How much time do we have?"

Kyle shrugged.

Great. Fat lot of help he was.

"What about the other shuttle?"

"Haven't heard from them," Francisco said. "And I don't see them in the view screen."

Sullivan's shoulders felt heavy. They needed to get medical help right away. Maybe those other aliens... "And the 'Enforcer' ship?"

"It stopped," Harvey said, pointing to a corner of the viewscreen. The ship just hung there, as if it was waiting to see if there was anything worth salvaging.

She huffed. "Damn it, if they're supposed to be the good guys, they should be coming to help."

"They might not even know we're here," Kyle said. "Too much debris."

She nodded. "Or maybe they don't know we're in the shuttles."

"Maybe they don't care," Harvey added.

"Do we have any way to contact them?" she said, now looking toward Emily.

"I have a theory," Emily said, her voice tentative, pointing to two rows near the bottom of one of the pads. "These icons seem to be for communications. If I can get them to work…"

"Those are communications *controls*," Kyle said.

"What's the difference?" Emily said, looking confused.

"The actual communications equipment is part of the shuttle," Kyle explained. "And this thing is so badly damaged, I doubt anything works anymore."

Emily's shoulders sagged and she let the control pad fall to her side.

"But don't give up," Colonel Sullivan said.

Kyle gave her a weak smile. "Never surrender."

Colonel Sullivan's knees started to tremble, and she braced her hand on the wall. "In the meantime, we need to come up with additional ideas."

Everyone looked at each other, but none of them spoke.

"Nothing?" she said.

"Pray?" a soft voice whispered from behind them.

"We're gonna need help," Harvey said.

L. D. ROBINSON © 2022

"Yeah," Doctor Samra put in. "I haven't seen any food or water on board, and who knows how long the air supply will last."

"Okay," Colonel Sullivan said, nodding at them. "Our first priority is to figure out how to not get torn apart when we hit the ring. Once we get through that, we can worry about this other stuff."

"Right," Harvey said. "Okay you people, let's start cracking on ideas here."

"I can keep working on the control pads," Emily said.

Colonel Sullivan shook her head. "I doubt the shuttle's thrusters work any better than the communications."

"It's not just that," Kyle said, "but the amount of speed we'd need is just too much."

Too much. Not words Sullivan was willing to accept. There had to be something she could do. Something.

She looked back at the viewscreen. The formerly smooth plane of the ring now looked bumpy, little shadows giving the thing texture. That couldn't be good. They were getting close enough to make out details. They were running out of time.

Maybe, if they were lucky, they could just slip through the ring without hitting anything. It was made of small pieces, wasn't it? She narrowed her eyes, trying to focus more on the mass of material showing on the viewscreen, looking for some place where she could see space from the other side. Small bits of dark appeared, here and there, popping in and out of existence.

"Kyle," she said, "how close together are the individual pieces?"

He glared at her, like he was about to go cross-eyed. "Lady, I'm not a ring specialist."

"But can we get through without hitting too much?"

Kyle covered his face with his hands, and Sullivan frowned. Was she asking too much of him? She stepped toward him, trying to formulate something to say to get him back working with her. And then, out of the corner of her eye, she noticed a dark line, running diagonally across the viewscreen. "Kyle, is that a gap?"

He dropped his hands and looked at the screen, then grinned. "Yeah. It's small, but probably big enough."

"Then we need to head for it," she said.

"But how?" Emily asked.

Okay, good point. Without thrusters, they would have to find something else to change the ship's direction.

That was it! "Physics," Colonel Sullivan said.

"Say, what?" Harvey tipped his head to the side.

"Is that door the only exit?" She pointed toward the hallway.

"There's an airlock in the starboard compartment," Kyle said.

She looked at her hands.

"The right side," Kyle said.

She let out a breath. For once, something was working in their favor. Not only was the right side opposite the part of the shuttle that took the brunt of the explosion, but it was on the side from which they needed to move. "So, if we throw something out through the airlock, that should create some... um, jet propulsion."

"Newton's second law," Kyle said. "The heavier, the better."

"So, what do we have that we don't need?"

Sergeant Harvey grimaced. "There ain't nothin' in here but those pad things."

She glanced around again. "Shoes. Everybody take off your shoes and put them by the airlock." She sat down and unlaced her boots.

"How are these little things going to make a difference?" Emily said.

"Even a small change in trajectory will make a big difference when you're going a long distance," Kyle said.

"Okay," Emily said with a nod, bending over to slip off her heals. Everyone else followed Colonel Sullivan's lead.

"Hurry!" Kyle said.

While everyone else worked to gather up all the shoes, Sullivan hurried out to the side compartment, to the controls in the wall beside the airlock. There were three buttons, and she needed to try each to see what it did and hope she didn't open both doors at once. Theoretically, the alien engineers should've created a failsafe mechanism to keep that from happening, but given their cavalier attitude about death, it was possible there was no such thing.

She pressed the top button, and the inner door slid into a pocket in the fuselage with a whooshing sound.

"You want us to put the shoes in there?" One of the civilians asked.

"Give me a second to figure out what I'm doing." She pressed the same button a second time, and the inner door slipped closed, landing against the side with a thunk followed by a couple of distinct clicks. That was good.

She pressed the second button, and the outer door opened, hinges and hydraulics swinging it to the left, with a faint whine of pumps.

"Hey," Francisco hollered from the cockpit, "I think that did something." Colonel Sullivan smiled. She hadn't expected any change of velocity from just a little air leaving the shuttle, but she'd take it.

She toggled the outer door closed, then pressed the third button. Air hissed loudly, probably re-pressurizing the space between the two doors. Amazing, she thought. The buttons were actually in a logical order. With the control pads being so alien, she was surprised to find this contraption easy to work.

She opened the inner door. "Okay, pile all the shoes in here."

Once that was done, she closed the inner door, then told Sergeant Harvey to press the outer door button when she gave him the command. She hurried into the cockpit, then moved into a position where the left edge of the screen lined up with the gap in the ring. As long as she could stay there, she would know if her plan was working. "Open the door," she called out.

The hydraulic actuators whined and thudded, and the shuttle moved ever so slightly.

She stared at the gap for a long moment, eyes narrowed as she tried to calculate the extent of the change.

Francisco furrowed her brows. "What's wrong, ma'am? It's working, isn't it?"

"Not enough," Colonel Sullivan said. "We've only moved a little closer to the gap."

"Dang," Francisco said, which made Colonel Sullivan smile at the mildness of the curse. The situation called for much more colorful language.

On the viewscreen, individual particles were resolving, and the edges of the gap were jagged and rough. "We need to do it again," she said.

L. D. ROBINSON © 2022

"I'm on it," Harvey said. He rushed back out, shouting, "Give me everything you can spare. Shirts. Jewelry. Glasses."

Sullivan tore off her shirt, shouting back to Harvey. "Everything! Get everything! I mean everybody needs to be naked!"

Emily gasped, but then she looked out to the screen and seemed to swallow her objections. She stripped off her gossamer dress and underwear. Everybody did the same.

In a few moments, they had a large pile of clothing, which they stuffed into the airlock. Strange, she thought as she looked at everyone. Most of them were avoiding eye contact, but the reality was there was nothing sexy about their condition. Only desperate.

Sullivan rushed back into the bridge and stared at the screen as SGT Harvey opened the airlock and then the nose of the shuttle veered slightly to the left. A few seconds later the thunk of the door closing rattled the vehicle.

Sergeant Harvey rushed into the cockpit. "Did we get it?"

She turned to him, deliberately looking only at his head and neck. "I have good news, and bad news."

His face fell. "Not enough?"

She indicated with her finger their original crash point, and then the new spot. "It looks like a spot that's more solid than the rest."

"Damn."

"If we can send out something else…"

Harvey shook his head. "We shot out everything, ma'am. There ain't nothing left."

She looked again at the massive expanse of particles, bits of dust and pellets of ice. How bad could it be?

"You sure we're in danger here?" she said, turning back to Kyle.

"Look more closely," he said.

She stared again at the ring, at the little gap she had put so much hope in, coming closer and closer. Yes, she could see the movement of the particles now. Even the edge of the gap fluctuated as it moved around the giant planet. And now she could see that the gap wasn't entirely empty. Occasional pebbles or even larger particles flung themselves through it. Even the gap was dangerous.

But what they were plummeting into now was surely a death sentence.

There had to be something else. "Maybe we can remove some of the bulkheads."

Harvey looked at the wall that separated the cockpit from the main compartment. "How the hell? With our bare hands?"

He was right. Even if such a thing was possible, they didn't have enough time to make it happen. But there had to be something else.

"Come with me," she said to Sgt Harvey. "Look for anything loose." With that, she began a systematic walk-through of the shuttle, glancing into each depressingly empty room, then looking at all the people, at naked frames both fat and thin, huddled together, arms wrapped around themselves against the chill.

Nothing. Absolutely nothing.

She turned to leave, then noticed one naked body lying on the floor, inert, a large black cavity where the chest should have been. Oh, god, could she do that?

No choice.

"Mendez," she said, pointing at the body.

Harvey glanced at the body, then back to her, and then his eyes bulged. "Ma'am, you can't do that. We don't leave our people behind."

She put her hands on his shoulders, squeezing them softly. "I know how hard this is. But I think he would want this. He's going to save us."

Harvey swallowed, then gave her a little nod, his eyes filled with moisture. "Damn son of a bitch has to be a hero, huh?"

She nodded.

Harvey turned to the biker-dude. "Hey, man, help me get this over to the airlock."

"Right," the other man said.

"We're about to hit!" Kyle called from the cockpit.

They picked up the body, now beginning to stiffen, and stuffed it into the airlock, grunting as they forced recalcitrant arms and legs into the tiny space. Something made a cracking sound. Harvey closed the door, then the airlock hissed as it cycled open and released the body into space.

"I'm sorry," Sullivan whispered. Then, she rushed back into the control room. This had to have worked, she said to herself. She'd just sacrificed the body of her dead soldier, and this had to be enough.

"Almost!" Kyle said.

She looked at the viewscreen, where the gap now took up half the screen. And what she'd thought were pebbles now grew into rocks. Boulders. Things as big as cars and houses. Solid. Hard.

"Damn, so close!" Francisco said.

"Mrs. Steiner," Colonel Sullivan shouted into the hallway.

"Wilco!" Harvey hollered back.

Colonel Sullivan listened to the sounds of the airlock operating, her fisted hands crammed against her chin, teeth ready to bite into her knuckles. This last one had to be enough. There weren't any more dead people left, and she wasn't about to order a live person out the airlock.

The shuttle jerked again. So close. So, so…

People crowded into the room, pressing her forward, so many naked bodies forcing her to lean against the work panel, cold against her bare skin.

She thought to ask them to back off, but from the looks of it there were only a few minutes left.

The ring particles continued to grow, edges resolving into crystal blades, the space between them filled with icy dust. And the gap widened and narrowed frenetically.

Then, the gap was all she could see. They were going to make it through. She held her breath.

Bam! Whoosh!

The air rushed past her, out a tiny hole in the fuselage. She barely had time to register what had happened. Her palm slapped against the hole, and then her entire arm screamed as the burning pain of freezing flesh radiated into her body.

Shards of pain pierced her, and a cloud of darkness snuffed out the light.

Chapter 57 — New Aliens

A voice spoke in the distance, random words floating into her awareness. A soft male voice telling a distant story. "Like the Dutch boy with his finger in the dyke."

Colonel Sullivan knitted her brow as consciousness slowly lifted the darkness around her. She opened her eyes. She was in a huge room, tall ceilings and distant walls, and she lay in a soft bed, while Dr. Samra sat beside her, dressed in a white smock, smiling at her, patting her uninjured hand. SGT Harvey stood behind him, grinning and nodding, his face gone angelic.

They'd all died and gone to heaven, she realized with a start.

But where were the wings? And why did

her other hand still ache? "We made it?" she asked.

"All personnel accounted for," Harvey said. "Them enforcers even brought back the bodies... Mendez and the old lady."

"Enforcers?"

She tried to sit up, but her left arm wouldn't bend. It had been encased in a glowing metallic box. No wonder she couldn't move it.

Dr. Samra pressed her back into the bed. "Just relax. You've sustained enough injuries to keep you off your feet for five or six years."

"You exaggerate."

He nodded.

She glanced around then. It was a large room, lined with beds, most of them filled with humans, and one woman wearing long robes, looking more like a monk than a nurse, patrolling the area. The overhead lights were bright and the air was filled with the smell of rubbing alcohol, but unlike any hospital Sullivan had ever seen, each bed had a large potted plant, and vines hung from a row of planters on shelves near the ceiling.

Her own bed was separated from the rest, nestled into the corner, and overhung by large green leaves. She relaxed back onto the pillow. "What happened after I passed out?"

"Francisco was ready to replace your hand with hers," Samra said. "And people were looking for something strong enough to put over the hole, something that wouldn't get sucked out. But when your hand fell away, the hole was gone."

"Gone?"

Samra's eyes glowed with excitement. "Looked like the hull was made of some kind of self-healing material." He glanced around. "And the medical technology here… we have to ask them for some of it."

"Of course." Sullivan let out a loud breath. But now, there were more important questions to ask. "You know where they're taking us?"

A nearby door opened, and two people walked into the room.

"Maybe you can ask them," Samra said. The newcomers walked up to Sullivan's bed, and as they approached, Samra and the other humans drew back respectfully.

The first alien was an old woman, her graying hair pulled softly away from her face, revealing ears with… fur? Tentacles? Looked like… Sullivan tried to think of something that had a similar appearance. Sea anemones, maybe.

Behind the alien woman, a young man waited.

"My name is Eanthis," the woman said. "You are Colonel Sullivan?"

Colonel Sullivan nodded. "Are you the 'enforcers'?"

Eanthis barked out a little laugh. "Is that what the Dakh Hhargash call us?"

Colonel Sullivan shrugged. "They wouldn't tell me much."

"I expect not. They refuse to communicate with any other aliens."

"So, you don't know what they wanted us for?"

The woman shook her head. "It seems to be something they want to keep secret at all costs."

"Interesting." Colonel Sullivan glanced back down the rows of beds where many of her charges lay. She was still responsible for all of them. She turned back to Eanthis. "Thank you for rescuing us." Now came the question she was afraid to ask. What did *these* aliens plan to do with them?

L. D. ROBINSON © 2022

"As soon as you're all well enough to transport, we will return you to your planet," Eanthis said, as if she had read Colonel Sullivan's mind.

"That's wonderful." That solved her immediate problem, but what would they do if the Dakh Hhargash made another attempt to kidnap people?

"But?" Eanthis said.

"I suspect my government is going to want to talk to you," Sullivan said. "Perhaps—"

"No," Eanthis said, raising her hands in a protective gesture. "We cannot provide you with space technology."

Colonel Sullivan stopped, staring at the woman with surprise. How had she known that would be the question? Did she get asked that question a lot? But there was a more important issue. "Then, how can we defend ourselves when these Dakh Hhargash come back and try to kidnap a bunch of us again?"

"That is a reasonable concern," Eanthis said, "but you needn't worry. Our mission in space is to keep more technologically advanced species from taking advantage of those who cannot defend themselves."

Colonel Sullivan frowned. That wasn't going to make people on Earth very happy. Human leaders, especially the military, would want to defend themselves, not rely on strange aliens to coddle them like children. Not to mention that now that they knew this kind of space travel wasn't only possible but common, they would want to join in with the other space farers.

But before she could start arguing with the aliens, she needed to know more.

"So," Colonel Sullivan said, "you'll protect us."

"Yes."

"And how long have you been doing this?

"Well over a thousand years." Her tone of voice held great pride.

Colonel Sullivan narrowed her eyes at the woman. "You, personally?"

Again, Eanthis laughed. "No, no. My people, my culture."

"And so for most of that time, you've been successful."

Eanthis glanced away, then gave an apologetic smile. "The Pelmians occasionally sneak onto your planet, but they only pick up isolated individuals and hold them for short amounts of time."

Colonel Sullivan's eyes opened wide. "You mean those stories are true?" Then, she waved the question away. "But these…"

"Dakh Hhargash."

"These Dakh Hhargash have never attacked us until a few weeks ago." She narrowed her eyes at the alien woman. "Was that their first try?"

"Oh, no. They've been coveting your planet for hundreds of years."

"And you were successful at keeping them away."

"Yes." She looked quite satisfied.

"Until now."

Eanthis wavered. "Yes."

"So, what changed?"

Eanthis's smile faded. "Changed?"

"Why weren't you defending us on these last two attacks?"

Now, the alien woman looked like she hadn't anticipated that question and didn't know what she was allowed to say about it.

The young man behind her whispered in her ear. Her brow crinkled, deepening the wrinkles around her eyes and on her forehead. "I can't make that kind of decision."

"You can recommend it," he said.

She looked thoughtful, then turned back to Colonel Sullivan. "I cannot address your concerns until I have spoken with the Council of the Protectorate." Her lips quirked in a quick smile. "They're part of the central government."

"I understand."

"And Brel has reminded me," she said, indicating the young man, "that you are the only captives ever to escape the Dakh Hhargash."

"Ever?" Colonel Sullivan said.

"Yes. It was quite an accomplishment. Such cleverness, the ability to succeed against superior capabilities… does this often happen among your people?"

Sullivan quirked a smile. "We call it guerilla warfare."

"Well, then…" She took in a deep breath. "If you have a name for it, it must be quite common."

"Common enough."

Eanthis shifted her weight. "I cannot predict the government's reaction, but I suspect we may want to work with you."

"I'm certain our government will be—"

"Just you," Eanthis said.

"Me?" Sullivan thought for a moment. "Eanthis, you said you would have to check with your government."

"Yes." Eanthis batted her eyelids, like she knew she was about to be forced into a corner. That was good. Meant she understood.

"What makes you think I can act any more independently?"

"I didn't..." She looked away. "Of course, if you must get their permission."

Sullivan then smiled at Eanthis. "I'm sure if your government and mine can come up with an agreement... an alliance, perhaps..." She wasn't certain how much more to say.

"Well, then," Eanthis said, raising her brows and smiling, "There is much to be done."

Chapter 58 — Landing

Once Kyle and Mr. Lorenzo got the Mralan shuttle pilot in communication with air traffic control, everything was set for the return to Earth. From there, the call was shuttled to the pentagon, where the brass offered to land them. But she told them she wanted to get back to her unit. It was soon enough, she hoped, that she wouldn't already have been replaced, and she could finish her brigade command, a necessary ticket to a promotion to general.

So, they landed on post back in central Texas, on the parade field south of the Corps Headquarters building. From here, ambulances took everyone to the hospital to be evaluated, and to have a short time to process what they had been through before they were reintegrated into their normal lives.

As requested by the aliens, a diplomat from the State Department was flying out to discuss what kind of alliance the U.S. would have with these people. In the meantime, they chose to close up their shuttle and wait inside.

Sullivan spent four days in the hospital, talking to counselors and getting her injuries treated. "You're in pretty amazing shape," the doctor had said, "considering what happened up there."

"Oh?"

"Looks like the aliens did a bit of medical treatment on you."

She ran a hand over her head. "I don't remember most of that."

"Well," the doctor said, "I don't know what the official stance is, but I'd like you to talk to the negotiators down there about the aliens sharing some of their medical knowledge with us."

Talk to the negotiators? What the hell was he talking about? "I'm not sure I'll be involved in any of the negotiations."

The doctor shook his head, one of those expressions that seemed to say, "Oh, brother, you really don't know what's going on, do you?" Maybe he knew something she didn't. In that case, the sooner she got released, the sooner she would find out what was going on.

"How much longer until I get out of here?"

"Soon," he said. "But for now, just keep resting." With that, he walked out the door.

She sighed. Resting was not something that came easily to her. She turned to the window, looking out over the stunted trees of central Texas, toward the main buildings on post, where things were happening and she wasn't part of it. Time to get back into the action.

"Patrice?" a soft, feminine voice said.

She spun around with a gasp. "Mama!" And then they were in each other's arms, Patrice clinging more tightly that she'd ever remembered doing before. Mama's fingertips dug into her back, but then she backed away and smiled up at Patrice.

"I told them you'd come back. But did they believe me?"

Patrice chuckled. "Really?"

Mama looked a little sheepish. "Of course, why would they believe me, when all this time I've been saying your father would be back, too?"

Patrice put her hand on Mama's shoulder, fingers wrapping around her tenderly. "It must have been hard all those years."

Mama reached up to Patrice's scar, running a finger over the gnarled indention. "I think he felt so guilty." Her lips trembled. "Before the accident, he'd always talked about what a pretty girl you were."

Patrice smiled. All the rancor she used to feel was gone, evaporated into space or frozen in the darkness between the stars. It didn't matter. She had her Mama, her siblings, her friends... well friends from previous assignments. She'd been too busy since moving here to really get to know anyone, but that was going to change.

"I've decided to get it fixed," she said, pointing to her cheek. "And the plastic surgeons are all fighting over who gets to do it."

L. D. ROBINSON © 2022

Mama grinned. "Your father would be…" She stopped, gulped, then took a deep breath, as though she was starting from the beginning again. "I am so proud of you."

THE END

L. D. ROBINSON © 2022

Dear Reader,

I hope you enjoyed reading *Fog of War* as much as I did writing it. Creating alien worlds, societies and technology can be very challenging, but also exciting when I think I've got it right.

As an author, I appreciate feedback from my readers. So, let me know what you liked, what you loved, and even what you hated. I'd be delighted to hear from you, because I'm always trying to make my writing better.

Finally, I have a favor to ask of you. If you're so inclined, I would appreciate it if you would post a review of *Fog of War*. Loved it, hated it—it doesn't matter. Just let everyone know what you thought. So, if you have time, point your phone camera on the QR code below and it will take you to my store, where you can write your review.

Thank you so much for reading *Fog of War*, and for spending this time with me.
In gratitude,

LeAnn Robinson

L. D. ROBINSON © 2022

ABOUT THE AUTHOR

LeAnn Robinson has been writing since she was in the first grade, and she sold her first book to a schoolmate for ten cents when she was in the third grade. She loves up-beat science fiction and appreciates writers who get their military facts straight.

LeAnn spent her first few years in the military enlisted in the U.S. Air Force, where she worked on the radar systems of fighter-interceptor aircraft. Following that, she used her G.I. Bill to put herself through college, signing up for the Reserve Officer Training Corps (ROTC) and getting her commission upon graduation. She majored in Geography, a multi-faceted discipline that gave her insight into cultures, governments, climates, and landforms.

She served in both the Signal Corps and the Ordnance Corps and was stationed in the U.S. and Korea. During her career, she deployed to Saudi Arabia for Desert Shield/Storm, to Somalia for Operation Restore Hope and to Kuwait and Afghanistan for OIF/OEF.

She now lives in Little Elm, Texas, just a little north of Dallas, where she studies astronomy, biology and anthropology, and anything else that can inform her creation of aliens and their worlds.

L. D. ROBINSON © 2022

CONNECT WITH LEANN ROBINSON

Check out my Facebook page: Search for "LeAnn Robinson Author."

Subscribe to my newsletter: http://leannrobinsonbooks.com. You can also send me a comment from the website.

Find me on Amazon at:
amazon.com/author/leannrobinson

L. D. ROBINSON © 2022

Made in the USA
Thornton, CO
12/27/24 17:48:13

81ba2459-6ce4-4dd3-92c3-55942cfa6fcaR01